From the author of CRAZY FOR GOD...

AND GOD SAID, "BILLY!"

a novel by Frank Schaeffer

"Schaeffer's gifts as a novelist are more than comic his writing has a deeper river flowing through it, one that is sensual and full of true grace." — **Andre Dubus III**
author of *House of Sand and Fog*

This is a work of fiction. The events and characters described herein are imaginary and are not intended to refer to specific places or living persons. The opinions expressed in this manuscript are solely the opinions of the author and do not represent the opinions or thoughts of the publisher. The author has represented and warranted full ownership and/or legal right to publish all the materials in this book.

And God Said, "Billy!"
A Novel
All Rights Reserved.
Copyright © 2013 Frank Schaeffer
v3.0

Cover design by Irene Johnson.

This book may not be reproduced, transmitted, or stored in whole or in part by any means, including graphic, electronic, or mechanical without the express written consent of the publisher except in the case of brief quotations embodied in critical articles and reviews.

Outskirts Press, Inc.
http://www.outskirtspress.com

ISBN: 978-1-4787-0001-2

Library of Congress Control Number: 2013913330

Outskirts Press and the "OP" logo are trademarks belonging to Outskirts Press, Inc.

PRINTED IN THE UNITED STATES OF AMERICA

Advance praise for *AND GOD SAID, "BILLY!"*

"I love this novel. *AND GOD SAID, "BILLY!"* is laugh-out loud funny from page one. It's downright insightful throughout and takes readers deep into the shallow psyche of a sincere Charismatic-Evangelical whose God fails him. That failure turns out, through a hilarious series of tragic-comic reversals, to be – let's just say something close to miraculous." — **Brian D. McLaren**, author/speaker/blogger

And God Said, 'Billy!' is honest, very funny and very serious. It's and sure to rankle those who believe that being human means being certain." — **Kevin Miller** director of *Hellbound?*

PRAISE FOR FRANK SCHAEFFER'S OTHER BOOKS

The God Trilogy (*Crazy for God, Patience With God, Sex, Mom and God*)

"But when the family business is religion, it is especially perilous. That is one of the central laments, anyway, of 'Sex, Mom, & God,' a new memoir by Frank Schaeffer. To secular Americans, the name Frank Schaeffer means nothing. But to millions of evangelical Christians, the Schaeffer name is royal, and Frank is the reluctant, wayward, traitorous prince. His crime is not financial profligacy, like some pastors' sons, but turning his back on Christian conservatives." — *New York Times*

"[Schaeffer's] memoirs have a way of winning a reader's friendship… Schaeffer is a good memoirist, smart and often laugh-out-loud funny... Frank seems to have been born irreverent, but his memoirs have a serious purpose, and that is to expose the insanity and the corruption of what has become a powerful and frightening force in American politics... Frank has been straightforward and entertaining in his campaign to right the political wrongs he regrets committing in the 1970s and '80s... As someone who has made redemption his work, he has, in fact, shown amazing grace." — ***Washington Post,*** **Jane Smiley**

'The book[s] shine ... A consummate memoirist, Schaeffer fills the narrative with interesting anecdotes... The sage conversation on a New York-bound bus with a distraught Asian girl is warmly resonant and a befitting conclusion to... [a] book of ruminations, memories and frustrated opinion." — ***Booklist***

"[A] startlingly honest work, which is part memoir and part religious history... Intriguing fare." — ***Church of England Newspaper***

"A work that alternates from heartwarming to thought provoking to laugh out loud funny... Schaeffer brilliantly guides the reader through an exploration of the Bible's strange, intolerant, and sometimes frightening attitudes about sex, and how these Biblical teachings, through the evangelical grassroots of the Republican Party, have come to dominate the GOP stance... Schaeffer's writing style combines intelligence, warmth, humor, depth and insight... Sex, Mom, and God is hands down one of the best non-fiction books of the year." — ***Kirkus Reviews*** **(website)**

"A fond and sometimes hilarious look back at [Schaeffer's] mother's child-rearing methods and the effect they had on him... Schaeffer's journey demonstrates that the world could be a better place if we were all able to reassess our beliefs and values-to examine them closely and glean only those worth saving." — ***Library Journal***

"Well worth reading, highly entertaining, and very informative about the recent history of American evangelicalism. It will appeal to readers interested in the world today, memoir, or religion."
— *Huffington Post*

"Part memoir, part revelation about Evangelical pathology, and part prescription for theological sanity, the book has much to recommend it." — *Patheos.com*

"Frequently entertaining." — *The Humanist*

"Part memoir, part theology, and part political commentary... An ambitious undertaking. But Sex, Mom, and God did not disappoint. Alternating between laugh-out-loud episodes and poignant reflections, Schaeffer recounts with candor the influence his mother had on both his beliefs and the beliefs of a generation of Evangelicals... His readers-believers and non-believers alike-will be challenged to reconsider their views about politics, sex, and religion." — *The Daily Beast*

"An unusual mix-part memoir, part exegesis on Bible-based belief systems, and part prescription for a more compassionate, human-centered politics for both religious and theologically skeptical people. Humor, at times of the laugh-out-loud variety, is abundant. And while readers will likely bristle at some of Schaeffer's conclusions, his wit, sass and insights make Sex, Mom, & God a valuable and entertaining look at U.S. fundamentalism." — *San Francisco Book Review*

"Frank Schaeffer reads similarly to George Orwell's 'Homage to Catalonia.' Orwell's book describes his growing disillusionment as he fought against fascism during the Spanish Civil War in the 1930s... like Orwell [Schaeffer] became disillusioned with the extremism he encountered. Schaeffer fled the evangelical scene in the early 1990s... He now has created a thought-provoking analysis of the social and religious struggles that continue to define American consciousness." — *The Roanoke Times*

The Calvin Becker Trilogy (*Portofino, Zermatt and Saving Grandma*)

"Poignant and hilarious, Calvin is immensely appealing.... Schaeffer ... is very funny, but we are never far from a sense that harshness and violence are real; we are never entirely sure how things will turn out... Calvin, the irrepressibly endearing hero of Frank Schaeffer's Calvin Becker Trilogy, is the son of a missionary family, and their trip to Portofino is the highlight of his year. But even in the seductive Italian summer, the Beckers can't really relax. Calvin's father could slip into a Bad Mood and start hurling potted plants at any time. His mother has an embarrassing habit of trying to convert "pagans" on the beach. And his sister Janet has a ski sweater and a miniature Bible in her luggage, just in case the Russians invade and send them to Siberia. His dad says everything is part of God's plan. But this summer, Calvin has some plans of his own." —**Richard Eder** *Los Angeles Times*

"The wonderful thing about this book is that it feels like a vacation.... And, like any really good vacation, it ends too soon." —***The Richmond Times-Dispatch***

"Beautifully written ... great insight and unselfconscious humor." —***Publishers Weekly***

"A wry coming of age tale ... splendid laugh-out loud moments."
—*Kirkus Reviews*

"A profound and sometimes painful look at the challenges of practicing faith, and a lot of fun to read." —*Washington Times*

"Calvin Becker is back in a timely, timeless story about the volcanic sexual curiosity of a fourteen-year-old boy born into a fundamentalist family so strict that he has never seen a movie, watched television, or danced (and has to hide his five copies of Mad magazine in the attic). It is 1966, and Ralph and Elsa Becker, Reformed Presbyterian missionaries from Kansas, are stationed in Switzerland, and on a modest ski vacation with their three children: tyrannical eighteen-year-old Janet, angelic Rachael, and our narrator, the irrepressible Calvin. But then, while at the Hotel Riffelberg, high above Zermatt, the fourteen-year-old falls into the hands of a waitress who, while bringing him his breakfast each morning, initiates him into ecstasies he can barely begin to comprehend. Told with warmth and humor."
—*Library Journal (starred)*

"Mr. Schaeffer's gifts as a novelist are more than comic: Saving Grandma has a deeper river flowing through it as well, one that is sensual and loving and full of true grace. This is a wonderful book!"
—**Andre Dubus III, author of** *House of Sand and Fog*

Baby Jack (a novel)
"The author lets each character speak in alternating chapters. (In heaven, Jack befriends a down-to-earth God who is a "wannabe

theatre director.") The reader marvels at how Schaeffer makes this concise chorus of social conviction moving and memorable by emphasizing emotion over description. By no means is Baby Jack another War and Peace. Think War and People instead."
— *USA Today*

AND GOD SAID, "BILLY!"

Other Books by Frank Schaeffer

Fiction

The Calvin Becker Trilogy

PORTOFINO

ZERMATT

SAVING GRANDMA

BABY JACK

AND GOD SAID, "BILLY!"

Nonfiction

KEEPING FAITH: A Father-Son Story About Love and The United States Marine Corps (Coauthored with John Schaeffer)

FAITH OF OUR SONS: A Father's Wartime Diary

VOICES FROM THE FRONT: Letters Home from America's Military Family

AWOL: The Unexcused Absence of America's Upper Classes from Military Service—and How It Hurts Our Country (Coauthored with Kathy Roth-Douquet)

The God Trilogy

CRAZY FOR GOD: How I Grew Up as One of the Elect, Helped Found the Religious Right, and Lived to Take All (or Almost All) of It Back

PATIENCE WITH GOD: Faith for People Who Don't Like Religion (or Atheism)

SEX, MOM, AND GOD: How the Bible's Strange Take on Sex Led to Crazy Politics—and How I Learned to Love Women (and Jesus) Anyway

Media and Bookclubs

Please contact Frank Schaeffer at

halfickett@gmail.com

ALL BOOK CLUBS WELCOME!

Frank will participate in book club meetings.

Contact him to arrange an appearance or phone/Skype Q&A

For
Brian McLaren, Peggy Campolo,
Gareth Higgins, Rosa Lee Harden,
Eric Elnes ...and the rest of my
Wild Goose Festival family

Contents

Chapter 1: My Big Break 1
Chapter 2: Living Off The Land 16
Chapter 3: Solly Epstein Said He Just Loves My Work! 30
Chapter 4: How to Write a Flashback 44
Chapter 5: BACK TO THE PRESENT (All Caps) 57
Chapter 6: A Strangely Prosperous Black Man 67
Chapter 7: The Polite Policemen 77
Chapter 8: My Welcome Party 82
Chapter 9: Preproduction Day One 92
Chapter 10: Betrayed 108
Chapter 11: I Meet My Crew 117
Chapter 12: Pat Robertson to the Rescue 127
Chapter 13: A Predestined Object Lesson in the Fear
    of the Lord 130
Chapter 14: A Good and Just Policeman 137
Chapter 15: Good Muti 145
Chapter 16: Seven Hundred Rand 150
Chapter 17: A High Level Relationship Bears Fruit 153
Chapter 18: He Would Also Mock Her for Eternity 157
Chapter 19: The Blue Pages 161
Chapter 20: This Rewrite Came As a Relief 166
Chapter 21: Mood Swings 172
Chapter 22: My Rewrite Was Good 180
Chapter 23: Goddamned Fucking Script Won't Quit 185
Chapter 24: Church 192
Chapter 25: Missed Me Did You? 199
Chapter 26: The Battle of Blood River 204

Chapter 27: O Heavenly King, O Comforter, the Spirit of Truth 212
Chapter 28: You Will Never Be Beyond Our Reach 222
Chapter 29: I Still Have a Career 225
Chapter 30: A Private World 234
Chapter 31: I Don't Understand 237
Chapter 32: How Will I Get Home? 241
Chapter 33: It's Not a Long Drive to Rossing 245
Chapter 34: The Suffering Martyrs 249
Chapter 35: Eat! 256
Chapter 36: Please Come Into My Clinic 261
Chapter 37: Go Say Christos Aeinesti 266
Chapter 38: Silence Is Peace 271
Chapter 39: Small Minded Reactionaries 281
Chapter 40: Brother Bernard's Story 292
Chapter 41: Life Confession 298

"He who seeks beauty will find it."
Bill Cunningham (*New York Times* photographer)

Chapter 1
My Big Break

Sometimes I got mad at God because everything He *does* is just so needlessly complicated. Nevertheless June 18, 1988 was a great day. My heart skipped a beat as the Lord said, "Billy this is the day!" God's voice was upbeat and cheerful like a car commercial announcer but even classier. He spoke just as I spotted the movie crew vehicles parked across the street from Image Engineering on Victory Boulevard. I'd been begging God to let me complete the task He'd set me in New Midian and allow me to return home to my darling little child before she grew up. After three years in New Midian, the place most people call Hollywood, I was on the verge of my big break.

They had lights on the street including 10-Ks, 2-Ks, even a Brute set up on the sidewalk next to a gun store. The grips were unloading dolly track. I felt that God's Wonderful Plan for my life was about to happen at last, that I was where He wanted me at the right time and place of His choosing and that NOW I was finally on the last mile of the road back to my little daughter Rebecca!

I'd missed almost three years of her childhood because of my obedience to the Lord. Rebecca was three when I left home and now she was almost six! What I'd thought would take a few months had dragged out into years. So by that morning most of the time I didn't let myself get too excited when good things happened. It would just mean that when things fell through as they had so often, I'd get that much more depressed. However on the glorious morning of June 18, 1988 I let myself imagine Rebecca's little arms hugging me again. I felt *so very close* to getting the movie made that God sent me to New Midian to direct.

"Yes Lord!" I screamed as I pulled into the parking lot of a Toys R Us that the crew was using as their base camp. A production assistant or a PA -- like we call the people in The Business who are really just interns running around not doing much more than bringing the important crew people coffee -- tried to stop me like I was just some tourist. I rolled down my window and I said in an authoritative voice, "I'm here to see Guy Chesney."

My sophisticated director's smile that I'd practiced for hours in front of my mirror paid off. So did speaking in my coolest laid back confident voice. Whatever it was that opened the door to this new (and as it soon turned out decisive) opportunity my smile let that worldly PA wearing a tight torn-on-purpose pair of Levi's know that I was only driving my ten-year-old Honda Civic because I chose to. My handsome "chiseled face" (like my wife Ruth called it when she declared that I was the handsomest man she'd ever seen), my long blond hair tied back in a ponytail, my using a Navajo handmade hair clip to hold my ponytail, made out of genuine sterling silver and real Sleeping Beauty Turquoise stones that I'd plundered three days before from a the Sharper Image boutique in Brentwood, let the PA standing in my way know that I probably had a new Mercedes someplace and was probably somebody important. That's why I never washed the Civic and drove it dusty and trashed. I was stuck with my car but nevertheless I wanted to turn a debilitating vehicle challenge into an opportunity and make my disgusting little car help me look like the weird-but-brilliant movie director type. I wanted my decrepit excuse of a car to send the message that I was so "into my craft" that I didn't care about what I drove even if (secretly) I was also a prophet of the Lord begging Him for a better ride and naming and claiming an abundance of good things, not to mention a way to complete His task, so that I could return to my wife and daughter.

So I had long since turned my vehicular weakness into strength by manipulating my car's loathsomeness against itself and instead of covering up the decrepitude of my car accentuating it. I had to signal to everyone in town that the person driving this humble junker was sophisticated even if I was just a wannabe director who had not yet gotten his big break. That's why I always kept the Matisse art book on my cracked dashboard.

The Lord had spontaneously delivered the art book plunder into my hands at a Boarders Bookstore when the girl at the checkout counter was momentarily distracted by a famous actress who had just walked in to do a book signing. At first I'd thought that God had led me to the store to meet the actress and that maybe that meeting would lead to my big break. When her security people wouldn't let me near her God said that I wasn't there to meet her but in order that I could plunder the store of several items that would soon be used by Him to further our cause. So the star's walking in and the way everyone turned to watch her presented a God-given despoiling opportunity to grab a very expensive art book off the "New Releases" table and walk out. I even put post-it notes (also despoiled from that same bookstore along with three pens and a package of greeting cards to send notes to Rebecca on) throughout the book to make sure people would think I really was into classy artistic stuff like that.

So anyway, the point is that on THE BIG DAY that PA's eyes flicked from the art book on the dash to my pile of fresh scripts stacked on the back seat and she shrugged. Then she pointed to the trailers parked in front of a Burger King and said, "Guy's over there by the honey wagon I think."

I was in! Yes Lord!

A *honey wagon* is Movie Business parlance for the truck with the chemical toilets in it used by the actors and crew on location. As I parked next to that toilet truck I named and claimed this Bible verse, "This day will the LORD deliver thee into mine hand; and I will smite thee, and take thine head from thee; and I will give the carcasses of the host of the Philistines this day unto the fowls of the air, and to the wild beasts of the earth; that all the earth may know that there is a God in Israel," 1 Samuel 17:46. Then I looked around for Guy Chesney for a while but couldn't find him. So I just hung out and watched everyone working.

I didn't know that this day would turn into THE DAY but I was already happy because I was on a set and that gave me a chance to observe and learn. So I had a clear sense of leading and that something big was about to happen. Seeing at least thirty people and ten equipment trucks made me shiver with joy because if this was their idea of a "low budget second unit shoot" which was how Guy Chesney had described it when we met and he invited me to the set, and if my meeting up with the Chesney worked out, and if he introduced me to his producer, and if Guy's producer read my stepping stone exploitation genre slasher script and gave me a deal *and* we made my movie *and* they hired me to direct it as my first picture, *and* if my movie did unexpectedly well, then I could count on a great fee package and maybe even some back end points of the profits. And then maybe *that* would open the door to a studio deal for making God's Movie! And when that happened then I could go home to my family! So anyway, to get all this going I was there to meet Guy, the production manager I'd met by "chance" in a restaurant a few days before when I was cruising for door-opening contacts and – for once – had actually met one.

The crew was shooting a car crash gag. A big black 1969 Cadillac veered off the road, across two lanes of traffic and smashed through a break-away sugar-glass window in the gun store location. It was another sign on that day of days! It was the same model of vintage car

AND GOD SAID, "BILLY!"

I'd decided I'd drive when the Lord blessed me: The front-wheel-drive 1967-1969 Eldorado. God had said He'd give me one (along with the new Mercedes I was asking for) just as soon as I made His Movie.

I had hung around a lot of second unit shoots trying to pick up hands-on knowledge to add to my screenwriting night class learning curve to prepare me for what the Lord had in store for me. I'd noticed that stunt guys like to make a big deal out of what they do. The set was crawling with stunt guys. Stunt men are king on a second unit of an action movie. The stars are nowhere in sight. It's only crew and macho stunt guys with eighteen inches of gut hanging over their Stunt Man Association of America belt buckles that are around when most stunts get shot. The bigger the 'gag,' what they call a stunt, the more dangerous it seems, the more they get paid. That's why every time there's a fall into an air bag or pile of cardboard boxes, a car crash, a slide off a motor cycle, or a full body burn, whatever, the stunt guys limp away. The other stunt guys play along even though the stunt men are the ones who talk the second unit director into doing the stunt in the first place. They say stuff like, "Hey! You only want me to fall sixty feet!? Shit! That ain't nothin'! Last picture I did with Burt I took a hundred and twenty fuckin' foot fall." They still complain about it later though and say that the second unit director was, "an asshole for makin' me do it!"

The crew was checking a dozen or so remote cameras that rolled on the crash, along with one in the front end grill of the car. After the assistant director gave the okay a cheer went up. The stunt driver slowly climbed out of the crashed car holding his knee. Everybody went over to the craft services table to grab coffee, bowls of cereal and packs of gum, whatever. Movie people love to eat free food because crews feel ripped off because the "above the line" important people on the set from the stars and the director to the producers are getting rich while all the crew gets is a paycheck like anybody else.

Eating the craft services food for free is one way to get even.

I never did find Guy Chesney that day. But God led me to Solly Epstein instead!

Solly was following a PA lusting after her. I could see this by the way he leered upon her flesh. I admit that I leered a little too until I rebuked myself and claimed several anti-leering Bible verses like, Matthew 5:28, "But I say to you that everyone who looks at a woman with lustful intent has already committed adultery with her in his heart." Obviously Solly had not read Galatians 5:16, "But I say, walk by the Spirit, and you will not gratify the desires of the flesh."

Solly was short, chunky and about forty five years old. He wore a white shirt and a cool Blues Brothers-type black suit but no tie. His shirt was open three buttons down and his chest hair was visible. He had a smooth round face the color of extra virgin olive oil. Solly's lust for the PA was his sin but before the Lord she shared some of the responsibility (like she did for my leering) because of her immodesty. She was wearing an absurdly short miniskirt. As I walked past the PA she pushed Solly away and said "No way Sol!" in a flirty manner that reeked of loose living and lapsed morals of the kind that the whole country was suffering from ever since we had turned away from God and our Christian Founding Fathers' vision for America. Solly sipped his coffee and saw me looking at him looking at her and he winked a very Hollywood Unbelieving Lapsed Liberal Jew-type wink.

"It's her way of saying 'yes,'" Solly said.

"Hi, Sol," I said, pretending I knew him because that's what the Lord said to do because I'd seen Solly's picture in the *Hollywood Reporter* and I knew he was an important agent.

"We met?" he asked.

"Sure," I answered with the godly lie the Lord laid on my heart that very instant. "I saw you over at a wrap party at John Kohn's."

"John's a mensch," Solly said.

"He said you'd like this," I said and held out my script instantly building the godly lie into a deftly constructed entirely fabricated back-story based on having read about that wrap party. "That's why I came over. John said you'd be here."

I had read about John Kohn in *Variety* and the *Hollywood Reporter*. He was an important producer with some good credits including "Racing with the Moon." There was no question but that the Lord's hand was on this "chance" meeting with Solly Epstein and the fact that I possessed deep background knowledge about just about everyone in town.

"Want to read my script before I send it over to Universal?" I asked.

"Universal my ass," Solly said and winked his leering Hollywood Unbelieving Lapsed Liberal Jew-type wink again.

"It's a sexy thriller," I said.

"Yeah, sure, it'll go to the top of the pile," Solly said and laughed and turned away *with my script under his arm.*

Yes Lord!

I called after Solly, "The production can be scaled down to meet a budget! There's nothing non-negotiable in it. Where it says ten cars blow up on the San Diego freeway it can be one car in Texas or some other right-to-work state, even a motorcycle. We can shoot in Florida if we have to!"

And then the Lord gave me favor in Solly's sight! He walked back over to me from the craft services table clutching a handful of dried figs and smiled a friendly kindly smile and said "Good for you. I get tired of writers married to their material."

"I'm not just a writer Sol. I only write material I direct. I'm working on something with John Kohn right now," I said.

"You DGA?" asked Solly.

"I can join the Director's Guild anytime I want to spring for the nine grand. Right now I'm working non-DGA. There are a lot of independent producers out there looking for non-DGA directors."

"John won't get his picture made, not after what happened with 'Shanghai Surprise,'" Solly said. "Madonna and Sean Penn really fucked him over." He stuffed a fig into his mouth chewed, swallowed the fig and lowered his voice to a friendly just-between-us conspiratorial whisper. "How do you feel about South Africa?" he asked.

"How do you mean?"

"The boycott, you know, 'Free Nelson Mandela,' 'We Won't Play Sun City,' all that political bullshit."

"What about you?" I asked.

"Guess it would depend on how bad I wanted to make my first picture," he said. "Where can I call you?"

Moments later I was driving back over Laurel Canyon. I had a song in my heart and a prayer of thanksgiving on my lips! I turned left onto Hollywood Boulevard, parked and raced to my room to check for Solly's phone call. On the drive I had named and claimed a message from Solly to already be on my answering machine. Who knows, I thought, he might even continue to represent me all the way up to and including getting God's movie made.

It was like everything I'd done had led to this moment, every detail including screenwriting night class. My stepping stone scripts might only be stepping stones to making God's movie but they followed the rules. Each of my scripts got better. I was so green when I first came to New Midian. Now I was a real writer. I'd learned that there always had to be something "really important at stake in a script" just like my writing teacher Hal Busby, said. These things "drive the character's quest." There are always "obstacles that make for conflict," and that "this is the heart of drama." Before I started to write stepping stone scripts I had "somewhat naively," like my friend Molly called it, sent God's script out to just about every producer in town. Before I left home Molly had been my co-music director at our church. We were close friends.

AND GOD SAID, "BILLY!"

The Bad Jews and other Secular Liberals, Humanists, Homosexuals, Socialists, Agnostics and assorted Atheists (even some Communists) said the movie I was led to make was going to be a "hard sell." Mostly they never returned my calls. The few who did read God's script laughed at me and of course that meant that they were unknowingly mocking God too for which they will answer during a long hot eternity. The one or two producers who talked to me said that I needed to make what they called a "genre film," as a "first step picture," in other words a "stepping stone to better things." This might be a "slasher flick" or a "horror picture" or even a "sexy thriller." Whatever it was it would be low budget and something to "break in with" before trying to direct a major motion picture like "The Calling." That was the title of God's script that He'd laid on my heart to write and direct. It was the reason I had left my family and come to New Midian. In screenwriting night class our teacher, the world famous script doctor and writing guru, Hal Busby, said, "Horror and exploitation films almost always turn a profit if they're brought in at the right budget and they're a good starting place for filmmakers. Sometimes small stepping stone pictures lead on to bigger things like John Carpenter's 'Halloween' that was produced on just a $320,000 budget but grossed over $80 million worldwide."

Like I said it was Molly who talked me into listening to the people in New Midian who told me to make a stepping stone movie first. Besides getting Words of Knowledge from the Lord and other prophetic utterances Molly was a very kind woman and just a few years older than me. I was in my 20s and she was in her 30s when I'd left home. Molly wasn't like everyone else in our church because I never felt she was judging me or keeping a sharp eye out for any backsliding I might be doing. And Molly was straightforward. If Molly didn't like something I said (or later after I'd left home that I wrote to her) she just said so and didn't say stuff like "I'll pray for you" the way most Christians do when they're really putting you down but doing it by pretending they love you. Molly was so normal that it was like she wasn't even saved. But because she was so nice too and a really great music director Pastor Bob (and mostly everyone else) let Molly be. And besides being generally liked Molly sometimes spoke in the Heavenly Tongue or interpreted other people's prophecies during worship. So everyone assumed she was close to the Lord in her own way even if she seemed somewhat worldly at times. Besides all that Molly was married to our youth pastor and he was very popular—at least for a while before he split our church.

The people in our church who weren't Real Christians left along with Molly's husband. Long before this split happened over the inerrancy of Scripture, our pastor, Pastor Bob, who later expelled Molly's husband, had started a new denomination. Pastor Bob was led to name our new church "The Reformed Charismatic Full Gospel Word of Life Church." Pastor Bob was the only Reformed Calvinist leader in America who also practiced the Full Gifts of The Spirit. So we got "the best of everything," like Pastor Bob said, "Solid Reformed teaching *and* uplifting Pentecostal worship!"

At first I rejected the idea of making a stepping stone movie. I wanted to direct God's Movie then race home to Seabrook, New Hampshire to my little girl Rebecca and to my wife Ruth, not build a career in the Movie Business. "I only came to town to make one movie!" I told Molly when I wrote to her. Molly helped me see that making a stepping stone movie might be part of God's Plan as the way to learn my craft so that when the door opened to make His movie I'd be ready and that the stepping stone movie might be the way to get that door open in the first place. So Molly was why I had finally written several profane, godless and downright worldly scripts and resigned myself to the fact it would take years longer to get God's Movie made than I had thought. And that's why I was on the set that day trying to pitch one of my stepping stone scripts to the production manager I'd met.

The point is that Ruth, Molly and I had had a close spiritual brother-and-sister-in-the-Lord-type of relationship. Molly was like a second mother to my little Rebecca. My chaste platonic attitude about Molly should have been because she was my sister-in-Christ. But to be honest the fact I didn't lust for Molly (like I admit I sometimes lusted for several of the other women in our church) had more to do with the way Molly was so close to my Rebecca than because of biblical absolutes and family values. Molly took care of Rebecca when my daughter would go over to play with Molly's three kids or when all our children were playing together in church while Molly and I rehearsed the music for Sunday worship. And since everything to do with Rebecca was sincerely, genuinely and completely sacred and pure as new-fallen snow to me it just didn't feel right to ever look at her favorite person -- Molly -- with lust in my heart. And besides all that my wife Ruth was absolutely by far and away the most beautiful woman in our church and always had been. So I had no excuses. And Ruth was warm and friendly in the "bed department" like she called "that aspect" of married life.

However Ruth was so very godly that I just never wanted to disappoint her by being too bold in disclosing just how tough it was out in New Midian, or about how hard I struggled sometimes when I felt far from the Lord. So it was a relief to be able to write sister-in-the-Lord-type stuff to Molly I'd never dare tell anyone else, not even to my super godly gorgeous good-in-bed wife Ruth. So after I was living alone -- *very alone* – in New Midian I wrote to Molly at least once a week just like I wrote to Ruth and Rebecca once a week too. But in my letters to Ruth and Rebecca I stuck to uplifting cheerful anecdotes about the doors God was opening for me. With Molly I told her the truth. And Molly confided in me too.

So I told Molly about what they were suggesting in screenwriting night class. I told her that it felt like making a so-called stepping stone movie would be a "compromise with Satan." I wrote that I felt like I would be "lying about God's power and that if I have enough faith I should be able to make God's movie right away just by naming and claiming His blessing."

Molly wrote back, "Billy, you need to do whatever it takes since God called you there. Don't worry about your 'stepping stone' movies being a 'kind of lying' like you put it. Even if it *is* a kind of lying remember that it's lying for God. Rahab the harlot lied to the king of Jericho about hiding the Hebrew spies (Joshua 2:4–5) and was rewarded. Paul says that, 'By faith the harlot Rahab perished not with them that believed not, when she had received the spies with peace' Hebrews 11:31. Her faith demonstration was to tell a bold godly lie and it was as good as accepting Jesus would have been if He'd already come and the godly lie led to her salvation. So just make your stepping stone movie already! Even if you think it's a 'lie' to do that it's really just a godly King David-type trick to get the secular producers to let you make God's movie…"

Standing in the hall outside my room I checked to see I had my key in the right lock. The light bulb was broken in the socket hanging from a foot of wire below the ceiling tiles. I kicked at the loose edge of the carpet in frustration when my key wouldn't open the door. A nasty urine ammonia smell came out of that carpet.

I didn't need to read the "Come to the office" notice taped above the handle of my door. I already sensed God was about to test me. See, each door in the Mayfair Estates had two locks. The tenant had one key and the management had the other in the office. When they wanted to get anyone's attention about missed rent payments they locked the door with that second lock. They did this to everyone. The lower halves of most of the doors in the hall were almost kicked to pieces. There was man from India and his wife in the office and they never were really asleep even if it looked like they were. They'd scream at me before I made it halfway across the floor to the box with the keys.

AND GOD SAID, "BILLY!"

So I lifted up my problem before The Throne. I knew I was not alone in that dark hall. I could sense that this was a satanic attack that God was allowing as a chastisement, though I wasn't sure what He was punishing me for. So maybe this was just one last test to prepare me for my big break because at last I had an *actual agent* interested in my work *and I couldn't even get to my message machine*!

But rent or no rent, back home in Seabrook I wasn't forgotten. In her letters to me Ruth always said that I was "held up unceasingly" by Pastor Bob and all the Spirit-filled brothers and sisters who shared the burden of my missionary director-for-Jesus call. So I joined my voice to theirs and prayed, "Oh Lord! Thou who hast led Thy people faithfully, Thou who didst impute faith to me and even righteousness please lead Solly to call me that I mightest fulfill Thy call to make it in The Business in order that I might be able to reach America for Thee, Oh Lord! So just open this door for me or just provide for me the three hundred dollars I need, as Thou provided the five smooth stones for David so he could slay Goliath, Oh Lord, I just beseech Thee!"

Then, in one of the most *direct leadings* I ever had and almost as sure fire as the time I was led to write down God's first draft of "The Calling," God sent me a vision of Arab women by a swimming pool. He put the details into my brain directly right down to their rolls of slick brown fat hanging over their bikini bottoms. God showed me that they were sitting by the pool at the Oakwood, by day, week or month furnished apartments over in Burbank. I knew that there, in the purses the Lord revealed to me in the vision -- clear as if they were actually floating in that dark stinking hallway -- that there would be that day's milk and honey.

God even gave me driving directions. It was revealed to me that all I had to do was drive down Hollywood to La Brea, turn left, then right onto Franklin, go up Highland, past the Hollywood Bowl to Barham and pull in the gate, with my old Oakwood Resident sticker prominently displayed on the dash. I had lived there the first month I came to town when I thought making it would be easy. That's why I still had the sticker. So the Lord even used the fact that I never cleaned out my car. I couldn't afford to live at Oakwood very long and got my much less expensive room after the seed money the church gave me ran out.

After showing me those handbags God had said, "Billy, be My Gideon today!" So I did just as the Lord instructed me by laying this passage on my heart, "And the LORD looked upon him, and said, 'Go in this thy might, and thou shalt save Israel from the hand of the Midianites: have not I sent thee?'" Judges 6:7-14.

When I got to Oakwood to do what God's servant Gideon did to the Midianites the Iranian security guard, the same one as when I was living there years before, glanced up from his little portable black and white TV, saw my old Oakwood sticker -- Yes Jesus! -- and waved me in. But no Midianites were by the pool! Then, in a flash I remembered that there were *two pools*. One God plus one believer is always a majority in any fight! "I will be with you" God told Gideon. And that's all that we should ever need to know.

The pool I was standing at was down at the lower end of the twenty-building apartment village. The other pool, sun deck, Jacuzzi and fitness center was on *the other side* of the complex at the top of the hill. The Midianite women were there! They were wearing lots of jewelry, the kind they sell on the Home Shopping Network, little glittery chains like women from India wear when they walk around the Beverly Center with red demonic Hindu dots on their foreheads. The Midianites had purses with initials all over them. I knew the rent was in those handbags like God said.

"Lord You have brought me to this promised land of Oakwood, just help me cross over to it on dry land! Just deliver these daughters of Hagar into my hand!" I said.

He did! He showed me what to do down to the smallest detail.

AND GOD SAID, "BILLY!"

The upper pool area was empty except for those three Arabs who lay oozed out like melting chocolate. One was face down, her worldly brown bottom bulging above and below her depraved copper-colored way-too-small bathing suit panties. On top her straps were unhooked. The two other Midianites were face up. I trusted Him to keep their eyes closed. I had to name and claim them closed. I couldn't see their eyes behind their rhinestone mirrored sunglasses. By faith alone I picked up a garden hose on the shady side of the pool next to the staircase that led to the fitness center. I pointed it at a bush, turned it on full blast, adjusted the nozzle from spray to a powerful stinging jet and waited for the water to get icy cold. Then I whipped around and blasted the three Midianites like God said to.

If they had thought it was only a joke the Midianites would have just run to the end of the pool screaming Arab curses. By yelling what God placed in my heart, "Death to Arabs! ISRAEL LIVES!" I convinced them to not just scream Arab curses but to also run all the way around the pool into the lower hall of F building.

Then I dropped the hose, ran around the pool and grabbed up the Midianites' Louis Vuitton, Gucci and Yves St. Laurent purses and dashed through the underground parking garage under Apartment G and ran on out to the parking lot and jumped into my Honda. The engine started right away which it never did so right there it proved I was in the Lord's Will. "Praise you, J-e-s-u-s!" I screamed and I made sure not to accelerate too fast. That would have made the Iranian look up from his TV and maybe take down my license number. But when God's Hand is on you everything works out fine and the gate guard didn't even turn his head.

Chapter 2
Living Off The Land

Plunder was the primary purpose of my Oakwood raid but God – who always uses any action to accomplish lots more than one thing in a sort of infinite many-birds-with-one-stone manner, had also used me to punish His enemies. For "God shall wound the head of His enemies, and the hairy scalp of such an one as goeth on still in his trespasses" Psalm 68:21. Arabs hate Israel and so are the sworn perpetual eternal enemies of the One True God. The Arab women clearly hated God otherwise why would they all have run around the poolside? If they had been in tune with God's mighty sovereign purposes they would have answered "Praise God!" when I screamed "Israel lives!"

Besides the plunder cash spoils there was a ring with rubies in one Arab's purse. I knew that the Lord wanted me to keep this for Ruth's Christmas present. I'd have to trust Him for the story of how I got it because it might make Ruth ask about things she didn't need to know. But I knew that when the time came to send it to her that God would give me a godly fib to tell. God had already led me to invent a pretend job as an assistant freelance director on commercial shoots in order to explain the manner of the Lord's provision of my needs to Ruth. Otherwise Ruth would have asked questions about what I was living on. Of course I had no actual day job because if I had been at work all day then looking for Movie Business contacts, doing meetings (if I ever got a meeting), going to screenwriting classes, writing scripts and waiting by the phone for calls to set up the productions (should God decide to bless me at last) could never have happened. In other words my full time work for the Lord had to actually be full time.

The people who left our church along with Molly's husband started another "church" up the road from ours in Hampton Falls. Then Molly's husband got found out to be having sex with a woman who wasn't Molly. So some of the backsliders who had followed him left his new so-called church and came back to us. And Molly left him too and also returned to us. Molly took her three young kids with her and came back and after she made a public confession of repentance and was reinstated by Pastor Bob as our music director. And a few weeks later when Molly asked Pastor Bob for permission to get a divorce, Pastor Bob said that Molly's divorce was Biblical because the false youth pastor had cheated on her.

Molly's girls loved to come over to Ruth's and my trailer because of all the paints and clay we had for Rebecca spread out on our picnic table. Ruth was a very creative person and a good mother. The children always begged her to read poems to them. Rebecca's favorite poem that Ruth most often read out loud in her lovely sweet voice began:

> "Over in the meadow,
> In the sand in the sun,
> Lived an old mother toadie,
> And her little toadie one,
> 'Wink!' said the mother;
> 'I wink!' said the one…"

Besides the ring, the Lord delivered $1,236 in cash to me. This was more than enough money for the rent and the back rent. God's bounty was welcome but not unexpected. We're not supposed to go through life defeated and not having enough money to pay our bills. God offers health, abundance, wealth, prosperity and success if we just have the faith to claim His victory of success. "Then nothing on earth will be able to hold those good things from us," I'd say over and over again while practicing smiles in front of my mirror. And I'd add, "You were born to win; you were born for greatness, you were created to be a champion in life!"

So breaking men's petty "rules," in order to keep God's Mighty Commandment to be Prosperous was the right thing to do. Jesus wants his ambassadors rich and happy so that others will want to join God's team. Satan wants us poor. Besides, just for practical reasons, if God's anointed aren't happy, fed and provided with relaxing treats we can't do the Lord's work effectively. That goes for churches, ministries and evangelical leaders and it also goes for individual prophets. And it's not like I was plundering for selfish reasons. The stakes can't get any higher than what I had been called to do!

God had told me that by making His movie we would unleash the final revival that would prepare the way for the End Times. Our movie was going to bring all the Bad Jews back to God. They would watch the movie and be convicted to return to Israel. Using The Law of Return, they'd become citizens of the Jewish State, in order that prophecy might be fulfilled. And then Jesus would return to take us Real Christians to Heaven in the Rapture. And then He'd kill all the Jews (except for the few who had become Real Christians) and the world would end.

Another reason God provided me with plunder is that He knew I was suffering a terrible loss for the Kingdom's sake. I was cut off from my family until the Lord's Word would be fulfilled. So He found ways to cheer me up. I needed plenty of cheering up! I missed Rebecca so much that most nights I cried myself to sleep. I'd think about all the lovely times when we were still together. Even hard times provided sweet memories, like the time she fell on the Newburyport boardwalk down by the Merrimack River. Rebecca was two when she chipped a front tooth and a few months later she had to have it taken out because it got abscessed. Because she was so young the dentist said she'd need to send her to a child specialist in Danvers and that Rebecca would need to have an anesthetic. I held her close and I could smell the anesthetic coming out of her when she breathed out as she woke up. Ruth carried Rebecca into our trailer but when Rebecca saw me she reached for me! I held her for hours and was telling her a long involved story about Jiminy Cricket. Remembering her warm little arms around my neck, her head against my chest and how I kissed the top of her head gently over and over always made me cry. I really pined for her.

Anyway, after almost three years of my ministry bearing little-to-no fruit and at a low point for me spiritually of missing Ruth and Rebecca I had called Pastor Bob. This was just before I met Solly and got my big break. I'd just reread my Rebecca Diary entry where I'd written down what she said when she turned three: "Today Rebecca announced: 'I will marry you Daddy!' 'Why?' I asked. 'Because you're so kind to me,' she said." After rereading that passage I had called Pastor Bob and asked if there might be some other way to fulfill God's Word instead of me not seeing my family until the Lord's Will came to pass. Pastor Bob said, "You need to stay there Billy, hard as it might be for you to understand God's mysterious ways." Then like always I was flooded with this lonely feeling of missing my little girl and I wept bitterly. Then I called Pastor Bob back. But all he said was that I had to stay where I was.

So after I dried my tears I turned on my answering machine and went to Ralph's Supermarket. The black security guard at Ralphs was no problem. The Lord always closed his eyes to my plundering just like He had closed the eyes of the lions when His servant Daniel was cast into the lion's den. The guard mostly spent his time playing with his keys and the mace can strapped to his shiny belt. Once in a while he'd do his security guard job and keep the homeless people hanging around the boarded up frozen yogurt bar across the street from panhandling from Ralphs' customers. Mostly he didn't do anything.

Sometimes I took things like dog food or even women's personal hygiene items in order to get what I really wanted. I didn't want dog food (or tampons or whatever) but I despoiled unneeded items along with what I needed because the extraneous items happened to be listed on the receipt I'd found in the parking lot trashcan. Then I'd put the hamburger or steaks or whatever else I really wanted in the bag along with everything else listed on the receipts. That way if the checkout girl bothered to check what was in my bag she'd see that the hamburger matched my receipt along with all the other items. So she'd believe me when I told her that I'd already paid and had come back into the store carrying my paid for purchases to look for my lost sunglasses. I'd even make sure that the receipts I used weren't more than a few hours old because I figured that if the checkout girl was unusually smart and/or vigilant if the time code stamp was too old she'd get suspicious.

Sometimes God sent along a special little encouraging treat to take my mind off missing Ruth and Rebecca and the rejection by the producers I was suffering for the Kingdom's sake. For instance there was the time I discovered Haagen-Dazs vanilla ice cream! I'd never heard of it until I had to stick three quarts of it into a bag so I could despoil the steak I actually wanted that day listed on a receipt I'd just found.

So after that I despoiled Haagen-Dazs vanilla ice cream regularly even though it sometimes took me hours of sorting through receipts in the trash to find Haagen-Dazs listed. Maybe I didn't need all that ice cream but in the Bible the Apostle Paul says God uses us believers for the advancement of God's work even when we have

AND GOD SAID, "BILLY!"

bad attitudes. "What then? notwithstanding, every way, whether in pretence, or in truth, Christ is preached; and I therein do rejoice, yea, and will rejoice" Philippians 1:18. And that's how it was when "in pretense" I wanted ice cream, even though I already had sufficient food. So maybe I plundered Haagen-Dazs vanilla ice cream in pretence and not always "in truth" but that was okay because in 2 Corinthians 12:10 it says "My grace is sufficient for thee: for my strength is made perfect in weakness. Most gladly therefore will I rather glory in my infirmities, that the power of Christ may rest upon me."

So most nights I ate my ice cream in front of my TV while sitting on the floor at the end of my bare mattress and glorying in my infirmities. Next to the TV I kept my Bible, my cassette tape player, the stack of sermons on tape by Pastor Bob, my stack of women's Bible study talks by Ruth, my electric frying pan, phone-answering machine and reading lamp. I also kept my Rebecca Diary there. I'd have it open to some entry like this one: "Rebecca looked so lovely today in her Easter dress. She was hunting for the eggs Molly and Ruth hid all over in the park. When Rebecca stood so still in that white dress between rows of daffodils it's like she was some flower fairy come to life from that book she loves so much. I was watching her and thinking that loving somebody this much is dangerous. How would I survive if anything bad ever happened to my precious child?"

I would stop eating, rereading my Rebecca Dairy or writing scripts when Pat Robertson came on TV. Then I'd intercede before The Throne right along with Pat and the other "700 Club" prayer partners. That was when I'd feel the most uplifted. Even though Pat wasn't a member of my denomination and he had "some theological problems" like Pastor Bob said, nevertheless Pat spoke to my heart. I just loved that happy chuckle of his!

After the show I'd get back to work on my stepping stone scripts. The way I wrote these scripts was to think of depraved things that typical Secular Humanists in New York City, who run the ACLU, hate Christmas and ban prayer in American schools would put in their scripts. That included nudity and F-words and gratuitous violence. However even when I had to pretend to be a God-hater in order to trick the actual God-haters that control New Midian into making God's movie, there was still a way that I secretly honored the Lord. You see my stepping stone scripts never had anyone in them taking the Lord's Name in vain. God told me that He understood why my characters had to use the F-word and do full frontal nudity but He commanded me to never write dialogue where my characters took His Name in vain.

I wrote to Molly about God's dialogue instructions. Molly wrote back, "You worry too much. Do whatever you've got to do to get this over and come home." At that time Molly was beginning to express her theological doubts to me besides urging me to come home almost like she wasn't fully in tune with God's leading any more. I began to worry about the eternal destiny of her soul when she wrote: "My parents still think very highly of Pastor Bob and don't understand why I'm starting to grumble. But I'd like to find a church where the pastor is a spiritual leader living a life that matches his rhetoric. How can I tell my parents I want to change churches without hurting their feelings?"

I wrote back: "I challenge you to stay at our church and try and work through your attitude problem. The Bible calls the church the 'body of Christ' for a reason. Despite the fact that our church may have some problems, we're still called to be committed to this body of Christ."

Like I said Molly's doubts were troubling me but we had both shared things we weren't telling anyone else. Being able to share pretty much everything with someone was helpful. And to be honest, maybe the fact that Molly was somewhat backslidden made it easier to share everything. Even before I'd left home I talked to

Molly pretty frankly about the little ups and downs in my marriage. I knew Molly had had fights with her husband too (back when they were still married) about the way he seemed to flirt with the younger women in the church, even though he was the youth minister. And she knew that sometimes I found it difficult to talk to Ruth about the fact I wished she'd spend more time with Rebecca and less time teaching Bible studies.

So anyway in my letters I told Molly the stuff no one else but God knew. For instance I had never said anything about my stepping stone scripts to Ruth let alone about what was in them. Ruth never even said "darn" because she said it was a "minced oath" in other words sounded like the swear word "damn." That went for "jeez" (too much like "Jesus") or anything else like that. The point is that Ruth was just too holy to be fully honest with. So I withheld information from her in the spirit of the biblical command to never needlessly offend our brothers and sisters in Christ.

So like I said by the time I was writing my stepping stone scripts Molly was entering her period of doubt. Her doubts escalated. Soon after she began to grumble about Pastor Bob, Molly really shocked me. She wrote, "The hardest thing in this church for me is my inability to ask real questions. All their opinions are 'based on Scripture.' If you question their opinions beyond the sweet, surface way of questioning a 'girl' can use, you are 'questioning the authority of the Bible.' They tell me I can't be a real Christian if I question. I know Pastor Bob will fire me if he learns what I'm telling you but I trust you."

I had to rebuke her but there was plenty of good news to share too. I'd share my joys with Molly like about how I'd take special Praise Drives to thank God for His blessings. I hoped these news items from my life would uplift her. So I told her about how I liked to drive down Sunset Boulevard through the heart of The Business. I told Molly and Ruth and Rebecca too because this was so positive, about how during my Praise Drives I'd name and claim every screening room and production office I passed. "Someday I'll work there!" I'd shout pointing at each one. "Yes Lord!"

Anyway, the day after meeting Solly I took one of my may-my-joy-may-be-full Praise Drives. I had a full tank of gas! I had money! I had a REAL AGENT interested in my work! He'd even agreed to read one of my scripts! So I hopped into my old Civic and drove past Fairfax and La Cieniga past the Sunset Plaza and all the giant billboards that line the Strip. Up close the billboards are ugly. But at sunrise on that Sunday morning of godly joy and with my rent paid and an agent having said he'd read my script, even the billboards looked pretty! Even the Marlborough man looked good that day!

Here's how I'd described this part of town to Ruth, Molly and Rebecca in a newsletter I'd sent them all: "At Doheny and Sunset, Hollywood stops and Beverly Hills starts. Tacky billboards, restaurants, offices, record stores, comedy clubs and apartments end and classy trees, streets, lawns, Armed Response signs, Mexican gardeners and nannies pushing strollers, start. Both sides of Sunset are filled with giant houses that cover whole lots. They're so huge they leave no yard unless you count two tennis courts as a 'yard.' Deeper into Beverly Hills the houses on Sunset at Benedict Canyon Drive, Roxbury and Whittier, have more land around them. I never name and claim those houses because even I know the limits of what I have faith to claim! (Just being funny!)"

Anyway, on that day's Praise Drive with Beverly Hills, Bel Air, Westwood and UCLA behind me I reached the bottom of the hill and turned right onto the Pacific Coast Highway and headed for Malibu and a breakfast of thanksgiving. The one-story white and green Malibu Inn sits across the road from the Pacific Ocean and the Malibu pier. The inn is the same kind of eating joint that I could have found back home out on Salisbury Beach, where sometimes I took Rebecca for pancakes, only the food in California was way better.

AND GOD SAID, "BILLY!"

The Malibu Inn is just a plain wooden building sided with New England-style clapboards. It doesn't look fancy. But inside it's decorated with hundreds of black and white pictures of the movie stars who ate there. Jane Fonda, John Wayne, Johnny Carson and other faces of dead and living stars said Hi to me as I walked in. I always smiled back at them because the Lord told me that someday soon my picture would be up there too! "Yes, Lord! And I'll bring Rebecca and Ruth here for breakfast too!" I said as I walked in.

On Sunday the actors, producers and agents who live in Malibu came to the inn to eat mushroom omelets served with apple butter and whole wheat English muffins. These muffins were served by girls in short black mini-skirts. These worldly girls didn't care if people seated at the counter could see their panties when they bent down to get more coffee filters. I think they did it on purpose. But in the Bible God says if you lead one of His children astray, it would be better if you were never born. So I got the lust tingle but they will reap the judgment.

After I ate I wrote my Sunday letter.

> June 20, 1988, Malibu Inn
> Dear Ruth and Rebecca,
> Greetings in the name of our Lord Jesus Christ! I met the most important agent in Hollywood who loves my work and wants to do everything he can to help "The Calling" get made.
> Rebecca it's your sixth birthday! I remembered! There's a surprise! (Ruth don't read this part out loud but it's the wallet here with 20 dollars in it for her to find in the billfold.) Rebecca, thank you for the wonderful picture you drew for me and your latest poem. It's up on my wall and reminds me every day how the Lord has blessed me with such a wonderful daughter and it's nice to have a reminder of good old

Plum Island beach too! You drew the heron standing in the tidal pool so well. I'm so glad you say you love birds and would like to have one as a pet. Maybe the Lord will provide that in His Own way.

I love you lots and we're close in Him even though we're far away from each other. Give Pastor Bob my love and tell him that his upholding of me is being answered! Say Hi to Molly and her kids too!

In His love your brother in Christ, husband and Daddy
Love and kisses,
XXX OOO

I finished the letter and put it in the big yellow envelope that I had plundered from a stack in a Xerox store. I wiped a smear of apple butter off the envelope, licked the flap and stuck on a couple of the stamps from a new 20-dollar roll that was in one of the Arab's purses because when God does something He thinks of every detail. As I pressed the stamps down I said a little ditty Pastor Bob taught us in Summer Bible school years ago, "Never a weakness that He can't fill and never a sickness that He can't heal! Moment by moment I'm under His care! Wherever I go, whatever I do, no matter how far or how long, Jesus Christ will always be there for me!" Because I had plenty of money I actually paid for breakfast rather than sneaking out and I left a nice tip. I could have walked out when the waitress went back to the kitchen for a minute but I never plundered unless God led me to and always took just what I needed (ice cream excepted) and no more and no less just like the Good Jews did with the manna.

But not everyone is given enough spiritual discernment to walk by faith alone and finish the race they have begun. The very same day I'd met Solly I received another distressing letter from Molly. She was starting to write in an angry way about her whole life and to question everything! Up until that letter the grumbling had been pretty standard backsliding. But with this letter she began to go from mere backsliding to edging towards the precipice of actual heresy.

Molly wrote, "After growing up in the End Times commune I got involved with Campus Crusade at age 17 and stayed with them until I married. Talking about evangel-o-bizarre-o-world, that's Crusade! All the staff was considered 'godly' and what they really meant by that was that they were infallible. So whatever the staff said or did was somehow 'from God.' To question the leadership of the Crusade elite was to question God himself. As a result, when I was in a staff training center and one of our 46-year-old staff and his 43-year-old wife took a sabbatical then he returned a year later with a hot 21-year-old new Mrs. Bentley, we just pretended it was the same Mrs. Bentley that he had left with, no questions asked! I've suppressed these memories for too long! My reason for reaching out to you again and again, Billy, is the sense that you may understand this struggle because you gave up so much to 'follow God.' At least I know you are serious about your faith. I'm so confused on so many levels."

After dropping my package with the wallet and letter in it in the mailbox right next to the Malibu Inn door, I drove along the Pacific Coast Highway to Zuma Beach. At the beach exit I turned off the highway and drove down a sandy track for about half a mile and parked by the side of the road that runs next to five miles of great beach from Le Chuza Point to Point Dume. I walked up the beach to the cliff that's always in the background of half the commercials on TV whenever they need ocean framed by rocks. As I walked I got busy thanking God for the sun on my face and praising Him for my rent and beseeching Him to watch over Rebecca and also that He'd restore Molly's faith. Suddenly I stopped dead. I stood so still that I started to sink into the sand with the surf washing over my feet because sitting on the beach opposite me about fifty feet away was

Solly. *And he was reading my stepping stone script.*

I could see the title "Blood Warrior." It was in the extra bold letters in 72 point type on my bright red cover. Seeing a Very Connected Agent reading my latest script was like I heard a choir of angels singing. Solly was sitting next to a worldly looking woman. Her bikini top was unhooked. She lay on a huge Budweiser towel, the kind you can win from KISS, FM, if you're worldly enough to want to listen to that kind of music and you're one of the first 100 callers. She had shapely thighs and a bottom like a trim apricot. Solly was slouched on a fold-out aluminum chair smoking a cigarette and reading.

At first I thought that I wouldn't say anything. "If you look over-eager it doesn't help. They have to need you more than you need them." That's what they said in "The Business of The Business" I read for night class. But then I thought as how this couldn't be a mere coincidence. I thought about how many details the Lord had just worked out to get me to be on exactly the same spot at exactly the same time that a Secular Bad Jew Agent was reading my script. Solly wasn't just skimming it but slowly turning my anointed pages. Solly wasn't even distracted by the woman he was with even though she was so close to him that I'm sure he could smell her perfume because I could from fifty feet away.

I waited for the Lord's instructions. Then the Lord said that I should walk about another fifty feet up the beach. When I got there He told me to sit down "real casual like" and to wait for Solly to finish reading. God said that when Solly was done reading that I should walk back past him and if he looked up and saw me, fine, it would be a sign. If on the other hand Solly didn't look up then the Lord said that at least He had let me see Solly reading my script as an encouragement to my heart. So while Solly turned the pages I sat nearby praising God and squeezing sand between my fingers. Then Solly turned a page and shook his head like he was saying "no" to somebody. Then he stood up and *pitched my script into the Pacific Ocean!*

AND GOD SAID, "BILLY!"

"Why?" I yelled before I could stop myself.

Solly jerked his head around and recognized me and yelled, "What the fuck?"

His worldly woman sat up then she remembered her bathing suit top was off and she crashed back onto her towel. Solly took a step toward me. I took a step toward him and then we both looked at my script rolling in the pounding surf. It slid up and down on the sparkling wet sand. Pages pulled loose from the brads and started to float away.

"What the fuck are you doing here?" Solly asked and he looked angry.

I smiled and tried to act calm. And then God did a miracle and placed His words in my heart in a flash. "I always come here on Sunday mornings," I said.

"What are you doing watching me like some goddamned creep?" Solly asked and his voice went up high and angry on the word "creep."

"I was walking along and I saw you reading my script," I said.

Then he seemed to snap out of his bad mood in an instant. His expression went from angry to a sort of thoughtful neutral, like he'd just remembered something, and then his face broke into a big sunny welcoming grin.

Solly laughed walked down to the water and fished out what was left. Then he walked back up the bank smiling and smiling and started to chuckle. He was holding my dripping pages and putting them back together and he smiled some more and said "Hey Billy, I was just pulling your chain! I saw you standing there way before you saw me! I'm afraid I get in lots of trouble because I kid around too much! This is really great work! You've got a really active protagonist here. Great work! Call me. Let's do lunch."

Chapter 3

Solly Epstein Said He Just Loves My Work!

On Monday morning at 10 AM sharp I called Feinstein, Goldstein and Epstein. I would have called earlier -- I'd been up since 5 AM waiting to call -- but no one important in New Midian does anything before 10 AM, unless it's an insanely early breakfast meeting which sometimes they set up at a juice bar or something right after Yoga or just before a dawn crew call.

Right off the bat Solly's personal assistant Jasmine said, "Hi I'm Jasmine, Solly's personal assistant. Solly wants you to know that he just loves your work! He wants me to ask you if today would be good for lunch."

I was able to remain cool, calm and collected and pretended to look at a day planner and answered, "Let me see Jasmine... sure, if I move a few things around today's fine."

"How about you meet him at Angeli's on Melrose, Billy, you know one block up from La Cucina."

"I know where it is," I said. "I do meetings there all the time."

"Twelve thirty?" she said and her voice was warm and full of a really deferential-type smile that I could clearly hear, the sort of deferential love-your-work voice-smile she probably reserved for Solly's

AND GOD SAID, "BILLY!"

top clients, clients I knew that included the three top screenwriting teams in town not to mention a hot new talent named Bruce Willis.

"Fine," I said calmly and without a trace of excitement, like this happened every day and I put a warm smile in my voice too so she'd know that I was a good guy and she'd keep my stuff on the top of every pile of scripts in the office whenever she could. I added, "Thank you so much Jasmine. I really appreciate all you do. Solly says he can't get anything done without you."

"That's so sweet of you Billy," she said.

I hung up and screamed, "YES, LORD! SOLLY EPSTEIN SAID HE LOVES MY WORK! YES, LORD! SOLLY EPSTEIN SAID HE LOVES MY WORK! YES, LORD! SOLLY EPSTEIN SAID HE LOVES MY WORK! YES, LORD! YES, LORD! YES, LORD! YES, LORD! YES LORD! THANK YOU JESUS! SOLLY EPSTEIN SAID HE *JUST LOVES MY WORK!*"

Then I sat down and reread (for about the thousandth time) one of my favorite parts of my Rebecca Diary. I read it with a joyful heart because the Lord was moving in my life and so I knew that I'd soon be back with my child. This was what I read: "I love her arms around my neck. I love how she is so used to being in my arms that she just kind of fits there as if she grew there. Sometimes we have what we call a 'Walking Picnic.' I carry her and bring crackers and apples and cheese and we walk up the beach to Sandy Point and she eats and I tell her Bible stories. Today all on her own without me even asking Rebecca leaned over and kissed me and said 'I love you Daddy.' We saw a dead cormorant and talked about all the reasons it might have died. Rebecca said 'I think it ate a bad bug' and then she said, 'I think he flew into a window.' And then a while later she said, 'Maybe Jesus forgot about him.' She is so smart and so advanced verbally! She's only three and knows Jesus is God and that God sustains the universe so that if a bird dies it must be because God 'forgot' him! Amazing vocabulary! Amazing grasp of doctrine!"

By 11 AM I was waiting in the doorway of a Sodomite bathhouse across from Angeli's. I didn't want to wait in Angeli's in case Solly was doing another meeting there first. I didn't want him to know I was over an hour early. Overeager doesn't pay in a town where cool and "laid back" is how everyone successful acts. I moved from the bathhouse entrance because the homosexuals kept giving me very homosexual looks. After that I stood next to the door of the convenience store in the gas station beside the bathhouse and watched the Indian behind the counter selling gas, big gulp slurpies and hamburgers. An hour later I walked over to Angeli's.

I sat down at the gray marble counter opposite the pizza oven. I ordered a Virgin Mary but I didn't drink any. With a full glass in front of me Solly would think that I had just arrived. My Virgin Mary was served with a celery stick just like a Bloody Mary. I ordered a Virgin Mary so Solly wouldn't suspect that I was born-again and protecting my temple of the Holy Spirit from alcoholic defilement. A Virgin Mary looks the same as a Bloody Mary so I could look like I was in the world but not actually be of it. I left it untouched because like I said, overeager doesn't pay and if the glass was empty it would prove I'd been waiting way longer than is cool.

There was a little girl at a nearby table and she reminded me of my Rebecca. The little girl dropped her glass and it broke. Her mother scolded her and she cried. Rebecca used to get nervous too if she broke something. But after she broke a plate I said "It doesn't matter, I love you more than anything we own so never feel bad if you break anything." After that Rebecca would tell me about anything she'd broken without being nervous.

Solly was twenty seven minutes late and he made me jump because he happened to walk up to me and tapped my shoulder at a moment that I wasn't watching the door but was watching the child at the table across from me and praying for my own little girl.

"Hi Billy!" Solly said, very warm and friendly.

AND GOD SAID, "BILLY!"

"I just got here," I said.

Solly glanced at my untouched drink (Yes Lord!) and called over a waitress with enormous breasts and asked her if our table was ready. She said, "Hi Solly! Did you get a chance to send my headshot over to Disney?"

"Sure," said Solly, "I'm waiting for them to call back. You look great!"

We sat at our table and she took Solly's drink order and walked to the back of the bar. "Nice tits but no ass," Solly whispered and winked. Then when the waitress brought Solly's drink he spoke up in a loud voice like he wanted to be overheard and to be noticed by the other diners and said, "I'll call Disney again today." Then Solly lowered his voice and leaned over the table and whispered, "Remember I asked about SA?"

"What's that?" I asked.

"South Africa," Solly whispered. "How do you feel about it? Remember I asked?"

"About South Afri--?" I said.

Solly cut me off. "Shhh!" he said and smiled and held up a finger to his lips. "Let's just call it S," he whispered. Then Solly raised his voice back to normal and said, "Yeah, so how do you feel about S?"

"Fine I guess."

"You'll work there?"

"On my movie?" I asked, trying not to scream with excitement.

"Could be or maybe on another script." Solly leaned forward again and whispered, "We can't be associated with this shoot though. Our agency organized the Hollywood Bowl Winnie Mandela benefit for chrissake."

"You'll represent me?"

"Hey with a talent like yours I'd kill to be your agent! Of course I'll represent you later! But on this deal I'm not going to officially be your agent. So let's just get this one done and then when you're back we'll do lunch and set up a plan to roll out your work. Sound good?"

"Yes!" I said and try as I would I couldn't keep the excitement out of my voice. But Solly gave me such a warm smile and looked so pleased at the idea of representing me that all my fears about not being cool enough evaporated and I calmed right down.

"You'll have to spend the Rand in S because they won't let you take money out of the country."

My excitement broke through again and what I said next came out too high pitched and way over eager. "Who wants to make my script?" I squeaked.

"Lots of people I'm sure but I just need this favor first. They start to prep in a couple of weeks. Interested? Do this one and I'll have your work on every studio reader's desk the day after you're back. Interested?"

I tried to contain my joy but I couldn't. I yelled out loudly in the Heavenly Tongue, "Agoia, ahoi, attache, zaneb shan-na-na-na-na!" Solly jumped and dropped his glass. The smashing sound of his wine glass hitting the floor brought me back to earth. Solly's smile turned to a frown and he hissed, "Jesus Christ!" and started wiping his lap with his napkin. Everyone was staring at me. But without missing a beat God told me exactly what say. "My valium prescription ran out. I'm a little edgy!" I said loudly. People laughed.

Everyone in New Midian takes prescription medications or sees psychologists or other false teachers to fill the empty place only Jesus can fill. So once I said the word "valium" that made everything okay again. Solly loosened up even though he kept blaspheming by muttering, "Jesus Christ!" at the same time he was smiling.

"Let me order you another one," I said and I did.

We didn't talk much while we ate the rosemary chicken we'd both ordered, or rather after he'd ordered for us both after he said this was the "best roasted chicken this side of a place I know in Florence."

AND GOD SAID, "BILLY!"

Solly was in a hurry to leave for a meeting with Bruce on the set of "Die Hard" and so we skipped desert. When the bill came I reached for it and Solly grabbed the bill and paid! I had the Arab's twenty crisp new 20 dollar bills ready in my pocket but never touched them.

I HAD JUST BEEN TAKEN TO LUNCH!

Solly wrote down the address of the producer of the S deal and he handed me the S script and said, "Read this little gem and then get your talented butt over to Rubin's. You're set up to meet at five. Don't be late. He can be a little difficult but he's one of the fine old school producers and a great contact for you. Goes way back with Mel Brooks and Cid Caesar, so don't let good old Ruby offend you. He's a little rude but in a friendly fatherly way. His little picture may not seem like much but it's a great way for you to get into the business. While you're out of town I'll position your screenplay. And send more of what you've got to Jasmine. She just thinks you're great."

At first I thought I'd go back to my room and read the script there but God said "Do a David." I knew what the Lord meant. In the Bible it says that David dreamed about being a warrior for God like I did about being God's movie director. David practiced for success by killing animals with his slingshot. This was long before the giant Goliath challenged God's Good Jews and God uplifted David. David practiced so often that he knew he was a warrior for God even before his success arrived and he started killing people. David named and claimed success against giants and all the thousands of other people he killed for God by killing lions and bears first. God honored David's practicing for success. So I drove up Sunset instead of going back to my room in order to practice for success in my own way. And while I drove the Lord gave me a vision of my little girl twirling and twirling as if she was the lead angel of the heavenly host dancing her way in front of my car through the traffic. So I crossed into Beverly Hills led there by the vision of my child leading me directly to the Beverly Hills Hotel!

I parked on Crescent Drive in a parking space that the Lord opened up for me when a Mercedes pulled out just as I arrived. The parking space was one block from the main entrance of the Beverly Hills Hotel. Everything was so clearly of the Lord that afternoon. Like I'd written to Molly, "There is not an area or detail in my life that God is not willing to help me out with, no matter how small." I'd written to her to try and help her see God's plan for each one of us more clearly after she'd written, "These days I seem to be speaking a different language than my church friends. Trying to see the world honestly is very, very lonely."

Anyway, I killed that day's practice lion by reading the S script sitting out in the open in the lobby across from the Polo Lounge! "Yes, Jesus! SOLLY EPSTEIN SAID HE LOVES MY WORK! YES, LORD! Put on your twirly dancing dress Rebecca! Daddy's coming home!"

With a script in my hand and my hair in a director ponytail and with the joy of the Lord in my heart I was already feeling like a "giant killer" even *before* the Lord revealed me to the world! See, I was naming and claiming success by my choice of where to read the script. You have to get the settings and the scenes in your life right. Scripts and life are the same. God knows how to write your scenes best of all. So you have to know when God wants you to jump into the scene He's written for you and act the part He wrote for you or even to throw in a little improvisation the way directors like Bob Altman encourage. You have to "act" because what we do is watched by both the hosts of Heaven and the hosts of Hell. It all has eternal meaning in the struggle for the salvation of the world and, like Job, we have to help God defeat Satan through our brave and faithful activities, say like by me claiming directing success by acting *like* successful directors hanging out near the Polo Lounge *before* God sent the actual success.

AND GOD SAID, "BILLY!"

Anyway as I sat down in the Beverly Hills Hotel acting like a successful director and looking the part before actually playing it for real, I heard God say "SOLLY EPSTEIN SAID HE LOVES YOUR WORK!" Then I heard God call "Action!" And I played the part written for me from before the dawn of Creation and asked a passing Mexican for a phone.

I asked in a commanding voice filled with self-confidence like I'd practiced in front of my mirror. I asked for the phone in the voice of someone that Solly Epstein represented. The Mexican obviously knew what a real Hollywood insider looks like and could sense I was important or soon would be. So he brought a phone on a silver tray while another bellboy carried the phone cord from the concierge desk across the floor so no one would trip over it. I'd seen them do this for other people when I'd hung out cruising for contacts. One time I saw them bring a phone – *the same phone I was about to use* – to Elizabeth Taylor!

As he handed me the phone the Mexican said "Here you are sir." I might as well have been Stanly Kubrick! I tipped him 10 dollars because, "He that is faithful in that which is least is faithful also in much" Luke 16:10. Then I pretended to dial and then said, "We start shooting next week. I never thought De Niro was right for the part!" And heads turned. I saw at least three well dressed super worldly women and one man in a three piece suit with a flower in his buttonhole look to see if I was anybody. One woman even smiled at me. And God said, "Billy you *are* somebody if I say you are!"

Then I read the script. The story was set near New Orleans. It was about a body builder and his aerobics instructor girlfriend. They go water skiing together. They're both great looking. After the engine of their boat breaks down they're swept into a bayou by a storm where they're washed up, "clinging to their overturned boat." The girl's bikini top comes off. So when they run up the beach to get help she's topless and stays that way for the rest of the movie exposing her, "hard cat-like body and pearl-pink, erect nipples," like the very worldly script said. The people who own the shack that Topless and Muscles go to for help are drug dealers. They spend the rest of the movie raping Topless and torturing Muscles. At the start of the third act -- that's the last part of a movie after the Motivating Incident and Characterization have been established -- Muscles gets loose and hides in a swamp. He comes back in the night and kills the drug dealers one by one in interesting ways. Then Muscles unties Topless and she gets to kill some of her captors too because she's a "fully liberated woman" and a martial arts expert. With one of them Topless, "bites off his engorged manhood" like the script puts it. That's why the movie's title is "Suck On This!" That's what Topless says as she chomps down.

Except for Molly, the folks back home would not have understood how it was God's Will for me to direct "Suck On This!" They didn't understand how The Business works. But even I never figured that my big break was going to be a slasher picture where someone bites off a penis. Talk about going deep under cover as God's secret agent!

At first I was shocked. But right after I read the penis biting scene and was feeling shocked God said, "You're my Daniel in Babylon Billy! Daniel served the worst king ever so he could be in the right place and the right time and I'm giving you 'Suck On This!' for MY purposes." Then God told me that nothing shocks Him. He reminded me that He's "seen it all," even when it comes to penises. He reminded me that told Abraham to get a stone knife and cut off the end of his penis -- talk about a test of faith! -- and to also cut off all the tips of all the penises of his slaves and his family-- talk about a test of leadership and the ability to get other people to do what you say! No writer has ever come up with anything as far-fetched as what God came up with. I mean why penises? Why not command them to cut off an ear lobe? So as soon as I remembered that circumcision is biblical I was praising Jesus for sending me a perfect stepping stone disguise. I mean no one would have mistaken "Suck On This!"

for a born-again movie starring Pat Boon or Cliff Richards.

On my way out of the hotel God suggested that I despoil the men's room. While the attendant was helping a man brush off his jacket I stuffed two monogrammed hand towels under my shirt and plundered a bottle of cologne, two combs and a roll of toilet paper. They never had that kind of extra soft quilted paper at Ralph's. Even with the bulges under my shirt and jacket I was protected. God closed their eyes and delivered the Beverly Hills Hotel spoils to me as a sign of confirmation that "Suck On This!" was indeed His Will.

So I was feeling so mightily uplifted that on the way to meet the "Suck On This!" producer I stopped and hurriedly scribbled a faith-claim note to Ruth and Rebecca, naming and claiming what hadn't happened -- yet -- but that *would happen* at my meeting, *if* I stepped out and claimed it in faith *before* it happened!

>Dear Ruth and Rebecca,
>Greetings in the Name of the Lord Jesus Christ! I just got hired by the top agent in Hollywood to direct a very important movie for a top producer! (Mel Brooks is involved!) I'm on my way to an important production meeting but I just wanted to share this great news RIGHT AWAY and claim the result of my next meeting in faith by saying it was *already* a great meeting *before it happens* because it has *already happened* in God's Predestined Plan! He's already written the script of our blessing and all we have to do is claim it and act our parts!
>In His Name, Love and XXX OOO,
>Billy and Daddy
>PS. Hug each other for me! I'll bring you both out here so soon now!
>XXX OOO

After I dropped off the faith claim note (at the new FedEx office on Sunset at Cory) for overnight delivery, I drove a couple of blocks up Sunset. I parked behind the Tower Records building.

Rubin Roth had a top floor apartment in a ten-story apartment building. When I rang the bell it took him a long time to answer. I watched a dead mouse floating around in circles in a plastic fountain next to the elevator. There were plastic statues of angels on the fountain with water squirting out of their mouths.

When Rubin answered the door he looked like he'd just gotten out of bed. He was short, fat and smoothing down what was left of his thinning greasy yellowy-gray hair. I towered over him. His belt was open. He had a coffee stain on his white way-too-tight pants. Rubin's hands shook when he buckled his belt. The way he was so falling apart looking just shouted out God's warning, "For the wages of sin is death" Romans 6:23. Rubin's entire aspect from his stained pants to his alcoholic's purple nose was like a warning from God to all Good Jews everywhere that they should rush back to the Promised Land and fulfill their destiny and not stay in America and wind up looking like Rubin! I had never met anyone so obviously far from the Lord's Plan for all His Good Jews. And this was even before Rubin went to the restroom during our meeting and I snooped around a little and noticed that the only book he had on his shelf was titled, "Anal Sex and Your Health."

"Sol sent over a copy of your script. It's a piece of shit," Rubin said. Those were the first words he spoke to me unless you count him shouting through the door after I rang the bell that I needed to wait and he'd be there in a "minute." He never introduced himself.

Yet his words did not discourage me in the least. Solly had said Rubin was a character, one of the "old school" so I took his pretend rudeness as a sort of act to test me. In fact I figured his rudeness was a sort of Jewish compliment, making me "one of the boys" so to speak, showing his actually respect for me by talking like we were old friends who could be rude to each other as a way of signaling that we went "way back" together even though we'd just met. So I followed Rubin with a song in my heart as we walked across his red shag carpet and past walls covered with gold-flecked wallpaper that was the same in the hall and living room and in all the other rooms

There were paintings of children with big sad eyes in clown suits with tears on their cheeks all over the place. The pictures were in gold and white frames. Pastor Bob had a picture just like one of Rubin's child clowns. Pastor Bob's picture was in the church basement with a sign saying, "Jesus loves the little children" under it. The picture was over the big yellow counseling couch where Pastor Bob kept Kleenex handy on the end tables. And like everyone said Pastor Bob was "really good with kids" and decorated his office with lots of stuff to "relate" to the children he loved to minister to. And there was another reminder of home in Rubin's apartment: it smelled like left-over macaroni and cheese. That smell made me think of our church basement which was God's gentle way of reminding me that the prayers of my home church were being answered at that very moment! And I loved that such an important producer from the old school would eat mac-n'-cheese! I mean it made him come off as so down to earth and real. So that put me at ease too along with his rudeness that was really a friendly way to break the ice. I mean he'd never have called my work "shit" unless he was really saying he liked it the way both Solly and Jasmine did.

"I'm working on something new," I said as I sat down and smiled my best director's smile.

"I don't give a flying fuck," said Rubin, continuing with his friendly banter that had the effect of making me feel so included.

Rubin poured out two glasses of whiskey. He handed me a glass and walked out from behind the bar and sat down next to me on a red velvet stool. The velvet was mostly worn off. The ceiling had mirrors on it. Rubin looked up and stared at himself. While I was waiting for the words I needed to answer Rubin's "rudeness" in a way that would get into the spirit of his way of friendly bantering and yet show respect, I noticed some posters of his movies on the mirror-wall behind the bar. I could see Rubin's name on "Blood Servant II - The Return." It said it was "A Rubin Roth Production." The poster was faded and looked like it was about thirty years old. It had a picture of a girl wearing a bra and panties being grabbed by a big man holding a bloodstained ax.

I slowly lowered my drink below the bar's rim and dribbled the whiskey onto the carpet. Rubin was staring at himself in the mirror and didn't notice me getting rid of the alcohol.

"I don't give a flying fuck about this fucking movie," Rubin said. "It's not a movie, it's a deal." He swiveled around on his stool and stared at me. "Take a piece of advice from this old Hebrew fagot and never bullshit people in this business," said Rubin and then laughed.

"I hope to learn from your experience," I said.

"We've got to shoot some fucking thing but the point is that investors in South Africa need a way to get their money out of South Africa before the shit hits the fan boycott or no boycott," Rubin said and laughed. "It doesn't matter what the fuck we make as long as it comes in on budget and is shot in thirty-five. We shoot all our shit in South Africa, three or four pictures a year and then sell it at MIFED to the Brazilians and other shit-for-brains markets. Then when the Schwartzas come out of Soweto, like they will any day now looking for Van de Merwe, Van Rensburg, Van Vuuren, Van-fucking-God-knows-what-else, whitey will have some money to start over with in the real world. That's because by investing Rand in my productions and with me selling my pictures in dollars they have a way to get some money out of South Africa even with their new restrictions on currency flight. So like I said this shit isn't a movie. It's just a deal. Understand?"

AND GOD SAID, "BILLY!"

"Yes," I said feeling flattered that Rubin was laying out his business plan in such detail.

"Like I told Sol you're not going to get paid besides your cash per diem and that's in Rand and no artsy fartsy bullshit, okay?"

"Please give me the words to speak," I prayed. "Don't let me seem over-eager. Amen and Amen!" Out loud I said, "I'll need to talk it over with Sol."

"Fuck Sol! He's already got his fucking fee for packaging all the above-the-line talent for this piece of shit," Rubin said and swiveled sideways so he could look at his profile in the mirrors. "All we needed was a director. He's been trying to find me one for months."

Rubin's face looked smaller and darker as it was repeated hundreds of times and faded off into the distance of the curved "hallway" made by the mirror-reflecting-mirror effect. "Don't bullshit a bullshitter! You know what I think?"

"What?" I asked in my best upbeat tone.

"You don't know your asshole from the Holland Tunnel. You've been in town for years sending out your fucked-in-the-ass scripts. I heard about you. There's nothing to 'discuss' with Sol. There are twenty thousand other creeps here who'll direct for free and suck me off into the bargain. You got thirty seconds to decide. Twenty-nine, twenty-eight, twenty-six…"

"O Lord Jesus I just thank Thee for this golden opportunity and this fine old school producer who has taken me into his confidence since obviously we're hitting it off!" I prayed. "I just thank Thee that I have found favor in the sight of Solly, Jasmine and now Rubin and that Thou hast raised up South Africa so that in Thine infinite wisdom so there's a chance for me to break into The Business because no one else will make a movie there because of the anti-apartheid boycott. So Lord I just thank Thee for the sanctions and for apartheid!"

"Okay Rubin," I said out loud. "Thank you so much for this opportunity. I won't let you down."

Chapter 4
How to Write a Flashback

When I got back to my room God told me to call Ruth. I hardly ever called home anymore. At first Ruth was quiet when I broke the great news. She remained silent in what I took for a "They yet believed not for joy, and wondered" Luke 24:41 kind of way. Then I heard her start to cry like she always did when she was extra moved in the Spirit. I could picture my darling Ruth standing on her long beautiful legs by our trailer's dinette set with her glossy blond hair swaying and joyful tears squeezing out of those big blue eyes of hers and then dripping off her straight perfect nose. I started to sing. After a while Ruth joined in. At first her voice was trembling but soon she was praising loud and clear. We sang our favorite hymn again and again. "We are one in the Spirit, we are one in the Lord. We are one in the Spirit, we are one in the Lord. And we pray that all unity may one day be restored. And they'll know we are Christians. By our love, by our love, Yes they'll know we are Christians by our love..."

After we'd been singing for twenty minutes or so I heard the phone bang against the wall. I said, "Ruth? Ruth?" but there wasn't any answer. I could hear Rebecca crying. She always got scared when Ruth was taken up in the Spirit and fell to the ground in a Heavenly swoon. Rebecca was crying and saying "Mommy! Mommy! Please

AND GOD SAID, "BILLY!"

stop! Please get up!" over and over again. And I was so lonely for my little girl that I was glad to hear her voice even if she was screaming in fear. It was better than nothing. I shouted "Rebecca! Rebecca! It's Daddy! Please talk to me! Don't be scared! Mommy's just visiting with Jesus!" But Rebecca couldn't hear me or could hear me but wouldn't come to the phone. The call petered out when Ruth began to mumble in the Heavenly tongue and by then I couldn't hear Rebecca anymore. So I waited and said "Ruth? Ruth?" but Ruth didn't pick up. Then I hung up.

Hearing Rebecca's voice made me SO homesick! It had been months since I had called home. After I'd been gone for almost a year Ruth had said that my calls upset Rebecca. Ruth said that every time I called it took Rebecca several days to calm down because she would be asking when I was coming home and Ruth would find her crying in her room. So Ruth said to "just stick to letters" since they, "have less impact on Rebecca and cheer her up more than your calls do." After that Rebecca sent me pictures she drew and little notes and I wrote letters and sent presents. And for whatever reason I just didn't call Ruth much after that either until it became a sort of unspoken thing between us that (emergencies or great news aside) the Lord only wanted us to communicate through letters.

Hearing Rebecca's voice was almost more than I could stand. I was struck down by grief. I lay face down on my mattress and cried for a while in spite of all the great news. I tried to revive myself by thinking over the fabulous meetings I'd had with Solly and Rubin. Then I thought about what had brought me to this moment of spiritual warfare where even though everything I'd prayed for was being answered my longing to see my child again just seemed to hard to bear. I was feeling *so torn* like Paul said in 2 Corinthians 4:8 "We are troubled on every side, yet not distressed; we are perplexed, but not in despair." I had finally gotten my big break and was set to direct a movie with a great old school producer! Yet my little girl missed me so much that she cried when she heard my voice and I cried too! So I lay there full of hope and full of regret and thinking back over all the twists and turns that had led me to this moment while trying to figure out if I could have done anything differently and still have done the Lord's Will.

Maybe Molly's doubts had begun to infect me. Or maybe it was just that all the years away from home were adding up. Or maybe it was some sort of Mood Swing caused by all the highs and lows that sort of ping-ponged my brain around. Whatever the reasons were, I was plunged into a flashback.

In screenwriting night class Hal Busby told us about how to use flashbacks. While lying face down in my dingy room alternately praising Jesus and weeping, I was literally flashing back to the steps that led to me lying face down weeping for my child and at the same time, thanking God for my big break but unable to find peace about any of God's marvelous provisions and flashing back to a flashback within a flashback.

Hal Busby said, "The purpose of flashbacks is to give the audience information that is needed to move the story forward. When a character recalls an important event from his past, that memory can be shown in a flashback. But the flashback should be a significant event, one that influenced the character's actions in the present. The word FLASHBACK (all caps) must appear at the right of the script page. When flashbacks are completed then indicate that with the words BACK TO THE PRESENT (all caps) on the left side of the script page."

So anyway here's my flashback I was flashing back to:

When Ruth and I both turned twenty God gave me favor in Ruth's father's sight and we got married with his blessing. Our church followed the Christian leader Bill Gothard's teaching on marriage where you could only marry with your parent's approval. We had Rebecca nine months later. Ruth became pregnant on our wedding night or it could have been the next day after breakfast or the day after that because we celebrated our fleshly union like Christ with His Spotless Bride the Church every day and sometimes more than once a day. She said once a week was plenty for her but that I should be rewarded for waiting.

I sure had waited! In fact I'd spent years worried that Jesus would come back before I ever had the chance to have sex. Ruth was so godly that on our wedding night she prayed over my male organ and dedicated it to the Lord before I penetrated God's Gift that she had saved for me. Ruth was so godly that she handed me a pair of scissors to cut the big pink ribbon she had tied around her hips to cover her Intact Gift with a big fancy bow. Ruth was so godly that a few seconds after I cut that ribbon and entered her she prayed over her Unblemished Spotless Blood Covenant Offering that she had just shed onto the sheet and then quoted 2 Corinthians 11:2, "For I have espoused you to one husband that I may present you as a chaste virgin to Christ."

Then in 1985 when Rebecca was almost three years and four months old, right out of the blue, God laid His movie script on my heart. I had always liked movies even though when I was growing up lots of Real Christians said I should not go to the movies. I did anyway. I snuck into them. And from the time I was fifteen on I subscribed to *The American Cinematographer* magazine. I'd even sent away for some screenplays and would read them and picture how each scene had been shot. Everyone at church knew I was "into" movies. I always explained that it was because as co-music director I got inspiration from the film scores on what could be used to make our music "contemporary and attractive to the young people." I'd even talked to Pastor Bob about this and how even though Hollywood was run by mostly Bad Secular Jews we could still learn from them how to reach the lost by using "contemporary methods." He had agreed.

Any way it was at a Wednesday night praise gathering that I

was drumming for that I heard the Lord speak to me as clear as if He was standing behind me on the platform where I was sitting below the overhead projector screen. I had Rebecca up on the platform with me like always along with Molly's kids. The children were dancing around. I used to give them bongo drums and tambourines so that they could also make a "joyful noise unto the Lord!"

And God said, "Billy!"

And I said, "Yes Lord!"

And God said, "I AM That I AM thus shalt thou say unto the children of Israel and to everyone else too, I AM hath sent me unto you. So write a script for ME and then go to Hollywood that thou shalt call New Midian. Take that place back for ME from the Bad Secular Jews who will not fulfill my Word and return to Israel and/or join Jews For Jesus."

"Okay Lord," I said.

"This is MY Manifest Destiny for All MY Peoples including the Good Jews and Real Christians," God said.

"Okay Lord," I said.

And then He said, "Here's the script outline in broad strokes that thou shalt write and direct. It shall be this story: It starts in a plane that is headed to LA. Passengers disappear and terror spreads through the cabin as the believers onboard are raptured and those left behind know that the apocalypse has begun. It goes from there. My movie is mostly about the Second Coming and Rapture, like Revelations but with more special effects and dialogue. Got it?"

"Okay Lord," I said. "I got it."

"Now get thee home and write down the rest," God said.

"Thy Will be done!" I said.

Then I dropped my drumsticks and started to cry right in the middle of the chorus of "We Adore You." We had been singing it for about three hours so everyone was pretty worked up and the kids on stage were getting wild and tired. So no one noticed I was weeping

AND GOD SAID, "BILLY!"

before the Lord except for my little Rebecca. She ran over to me and put her arms around my neck and asked, "Daddy why are you so sad?" "Don't worry sweetie it's just the Lord is speaking to me," I answered. I guess everyone else just thought that I was being moved by the music. They didn't know it was an End Times prophecy – correction -- *The* End Times prophecy!

I rushed home and wrote the script on four yellow pads in one night. I started it on the only paper I could find and that was a stack of Rebecca's drawings. Back then her drawings were mostly squiggles made with markers and crayons. She was just starting to draw faces. So Scene 1 of "The Calling" was written down on the back of one of her big splotchy clown drawings copied from the clown in Pastor Bob's office she liked so much. Maybe someday (I thought) these sweet drawings mostly of splotchy scribbles on the back of the first historic pages of God's script will be in a heavenly museum of some kind along with the original tablets of the Ten Commandments, the Ark of the Covenant, maybe the seeds of whatever the fruit was Eve gave Adam, the club Cain murdered Able with and all those other things that played a significant role in the unfolding of God's Plan of Salvation.

So anyway, here's the story that God wrote through me on the back of Rebecca's drawings. Nuclear-armed America and Russia (the "King of the North") and nuclear-armed China (the "Kings of the East") attack the nuclear-armed Muslim Antichrist in the Valley of Megiddo. The three nuclear powers would rather destroy the world than suffer defeat at the Hand of God. They belong to their fathers Satan and the Antichrist that both want to be like God. When the three nuclear powers are gathering into the Valley of Megiddo for a nuclear showdown at the moment when the three armies are detonating nuclear weapons and Washington is nuked and the IRS is finally eliminated along with the Environmental Protection Agency and the Federal Reserve and Planned Parenthood, then all the

Unbelieving Bad Jews running the ACLU who will not return to Israel or join Jews For Jesus, are melted. This happens in New York and in LA. This results in a nuclear chain reaction. If Jesus didn't return in the nick of time (He does!) everyone would die. Then the sounding of the Seventh Last Trumpet happens, just like Matthew 24:31, 1 Thessalonians 4:16, 1 Corinthians 15:52 and Revelation 11:15 make so very clear. And the pouring out of the Seventh Last Bowl of God's Wrath destroys the three armies that are gathered at the Battle of Armageddon.

That's what God told me to write only in lots more detail. Like all born-again believers filled with the Holy Spirit I had often heard God's voice speak to my heart about stuff like where to park or who to marry, but I had never actually heard Him speak *out loud* before that night. So of course my hands were shaking the whole time He was dictating His screenplay, like I'm guessing Moses' hands shook when he took off his sandals before the Burning Bush. I mean "hearing" God "speak to your heart" can mean lots of different things to different people. But actually hearing His voice as certain sure as if you were wearing a good headset is another matter. So there was plenty of reason to tremble!

Ruth and Rebecca came home a while later but I just waved them off and kept writing. And the Lord moved them to quietly go to bed and not disturb me. Later Ruth said she felt a "real presence" in the trailer when she had walked in. After writing down a few more scenes on Rebecca's drawings I had run out of paper and so I went out to the all night CVS and got more paper. God graciously waited up for me until I got back. (We lived in the Vista View Trailer Park, Seabrook right across from the nuke plant. CVS was only five minutes away.)

Then I'd used up three and half Bic pens and four yellow pads by the end of that night. By the last page writing by the dawn's early light I could see that my handwriting had turned into a big messy scrawl because my hand was so tired and cramped up. But God had picked the right man to dictate His script to!

First off by reading all those movie magazines I understood God's movie jargon like "Fade Up" and "Dissolve To" and "VO" (for voice over) and so on. Clearly He had long since prepared me to receive this revelation. But there was a second and even bigger reason God chose me: You see, I have a "special sort of memory ability," like the hermeneutics teacher at Bible school once called it. Another teacher (who wasn't as spiritually discerning) said that I'm an "idiot savant." They made these comments because ever since I was a child I have always remembered everything I read or hear. I mean I can recall *every single word*, even words I don't understand, even foreign words, even words spoken in the Heavenly Tongue that I hear or read. No kidding! For instance, I won every Bible quiz in Sunday school until they stopped letting me compete since no one else ever had a chance to win. Say the first few words of any Bible verse (or a script) and I can finish it and give the reference too.

Anyway, I scribbled furiously from 9:45 PM until 8:21 AM—solid! And when little Rebecca came in at 7 AM, carrying her favorite stuffed toy, her "Lamby" that she always had with her and looking so very sweet, I just waived her away and she got back into bed with Ruth. And later when Ruth said she had to go to work and came in wearing her Market Basket checkout girl uniform and nametag I didn't even look up but just said, "God is speaking to me!" And since Ruth was so very Spirit-filled and holy and pure-of-heart she sensed that I was in the midst of a miracle and she said "Praise Jesus!" and tiptoed out.

When I got to the end of the story where God creates the new Heaven and New Earth God said "That's it! Fade to black!"

The day after I wrote "The Calling" the Lord spoke to me through Ruth's and my friend Molly. This was after dessert during our Thursday pot luck. Right after we ate cherry jell-o and before the children's Bible quiz, Molly had it laid on her heart that the Lord would use me mightily "in the dark pit of Hollywood that is the New Midian."

Her Word of Knowledge was confirmed and interpreted by Pastor Bob himself. Then Molly spoke a second prophecy in the Heavenly Tongue and Pastor Bob interpreted it while Molly's children hung onto her hands looking scared. Molly's utterance in tongues that Pastor Bob interpreted was, "Shabaz, waguloo, do, do, do banz, shan, na, na!" Pastor Bob interpreted that as, "Thus saith the Lord, you Billy shall not see your family again until God's Will has been made perfect in your weakness!" Then Pastor Bob laid hands on me and I fell to the ground slain in the Spirit. I lay there for over an hour. Some people wanted to call 911 but Pastor Bob rebuked them for their lack of faith. He sent Rebecca and Ruth home because Rebecca was having hysterics because she thought I was dead.

The amazing thing was that *Pastor Bob didn't know I had been led to write down God's script the night before*. When I woke up and told them I had written the script already everyone agreed that there was no question of it being a "mere coincidence." Then at the end of that pot luck supper Pastor Bob said, "Billy, thus saith the Lord! As you continue your communications with God a time will come when He will tell you The Plan for your life. This Plan will seem so fantastic that you will know that you are incapable of doing it. Remember, if you use God's power, you can do anything. With God all things are possible! Amen?"

"Amen!" I shouted.

Then Pastor Bob said, "All you have to do is take one step at a time and God will make the Plan come true! But first you need to take a big step of faith! Amen?"

"Amen!" I answered.

"And that step for you," Pastor Bob said, "is that you need to obey God's call and leave home and leave your precious wife and child here and go alone into the wilderness to hear God's voice and not come back until the task He set you is complete. Amen?"

"Amen!" I shouted along with everyone else.

So just like Abraham with Isaac I was called to sacrifice my child. To be honest I was thinking I could fulfill my call in months, not years. That just goes to show how little I knew about the Movie Business even though I had read so much about movie making, or about God's sense of time. I was never any good at math and maybe had just never figured out to add all the time making God's Movie would take, even if everything had gone smoothly, which it didn't.

With Abraham God said at the last moment not to kill anybody but I had to go through with my sacrifice. I left home when Rebecca was three. By the day of my big break when I met Solly, Rebecca was six! I'd been away three years! During that time I never broke my Covenant Call laid upon me and so I obediently stayed away from home that whole time!

After I had been in New Midian 6 months Pastor Bob called and said that I needed to become more like the Apostle Paul. "He didn't depend on any mission board," Pastor Bob explained. "Paul says twice that he worked in order not to put an obstacle in the way of the Gospel, so his message wouldn't become suspect to the Gentiles. He did not take money from anyone, so he could be free from all men and speak only for God. That's why we shouldn't send you any more money Billy."

Pastor Bob didn't know it but he was laying the foundation for God to do many mighty miracles on my behalf because after Pastor Bob quit sending the gifts the church had been collecting for me I became totally dependent on the Lord's provision. That's when I began to live off the land and to despoil and plunder in the biblical manner. And at that same time God laid it on my heart about how to relieve my sexual needs because "All things are lawful unto me, but all things are not expedient: all things are lawful for me, but I will not be brought under the power of any" 1 Corinthians 6:12.

From then on since our project was taking lots longer than I'd figured and I hadn't seen Ruth for half a year, God let me do what I needed to do to relieve my carnal desires once a week. But He did one of His great two-for-one things because the way God led me to relieve my carnal desires also became a powerful witness for the gospel in a mission field few reach.

I'd reach above the refrigerator and get down the brown plastic bread loaf-shaped box. It was stamped with the words, "The Bread of Life." In the box there used to be five hundred three-page booklets the size of a match books. The box of booklets had been sent to me free of charge by Campus Crusade for Christ. With the box of tracts I got a letter from Bill Bright the founder of that fine ministry. The letter said, "Dear fellow warriors for Christ help me to conquer the world for our Lord! Use these enclosed Four Spiritual Laws to bring all you meet to Christ."

I didn't exactly carry out each step of the witnessing program as outlined in Bill's letter. I'd stuff ten tracts into my pocket along with a bunch of dollar bills, leave my room and walk across Hollywood Boulevard, down Alta Vista, past Ralph's and one block up Sunset to the corner of Courtney where my missionary outreach took place.

The Totally Nude Club was usually pretty empty when I went in there in the early afternoon. The girls' cages were made like bird cages only the bars were a lot further apart and the cages were girl-sized. The girls' act was to swing from the trapeze in the cage and do all sorts of stuff like the splits so you could see their Womanly Gifts up close. The cage floors had red, green and blue blinking lights in them and that meant that even though it was dark in the club the parts of the girls' Gifts I needed to study up close were clear. I'd get out a dollar and take a copy of the "Four Spiritual Laws" out of my other pocket, fold it into the dollar, face down, and then put the Laws wrapped in the dollar on the floor of the cage. The girls always

AND GOD SAID, "BILLY!"

picked the Laws up along with the dollar.

What the girls stuffed into their panty tops along with the dollar bills was: "Law 1: God loves you and offers a wonderful plan for your life. Law 2: Man is sinful and separated from God. Therefore, he cannot know and experience God's love and plan for his life. Law 3: Jesus Christ is God's only provision for man's sin. Through Him you can know and experience God's love and plan for your life. Law 4: We must individually receive Jesus Christ as Savior and Lord; then we can know and experience God's love and plan for our lives."

After the part where they took off their panties and got "totally nude" (as advertised on the billboard) they just picked up the "Laws" along with their panties and garter belts and other stuff they had just taken off and walked backstage at the end of the show. Then a new song started pounding out its worldly demonic beat and the next girl came out and climbed into the cage and I had the opportunity to witness to her.

There was a big turn-over. From one mission out-reach revival to another so I hardly ever saw the same girls. I guess some of the girls quit because they'd read the Laws and invited Jesus into their hearts and called the 800-number for the follow-up materials. Whatever the girls did God told me to return to my room after each mission and "relieve your carnal desires for all things are lawful for you." He said that the passage in the Bible about Onan being killed for casting his seed upon the ground wasn't about me relieving my carnal desires but only about how Onan disobeyed God when the Lord told him to get his dead brother's wife pregnant and Onan didn't and pulled out during intercourse. God told me that to masturbate is "usually wrong because to lust is the same as adultery but if you only picture Ruth when you ejaculate I'll give you the special spiritual gift of chaste masturbation."

Molly wrote, "Billy you're so full of self-justifying crap 'chaste masturbation,' are you kidding? But who am I to judge you? I don't feel I met my parent's expectations. I'm tired of trying to be something I'm not, nor ever will be. When I grew up on that End Times farm in Vermont I confessed to our pastor I had doubts (even back then) about praying for the nuclear war to devastate the rest of America and he said I had a demon. For a while the exorcism stuck and I went into the Lord's work full time with Crusade and later married and my husband and I came to Pastor Bob's church. My life has been a spiritual battleground especially since the divorce. But I don't want to see my children as a 'battleground' in the war between God and Satan. I think about raising my children secular but yesterday when my daughter asked me 'who made this rock Mommy?' I said 'God did.' I said this before I even thought about it. So maybe that's what I really believe deep down. I mean I gave that answer, not some complicated stuff about doubt. But I don't want to train my children up into unquestioning obedience to me that transfers to God."

I didn't hold Molly's doubts against her or even her tempting me away from my call because the Lord told me He was using her backsliding to test me. I never told Pastor Bob on Ruth. I figured what with her ex-husband and her having already been kicked out of our church once because of his apostasy, it could happen again. I knew Molly needed the music director job now that she'd been reinstated.

Chapter 5
BACK TO THE PRESENT (All Caps)

It only took two weeks to get a passport, my visa and my guest union membership of the South African Film and Television Association (SAFTA). When Rubin got my passport back from the South African consulate there was a piece of paper folded in it saying that I was a "temporary member of SAFTA." It said I was a director. My member SAFTA card was about the size of my driver's license. My number was T5-397. It was the first time I saw my name listed as a director on anything official and this made the Lord's provision seem so very precious and real because up until then the unfolding of the Lord's Plan just seemed too good to be true. I read the word "director" on the card over and over again.

Rubin explained that the deal with the South Africans was that the director, producer and "first and second highest paid stars," had to be Americans. He said it was to guarantee international sales. Then he said (old school jokingly) "That's the only reason I'm taking you. I'm telling them you're a hot new American director and this is your third picture so don't fuck it up if you meet any of these rubes. Tell them you directed 'Halloween II' or some fucking thing." Then Rubin told me he had cast the male lead already (what he called "Cocksucker One") and the female lead all set (what he called, "Cunt One") and that they that had enough "name recognition so that a bunch of Afrikaner sheep-fucking farmers who think that Linda Blair is a star will be impressed."

Our stars names were April and Karl. April had been a regular on "Hawaii Five-O." Karl got a speaking part in "Cool Hand Luke" but he was the only actor with a speaking part in that movie whose career didn't take off after the picture was released. Rubin said Karl spent "most of the 1970s lying face down in his own vomit." Karl was forty-something. The script called for him playing a twenty five-year-old. April was about forty, maybe closer to forty five and she was going to play a girl of eighteen. April's body looked terrific at least when it was encased in tight black jeans and even tighter T-shirts but her face was way too old. Rubin said that all she needed to do was to "Stick another couple of bags of silicone in each tit and look the other way when we shoot a close up!" He said this to me right before Karl and April and me met with Rubin to get introduced just before I left for South Africa. That meeting was when Karl asked for more money. He brought along a copy of *Variety* with an article about the South Africa apartheid boycott. The headline said "SAG Says Nix to SA Pix." Karl tossed the paper down and asked Rubin if he expected him to, "End my career for a lousy ten grand?"

"What career?" Rubin asked. "No one's going to know where this piece of shit was shot. We'll thank the government of Zimbabwe in the credits like always. Why are you busting my chops this time around? You never worried before."

"It's the worst piece of crap I ever read," said Karl.

"So rewrite it," Rubin said.

"I'm not letting Karl mess with my lines," said April.

"Fuck with your own lines then," Rubin said and laughed.

April turned to me and said, "Maybe we should ask our 'director.'"

They all laughed. I knew they were laughing at me because in their unregenerate minds the movie was a joke and just a way to earn some money for the trouble of flying to South Africa for the 16-day shoot. And I knew April was being sarcastic because most directors get to pick their stars and mine were picked by Rubin and Solly. But I also knew that if the Lord be for you who can be against you and that what was a joke to them was part of a Larger Plan they had no idea about because "The natural man receiveth not the things of the Spirit of God: for they are foolishness unto him: neither can he know them, because they are spiritually discerned" 1 Corinthians 2:14. I also knew that Solly believed in my talent and so did his assistant Jasmine. For all I knew she'd be a studio chief someday and that might happen any time. There were lots of stories about personal assistants suddenly finding themselves on the fast track and she'd been supper friendly. So April and Karl's rudeness didn't get me down. And of course Rubin was just being Rubin with all his old school brusque humorous charm, that could be mistaken for meanness but really was his way of expressing admiration.

Rubin and I flew to South Africa two weeks ahead of Karl and April because even our "it's-a-deal-not-a-movie" production needed some preproduction. I took a taxi to LAX and waited on the curb for Rubin like he told me to. Rubin arrived in a stretch limo. I spent more or less the last of the Arab's plunder on that cab fare. He had said he'd pay me back for the cab fare but never did. I had had to pay the next month's rent on my room so they would hold it for me so I was pretty low on cash. When the limo driver opened Rubin's door Rubin didn't get out. It was only 8:00 AM but Rubin was asleep with an alcoholic drink in his hand and it took the driver and two skycaps to wake him.

From the first minute of our trip Rubin lived it up in the worldliest reprobate Bad Jew way, even for an old school curmudgeonly type. "And even as they did not like to retain God in their knowledge, God gave them over to a reprobate mind" Romans 1:28. When we checked in Rubin handed me a coach ticket then he headed for the TWA First Class lounge.

I knew that Karl and April were flying First Class too as part of their deal memo because I heard Rubin yell that fact at Karl when he was asking for more money. So of the four of us above line talent needed to greenlight the South African investor's money, I was the only one flying Coach. The only reason that Rubin wasn't swallowed up by the sidewalk at LAX when I asked for my cab fare and he said "Go fuck yourself," was probably because I was standing there explaining to God that appearances aside Rubin actually was okay and had once been associated with Mel Brooks. Or maybe Rubin was temporarily spared because God still needed him to produce the "Suck On This!" stepping stone production to get my career going.

No wonder Rubin wanted to fly First Class! Our trip was 37 hours long! There were no direct flights anymore from America to South Africa because of the international boycott of apartheid and because black-run African countries didn't let planes on their way to white-run South Africa overfly the rest of the continent. So we had to go to England first. Then we had to fly from London way out over the Atlantic so we wouldn't get into the black run nations' air space. According to what Rubin joked in his earthy manner, that way we'd have "time to think about Nelson Mandela jacking off in jail."

On the flight to New York I opened up my copy of the "Suck On This!" script on my tray table to get a pretty girl with a big red mouth and nice perfume sitting next to me to ask me if I was working on a movie. I pretended to be making notes. I figured that this would be a great ice breaker to share the gospel with her because our responsibility is to lovingly show forth Christ leaving the results of our witness in the hands of Him for whom we have borne testimony "So then neither is he that planteth anything, neither he that watereth; but God that giveth the increase" I Corinthians 3:7.

AND GOD SAID, "BILLY!"

My evangelistic trick worked and she did ask me about the script so I told her I was going to Zimbabwe to direct a production for Universal Pictures. When she asked about what other movies I had made I told her that my last picture was "Blood Simple." She squealed and asked how my brother was. I wasn't expecting a girl with a Southern kind of big frosty sprayed-solid hairdo and a dumb gooey accent to know that the Cohen brothers made that movie. I only knew because of night class.

"Give me the words, Lord!" I prayed and I also apologized to God for making up my own story about directing "Blood Simple" instead of waiting for Him to inspire whatever godly lies I needed to tell to evangelize her. Nothing works if you do it in your own strength and I had charged ahead into this witnessing trick without first asking God for His direction, even though Psalm 27:14 teaches that we are to "Wait on the Lord." So I backtracked until God gave me His direction. Meanwhile while I was waiting for new instructions I explained that I had only been an associate producer on "Blood Simple" but that I was directing a new movie. She asked me who was in it. God still didn't speak to me so I was just vamping and saying whatever I could think of.

"Jimmy loves the script," I blurted.

"Jimmy who?" she asked.

"James Caan," I said.

"He's one of my favorite actors!" she squealed.

"We play racquetball together," I said.

"Wow!" she said and her big blue eyes opened wide.

Then she wanted to know what a grip is. I asked God what to say and at last He jumped in and told me to make "casual conversation" and then He'd open the door and tell me when to present "the spiritual knock-out." So I explained about the grips who move the camera dolly and how the gaffers set lights and about the continuity girl who keeps track of everything. Then after telling my witnessing target more about how movie crews work God said to jump right in even though in Pastor Bob's sermon on "How to Talk to Strangers About Jesus" he said, "One good ice breaker besides asking about them is to say you're taking a survey. Ask the target a series of questions related to current events like, 'Do you think marijuana should be legalized?' Then end your survey with these two questions: 1) If you could ask God one question what would you ask Him? 2) If God was to ask you why He should allow you into Heaven what would you say? Then share the gospel. Surveys work well for softening up the lost target for the Holy Spirit to work on because questions are non-threatening."

But sometimes God says to just go for it. So I didn't pretend to be interested in her life. What God told me to say instead was, "People ask me how I've been so lucky to make it big in the movie business. I tell them it's not luck! Jesus loves me just like He loves you. He has a Wonderful Plan for your life too if you'll invite Him into your heart right now."

"I already have!" she said and her wide mouth shaped itself into a big wet smile with a smear of lipstick on her perfect white teeth.

"You're already born-again?" I asked.

I was surprised because my spirit hadn't recognized hers. She seemed very worldly. Usually I can tell if somebody is born-again. This is what Paul was talking about when he said, "The Spirit itself beareth witness with our spirit, that we are the children of God" Romans 8:18. But nothing about her gave me a revelation in my spirit or showed me that she was cooperating with God. She just seemed too normal.

"I've been a believer since I was a little girl!" she said. "I accepted Jesus as my personal savior with Miss Melinda in the second grade Sunday school class, on the fifteenth of May, 1966 at ten-forty-three in the morning!"

"Praise the Lord!" I said. And I meant it. Even if my spirit didn't bear witness to hers I thought that maybe I'd missed something and should stick with this verse, "Now therefore ye are no more strangers and foreigners, but fellow citizens with the saints and of the household of God" Ephesians 2:19. My newfound sister-in-Christ leaned way over and gave me a big hug "For through him we both have access by one Spirit unto the Father" Ephesians 2:20. Her perfume smelled good. Her breasts pushed against me. And her breasts-shoving-into-me hug gave me a deep tingle that I asked God to forgive since she was a sister in the Lord and "In whom ye also are built together for an habitation of God through the Spirit" Ephesians 2:22.

"How wonderful to meet a brother who's a real movie director!" she said.

"God raised me up as a witness to The Business," I said while rebuking Satan for crashing the image of this girl's naked body into my brain.

"Praise the Lord!" She said and clapped her hands so hard that the man sitting in 36-C woke up and glared.

"I know the Lord is going to give me the chance to bring people to Him through my movies." I said while feeling ashamed that I'd noticed her nipples under her sweater upstanding after our hug.

"I can't wait to share this with our young peoples' fellowship back home in Manassas!" she said.

When our time of fellowship (and, to be honest, my Satan-directed lust) was done she got up to visit the rest room. She left her purse on her seat. God told me to look into it. That surprised me. Why would He want me to despoil a believer even if she seemed weirdly normal? But His voice was clear so I said "Okay Lord, Thy Will be done." And I opened her purse just to check it out all the while trusting God's very specific Word to me because He always has His reasons. I was sitting in the aisle seat and she had the window seat. The middle seat was empty so no one could see what I was doing because I kept her purse below the rim of the middle seat armrest. There was a pink wallet, three "super-absorbent" Tampex, three Light Day's panty shields (I guess she was a heavy bleeder like Ruth) and two booklets of the "Four Spiritual Laws," some car keys, two letters from somebody in Oklahoma City and what I thought was a Folgers single coffee serving packet.

It looked like the single servings I kept on my shelf in my room in New Midian, when I could find a receipt in the parking lot with that kind of convenient single serving coffee product on it. So I picked up one of these little packages and then realized it wasn't an individual single coffee serving. It was a condom!

I knew my so-called newfound sister in Christ wasn't married because I had told her about Ruth and Rebecca. I said we all lived in Beverly Hills, because even most born-again people often didn't understand about how -- if you give up wife, children, lands and goods for Him – God will reward you tenfold. I had told her how I'd sing to Rebecca and make up silly rhymes about 'Fly so high to the sky!'" She had said, "How great! I'm praying that the Lord leads me to the husband of His choosing. Right now I'm not even engaged! I'm *sooo* single! I can't wait to have a Christ-centered family of my own! I plan on homeschooling my children! I want lots of kids!"

"Not even engaged!" she had said. "*Sooo* single!" she had said! I thought about these words as I held that condom packet between my thumb and forefinger feeling the slippery pre-lubricated contents slipping around inside the package as I rolled the rim around. "For by thy words thou shalt be justified, and by thy words thou shalt be condemned" Matthew: 37. Now it was clear to me why when I hugged her I'd been so tempted! She wasn't a sister in Christ at all but a false believer wolf dressed in sheep-type clothing and that's the worst kind of unbeliever. Jesus warned us, "Beware of the false prophets, who come to you in sheep's clothing, but inwardly are ravenous wolves" Matthew 7:15. Jesus also said, "Behold, I send you out as sheep in the midst of wolves" Matthew 10:16. And Paul said, "I know that after my departure savage wolves will come in among you, not sparing the flock" Acts 20:29.

I hadn't been tingling over a sister in Christ with unfortunately erect nipples but was aroused in the flesh because she was a sinful female wolf of the worst kind! "Of the woman came the beginning of sin, and through her we all die" Ecclesiastes 25:22. No wonder God told me to check out her purse! It turned out that He'd put her next to me for a reason and that reason wasn't for me to share the Good News with her but so that God could take action against her through me.

Then I saw she had two more condoms! Just how much fornication was she planning?

It made me so sad that someone could be so hypocritical and lie about her relationship to Christ so blatantly. But sad or not I was thankful that God led me to those condoms. I was thankful that God revealed this wolf's real character in time otherwise I would have thrown my pearls before swine and kept sharing the Lord with a false believer and also I wouldn't have known it was time to despoil her of the 78 dollars I found in her wallet after God said, "And I will give it into the hands of the strangers for a prey, and to the wicked of the earth for a spoil; and they shall pollute it' Ezekiel 7:21."

I left her credit cards and about 15 dollars in cash just in case she glanced into her purse before we got off the plane. I should have trusted God for everything in her wallet and taken it all like He said to. Maybe reading Molly's doubts and struggles was weakening my faith. But that's the risk anyone takes trying to help others, like doctors sometimes catch typhoid from a patient I was at risk of catching doubt but glad for the honor of being the one sent to encourage Molly in the Lord.

After I took the money and put that wolf's wallet back in her purse I sought God's guidance over the condoms and right away He laid this verse on my heart, "This is the word of the LORD, which he spake by his servant Elijah the Tishbite, saying, in the portion of Jezreel shall dogs eat the flesh of Jezebel" 2 Kings 9:36. So I knew what I had to do when False Christian Whore Wolf went to the rest room a second time just before the last snack service. I pressed the stewardess call button and I asked her for a pair of toy pilot's wings to take to my daughter. I knew that if False Christian Whore Wolf was ever going to come back to the Lord He'd have to chastise her mightily, "For it is impossible for those who were once enlightened, and have tasted of the heavenly gift, and were made partakers of the Holy Ghost, and have tasted the good word of God, and the powers of the world to come, if they shall fall away, to renew them again unto repentance; seeing they crucify to themselves the Son of God afresh, and put him to an open shame" Hebrews 6:4-6. That's what the little plastic pilot wings had been put on that plane for by God as part of His Plan from before the Creation. It was the Lord's way to deliver a pin into my hands.

The handy pin was perfect for perforating the three condoms. God was giving False Christian Whore Wolf a last chance to repent by offering her a little tough love. That way she'd have a chance to both repent and keep the baby and marry the father and bring that child to the Lord and raise a godly family and home school her child, like she said would or get an abortion and murder her baby and turn from the light forever. Either way a pregnancy would turn her mind back to the Lord.

When we were in our initial approach to New York City our plane was routed over Boston. The plane banked and I glimpsed the Seabrook nuke plant and the *actual trailer park* Ruth and Rebecca lived in. *I was so close to my daughter.* I would have loved to have been allowed by God to at least change planes in Boston so I could have hugged Rebecca. When we landed in New York there were tears in my eyes.

Chapter 6

A Strangely Prosperous Black Man

After flying six hours from LA to JFK, then eight hours from JFK to London it felt like we should be done with the trip. But I had to wait in London from 8:00 AM until 5:45 PM. I changed a little of the plunder I despoiled from Christian Wolf Whore into pounds. I drank tea and ate a stale cheese sandwich that in the States you'd send back and complain about even if you were plundering it. Rubin disappeared into the South African Airways (SAA) First Class lounge. I wandered around the duty free stores, restaurants and crowded hallways all day. The whole airport was under construction. Everything was boarded up with plywood but so used and dirty looking that it seemed like it had been that way for years even though the signs said "Excuse the *temporary* inconvenience while we build the new Heathrow." I looked at the English workmen. They were drinking what I guess was tea out of thermoses. They didn't seem to do much work. Pastor Bob once said that the English gave up on their Reformation heritage and that these days less than two percent of them go to church "and that's to any kind of church at all let alone to a church with good Bible-believing teaching." He said that as far as he knew there were "no Real Christians left in England" and that

"The England that produced the King James Bible is now as godless as France."

When we boarded the South African Airways plane I expected it to be primitive. I figured an African plane would be like aircraft in World War II movies where they all sit sideways in long rows on a metal bench facing the middle. I didn't think it would even be a jet let alone expect seats as wide in Coach as the First Class seats were that I saw Rubin sitting in on TWA. I was surprised by how beautiful the SAA stewardesses were. I'd been expecting black women something like the sullen girls selling popcorn at the Beverly Center Cinema Cineplex Odeon. On SAA all the stewardesses were white and looked like models. Their hair was French braided the way Ruth wore hers sometimes. When she wore her hair that way Pastor Bob always said that she looked the way Queen Esther must have looked in the king's court. The SAA stewardesses spoke softly in a fancy accent that sounded high class but different than American or English accents. Their accents were more like the Australian seminary students who came to our church for two months each summer, except the seminary students were all men since our church followed the Bible where it says that women must not preach in church. The Bible is very clear which is why Ruth only taught Bible studies and never preached. Paul says, "But I suffer not a woman to teach, nor to usurp authority over the man, but to be in silence" 1 Timothy 2:12. The seminary men were sent to us by what Pastor Bob said was the last good seminary in Australia that still taught the inerrancy of scripture and had "stuck to good Dutch Reformed theology."

The drinks were free on SAA, even the alcoholic ones. Free for everybody not just for the First Class passengers, not that I drank any alcohol. And you could stretch right out. The space between the seats was at least twice as wide as on TWA. I could recline my seat way back. The pillows had cloth covers not plastic stuff that balled up behind my head like on TWA. The food was served on glass and china and was as good as any I ever despoiled, even the time I ate at Spago's on June 23, 1984 to celebrate my wedding anniversary (in spirit) with Ruth. (I climbed out the bathroom window after eating some really great angel-hair pasta with goat cheese and thyme.) I couldn't even imagine what Rubin must eating in First Class since grilled inch-thick juicy tender mouth-watering veal was what I was eating in Coach. The croquets were crunchy and delicious. A salad and French-style bread (as good as any I ever despoiled in Santa Monica from my favorite bakery) were served and they walked down the aisle offering us more of the little crusty rolls. For desert I got a choice between Baba au Rhum and a Flan. I ate both with thanksgiving.

After all I had heard about South Africa and apartheid it surprised me that they let a black man sit next to me. I figured that they'd make the blacks sit in the back. I'd even planned to walk back to Third Class (or to wherever SAA put their black passengers) and share the gospel with them. I had even picked out a verse to share with the blacks about the Ethiopian eunuch. I planned to tell them that he was one of the first Christians and that this proved that black people can be saved. Pastor Bob said in his sermon on race differences: "Turn with me in your Bibles to Genesis 9. We read, 'Then Noah began farming and planted a vineyard. He drank of the wine and became drunk, and uncovered himself inside his tent. Ham, the father of Canaan, saw the nakedness of his father, and told his two brothers outside. But Shem and Japheth took a garment and laid it upon both their shoulders and walked backward and covered the nakedness of their father; and their faces were turned away, so that they did not see their father's nakedness. When Noah awoke from his wine, he knew what his youngest son had done to him. So he said, 'Cursed be Canaan; A servant of servants. He shall be to his brothers' Genesis 9:20-25. There's no proof that Noah's son Ham was cursed with an inability to be of the Elect even though it is very clear he became the first black man as a result of his sin and that all his descendants would bear the mark of black skin. Clearly the black race is the servant class as the Bible teaches us. But the Bible also has stories in it about slaves who came to Christ. So blacks too may be saved even though they are born to serve whites as the Bible teaches us. In Heaven born-again blacks will have been healed and have white skins at last."

The black man sitting next to me had on an expensive looking suit, a white shirt, cuff-links, and a yellow silk tie. He was about 6 feet tall and His head was bald except for a fringe of white hair. He was prosperous looking but weird looking too because there were scars on his cheeks left by some kind of pagan tribal ritual like Pat Robertson showed on the 700 Club when he explained how Africans did "pagan cuttings" on each other. So I knew that this black man wasn't born-again because he was literally marked as a child of Satan. He was worldly too and ordered whisky and had cigarettes in his shirt pocket.

The black man said he'd been visiting his family in London. I didn't tell him anything about myself. Rubin said we'd tell everyone we were making the movie in Zimbabwe and this plane was headed to South Africa. So I figured that I'd better just keep my mouth shut. For all I knew this black man had Liberal friends in Hollywood who would rat us out. So I asked the Lord for direction and He said to just say I was visiting a friend. The black man told me that he was a doctor. When he talked he sounded like somebody upper class in those old English movies called the "Ealing Comedies" we watched in night class. He didn't talk like any black man I'd ever met. He even turned his headset button to channel number 4. Number 4 was for classical music. He said, "Isn't it extraordinary that an aircraft like ours has sufficient fuel capacity to fly from London to Johannesburg nonstop while circumnavigating the western rim of the continent?"

"Where'd you learn to speak English so well?" I asked.

"In secondary school," he said.

"You went to school in England?" I asked.

"I went to primary school in Pretoria. We studied in Afrikaans and spoke Zulu at home. English was our third language after Zulu. I did UNI at Cambridge and medical school at Harvard, notwithstanding that education is viewed as a part of the overall apartheid system, which includes the homelands and urban restrictions, pass laws and job reservation. I was one of the fortunate few and received a scholarship from the Anglican Church. The powers that be tolerate a few successful blacks as their version of a Potemkin village."

"A what?"

"The fraudulent settlements built at the direction of Russian minister Grigory Potemkin to trick Empress Catherine II during her visit to Crimea in 1787 in order to give the impression that everyone was prosperous and well. The Germans did the same thing with their 'model' and 'happy' concentration camp of Theresienstadt. In 1944 the Nazi government used the camp to hoodwink members of the Danish Red Cross by taking them on a tour of this 'ideal' camp. A few educated and successful blacks like me serve that purpose for the South African government. We're the model 'camp' they show off to prove that thirty three million blacks living in abject poverty and fear are happy. And yet what can I do? To reject my assigned role would be to offer the racists further 'proof' that we're inferior. At least a few black people like me hold out hope by our very existence, even if we know we're also used as window dressing."

"What do regular people speak in South Africa?"

"Afrikaners speak Afrikaans and they try to make everyone else do so as well. The English speak English and never use Afrikaans if they can help it. The Indians speak Hindi and the Cape Coloreds have a very colorful, no pun intended lingo of their own. But almost everyone speaks at least some English as well as their tribal language."

The second time the black man got up to go the bathroom I hunkered down in the dark and peered into his duty free plastic bag. All he had were four cartons of Rothman's cigarettes. After I looked through his wallet that I found in his jacket, I unzipped his SAA airline bag. He had put it under the middle seat. There was a bottle of perfume, a copy of *The Lancet* magazine, neatly folded clean socks and underpants, a leather toilet bag with the usual toothbrush and stuff and two square metal cans of something called Earl Gray tea and a stethoscope and a blood pressure cuff. I picked up the stethoscope to take a better look. I had just put the ends in my ears to listen to my heart, like I used to do when I went with Grandma to the doctor in Newburyport when I was a kid, when I felt a tap on my shoulder. I turned around as slowly and as casually as I could and looked up from where I was crouching. My head was jammed against the pouch that had the magazines in it. If I hadn't been so tired I never would have taken as long going through that black man's stuff let alone absentmindedly tried out his stethoscope!

When the black man caught me I knew right away that I was outside of the Lord's Will. God never said to look at the black man's stuff or to despoil him. I hadn't asked for direction. I had never been caught before during almost three years of God-ordained predestined Spirit-filled wall-to-wall plundering. I'd even run little confidence-building spiritual tests. One time I picked up a twenty pound frozen turkey and just walked out with it right past a Ralph's checkout girl. And no one even looked at me.

But at the moment I stepped outside God's Will and plundered the black man without God's telling me too God removed His protection. Ice cream was one thing but this was stepping out of the Lord's Will on a bigger scale. So He let me see what it would be like if I quit living by faith alone. When that black man tapped my shoulder I could feel God was angry. In the darkened cabin I couldn't see the expression on the black man's face and that made it worse. I held up his stethoscope and said, "I saw this was sticking out of your bag. I always wanted to be a doctor," and I tried to laugh.

The black man didn't say anything. He reached over and clicked the armrest switch for the overhead reading light. The blinding light hit me right in the face but left him in the dark. So I could see even less than before. I handed back his stethoscope. He slowly folded it up and put into his bag. He zipped the bag shut. I still couldn't see his face. The only illumination was the pool of light on the seat from the overhead reading light.

When he spoke it was in a low quiet voice. "In South Africa the laws against theft are rather rigidly enforced," he said.

"You don't think I was stealing, do you?" I whispered.

"I observed you for a full ten seconds or so. My stethoscope was not 'sticking out' of my bag. I think I'll have a chat with the steward."

The black man walked up the aisle to First Class.

"Lord! Please help me!" I begged.

"Forsake Egypt Billy!" God said. "Forsake the ways of the world! If you're not doing it MY Way then you're not walking by faith!"

"Yes Lord," I answered feeling relieved that God was still talking to me but frightened by God's voice. His baritone sounded unusually stern.

"Announce your intentions so Satan knows that he doesn't have any power over you," God said. "Return to worship Billy! Make it your priority to get before ME as Abraham made it his priority to get back to MY altar in Bethel. Do it now!"

"My life is in Your hands," I prayed.

Then a new Word came to me in a flash. God said *exactly* what to do. He said it in a loving and gentle voice all warm and fatherly. And I did it! And after that I *knew* that I was back in line with His Will.

After I followed God's new instruction I jumped up and walked to the back of the plane past rows and rows of people sleeping with their mouths open. I pushed past the curtain that hung across the door of the rear galley. The galley smelled like orange rind and coffee. A steward and two beautiful stewardesses were sitting in the backward-facing fold down jump seats they sit in for takeoff and landing eating off trays held on their laps. They were eating food from First Class, whole lobster tails with caviar and chopped egg.

"Excuse me," I said.

They looked up and smiled.

"How may I be of assistance?" asked a steward. He put down his tray and stood.

"Excuse me but the guy next to me tried to steal from me," I said, telling him exactly what God told me to say as part of His New Plan.

"Really?" the steward exclaimed. He looked shocked.

"I went to the bathroom and when I got back I noticed the black man next to me putting down my jacket that I left on my seat. He pretended he was looking for a pen or something."

The members of the cabin crew didn't say anything and just kept staring at me. "Please Lord!" my spirit cried out. Then God gave me the words. I said "A minute ago when he got up to go the bathroom I checked. My wallet's gone!"

"Please wait here," said the steward, "I shall inform the Captain." He stepped into the aisle then poked his head back through the curtain. "Which seat are you in?"

"Twenty-one F."

While the steward was gone God gave me one of His refresher courses. The stewardesses avoided looking at me and sat in silence. I kept my eyes on the curtain while God said, "Acting is communication Billy! This little galley is your stage tonight! The whole Host of Heaven is watching! The audience should always feel drawn in by your performance. Break a leg!"

Five minutes or so after the steward left he opened the curtain. The captain was with him. He was tall and impressive looking and

AND GOD SAID, "BILLY!"

had short white hair. "Now look here," said the Captain in a classy Masterpiece Theatre-type English accent, "This is a devilishly awkward business. This chap you've accused of theft says the same of you. While you were here in the aft galley lodging your complaint he's been up at the forward galley saying much the same."

I was dumb-struck. At least I hoped I looked dumb-struck, just like God had directed me to act.

"I'll be!" I said and shook my head as if I just couldn't believe my ears.

"Nice work!" whispered God, "You've got a good free-flow of emotions and impulses expressed in your body and voice going on here!"

"It's your word against his sir," said the Captain.

"But my wallet's missing! What does he say I took?"

"He says he saw you going through his personal effects."

"At home we'd know what to do with a black man who said something like that," I said. And I tried to make my voice Southern sounding when I said *black man* to let them think that I didn't mind about apartheid and wasn't a Liberal. The Captain's face turned red. The red started at his white shirt collar and worked its way up his tan neck like a paper towel soaking up spilled cranberry juice.

"I'm afraid you're laboring under a misapprehension about South Africa sir. The fact that Dr. Mzamane is a black is irrelevant."

This stumped me but made me even more thankful for the Word God had put in my heart when I had cried out for guidance right after the black man caught me.

"Search him and search his bags. My wallet's gone," I said.

"Sir we cannot search passengers. If you want to lodge a complaint you can do so when we arrive in Johannesburg."

"Ask him if he minds. You're personally responsible if you don't at least ask him."

"I shall see what can be done," said the captain.

He was still flushed as he turned and ducked back out through the curtain. Red blotchy welts like slap marks covered his neck. No one said anything. I studied the stainless steel coffee maker, water dispenser and microwave ovens until the captain came back. When he did, about a minute later, he said, "Dr. Mzamane has graciously volunteered to be searched. The chief steward's going through his personal effects now."

"Thank you J-e-s-u-s!" I prayed.

You see God had led me into this new battle just like he led Joshua. Joshua followed God's instructions for the destruction of Jericho. For six days the army marched around the city. On the seventh day they marched seven times and shouted and the walls fell down flat. The Good Jews ran in and killed every living thing except Rahab the Harlot and her family. With my great wall-smashing God in charge I knew they'd find my wallet in the black man's duty free bag. I had obeyed the Lord and shoved it down between his cartons of Rothman's cigarettes. That's where God told me to plant it when the black man had walked up the aisle to report me.

Chapter 7

The Polite Policemen

When I got off the plane in Johannesburg the first thing I noticed was that they didn't have passenger ramps like in the States. I walked down a three story staircase built over the back of a truck that drove up to our Boeing 747. The sky was a dirty pale blue. It was warm but not hot. I was so tired and nervous that I felt like I was floating down those tall stairs. The airplane engines looked so huge from up close at ground level. Nobody from the crew even glanced at me or spoke to me when I got off the plane even though they were saying goodbye to the other passengers. I felt like one of the lepers before Jesus made them clean.

I saw Rubin with the First Class passengers on the other huge staircase parked on the other side of the wing where the First Class passengers were disembarking. He didn't look in my direction and was hanging onto the rail and having trouble walking down the stairs.

A policeman was waiting for me on the ground. The steward I talked to in the galley was standing next to him and pointed me out with a nod. The policeman was white and polite and said, "Welcome to South Africa sir. I hope you don't mind following me. We have some questions to ask you." He didn't say anything more and walked off ahead of me. He was dressed in a gray-blue uniform that looked loose and sloppy compared to American cops. The policemen led me past the line of passengers holding passports and waiting in rows at the customs windows. He walked me to the head of one of the lines and stood next to me while I cleared customs.

Overwhelmed by a rising wave of anxiety and before I could stop myself I blurted, "I just claim God's promise today!" The policeman glanced at me but didn't say anything. Then we walked through the Jan Smuts Airport main terminal hall. It was one huge open building the size of an NBA basketball arena but filled with newsstands, coffee bars, liquor bars and gift shops. The square columns that held up the roof were covered with gray marble and the floors were covered with some sort of fancy polished stone. White people speaking English and Afrikaans and blacks with skin colors ranging from coffee ice cream light brown to pitch black and all speaking gobbledygook pushed baggage carts loaded with boxes and huge bundles.

There were dozens of policemen with shotguns and machine-guns pacing around. Rubin had told me not to freak out because working in South Africa was "no more dangerous than shooting a movie in downtown LA." That was during the meeting when Karl asked for more money. Karl kept yelling, "All our asses are on the line. They're in a fucking war!" and Rubin yelled back, "It's no worse than here! The media talk about the ANC bombs but when you're over there everything's fine. You've never had any trouble there. You know that!"

Even in the midst of my many sorrows God perked me up. He did it while I was following the policeman through the airport weaving our way through all the luggage carts. God reminded me that He'd always helped the Good Jews and Christians who had also been in tough spots. "You're in a mighty army of one Billy!" He said right out of the blue in His most upbeat announcer type voice. "You're part of MY Big Picture! When I sent My Son to give the

AND GOD SAID, "BILLY!"

Jews a last chance Satan talked King Herod into killing all the newborn male babies in Bethlehem to try and kill Jesus in order to screw up My Plan. Satan knew I was going to fulfill My Plan of bringing the Jews back to Israel just like Satan knows you're here in South Africa to make the stepping stone movie that will get you into The Business and open the door to make MY movie. You'll win just like any three of MY Good Jews can beat a whole stinking Arab army of tens of thousands!"

"Thank You!" I prayed out loud.

"Don't mention it," said the policeman glancing over his shoulder.

When we got to a small room at the end of the hall there were two white and one black policemen waiting for me. I was surprised that there were black policemen in South Africa. They all wore the same gray-blue clothes as the white cop who had met me. And they were all polite.

"We're sorry to trouble you sir but we must ask you to file a complaint if you wish to pursue this matter further," said one of the white policeman.

"I got my wallet back so it's okay now," I said.

"If you wish to file a complaint you may do so," said the black policeman sitting behind the desk.

"I've come here to direct a movie not to get anyone into trouble," I said, and I laughed as friendly and casual as I could and looked around at them. None of them smiled back.

"Tough crowd!" God whispered.

"Dr. Mzamane has filed a complaint sir," said the black policeman behind the desk.

"But he's the guy who did the stealing!" I said in the shocked sounding voice God told me to use.

"Sir if you file a complaint yours will be investigated as well as his. In any event we must ask you to leave your passport with us for the time being."

"But my wallet was found in *his* bag!"

"Yes sir, we have a signed statement by the captain confirming that fact. Dr. Mzamane is the head of the cardiac unit at the Baragwanath Hospital in Soweto. He has asked us to dust his wallet and belongings for your fingerprints. He says he is missing a significant quantity of Rand."

I felt cold, just like Jesus' human side that shared our sufferings and took them upon Himself probably felt when he was standing before His accusers. "Thou knowest all things," I prayed. "Thou knewest even before Creation that You wouldst tell me to plant my wallet in his bag."

"But I never said it would be easy," said God and chuckled.

The three policemen were staring at me. I tried to think of a heartening Bible quote but couldn't. I had never heard God chuckle like that before and was kind of freaked out. He sounded just like Pat Robertson! Was He laughing at me by mimicking Pat? I began to tremble. I tried to steady myself by reading the poster that was on the wall behind the policeman's desk: "Join the South African Police. The SAP is the most professional force in the world. Pay! Training! Benefits! A lifetime career!" The recruiting poster had a picture of a black traffic cop stopping cars to let happy white school girls in blue and white checked uniforms cross a street. It made me think of Rebecca. I teared up.

God spoke again. This time He sounded more sympathetic and wasn't chuckling. He said, "I'll bet some of the apostles would have loved to be home with their kids too instead of on nonstop missionary journeys all over the world. Hang in there Billy." Then God filled me with a vivid uplifting picture of the old days back home as if He was promising to restore me to those times again soon if I'd just hang in there now and stay the course He'd set me. It was suddenly like I was watching a vivid home movie of my own life. Rebecca liked to sit up on the counter when I cooked. That's the "home movie" God played in my brain just like He encouraged the wandering Good Jews to name and claim milk and honey when they were lost in the wilderness. I used to let Rebecca toss the pieces of the haddock in the cornmeal that I was about to fry. I didn't care if she spilled the cornmeal all over. The key to getting her to eat healthy food was to let her enjoy cooking it and then to put out the good stuff first and let her graze on it instead of loading a plate with everything at once at dinner. So I'd hand her string beans or broccoli or fried fish right after we cooked them and we'd both snack before we sat down or even said grace for dinner. I'd tell her she was a real cook. "I'm helping you Daddy!" she'd say as we ate right off the serving dishes…

"I can't believe this," I said.

"Nevertheless sir we must ask you if you would be so kind as to give us a sample of your fingerprints. You may wish to alert your consulate," the black policeman who was sitting behind the table below the poster said. He had a stamp pad in front of him and some sheets of paper with boxes printed on them. He pointed to the stamp pad.

"Sure, you can have my prints," I said, "Who knows what I touched or didn't touch during a fourteen hour flight!"

Chapter 8

My Welcome Party

Even though I was pretty sure Rubin liked me I was worried that Rubin would be furious because of waiting for me being he was an old school pro and all. When they let me go and I came out and couldn't find Rubin I figured he'd left without me. Then I saw him on the other side of the glass partition waiting inside the customs area. The Lord had delayed good old Rubin for me by moving the customs inspectors to open all five of his suitcases. They were going through his clothes and even opened his toothpaste. When Rubin finally came out of customs and found that no one was there to meet us he muttered, "Leslie's been out here so long the fucker's on African time." Then Rubin said he'd known Spink since they produced "Zulu Zombies" in 1976 and that they had worked together ever since. Rubin said Spink was "okay for an old Limy lush."

I decided to wait until we got to the hotel to explain to Rubin about the police and how they had kept my passport and told me not to leave Johannesburg until they contacted me. Anyway there was no time to talk. As soon as Rubin walked out to the curb black men of all ages crowded around us asking if we wanted a taxi. Rubin sat down on a suitcase and closed his eyes so it was up to me to keep them away from our stuff. They wanted to pick up our suitcases and stick them in their taxis.

AND GOD SAID, "BILLY!"

That was the first time the blacks called me "Master." Some of the younger blacks trying to grab our bags said "Taxi boss?" and some said "May I help you sir?" Being called *sir* or *boss* wasn't new. Mexican gardeners in the Beverly Hills Hotel called me sir too when God led me to sneak into the bungalow area to despoil the extra thick soft toilet paper. But when the older South African blacks shouted "Taxi Master?" and "Here Master!" it felt biblical.

Being called *Master* was like I'd stepped back into ancient Israel. Abraham had slaves and Paul told born-again slaves how to treat their masters. He said "Let as many servants as are under the yoke count their own masters worthy of all honor." Timothy 6: 1. Paul would have liked South Africa. The older taxi drivers were calling me Master and treating me with the respect Paul told slaves to show their betters. When Leslie Spink pulled up I was thinking about how Paul said slavery was okay and how that meant that apartheid was probably biblical too.

Spink's van had a zebra logo painted on the side above the name "Safari Productions." "Les, you old bastard!" yelled Rubin. He didn't introduce me. Spink had to ask who I was. "Some fuck I met on the plane," Rubin answered. They both laughed. "Welcome to South Africa," said Spink in a cockney English accent that in movies (like "Mary Poppins") lets you know the guy talking that way is working class. In screenwriting night class Hal Busby had said, "People are often able to make instant and unconscious judgments about a character's class affiliation on the basis of his or her accent. Always note the correct accent for region or class when writing a part for a British character." Then he had shown us a video of clips from various movies illustrating how to classify British accents by region and class.

Spink smiled and stuck out a big soft freckled hand for me to shake. He was about fifty years old. He was friendly. I hoped God would reward Spink for being so nice to me and had elected him for salvation.

If he'd been elected, even though I never got the chance to witness to him, someone else would come along and tell Spink the gospel.

Spink invited us over for a braai. *Braai* sounds like *bry* and means a barbecue. So a few hours after taking naps at the hotel Rubin and me were sprawled on chaise longue chairs behind Spink's huge house. We were sitting with Spink and his wife Margo. Margo was friendly and had light blond hair. She spoke in an upper class English accent. She wore lots of makeup and had crusted-up long eyelashes with so much mascara clumped up on them that she looked like she had black eyes. Margo chain smoked and was pulling cigarettes out of packages of Benson and Hedges that were scattered all over the patio on chairs and tables. She was a small woman with a pretty face that reminded me of a tired and older looking Marilyn Monroe. And Margo had a nice firm little bottom. She had huge breasts and was at least forty five years old but wore clothes like a flirty Beverly Hills teenager. That night she had on tight gold jeans and a matching gold jean jacket open over a pink halter top that was low cut.

"Sorry it's just Margo and me and a garden full of kaffirs," Spink said. "Ten years ago we'd have had twenty or thirty movie people here to welcome you Billy. They'd have been from all over the world. Before the bloody sanctions there were more international productions in South Africa than in the UK, Australia and Germany combined. Hundreds of bloody commercials, thirty or forty features a year, television too." Spink sighed. "Those were the days my lad. Fuck Martin Lucifer Coon! Cheers!"

One of Spink's "boys" (what they called their black servants) who looked like he was about one hundred years old handed me a plate loaded with slices of sausage. He called me Master and never looked at me but kept his head and eyes down like a dog that's afraid of being hit. After serving us the old man limped back to a fancy three sided log cabin-style outdoor bar on the other side of the swimming pool. The bar was lit by dozens of flaming torches stuck in holders around it.

Suddenly there was deafening squawk above me. I ducked and dropped my plate of sausage. I looked up and saw that the noise had come from a peacock screaming. It sounded like the squealing brakes on a train mixed up with a truck horn. The bird was perched on the roof of Spink's house. It was standing on thatch made of tightly packed reeds at least two feet thick that -- when he was showing me around earlier -- Spink had said was "the traditional South African roofing material and bloody expensive too."

"He made you bloody well jump, didn't he?" said Spink. He was laughing hard. So were Margo and Rubin.

"Watchdogs with wings! Even better than geese," said Margo. "They'll scream bloody murder if a kaffir so much as looks down our lane. They never sound off for whites. Clever birds! Look!" Margo pointed to the driveway that led up to the road. In the moonlight I could see a couple of men running. Spink grabbed a huge flashlight off the coffee table and blasted them with light. When the light hit them the black men went from running like joggers to sprinting. As soon as they were out of sight the peacocks ruffled their feathers and settled down.

"Why are all the blacks around here always running?" I asked. "I saw a bunch more running on the way over."

"The kaffirs know that if they slow down we'll bloody well shoot them," Spink said and laughed. He lifted his jacket and I saw a pistol stuck into his pants. His big belly was wrapped around it. Seeing the pistol nestling into his hairy flesh gave me a sick pit-of-my-stomach feeling like I'd just looked over a cliff. Margo giggled and tapped my arm with her bright red fingernails and then opened her gold handbag that was lying on the coffee table. She took out a little pistol with a shiny chrome barrel. The barrel reflected the torch flames and made the gun look like it was on fire. "We all need these," she said. "I'd lend you a spare from Leslie's arsenal only it's a pity you're American because you need to be a white South African or at least a permanent white resident, to carry one. If you shoot a kaffir without a proper license there's no end of a row. The Afrikaners are such sticklers for regulations and they have it in for us English speakers. Never mind my dear, you just stick close to me and I'll protect you."

"But seriously," said Spink, "our kaffirs run because the Zulu always lopes about. They're an energetic inventive lot, run, dance you name it. And they're not as gormless as they look. When the authorities outlawed tribal drumming the kaffirs invented a new way to drum. They call it 'gumboot dancing,' and pound out their rhythms on the boots they wear in the mines. Rather clever really. Those two you saw run past just now must work up the road at the gravel pits and are on their way back to Alexandria Township. Bloody good stamina, might as well be Kudus! It's marvelous."

On the way over to Spink and Margo's I had seen lots of black men running. This was right after another one of Spink's servants (one with two fingers and an ear missing and who looked like he was about eighty) drove to our hotel to pick us up. "How come all those people are allowed on the highway. Where are they all going?" I had asked Spink's driver as we passed thousands of black men running in the breakdown lane of the highway.

"Alexandria Township, Master," said the driver.

Some of them wore suits and carried briefcases. Hundreds more were crammed onto every sort of truck. I had never seen people packed so tight shoulder-to-shoulder standing up in the back of open trucks. Rubin slept the whole way to Spink's place. He was slumped down in the van's front seat. His head bounced against the window. There was a big wet smear of saliva under his cheek. I was sitting behind the driver. Right after we left the hotel we passed a row of stores and office buildings that could have been in Santa Monica. Then we drove past dusty vacant lots like you see around Fontana in the desert on the way to Palm Springs. After that everything got really strange and different from America. Shacks the size

AND GOD SAID, "BILLY!"

of garden sheds all crammed together stretched as far as I could see. "Do people really live in those?" I asked pointing to the thousands of huts made out of scraps of plywood, tin, cardboard, cinder block and whatever else. They were crammed in rows behind mounds of trash.

"Yes Master. I live just over there," the driver said pointing.

We drove along miles and miles of rusted chain link fence. Behind it were thousands more shacks. Thick haze hung over the township thicker than the smog you see in New Midian even on a smog-alert day. The driver said it was the cooking fires that made the air so bad. Shafts of sunlight cut fingers of dirty pink through the air but otherwise it was dark under the smoke. The red setting sun glinted on muddy puddles and ditches between the huts. Mothers with babies tied to their backs by blankets wrapped around them and knotted up with a twist of cloth across their breasts were walking along the roads. Women squatted in front of the sheds next to fires. Women were walking on the highway carrying bags and boxes on their heads. Men, women and children all walked, ran and jogged down through gaps in the fence into the alleys and were picking their ways around ditches and puddles. Some of the children wore school uniforms that looked like what kids in America wear to Catholic school, gray and blue plaid skirts, white blouses and knee socks for the girls and gray shorts, white shirts and ties for the boys. The smoke from the fires wasn't like campfire smoke at summer Bible school on Lake Winipeesauckee. This smoke had wood smell in it too but it also had a weird smell of cooking that was sickening like they were boiling garbage and burning meat.

After driving past miles and miles of township shacks we drove through some open "veldt" (grassy prairie-type land) and then along a street with huge swanky houses on each side that were behind high walls and that looked like the biggest houses in Beverly Hills. All I saw there were black gardeners and white people in tennis shorts or other country club-type golfing outfits. There were as many brand new Mercedes, BMWs and Audis as on Rodeo Drive. Then we turned off the street that was winding through the swanky neighborhood onto an unpaved dusty track. Dust mushroomed up around us and when we passed a car. Our van filled with dust just like somebody had tossed a bag of flour through the window. Rubin woke up coughing.

"Jesus! What the fuck?" he shouted.

"Dust from the road," I said.

"Get your brain out of your ass and shut your goddamned window!"

"Yes Master, sorry Master!" said the driver.

"Not you asshole, the moron in the back seat who opened his fucking window," said Rubin.

"Yes, Master, sorry Master," said the driver.

So that's how we got to Spink's place. I put down Ruben's needless rudeness to jet lag, though I did begin to wonder if Solly was entirely right in describing Rubin's manner as nothing more than old school sarcasm or whatever. He really did seem to have an edge that went beyond that. I'll bet he never talked to his friend Mel Brooks that way. Anyway, as soon as we arrived and before he even showed me around, Spink poured me a glass of whisky. "That'll warm you up lad. Cheers!" Spink said.

"If you get chilly I'll send a boy in for a cardigan," Margo said.

I pretended to sip. When no one was looking I dribbled out enough onto the ground to make it look like I was drinking, but not enough so that Spink would call the black servants to fill my glass again. The rest of them were drinking like crazy proving by their slurred speech and carrying on that "Wine is a mocker, strong drink is raging: and whosoever is deceived thereby is not wise" Proverbs 20:1. Watching them defile their bodies with alcohol and tobacco my heart ached for Spink and Margo and I tried to ache for Rubin too but that was tough. Like Pastor Bob said about Molly's husband

and those who left our church with him when we split, Rubin was "clearly incapable of repentance."

If Spink and Margo had asked about why it's wrong to drink since the Bible has lots in it about Good Jews (and even the first Christians) drinking wine, I would have told them that yes there's six hunderd and thirty seven references to wine and drinking in the King James Bible and some of them make it sound like wine's okay. But that's because some people think that when wine is mentioned it only means alcoholic wine. That's not true. The thirteen different words in the Bible translated as "wine" have "a range of meaning in the Bible, from grape juice, to concentrated grape syrup to alcoholic wine," like Pastor Bob said when he explained why we used grape juice instead of wine for communion.

Margo's hands shook when she lit her cigarettes from the gold lighter she kept handy in her purse along with her gun. And in her drunken stupor she sat very immodestly with her legs wide open on the chaise longue across from me with her super tight jeans riding way up. So that was why I had to all of a sudden go to the restroom and take care of my needs. But I did remember to think of Ruth at the last moment.

I had never seen people drink or smoke so much even in New Midian. Margo and Spink were drunk when we arrived and got drunker until nobody on the patio except the blacks and me could even walk. Spink was collapsed in his chair. Once in a while he dragged himself over to the barbecue pit and pretended to cook. The one steak he tried to turn over fell on the ground. The blacks all said "sorry Master" over and over until Rubin yelled at them to shut up. And the steaks weren't even all that good, not as good as the steak and eggs at Cantors in New Midian. They were overcooked and had been marinated in something too sweet. So on top of the drinking these worldly people couldn't even get their food cooked right.

FRANK SCHAEFFER

When he wasn't pretending to cook Spink told stories like this one. (He was so drunk he was slurring his words.) "When we left England in sixty-three and we came out to Rhodesia," Spink said, "I was line producer on 'Jungle Fever.' It was Max Stern's last picture. You remember old Max don'tsh you Rubin?"

"What a cocksucker! Fuck him!" Rubin grunted.

"At any rate when Ian Smith packed up and the bloody kaffirs took over they put up thish statshue of a kaffir holding up a broken chain to shymbolize their new-found, bleeding freedom or some shuch kaffir rubbish! The day it was unveiled by all the wog dignitaries in fancy dressh we found that one of our white chaps had got a bucket of paint and in the night and had painted a message on the pedeshtal! Know what it said?" Spink laughed so hard he had to hand his drink to one of his boys, "It shaid . . . it shaid, '*A kaffir will break anything!*'"

Rubin didn't even smile. Spink was reaching over and trying to slap Rubin's back but missed and so just waved his arms in the air spilling his drink.

"Don't you bleeding well get it, Ruby? Broken chain . . . 'A kaffir'll break anything!' You should've seen the kaffirs skip about and try to rub it off. Even Joshua Nkomo was blushing! His ugly black mug turned a lovely purple!" Spink roared with laughter and gave the black man who was trying to mop up Spink's spilled drink a shove that made the old man fall.

Margo stopped laughing long enough to drain her glass. The rim was crusted up with pink lipstick. She said, "They've made a bloody balls-up of everything. There used to be a decent film lab in Salisbury, best lab in Africa. Once the bloody kaffirs took over first batch we sent in for processing never came back. The kaffir they put in charge was Robert Mugabe's brother-in-law. The twit forgot the film in the developer and melted it!"

"Kaffirs!" Spink muttered.

Margo lifted her glass. "To Joshua-bleeding-Nkomo and Robert-fuckhead-Mugabe!" she shouted. "Give it twenty years and they'll have Rhodesia -- excuse me I mean *Zimbabwe* -- ready for colonization again!"

Rubin finally got the joke about the statue. He started to laugh. He laughed until his drink spilled. He shouted, "Gotta take a fuckin' leak, Spinky! Where do I piss for Chrisake?!

"In your bloody trousers!" yelled Margo.

"Show Mashter Rubin to the lavatory," shouted Spink

Rubin tried to stand. Three of the black men had to help him. When he was about halfway to the house he wrenched his arms away from the men and turned around and shouted, "Too fucking late! I've pissed my pants!" His soaking wet jeans were steaming in the cold air. Spink and Margo fell sideways laughing.

Chapter 9

Preproduction Day One

At 10 o'clock the next morning Margo drove over to the hotel to pick Rubin and me up for our first production meeting. Margo was wearing skintight black jeans and a black T-shirt with the words RICH BITCH on it in letters made of rhinestones. She had a white sweater draped over her shoulders. When Rubin came down to the lobby he didn't even look at me. All he said was, "You still here asshole?" He had on wrinkled khaki pants and a white T-shirt and the same dirty tennis shoes he always wore. He should have been over his jet lag by then so I really began to wonder about him. Nevertheless I was feeling great. So what if my producer was a little grumpy? The Movie Business is full of stories about producer/director relationships that were far from easy and yet like steel forged by fire produced great movies. So all Rubin got from me was a sincerely cheerful upbeat smile filled with sincere goodwill. I figured nothing could get me down that morning!

I had tied my hair back in my best director ponytail as I prepared to pick up the mantle of directorial leadership God had laid upon me. I was wearing a new black leather jacket, new jeans and a plaid shirt just like Martin Scorsese wore in the picture on the wall at screenwriting night class taken on the set of "Taxi Driver." And I was wearing a viewfinder around my neck. I had plundered it from another student in screenwriting night class.

I despoiled the viewfinder a year before God delivered Solly and Rubin into my hand when I was at a spiritually low point. It was right after Ruth told me that talking to Rebecca on the phone made my little girl too upset so that from then on my only communication with her was through letters, notes and pictures. I had asked myself this question: "Do you believe enough to lay everything on the line? Or, do you only believe in God's Sovereignty when everything's going your way?" That night I had laid my hand upon the viewfinder when I saw it in the student's open backpack. I named and claimed a directing job and said, "I believe God for this viewfinder for the sake of the Kingdom." Then I despoiled it as a declaration of faith.

The viewfinder was just another example that God always has a covenant relationship with His prophetic servants and provides foreshadowing tokens of His Promises before He delivers them. He does this so that His servants won't give up. In the Bible tokens are often given as signs for the servant needing encouragement to keep his part of God's Covenant. My viewfinder was just one more token in a long line of promises kept. The first Covenant God made was with Noah. God told Noah to build the ark just like He told me to write "The Calling." The ark was not only for the saving of Noah's family but it was also for the saving of God's whole creation just like God's movie would begin the events leading to the Return of Christ and the New Heaven and New Earth. Noah agreed with God so God honored him just like I agreed with God and plundered my Pocket 11:1 Director's Viewfinder, "a proven accessory for directors, cinematographers, production designers, set builders and location scouts in the film and television industry" like it said on the box.

Well *at last* this was the day when the viewfinder would be put to use. So even though all Rubin said that morning was, "You still here asshole?" I had a song in my heart and cheerfully answered, "Good morning Rubin."

"Why the fuck are you wearing a viewfinder you jackass?" he said. "It's just a fucking production meeting! Jesus!"

That Unbelieving Bad Jew's rebuke of God's Covenant Viewfinder was too much even for my Spirit-filled cheerfulness. Suddenly I realized that Solly had been wrong about Rubin. The scales fell from my eyes. From then on I knew that "old school" or not, former pal of Mel Brooks and Cid Caesar or not, Rubin might as well have had a label stamped on his forehead, "Secular God-Hating ACLU-Type Left Wing Communist Democrat-Voting Abortion-Promoting Bad New York Jew Homosexual Who Won't Return to The Promised Land and Fulfill The Manifest Destiny of America and All Good Jews and Real Christians!" Or if that would have been too much to fit on one forehead, a big red "666" tattooed on his pasty face would have done fine.

So bounced from cheerful to brooding in an instant and I prayed a shortened version of Psalm 109 against Rubin in my heart. This was spoken directly by the Holy Spirit through me as I prayed: "Hold not Thy peace, O God of my praise; for the mouth of Rubin and the mouth of the deceitful are opened against me: they have spoken against me with a lying tongue. Rubin compassed me about also with words of hatred; and fought against me without a cause. Set Thou a wicked man over Rubin: and let Satan stand at Rubin's right hand. Help me, O LORD my God: O save me according to thy mercy: That Rubin may know that This Viewfinder is from Thy hand; that Thou, LORD, hast done it."

"We received a rather odd call from the SAP this morning," said Margo interrupting my prayer as we settled into the van, with me in the uncomfortable back seat, of course.

"Tell us about it some other time," muttered Rubin. "Right now just get me the fuck outta this hotel."

As we drove out of the carport Margo glanced at me in the rearview mirror and asked, "What have we been up to? Have we been very naughty?"

AND GOD SAID, "BILLY!"

"Naughty? He's the most boring little prick I've ever met," Rubin muttered.

"Well at any rate we received a rather odd call this morning from the SAP."

"What the fuck are you talking about?" Rubin asked.

"The South African Police want to verify that Billy's actually working for Safari Productions and that Leslie will vouch for him. Seems he's been accused of theft," said Margo and giggled.

"Give me a fucking break! What the fuck did you steal you little prick?" shouted Rubin.

"It was on the plane from London," I said. "The black guy next to me tried to steal my wallet. Now he's claiming I stole from him."

"I'll fucking sue Sol for dumping such a whacko on me. Margo did you count the spoons last night after this klepto left your house?"

"Help me, O LORD my God," I prayed, "Let them curse, but bless Thou: when they arise, let them be ashamed; but let Thy servant rejoice. Let Rubin be clothed with shame, and let him cover himself with his own confusion, as with a mantle. Amen and Amen!"

"How could I help it if some black man tried to steal from me?" I said.

Rubin turned all the way around to stare at me with his mean bloodshot eyes. "Schwartza or not, that's a hell of a way to start a picture," he snarled.

Margo shuddered and said, "The least they could do is to keep them off airplanes! It's bad enough they let them stink up the theaters and shops these days with all this relaxing of the race laws. A few years ago you'd never see them in our best shops let alone on an airplane! Do you know that when Leslie and I first came down from Rhodesia he said, 'At last we're in a country that knows how to deal with these people.' Now it's all happening again right here. The kaffirs are practically allowed to do anything. They'll be letting Mandela out next!" Margo sighed, licked the tip of her finger, looked at me in the rear-view mirror, smiled and smoothed her plucked pencil-line thin eyebrows.

"This one claimed he was a doctor," I said.

"Witch doctor most likely!" Margo laughed, "you should see their bloody muti shops. Positively stink with bacteria."

"What?" I asked.

"Tribal medicine shops with bits of rhino tooth, dried monkey gall bladder, roots, skins, ostrich eyes for sale as 'medicine,' pinch of this, bit of that, whatever the sangoma – that's what they call their female witch doctors – tells them to take."

"Enough with the fucking travelogue!" shouted Rubin, "What the fuck'll happen to the package if they arrest this prick? How am I supposed to find another American director for the requirement?"

"Grind him Lord! Make him my footstool!" I prayed.

"No worries," said Margo, "even in the new improved South Africa a kaffir's still a kaffir. If he makes any trouble we know what to do." Margo nodded to me in the rear view mirror. She winked then lit another cigarette and blew lots of smoke out of her nose. Then she smiled at me in a way that fired up a lust-tingle. This tingle was way past just a regular loin tingle and was a demonic attack from the Demon of Lust. And suddenly I was aware that God was warning me that Margo might be used by Satan to derail His Plan for me. And nothing would please Satan more than to waylay me with adultery on the very Day of the Lord's Deliverance. So I dropped my hands into my lap, laid a hand over my penis and cast out the Demon of Lust.

"Leslie's not an honorary member of the Broederbund for nothing," said Margo.

"What's that?" I asked.

"The oldest association of Afrikaner leaders. Occasionally they make an Englishman an honorary member. Leslie's one. He can't go to their secret meetings but he knows who to bloody well call."

AND GOD SAID, "BILLY!"

"I've got the runs," said Rubin.

"How lovely," said Margo, "Shall we stop and get you some medicine?"

"What do you think Sherlock?"

Margo didn't answer. I saw a muscle twitching in her nice shapely jaw. No one liked Rubin. He was way too worldly even for worldly people. A minute later Margo pulled into the parking lot of a huge mall. It looked kind of like the Beverly Center except it was cleaner and more spread out.

"Sandton City is our swankiest shopping center," Margo said and smiled at me.

There were dogs mating in the parking lot. Margo laughed and pointed. But I knew where the Demon of Lust I'd just cast out of my loins had gone just like Jesus sent all those demons into the suicidal Gadarene swine. Those pigs committed mass suicide and I don't know where the demons went next but the dogs were humping so crazily it was clear where my demon had gone. And that was just another sign to me that great things were unfolding and that I was now entering directly into spiritual warfare toe-to-toe with the Devil.

We walked into a big atrium and past a lot of fancy-looking stores that reminded me of Sharper Image back in New Midian, but not before Margo was stopped and had her handbag searched. Rubin and I were checked out too. Rubin was furious, "If they want to stop the ANC from blowing the fucking place up how come they let some Schwartza search us?" he asked.

"It's sheer madness," said Margo, "all the kaffirs are in the ANC no matter what they say. He's probably the cousin of the terrorist who set off the bomb this morning in the Randburg post office."

"This place has sure as hell gone the fuck downhill since I was here last," said Rubin.

The black man searching us didn't say anything even though

Rubin and Margo were standing right in front of him talking about him so rudely. He looked like he was about forty and had white gloves on and was tall, very black and very polite. When he was done all he said was, "Thank you, sir," and turned to the next person.

"I don't get it. Why are they allowed to search white people?" I asked Margo as we walked down a fancy marble hall past store windows full of fur coats and Omega watches and lots of other Beverly Hills-type stuff.

"Why do some white Americans celebrate Martin Lucifer Coon day?" Margo said, "We have bloody kaffir-lovers here same as you."

Margo led us to a big pharmacy. It smelled like Charlie perfume. The smell reminded me of Ruth on our wedding night at the Essex Inn in Newburyport. We became one flesh on a four poster bed there and besides the loin ribbon Ruth wore that she invited me to cut she wore so much Charlie perfume that I got dizzy. Whenever I smelled Charlie perfume I thought about Ruth's intact chaste hymen and offered thanks for it again just like I had that night after she asked me to cut the ribbon then opened her legs wide and told me to examine her Gift and check that it was intact and tight shut as a pink little trap door. It was.

Nine months later to the day as Ruth fed Rebecca for the first time from her beautiful breasts and we talked about how someday this sweet tiny little seven pound six ounce baby nestled at her bosom would be old enough to notice boys Ruth said, "Courtship shouldn't start until a daughter is ready for marriage. A son must also receive training like my mother gave me on the Biblical duties of a future husband. Mom said that a son must be instructed in the scriptural teaching about how to exercise headship over women. Dad left Mom before I was born because he was a total unregenerate pagan and Mom got saved so he left her because she kept trying to lead him to the Lord. I was trained up to look for a godly head of my future family."

AND GOD SAID, "BILLY!"

"May I help you, sir?" said the black woman behind the counter and she smiled at Rubin. She had high cheekbones and looked like a black version of Cher.

"Don't know," said Rubin "When do you get off work?"

I was thinking that maybe I could despoil this pharmacy of a bottle of Charlie and send it to Ruth for our next anniversary.

"Sorry, sir?" the woman said.

"Never mind, I got the runs," Rubin said.

"Sorry?"

"The shits! Jesus Christ! Do you speaky de English?"

When the woman handed Rubin a bottle of Kaopectate he tore off the lid and swigged it right then and there. The Kaopectate was the regular American brand so I figured out that the pharmaceutical companies weren't boycotting South Africa any more than I was.

As we walked out Margo explained that the production office was in what had been a farmhouse near a suburb called Lone Hill about halfway between Johannesburg and Pretoria. It took about 30 minutes to drive to the office from the hotel not counting the stop to get Rubin's medicine. When we pulled into the drive we parked next to a thicket of bushes with inch-long hooked thorns that Margo said were called the "wait a minute bush" because if you got stuck in one you couldn't just pull away but had to wait a minute to untangle yourself or get your skin ripped. The yard was covered with these bushes. There was some rusted out farm equipment parked in the fields that surrounded the office and the thorn bushes were even growing out of some of the rusting tractors. Whoever owned the place must have quit farming years before and just walked away.

As we pulled up next to the big rundown single story stucco farmhouse a pack of dogs ran up to our van barking like crazy. A couple of white miniature poodle-type dogs and three big ones (Rottweiler and Great Dane mixed breeds) ran up to us. The dogs wagged their tails and jumped up on Margo and she smiled and patted them and said "There, there, good boy."

It was cold and the gray sky looked like it might snow. I could smell cooking fires just like in the township we'd passed the night before. As I stepped out of the van the dogs ran over to me with their tails wagging but then an old pickup truck pulled off the road and rattled down the drive and parked next to us. Two blacks were in the cab. The dogs left us and tore over to the truck barking and snarling and throwing themselves against the doors. The blacks sat frozen in the cab until Margo called the dogs into the house and closed the door on them.

"Kaffir dogs," she said. "Won't bite whites but a kaffir is another matter. They'd have kept those two sitting in their bakkie all day or chewed them out of it more than likely. We keep the little dogs to wind up the big ones. Last week they bit a plumber's assistant then the big ones joined in. You should have seen that little darkie run!"

Rubin laughed and said, "I hope they don't bite old Hebrew queers!"

"They know better than that," said Margo. "But the poor things get terribly confused by Packies and especially by Cape Coloreds. Sometimes they bite them but sometimes they don't. Depends how much kaffir blood they smell in them. They're clever too, know all our kaffirs and never bother them in the least."

Rubin put his arm around Margo's shoulders and pulled her close. "All you fuckers have Schwartza blood in you. Those Dutch pricks started dicking everything in sight when they waded ashore. I'll bet there's not one genetically pure white South African."

Margo yanked herself away from Rubin and angrily snapped "I'm one hundred percent British mate!"

What had once been a living room was now the reception area. Spink's office had been a master bedroom and was still papered with red and orange flower wallpaper. The wallpaper was faded but there were darker square-shaped patches where there had been dresser drawers and paintings on the wall. Spink's metal desk, his chair and a dented metal file cabinet were the only furniture in his office. There were no pictures anywhere, just a big map of South Africa and another one of Johannesburg pinned to the wall with thumbtacks. The chipped metal office furniture looked like the beaten up stuff you see in high schools when they sell off used equipment. Another bedroom was Margo's office. Margo was Safari Films' production manager. Spink was the producer. Veronica, a scrawny dried-out looking Englishwoman of about 40-years-old was the production secretary. She didn't have much to say or an office and sat in reception area at a small desk with the office phone switchboard and a huge IBM electric typewriter.

There were half a dozen empty rooms opening off the hall that Margo said would be our production departments. There were handwritten signs taped to the doors designating which rooms were the wardrobe, makeup and hair departments. One was marked "Stunts & Effects" and others already had the names of our stars, Karl and April taped to the doors. Margo said they'd produced all of Rubin's "rubbish pictures" out of this house and that it had "quite a history" and had "seen some jolly times you wouldn't believe."

As we walked in Spink stumbled out of his office and shouted "Top of the morning!" Then he tripped on the loose carpet and fell flat.

"Jesus, Les, what the fuck?" muttered Rubin.

"The boys and girls will all be here in half a sec," said Spink laughing as he stood up.

"Had a bit of an early breakfast did we darling?" asked Margo.

"Jesus, Les," Rubin said, "How the fuck are we going to work if you're already pissed first thing? We have a movie to make!"

"Oui mon capitaine," Spink said and saluted.

A door crashed open and a small black woman with a baby tied to her back by a blue blanket ran in from the kitchen. "Janque fighting too much," she said.

"Bloody hell, Johanna," said Spink, "Margo go and see about it. Mistress Margo will go see."

Margo followed Johanna out of the room.

"Bloody savages," said Spink. "They'd sooner kill each other than piss! Saves us the bother of doing it, that's bloody something."

"You call this a goddamned production office?" muttered Rubin. "Every time I come out here you get more Third World."

"Bring us a real picture with an actual budget and you'll have a swank production office," said Spink.

Margo marched back into the room.

"They've gone at it right and proper this time. The bloody kaffir who drove up in the bakkie has gone and smashed Janque with a bloody great brick."

"Is he dead?" Spink asked.

"Looks as if he's had a good bit of his ugly mug caved in," said Margo.

Veronica just kept typing. She didn't even look up. She had only moved once since we walked in and that was to shake my hand. Behind the kitchen there was a courtyard. Like most of the houses I saw where white people lived our production office had a high brick wall around it. Built into the corner of the wall behind the kitchen were a couple of sheds that Spink's blacks and their wives, relatives, babies, cousins -- whatever -- lived in.

When I stepped out the back kitchen door I learned where the scent of fires and cooking was coming from. It was like some kind of mini township back there. I never did figure out what all the dozens of blacks living out back did or if they all belonged to Spink or just came with the property when he rented it. None of them were on the movie crew. Different ones would bring in tea and once in a while I'd see some of them raking or sweeping outside or digging in garden plots out on the hill or hacking away at the thorn bushes. Most of them had bare feet. A couple of the children wore school uniforms. Most of them just seemed to hang around or squat in the dust next to big pots of what they called Mealie-Meal, thick cream of wheat-like stuff made out of ground up white corn meal that the blacks seemed to live on.

Some blacks were standing around somebody lying on the ground. One old woman was squatting in the doorway of a shack wailing. A couple of toddlers dressed in rags stood next to the black lying on the ground looking down at him. His blood made a big puddle around his head. Little red rivers were spreading out in the cracks between the paving stones. My knees felt watery. I went back inside.

After Margo came back from delivering bandages she poured me a cup of tea. That was right after she washed the blood off her hands. It made me feel sick to hold a cup where the handle was wet from her hands that I knew had been bloody a minute ago.

"By the way these came for you," Margo said when she put down the teapot. She handed me two envelopes. Who would send me anything here I wondered. Then I remembered that I had sent Ruth and Molly my contact information that Rubin gave me a few weeks before we left. My South African address was the Lone Hill production office.

When I read the letters my hands got so numb that I had trouble holding the papers. I wanted to scream but Margo was watching me. So when I finished reading I walked to the corner and sat down next to the window in another foldout chair and reread the letters with my face turned away from the room.

>Ephraim King
>Attorney at Law
>Courthouse Square

Portsmouth, New Hampshire
Via Federal Express, Overnight International Service. (Return Receipt)
Mr. Billy Graham
C/o Safari Productions
101 Lone Hill 1438
Johannesburg
Republic of South Africa
Re: Graham vs. Graham
New Hampshire Superior Court
#123450
July 10, 1988
Dear Mr. Graham,

We are the attorneys for your wife Ruth Graham, who is the plaintiff in the above-entitled divorce action pending against you in the New Hampshire Superior Court in and for the County of Rockingham. The action has filed upon the grounds of your willing absence for five years without the consent of your wife; in view of your continued absence from her and your matrimonial domicile for the past five years despite her requests that you return, it is apparent that there can be no issue with respect to the existence of such grounds and her right to a divorce. You will note that she does not seek any property from you, or any alimony or child support.

Under New Hampshire law our client has the right to retain exclusive custody and guardianship of Rebecca, the child of the parties and Ruth is asking the Court to confirm those rights to her.

Mr. Stan Walsh, the Vice Consul of the United States of America in South Africa will take your acknowledgment of service and return it to the Clerk of the Superior Court for entry in the Court file in this matter. We will provide you with an attested copy of the divorce decree when it is granted.

Please provide me with a new address in case you move from your current location.

Very Truly Yours,
Ephraim King

The letter in the second Fed-Ex pack was in a pale lavender envelope. Inside I found a card with a picture of a robin on it. It was from Molly. Her letter was typed and folded into the card along with a picture of Molly, her kids and Rebecca.

Billy,

"Pastor" Bob used your "call" as an excuse to take Ruth. Most of the "brothers and sisters" have remained with Bob, even though he's an adulterer and liar not to mention the world's biggest hypocrite. I'll bet he's been working on this since the day you left. Even you must have noticed how he looked at Ruth. Bob steals from everyone, wives, music, sermons, he's fake from the knees up —correction – from his toenails up! He pulled all my original music off our worship list and then plagiarized it and rereleased my songs under his own name. He knows I need the paycheck and so he knows I'll pretend I haven't noticed! Pastor Bob was too young to serve in WW2, avoided service in Korea, and has trampled government rules on tax-deductible church organization and has mixed his private interests with his 501-C-3 "ministry" blatantly. Over time his church movement, like its founder has become increasingly legalistic, homophobic, politically far right wing, and fundamentalist… except when it comes to Bob personally! Then it's okay for him to break all his own rules! He's given me every reason to reject everything he stands for. Nevertheless, I feel like I have committed my own full and final apostasy and am somehow marking time until my eternal damnation. I now know that nothing I once believed is actually true and yet I feel emotionally tormented with constant guilt for walking away from the lies. Take it from me; it's hard to reorient yourself into a fact-based existence after a lifetime spent in la, la land.

The reading I've done (Kierkegaard to Huxley) has helped me understand another way of seeing that is as simple as it is complex to live by. Fact-based life is harder in a way but at least it's real. The point is we can become as mentally healthy as the degree of the depth that we are willing to invest in exploring the biological basis of personality (not to mention sexual orientation) and the way it interacts with our family background.

I am now happily involved with a very kind and spiritually profound woman who loves my children and honestly I'm living a much more mutually peaceful and emotionally fulfilling life than I ever had while pretending to be straight. I'm also not letting anyone in church know about this. We met when she was papering and painting the kids' bedroom and things just sort of happened. (She works for a decorator part time.) Lilly, my partner is blessedly secular and hang-up free and we keep our relationship secret for now. Lilly is finishing up her Master's in neo-natal nursing but once she has that we'll be economically free to blow off Pastor Bob and go our own way. For now people in the church just think their music director is renting a room out to a stranger. We never go anywhere in town together. I never let the kids see us together in the house in "that way." Lilly sleeps in a separate bedroom and we wait until the children are asleep (or in school) before I go to her room or vice versa.

Are you shocked? I know you'll keep my secret just like you know I won't show anyone here your latest "stepping stone" script you sent me. If I did it would be a tossup as to which one of us those sanctimonious pricks would burn at the stake first!

I'm still seeing precious little Rebecca almost every day because Ruth (stupid as she's been about Bob) says so much else has changed that she wants Rebecca to at least have "a little continuity" in her life since Rebecca and my kids are so close. Of course Ruth doesn't know I'm "living in sin." Bob still claims your calling to Hollywood was authentic and says that the only reason he's taken up with Ruth is because his wife "left him spiritually," and that God "led him" to Ruth "in a dream" (no kidding) that "revealed" to him that you have committed adultery "almost every day" in Hollywood and so are "no longer biblically married." As for his poor dumb wife believe it or not Nancy hasn't fought back at all and even though he's abandoned her she has gone along with what's happened and dutifully moved out and went to live with her sister! She's a completely browbeaten women and as servile as a "submissive" third wife of some Saudi prince. Talk about being literally and totally under the sway of a cult leader. Amazing! And I'm a total hypocrite too because I know all this is awful, false and lies, lies, lies and yet I need the music director paycheck for a while longer and so I stay. So much for my commitment to truth. You deserved a better wife, church and friend.

Love,
Molly

Chapter 10
Betrayed

If two moons had appeared one night I would have been no more shocked than I was by what Ruth had done. Ruth was so godly that she used to say "The only three words a Christian wife needs to know are submission, submission and submission!" Ruth was so godly that she broke fellowship with her best friend because that girl had continued having fellowship with her own mother after her mother divorced her dad for beating her. Ruth had said "Real Christians stay in a marriage and pray it through, no matter what!" Ruth was so godly that the week before we got married in the talk she gave to the "Matthew 19:4-6 Marriage Preparation Seminar" she had said: "Like you all know back in 1964 Bill Gothard was led by God to reclaim marriage from the Liberals. He did this by developing his six-day seminar Institute in Basic Youth Conflicts. Gothard teaches us that that young people must live with their mothers and fathers until marriage or forever if they remain single, just like he does because he's unmarried like the apostle Paul was. So raise your hands if you are virgins. Now if you didn't raise your hand let's all bow our heads and ask God to just recreate an intact hymen in you girls who made that mistake. The Blood of Jesus is powerful enough to heal your hymens! He bled for you so you can bleed for Him on your wedding night! Gothard teaches that God can even reverse the effects of a C-section, so what is restoring a mere hymen to a God like that? As Gothard prophetically wrote, 'A couple who is contemplating vaginal birth after cesarean should ask the Lord to give them a specific portion of Scripture that they can claim for the birth. Both the father and the mother should memorize and meditate on this passage and use it to conquer any fear that may come during the pregnancy or delivery.' So just like Gothard proved that couples can name and claim this scripture passage for a renewed Vaginal Covenant Birth after the sin of a faithless C-section, so too the Lord has shown me that they can also claim a recreated hymen if they'll just believe God hard enough for it! Amen?"

"Amen!" we all yelled.

So all the years I was called to the mission field in New Midian I always figured that Ruth was so pure that Satan wouldn't even bother trying to tempt her in the flesh. If she suffered from anything it would be spiritual pride not sin like most people mean when they use the word which usually boils down to what men and women do with their fleshly parts between their legs.

Ever since I was called to New Midian I felt a lot less spiritual than Ruth because Satan often made me think about committing adultery. But I never fell. I prayed away my lust. When I prayed for Ruth it was like I prayed for Rebecca when she was a baby. All I ever asked God for was to keep them both safe from car crashes, illness and other clean regular non-genital stuff like that. Sin didn't even come into it. But I always asked Ruth to pray for me because I was the one being tempted by a girl called Sadie at screenwriting night class, after I saw the way she looked at me and heard her tell another girl she thought that I was "cute." That was the real reason I signed up to take all 22 of Hal Busby's screenwriting classes, twice. It was because Sadie said she was going to repeat the class too because like she said, "Hal Busby is so brilliant so I don't want to miss a word!"

To pay for the night classes I sneaked into the Oakwood storage area under H-1 Building 3 different times and despoiled five brand new TVs still in their boxes and twenty new pool cues and a complete set of new hand weights and fifteen speaker phones. God blessed my plundering even though my motives were sinful. All I really wanted to do was stay in class to look at Sadie. But God blessed my Sadie temptation anyway because 1) I never fell and 2) My temptation was what motivated me to take the screenwriting classes a second time and God knew that I'd need to perfect my craft in order to perfect His script. The point is: I might have plundered once in a while when God didn't tell me to but I resisted Sadie, and yet Ruth *did not* resist "Pastor" Bob!

My point is that Ruth was so godly that even masturbation became a holy thing pleasing unto the Lord, *if* my final thoughts were about her! So when I fulfilled my needs I played the tapes Ruth made just for me of her reading out loud or I played the tapes of her talks to our women's group.

Ruth called the tapes she sent me my "bedtime stories." I had told Ruth about how I used them -- for both Biblical instruction and also for monogamous arousal. We'd prayed about my needs on the phone and she said that the Lord gave her peace about what I "had to do" because "men have those impulses and you're directing your fulfillment to me so it is of the Lord."

So on the days God led me to relieve my needs I pictured Ruth reading Bill Gothard's books out loud or reading RJ Rushdoony (another great theologian) out loud and then I'd take an imaginary God-anointed tour of my wife's body starting on her hands holding the book she was reading from. Then I'd travel up her arm and over her big breasts and then slide down under her godly floor-length-Little-House-On-The-Prairie-type skirt and push her plain white full-coverage extra-modest panties aside and claim my view of my God-Ordained Blood Covenant Spousal Property. And the words she was reading from RJ Rushdoony's "The Philosophy of the Christian Curriculum" drove my thoughts of Sadie's miniskirt right out of my mind and helped slam the door in Satan's face. It got so that if I even heard Ruth say the words "RJ Rushdoony" or "Bill Gothard" I got an erection. And there were certain read aloud passages I liked best on the tapes. I liked one RJ Rushdoony passage in particular. "'If humanism can retain control of the schools,'" Ruth read in her sweet soft voice, "'the logic of education will then create more and more modernism, because modernism is simply humanism in charge of the church. It will turn evangelicals into neo-evangelicals and neo-fundamentalists. It will produce, in the supposedly Bible-believing churches, a faith having the form of godliness but lacking the power thereof. The recovery of the power of godliness requires a radical break therefore with humanism and humanistic education. It means that a thoroughly Biblical doctrine of education must govern the Christian school.' Page one hundred and sixty one." Ruth always read out the page numbers. And as she read "page one hundred and sixty one," in her soft godly voice, I'd ejaculate.

So after thinking about how Ruth would have been the last person I knew who might commit adultery, I reread both letters. When I brushed my cheek I found my face was wet. Margo was staring at me. Spink and Rubin had gone into Spink's office and closed the door. Veronica never looked up from her typing. If she knew I was crying she pretended not to see.

I tried saying a comfort verse, "For the Lord will not cast off for ever but though he cause grief, yet will he have compassion according to the multitude of his mercies" Lamentations 3:31-32. It did no good. I felt no reassurance. I tried another one from Psalms 30:5 "Weeping may tarry for the night, but joy comes with the morning." I didn't receive even a hint of peace. I tried one more verse from 1 Peter 5:6-7 "Humble yourselves therefore under the mighty hand of God, that he may exalt you in due time: Casting all your care upon him; for he careth for you." I was humbled all right, on my face, groveling before God whimpering like a run over dog. My O-so-holy wife was gone! My pastor had betrayed me! My friend Molly was condemned to Hell for the unnatural practices she had chosen by carnally living with another woman! And my producer and production manager were meeting behind a closed door at that very moment and hadn't even included me!

Something snapped or more like it broke. One moment I was following my calling. The next moment I was falling into doubt bordering on outright rejection of God! It was like a dam breaking sending a wall of rushing water flooding down a valley sweeping away the landmarks I'd always figured were permanent. Maybe my downfall started when I discovered that Rubin was really rotten and was so plunged into disappointment. And before reading the letters I'd had suffered discouragements but I'd always blamed myself and prayed for more faith. Now I was wondering if the problem was that there might be no one to pray to or that if there was someone to pray to maybe He wasn't who I thought He was.

"Either way I'm alone," I said out loud and choked back a sob.

"No you're not," God chirped.

And now on top of everything God was talking to me in Jiminy Cricket's voice! Really!

God's new chirpy little voice was sinister. It was even scarier than His usual deep Jason Robards baritone He'd used on me ever since I first began to hear God actually speak to me out loud. And He was chirping at me angrily! In 1 Kings 19:12 it says God speaks in a "still small voice." But I'd never known what that still small voice sounded like. I figured it meant He just talked quietly sometimes. No one said anything about Jiminy Cricket!

"And if you give up on ME and MY movie" God said in His new nasty little shrieking chirp, "before we have a studio deal then Rebecca winds up like King David's love child. Got it? You can bet on that!"

"Are you quite all right my dear?" Margo asked gently.

I couldn't speak. God had shocked me into quivering silence. What He'd threatened and the voice He threatened me with was just insane! I had doubted God's call from time-to-time, though I hadn't dared to ever put such thoughts specifically into words before. Rather I just let a feeling of emptiness enter my brain sometimes as if I was trying on a little godlessness like a jacket that I knew wasn't the right size but wanted to (briefly) try on anyway just to see how it felt and how I looked in it. But now I had let my innermost suppressed and forbidden (very occasional) thoughts be expressed in the actual rebellious words "either way I'm alone."

And God had hit back hard and below the belt! He had just threatened to kill Rebecca because what had happened to King David's illegitimate love child (that David conceived with Bathsheba) was that God punished King David by killing David's innocent baby son!

"Bad news from home?" Margo asked glancing from my face to the letters and back.

I still couldn't speak. I didn't trust my voice not to break down into wild weeping or maybe screamed curses.

"You're positively white as a sheet my dear," said Margo. "Do tell me what's wrong."

"Tell her your aunt was crushed by a train," chirped God. "And quit sniveling!"

"My aunt was crushed by a train," I whispered.

"I am terribly sorry. Was she very dear to you?" asked Margo.

Margo gave me a hug. And this thought crashed into my brain: Wicked worldly Margo is much nicer than God! Compared to God even Rubin seems like the nicest person I ever met! Maybe there is no God! Then another thought crashed into my brain: But if there is no God, then who is talking to me? I pushed back that ultimate doubt and said to myself, "And if God exists maybe He's not a loving

FRANK SCHAEFFER

God after all! Maybe He's there all right but not nice! Maybe it's atheism that's just wishful thinking because He's there all right but I'd be better off if He wasn't!"

Margo said, "I'll fetch you a cup of tea. A good cup of tea is what you need." And she went out to call for Johanna.

In the Bible God doesn't act nice a lot of the time but there's always a reason, or at least I used to think there were "reasons" until my wife dumped me, my pastor betrayed me and my best friend turned into a lesbian and called our church "la, la land." I used to figure that God has to chastise backsliders and destroy the wicked. But in the Bible stories He's nice to His own people when they do what He wants. So I could always feel safe with God because I'd read the parts of the Bible where He was being kind and claim those passages for myself. Now it was like the thought that God might be mean to everyone -- no matter what they did to please Him -- stripped away my belief that, sure, He might test me now and again or smite the wicked once in a while or kill a love child here or there to make a point, but that in the end He'd always be nice to me and somehow things would work out.

Johanna came into the room with a tea tray and set it on the table next to me. Margo poured out some tea, added the milk, and also buttered some toast Johanna had brought in. "There, Luv," Margo said. "Steady on, have some tea and toast. Works wonders."

"Thank you," I said and picked up a cup and sipped.

The tea did taste good. I sipped more tea and thought about God betraying me.

Up until the moment those letters arrived I always figured that the people who disappointed God had it coming even when His chastisements seemed a little over the top, for instance when God killed fifty thousand people who just happened to be nearby when some other men looked into his Ark of the Covenant (thereby breaking one of the hundreds of rules Good Jews must keep) and, as described in 1 Samuel 6:19, God "smote the men of Bethshemesh, because they had looked into the ark of the Lord, even he smote of the people fifty thousand and threescore and ten men: and the people lamented, because the Lord had smitten many of the people with a great slaughter."

But what if God just made up the rules as He went along? What if He was just a bully and had been looking for any excuse to slaughter fifty thousand Jews as a sort of rehearsal for killing six million of them a few thousand years later? I mean these were His "chosen" people!

Maybe, I thought, I'm in the same fix so many characters in the Bible stories found themselves in when, like Cain, for instance, nothing they did could ever get God to like them because even though they sacrificed to God, He rejected their sacrifice as the "wrong kind" and hated them for trying to please Him the wrong way. What if the wrong sacrifice in the Genesis 4 story about Cain and Able was only "wrong" because God said so and not for any real reason? What if He liked setting traps for people who were doing their best? Cain brought fruit to God as his sacrifice but God wanted a lamb so He rejected Cain. And that rejection started a cycle of events that wound up getting Able – who had brought the "correct" lamb God demanded -- killed! What was wrong with the fruit to begin with? Maybe it was only a stepping stone-type sacrifice and Cain would have gotten around to bringing a lamb later. Or maybe Cain just didn't like the idea of slitting some poor little lamb's throat! All God had to do was say "That's nice fruit. Thank you Cain! Good job!" just like any good parent would say to their child whatever she brought them. But no! God rejected Cain and then Cain killed Able and all because of the jealousy God stirred up! They were fine until God showed up! So both Cain and Able were screwed and all because God just couldn't bring Himself to be minimally polite about receiving a fruit basket!

God interrupted my theological reverie by laughing in a high-pitched shriek that made me jump and spill my tea. Then He chirped, "Billy, stop worrying about Cain and Able. Think about Elijah instead. He got discouraged too after what happened on Mount Carmel. He was as disappointed then and, to be honest, as pissed off with ME then, as you are now! Of course I'm nice! I can prove it! I'm talking to you aren't I even though you've put a very negative spin on the Cain and Able story. I haven't struck you down even though I know what you've been thinking! Also, you have the Viewfinder Token of MY Covenant around thy neck! Who led you to that Viewfinder? So just calm down, drink your tea and eat of the toast given to thee by Margo with very nice marmalade and then rededicate your life to ME! And by the way, I was just kidding about killing Rebecca, so quit whining!"

"Okay," I whimpered, and tried not to let God hear what I was really thinking while I mopped the tea off my jeans that He'd made me spill. As I dabbed my jeans with the napkin that was on the tray I was remembering what Molly wrote to me a few days before I left New Midian for South Africa. For once I was hoping her doubts might be right! I mean maybe I *was* "just hearing voices" like she said I was. I sure hoped so!

Chapter 11

I Meet My Crew

Directors are supposed to choose their crew members. But I didn't get to interview any directors of photography, grips, gaffers or make-up artists just like I only met Karl and April after they were hired by Rubin to star in our movie. The crew that wandered into Safari Films' production office was already on board. The way the crew was hired was just another insult to me to add to the mocking of my viewfinder by Rubin, not to mention God's "just kidding" Jiminy Cricket threats against Rebecca.

Everything was turning to garbage on the same day. What Molly had written to me just before I'd left the States was starting to make sense, either that or her undermining of my faith through all her letters was being used by Satan to cause me to slip into a terminal death spiral backsliding episode of apocalyptic proportions. She'd written: "I have always had many more questions than answers. My life began to change when my first child was born. This event affected me in the same way that Rebecca's birth affected you. I saw it as ineffable, full of mystery and wonder. It had more to do with meaning and purpose, less so with biology or theology. All the 'God talk' just seemed so cheap after my living breathing daughter was placed in my arms. All the talk about life being 'meaningless unless you have Jesus' seemed so stupid. The deepest experience of my life – my first child's birth – was something shared by millions of women who didn't 'know Jesus' and therefore, according to my theology were living 'purposeless' even 'meaningless' lives. Now I define myself as my children's mother. That is where my true meaning is."

The tea had helped but it hadn't restored my faith. The problem was that I agreed with Molly more than I wanted to admit. My true meaning was Rebecca. The merest touch of her little hand on my cheek was more real and more powerful and more filled with love and truth than a lifetime of trying to rev myself up to "know" God through a thousand hours of sermons, singing and fellowship.

Even after drinking three cups of tea and eating all the toast it took a huge effort to keep my head in the crew meeting. All I wanted to do was run screaming from the room. God might have said He was "just kidding" about killing Rebecca but how long would it take to get back to her and see her again? I knew that I was going to have to make more stepping stone movies before I got my big break with or without God. And God's movie was such a big budget effects picture that by the time it was produced and distributed it would be a couple of years after the production was even green-lighted. Yet if I quit now, God's "kidding" threat was out there hanging over my daughter's head like a wrecking ball on a fraying thread! If there was just a one percent chance God was real and on top of that He had meant what He said I couldn't risk His wrath being poured out on my dear child.

So I decided that I'd stick with the program. I even said a few "I love you Jesus!" and "Thank You Lord!" prayers to rev myself up again and to keep God in a good mood. But the bad thoughts kept crashing in. Why, I thought, did God kill King David's baby? And why did God the Father and God the Holy Spirit gang up on Baby Jesus and make Him pay for other people's sins? It would have been fairer if All Three of Them came down to die for the world they'd screwed up! Why just pick on The Kid?

AND GOD SAID, "BILLY!"

"STOP!" I yelled, trying my best to cut off these dangerous thoughts. Veronica glanced at me and rolled her eyes. "I'm sorry!" I said. "Praise Your Holy Name Jesus! I love You Jesus, Shan-na-na! Amen!" Veronica just shook her head and muttered something that sounded like, "Simply barmy, bloody hell this really is the limit!" So I stopped saying things out loud.

Then God reverted to His best Jason Robards calm fatherly baritone and said, "Cheer up son! I know you love ME. We all get down once in a while. Hey, I once repented of the whole of Creation. Movie directing is a battle for everyone but yea I AM with thee always. Even though Coppola got to cast his own movie and hire his cameraman nevertheless he suffered set-destroying typhoons and fired Harvey Keitel and then there was Martin Sheen's heart attack and the extras walked off and Brando turned up so disgustingly fat that Coppola shot Brando's scenes in the dark and people started calling Coppola's movie 'Apocalypse When?' Brando and Coppola served Satan and yet their movie won the Palme d'Or! So imagine what *I* can do for you since your co-Screenwriter is The Living God and your executive producer is Jehovah!" Then God's voice shot way up so high He sounded like a parakeet having hysterics and He screamed, "*I smell Oscar!*"

God had yelled "*I smell Oscar!*" so loud that I glanced over to Veronica to see if she'd heard Him. But she just kept on typing. Still, what God had just said did begin to revive my spirits. I mean I was questioning His very existence and yes, Rebecca was more real to me, but nevertheless, He sure knew how to get to me by throwing in all that night class movie lore. I felt grudgingly encouraged despite everything and briefly felt my doubts evaporate into a sort of grudging faith. Also, the crew was arriving for our first production meeting. So I just had to get with the program or just give up for good. I decided to soldier on with both God and my movie making debut.

A young man was slouching across the room to meet me. "Jonny, special effects and prosthetics on this bloody marvelous show," he said.

"I'm Billy the director pleased to meet you," I said, standing up and walking over to him.

Jonny looked like he was about thirty and had stringy dirty long yellow hair and a shark's tooth dangling from a pierced ear. He had an English lower class accent. Johnny was white. There were no blacks or even Afrikaners on the crew just English South Africans and one very nasty German. Johnny wore torn Levi's and a white T-shirt. He didn't hold out his hand to shake mine but lit a cigarette instead and said, "I suppose they flew you in all the way from Hollywood. I suppose they had a budget for that even though Les says we'll be lucky if we even have the budget for a decent blood mix let alone any actual prosthetics."

Jonny's rudeness jolted me and gave me something easier to handle than all the big questions about my eternal destiny let alone God's character. And, yes, first off, God was right and Coppola *had* put up with terrible circumstances and he hadn't given up! Nor world I! Secondly, the point is that even if I followed my doubts to where Molly had gone – into outright apostasy – I'd spent years trying to get into The Business and hundreds of hours perfecting God's script, let alone the twenty two screenwriting night classes I'd taken twice. I wasn't about to flush away all that time invested in night class even if my only motivation had been to sit in of Sadie and look up her skirt. I'd still learned a lot about making movies.

And I admit it: My ego was on the line! I'd shown Hal Busby God's script and two of my stepping stone scripts. And I knew that he didn't think much of me let alone think that I'd get anything I wrote made. He'd been "encouraging" and polite but the expression on his face when he'd handed back God's script and said "It's very interesting but you might want to be focusing on the hero's moral and emotional growth and dig deeper within," was condescending. And there were producers all over town who had laughed at me. I wasn't about to let them have the last laugh. So right then and there deep in the midst of my very own Pilgrim's Progress-type of "slough of despond" and as the crew sauntered in I decided I would stick with it and make this movie come hell or high water. I decided to hedge my bets too and drive away my doubts as best I could. So I squared my shoulders and – as it were – stepped up to the plate to take another swing at whatever God decided to pitch me that day in the way of His latest curve ball. I mean, sure everything was awful but hey, this was an actual production meeting wasn't it? I was now *in* the Movie Business wasn't I? So God HAD answered prayers hadn't He?

Yes Lord!

"Drastic Mood Swing" is what they call this kind of thing in screenwriting class when a character has an "emotional breakthrough." Mine was helped by recalling lots of good get-going-again-type sayings I'd tucked away over the years and stored for just such a time as this. And right then they all kicked in. Maybe it was God talking to me (not so much verbally for once but by placing these sayings on my heart in the more usual manner) or maybe it was me talking to me, but either way the good sayings worked their good on me (along with the tea) and my drastic Mood Swing was upward. Here's what poured into my heart, 1 Philippians 3:14, "I press on toward the goal to win the prize to which God in Christ Jesus is calling us upward," and "When the world says, 'Give up,' Hope whispers, 'Try it one more time,' and Hebrews 11:1 "Now faith is the assurance of the things hoped for," and "Consider the postage stamp: its usefulness consists in the ability to stick to one thing till it gets there," and "Difficult things take a long time, impossible things a little longer!"

"I wonder what it feels like working on a real film instead of a Leslie Spink wank-off special?" Jonny asked me. "Have you ever worked on a real movie?" Jonny turned his back to me before I could answer and walked over to Penny, a tall pretty girl with red hair and pale creamy skin who had just walked in.

"I thought you said you'd never bend over for these bastards again," Penny said to Jonny.

Spink stumbled out of his office, "Afternoon lads," he called to the arriving crew members. No one returned Spink's cheery greeting as he staggered to one of the folding chairs Veronica was setting out. He fell onto it with a groan.

Penny walked over to me. "Hi," I said, the way Stanley Kubrick would have greeted a new crew member with a friendly yet commanding voice.

"He's our director all the way from Hollyfuckingwood," Jonny called out from across the room. "Look he must be the director because he has a viewfinder!"

Penny, Jonny and three more crew members who'd just arrived laughed fit to bust.

"Now, now, lads, show some respect," said Spink.

"Ooh can you get me a job in Hollyfuckingwood? I'm Penny and I'll do anything!" said Penny.

"Now, now lads!" said Spink. "We have a movie to make!" Spink was smiling at Penny and Jonny like he was talking to naughty children. Penny ignored Spink and said, "Give us a fag Jonny." Then Jonny tapped out a cigarette (which is what they call "fags") and lit it for her then handed it to her.

In the next ten minutes the rest of the crew arrived. They mostly seemed pretty young except for Martin Luther. It turned out that all 12 of the crew members hated Rubin and so they hated Spink too for working for him. And so they hated me because Rubin had hired me. But since there was so little work in South Africa for movie people since the boycott started, they had to take whatever Spink brought them.

AND GOD SAID, "BILLY!"

If Marin Luther had been anyone else I would have made some friendly joke about his name to break the ice. But as soon as I saw Martin Luther's face I knew jokes were out. Martin Luther was our director of photography. He had bad acne scars and his eyes were too close together. He was about 60-years-old, had a heavy German accent thinning hair and dandruff, and never looked at me. When Margo introduced us he stared at my feet and said, "Ve vill verk vell together if you do your task unt I do mine. Then ve vill verk vell."

Rubin had been in his back bedroom office as the crew arrived and when he walked in he plunked himself down in Veronica's desk chair while she was setting out the folding chairs for everyone. Martin Luther ignored him. No one looked at Rubin except for Veronica who shot him a furious glance because he'd taken her chair. Then Spink called his crew to order with a lot of, "now, now lads."

Martin Luther sat hunched over a copy of *The American Cinematographer*. He only glanced up to answer Spink's and Rubin's questions about the schedule and how long it would take to shoot this or that scene. Martin Luther's answer was always the same, "I vill take the time necessary to do vat I vill do!" Once Martin Luther spoke he'd look back down at his magazine and turn a page.

It was bad enough that they had hired everybody without asking me but Martin Luther was the worst person I've ever met, besides Rubin. For instance I tried to answer one of Rubin's questions about how long it would take to shoot the scenes in the water with the stalled boat and Martin Luther interrupted me. "How much verk haff you done in a tank?" he asked in a whiny German accent that sounded just like those bad actors playing Nazis in old movies.

"Well, not actually in a tank," I said, and then I lied, "but I've shot some water scenes up at Zuma, a big beach near Hollywood, I've worked with people in the water."

"A tank is very different. I have shot many hundreds of scenes in ze tank," Martin Luther said and went back to reading.

The great directors always stick up for their creative vision. So I tried to further rally my spirits and spoke firmly and loudly and said, "Maybe we ought to use the real ocean. It would give us wider shots."

"Jesus Christ!" Rubin shouted, "Do you know where the fuck you are? Fuck me but this is Johannesburg! You see any ocean around here? We shoot in a fucking tank! Jesus!"

The whole crew laughed at me. Every single person there shot me a smartass smirking glance.

"What about when they first go down to the water on the beach?" I asked, and I felt my cheeks getting hot and knew I was blushing.

"We vill shoot zat at ze Roodeplaat dam. Once zey are in ze vater it vill be in ze tank," Martin Luther grunted.

He turned a page.

"Strike him, Lord!" I prayed.

Jonny and Penny exchanged glances and giggled. Penny lit another cigarette. "Such a happy family!" she said.

Spink held up the Production Board.

"Lads, lads, it's all arranged. Look, the Day-Out-of-Days as well as the board makes it beautifully clear."

Spink's hands shook so hard that a long thin strip of cardboard fell out of the frame of the board.

"Jesus Christ! Can't you even get your goddamned schedule board to work?" Rubin asked.

"There goes my favorite rape scene!" Spink said and laughed and then winked at me. He fumbled around and after a while stuck the schedule strip back into place. Each strip represented a scene. "Look, I've gone and put all the rape scenes here," said Spink and pointed to the middle of the board. "We'll do the bleeding rapes on days eight, nine and ten."

"Jesus Christ!" Rubin yelled, "Three fucking days to shoot some shit-for-brains fucking that bitch?"

"There's wind and rain, the fan will have to be going. The water's cold as well. April will need to warm up between takes. Besides Martin wants to shoot a little under the water, didn't you say so Martin?"

"Fuck Martin Luther! Shoot the rapes in one fucking day. Jesus Christ, we shot the whole drowning scene in 'Tie Me Fry Me' in one fucking hour! Attila the Hun will do what he's goddamned told!"

Martin Luther didn't look up but he turned a page so hard it ripped. Spink licked his lips and smiled and said, "Whatever you want, Rubin. You're the boss, mate."

"You got that right!" said Rubin.

After the production meeting ended Veronica handed a script to each of the crew members and a schedule and whatever memos they needed for their departments. Then Margo drove me back to the Rosebank Hotel and Rubin stayed with Spink to discuss the details of the shoot that were supposed to be the decisions the director should have been making. None of the teachers in night class ever said how it would be.

"Would you like to talk about your aunt?" Margo asked while we were driving.

"No it's okay," I said.

Margo reached out and patted my knee.

"Rotten luck luv," she said.

We drove in silence. It had started to snow.

Margo said she bet I was surprised that there was snow in Africa. That's when I first noticed the snow. When Margo said the word "snow" my brain clicked back to Rebecca. She liked to make what she called "snow babies." That's what Rebecca called snow men. We were making one once when she was two, and she leaned over and took a bite of the snow baby's nose. She loved carrots and we'd just stuck one into the snow baby's face for a nose along with seashells for eyes. She bit the carrot and was about to take another bite when I'd said "Let's not eat the snow baby's nose. I'll get you another carrot."

Then we built three more snow baby's "A mommy a daddy and me," Rebecca called them. I used water-based markers to stain the snow so we could draw eyebrows. We played until Rebecca got too cold then we went inside and she took a sink bath. Rebecca sat in the kitchen sink chest deep in warm water and ate apples. I got all the plastic measuring cups out and we played with them and I mopped up the spilled water off the trailer floor.

Chapter 12

Pat Robertson to the Rescue

After I got back to my room I started flipping between the three South African TV channels to calm myself. Then I heard Molly's voice. When God talked to me I mostly thought it really was Him, though lately I was hoping it wasn't. When Molly talked to me even I knew that her "voice" was only in my head, maybe a sign of stress or something. I mean even Charismatic Christians full of the Holy Spirit don't believe in teleporting or whatever else kind of ESP or whatever it would take for Molly to talk to me direct. But we do believe God can and does do that. But knowing that from both a theological and scientific point of view it couldn't really be Molly didn't make her voice seem any less real. And just because what she "said" was mostly stuff I'd read in her letters, hearing her say it still freaked me out when she said, loud and clear, "We isolate ourselves by our self-determined 'absolutes' and in the end we discover that the poor 'lost' world we were trying to convert to our version of Jesus showed great restraint and patience toward our self-righteous pious arrogance."

Like I said, hearing Molly's voice scared me. I felt like I was falling. I mean how many people were going to start talking to me?

Then Pat Robertson suddenly appeared on a channel I flipped to. It was such a relief to hear a familiar voice coming out of a TV instead of in my head. Talk about a Word in time being like a refreshing spring of clear water in a parched land! I had had no idea South African TV broadcast Christian TV let alone The 700 Club. "Praise Jesus!" I shouted, "Praise Your Holy Name! Praise You! Praise! Praise! Praise!" I jumped up and down on my bed. I was screaming "Praise Jesus!" to drown out Molly's voice and to drown out my fears too.

Pat and his Spirit-filled sidekick Ben Kinchlow were deep in intercession. To see Pat's beautiful sweet smile, to see Ben's chocolaty black face all screwed up as he prayed his heartfelt prayer uplifted my heart so much that I saw sparks of heavenly light. I couldn't stop crying over the joy and comfort that I felt pouring over me along with Pat's actual not-just-in-my-head cheerful chuckles. I still felt like I was falling but now I'd slowed down. It was more like plunging through warm water.

Ben was interceding for, "Someone who's being tested right now in their relationship with the Lord and in their marriage and career." Pat nodded and agreed in the Spirit and smiled and chuckled in his kindest way and hissed, "Yes-s-s Lord! This person is so worried about their child too! Yes-s-s-s-s-s J-e-s-u-s-s-s-s-s, Amen and Amen!" Ben prayed, "Lord, we just agree together to just bind on earth what we just bind in Heaven. We just rebuke the spirit of testing that our brother is experiencing! We just claim your promises to be with him in this time of trouble Lord. In Jesus' Name we just rebuke Satan's attack on our brother and on his faith, family, career and child!"

I burst into tears. This Word was so specific it was clearly for me!

"I rebuke you Molly!" I screamed. "I rebuke you demon of doubt!"

I got down on my knees in front of that TV set. I laid my hands on the cold glass screen and prayed "Forgive me for reading Molly's letters of backsliding doubts! Heal me from her doubts Lord! Drive her voice from my mind! For like Eve with Adam the woman misled me!"

AND GOD SAID, "BILLY!"

The static electricity on the screen made the hairs on my arms stand up. My palms started to feel warm then got hot even though the screen stayed cold as ice! I had my sign! "Thank you!" I cried out. The indwelling of Pat flowed into me as Ben said, "Yes, Pat, He can meet all our needs and heal even our doubts!" Pat and Ben chuckled with Spirit-filled joy and I giggled and rolled around on the floor and agreed with them in my spirit as tears flowed down my cheeks. Then I leapt to the bed and jumped up and down higher and higher. It was my own Pentecost of spiritual revival all alone in the Rosebank Hotel way off in darkest Africa. Pat leaned forward in his chair and looked deep into my eyes. His blessed smile filled up the screen. "No matter where you are or what you did, or how far from home, or how desperate you feel, the Lord is close to you now!" Pat said. "That's right Pat, that's right," answered Ben and chuckled.

I knew that Pat could see me jumping for joy on that hotel bed from way over there in Virginia Beach. I knew that was why he was chuckling. Even though the show had probably been taped months before it was to *me* that Pat's Word of Knowledge was sent. So I said 1 Peter 5:6-7 "Humble yourselves therefore under the mighty hand of God, that he may exalt you in due time: Casting all your care upon him; for he careth for you" and the verse kicked in and did what it was supposed to do. My faith was working again!

"Amen!" I screamed, and with a last mighty leap on the bed I smashed my head into the hotel ceiling.

It was made of concrete. When I regained consciousness I was so dizzy with restored Heavenly Joy that I lay right where I was on the floor. I had a huge bump on the top of my head and a loud ringing in my ears. But the ringing was driving away my sorrows and was like the comforting sound of the surf rippling on the shores of the Sea of Galilee.

Chapter 13
A Predestined Object Lesson in the Fear of the Lord

In the morning Veronica took Martin Luther and me to block the locations. I had woken up in a good frame of mind. God had used Pat to bring me back to Himself! I brought my viewfinder to line up angles to shoot the scenes from. Martin Luther had his viewfinder too. Veronica had picked up Martin Luther first. When they pulled up at the Rosebank Veronica climbed out of the car and she flipped her seat forward and stood back to let me climb in. It was an old two-door Toyota Corolla. Martin Luther didn't bother to look up from the *Johannesburg Star* he was reading. He was riding in front.

Some cameramen call their directors "sir" as a sign of respect. Martin Luther didn't even offer me the front seat. So as we drove off I laid my hand on the back of his seat and prayed, "The wicked in his pride doth persecute the poor: let them be taken in the devices that they have imagined" Psalm 10:2. But even Martin's rudeness didn't spoil that moment of restored faith. My Mood Swing was okay for the time being.

At first we drove through suburbs that looked like LA. The only thing that wouldn't have been in any California suburb were the throng of black men in suits striding up the roadside. According to the road signs we were driving into Johannesburg from the east. I peered over Veronica's shoulder at the skyline. Martin Luther's paper blocked most of my view. He held it up on purpose. From what I could see out of the side window the city was mostly gray office and apartment buildings. There was a tall thickset concrete communications tower with lots of microwave dishes and antennas on it towering above the city.

Downtown Johannesburg flashed past as we drove along an elevated ring road. Then I saw the first mine dump on the edge of the city. It looked like a huge square sandcastle with a flat top about the size of 5 football fields. More mine dumps appeared as we drove out of the city. Veronica was friendlier than she had been in the office and started to explain how the mine dumps were made out of tons of rock crushed to sand that had been pumped out of the gold mines since the 1880s. "The largest cover hundreds of acres and are hundreds of feet high," she said. She explained that the sand got pumped to the top in "liquid slurry" year after year one layer at a time. The water drained away leaving caked sand. Cyanide was the "extracting agent for the gold," she said and so nothing grew on the dumps because they were laced with poison. "Sometimes criminals burry bodies on them but they're stupid because the chemicals preserve the corpses and therefore the evidence, intact. That's what an article said. It was by a retired police pathologist who worked in the morgue."

"What does Spink think we can shoot here?" I asked.

"The beach and island exterior," Veronica said. "We'll do the water scenes up at the dam and the water action in the studio tank. There's no sand at the dam so the dumps will have to do for beach. That's where the cabin exterior set will be built as well. No problem blowing it up in the final scene. There's nothing out here."

"Do not speak. I vish to read undisturbed," Martin Luther said. Then he turned a page.

The headlines were "Winnie Calls for General Strike" and "Five More Necklacing Victims Found in Soweto." Veronica ignored Martin Luther and just kept talking. I asked her questions to show him I wasn't going to be intimidated. I had to put my foot down about who was in charge.

We arrived at the gate of the mine dump we were going to use. A Toyota bakkie (pickup truck) with a black driver was waiting for us. The driver waved to us out of the window. I was the only one who waved back. The bakkie was parked at the side of a dusty track that ran next to a silvery pipe about 2 feet in diameter. Veronica said it was the slurry pipe. The pipe ran along the road then cut up the steep side of the mine dump to the top. She said this was an active dump and "still growing." No one spoke as we followed his bakkie along the base of the dump. Then we drove up its side on a bull-dozed track that zigzagged around the dump to the top. Even with the windows and air vents closed the powdery dust kicked up by the bakkie ahead of us made my eyes sting. When I licked my lips they tasted bitter. Veronica glanced in the rearview mirror and noticed me licking my lips.

"Never mind the dust. It's only cyanide!" she said and laughed.

Martin Luther coughed. "Ve must thank Leslie for choosing zis place!" he said. "Next time you vill tell ze kaffir to follow us!"

We were about three hundred hundred feet above the cow pastures that surrounded the mine dump and bouncing up the road at about twenty miles an hour. I could feel the tires slide in the sand at each corner. I looked for a seatbelt but there wasn't one. "Bloody cheek!" shouted Veronica after we hit a deep rut. "Bloody kaffir! He bloody well knows we haven't got all-wheel drive like he has. He's bloody well trying to kill us! Damn him!"

When Veronica said "Damn him!" it was like she'd proclaimed a Biblical bind-in-Heaven-and-on-earth-type curse because the pickup disappeared. Its dust billowed past us and then the air was clear. Veronica stopped and yanked on the hand brake and jumped out. Martin Luther stayed put. I was stuck in the back because at first I couldn't find the latch on Veronica's seat. I scrambled out after I discovered how to open it.

There was a set of tire tracks cut deeply into the sand. The tracks led over the side of the dump. I heard the muffled sound of metal crunching. I looked over the edge. The bakkie had stayed right side up for about the first 50 feet. The tire tracks ended where it had flipped over. Then there was a rut for about another fifty feet where it slid on its side. Now the bakkie was slowly rolling over and over and nearing the bottom. It almost stopped between each roll then flipped over again then almost came to rest before making another flip.

I stepped over the edge and started to slip-slide down the side.

"Stop!" Veronica screamed.

I stopped.

"What the hell do you think you're doing?" shouted Veronica.

"See if I can help the guy," I said.

"Not bloody likely! The sides aren't stable. You'll fall into a sinkhole and never be heard of again!"

"What should we do?" I asked, as I crawled back up over the powdery edge onto the track.

"Come back tomorrow with a new kaffir I expect," said Veronica, and she giggled.

After the bakkie hit the bottom Martin Luther got out of our car. The pickup had landed upside-down in a wide ditch. The ditch was filled with murky water. Smoke poured out from under the hood. The cab was squashed flat. I had never seen anybody die before. I knew that if the driver had survived the cab being crushed that he was dying right at that very moment trapped in the cab sliding under the water. I felt like crying.

"When we get back to the office Les will call the mine's management to complain," said Veronica.

"What do we do?" I said.

"I suppose we'd better drive up to the top so we can take a Polaroid or two of the location and then turn round. It's too bloody narrow just here," said Veronica.

The bakkie sank deeper into the ditch. A cloud of yellow and green water oozed out around the truck.

"He's sinking!" I shouted.

Martin Luther opened the trunk of the car and pulled out an aluminum camera case. He snapped the buckles then grabbed a Sony Betacam BVP-3 from its foam nest. Martin Luther stepped to the edge. I heard a hum as the zoom adjusted just as the bakkie tipped up and then with a gurgle -- that I heard after the truck was gone because of the time it took for the sound to travel to us -- it sank. Moments later only the front bumper was showing above the water.

"Go on," Martin Luther muttered, "Finish ze shot."

The bakkie slid out of sight. Yellow and orange sludge spread out then sank back under the scummy green water.

"Wunderbar!" Martin Luther exclaimed and kept his camera rolling to record the cloud of rainbow colors spreading on the water where the truck had been.

I understood what God was telling me. The man in the bakkie was killed as a demonstration of God's power. God had forgiven me for my faithless outburst and bad Molly-type thoughts but He wanted to remind me of Who is in charge! Well, He sure had gotten my undivided attention!

That should have been *me* squashed like a bug! God was showing me that His swift justice will always be fulfilled one way or another. He was telling me to never read Molly's doubt-filled letters again. God was telling me to never have thoughts about Him that I wouldn't want Him to know about and be willing to say out loud in front of His Throne on Judgment Day. Of course the bakkie driver that God picked to kill as a demonstration of His love for me must

AND GOD SAID, "BILLY!"

have done something to deserve it. Just like God works everything together for the good of those who love Him, He also works everything together to punish the wicked. He's able to bring everyone's story together in a way that lets Him overlap swift punishments with warnings and blessings just like He did when He killed six million Jews and yet *also* used the Holocaust to help Israel get going since it resulted in more Jews returning to Israel and made everyone else, especially Harry Truman, feel sorry for the Jews so that they gave them Palestine to be a country of their own again after a two thousand year break.

God had to work lots of stuff together to get His prophecies *about* his prophecies fulfilled! In 1917 God got Chaim Weizmann to get the British to issue a statement favoring the establishment of a Jewish national home in Palestine. The statement called the Balfour Declaration was payment to the Jews for their support of the British against the Turks during World War I which God had unleashed so that the Jews could get in good with the British. After that war, the League of Nations ratified the declaration and in 1922 appointed Britain to rule in Palestine. And that's why there had been a British Empire to start with, all so God would have them ready to do what He needed done for His Chosen People all those years later. So the Good Jews got optimistic about the establishment of a homeland and all of a sudden Zionism seemed like a real deal instead of their version of something like the Quakers or whatever that just came and went. The Good Jews newfound optimism inspired the immigration to Palestine of Jews from many countries, particularly from Germany when Nazi persecution of Jews began. So Hitler was God's master stroke to help the Jews do the right thing. Then at midnight on May 14, 1948, the Provisional Government of Israel proclaimed the new State of Israel! Then President Truman recognized the provisional Jewish government right after he'd nuked the Japanese to finish the war that God had started to get Israel going again in one of His typically complicated but effective long term plans to carry out His even longer term plans. Then On May 15, 1948, the Arab armies invaded Israel and the first Arab-Israeli war began between the children of Hagar and the Jews, something that took God over six thousand years, two world wars, the Holocaust and so forth to make happen. In other words God really can kill an infinite number of "birds" with one stone and weaves all our stories together into One Big Wonderful Plan!

"I'll never grumble again!" I shouted and pumped my fist into the air to salute God.

"You do say such odd things," Veronica said and giggled.

Chapter 14
A Good and Just Policeman

When we got back to the production office Margo told me that the police had just called. "They would like to interview you this afternoon at the central police station at John Vorster Square in Johannesburg," she said. Before I could answer Veronica blurted out, "Martin's taken the loveliest video of some silly little kaffir sinking into a pool at the mine dump. It will be perfect for the blooper reel at the wrap party!"

When Martin Luther walked in Margo said, "What's all this? I hear you took a super video."

Martin turned his back on her and marched down the hall to the room with a sign on the door that said "Camera Department." Margo flushed and shouted, "Leslie, our sodding little fuehrer is back. Apparently he's been drowning kaffirs."

"Good for you my boy!" Spink yelled from his office, "One down, thirty million to go!"

"Now then luv shall I go with you? Or would you like to borrow the van?" Margo asked.

"I don't know the way," I said.

Margo smiled and patted my arm. "Poor lamb they haven't abolished hanging here you know," she said and laughed. When Margo made her joke about hanging I heard Spink laughing and there was a crash. "The old bastard's fallen out of his chair," said Margo. She took me by the hand and led me down the hall and shoved Spink's door open. He was still laughing even though he had hit his head. There was a little blood above one ear. He was laughing so hard he could hardly talk.

"This takes the bloody c-c-cake!" he said, "Our director's arrested before we shoot a foot of film!" Spink struggled to a kneeling position. Pulling on the corner of his desk he stood up while Margo picked up his swivel chair.

"Have a drink!" said Spink as he crashed heavily back down in his chair.

"What do you think I should do?" I asked.

"Do?" said Margo. "Tell those Afrikaner twits you didn't come all the way from America to be harassed by some uppity gollywog!"

"How about if they believe him and not me?" I asked.

Margo patted my shoulder and then put her arm around my waist.

"This isn't America thank God. No worries luv."

Spink picked up a wine bottle and tried to pour. When nothing came out he reached into the filing cabinet and shoved some loose papers, two pistols and a box of ammunition aside and pulled out an unopened bottle. Margo handed me a glass and picked up another glass.

"Boschendal Blanc de bloody Blanc. Marvelous," Spink said after he got the cork out and poured me a brimming glassful. "Bottoms up," he said. I held up my glass and clinked glasses with Margo and Spink but I didn't drink. Spink and Margo stared at me. "Bottoms up lad. To sanctions busters everywhere!" Spink roared. I still didn't drink.

"It's bad luck not to drink after making a toast," said Margo. "Drink up luv."

I was shook up from seeing the driver drown. I was even more shook up by the news that the police wanted to talk to me. I'd kind of hoped that this particular fiery dart would just go away and that the Lord would spare me another testing. I cried out inwardly, "I'm feeling far from You Lord!"

"Drink up luv," Said Margo. "If they cut off your balls it will hurt less if you're a wee bit tight."

Then God surprised me because in His friendliest Jason Robards voice He said, "'Give strong drink to him that is ready to perish, and wine to those that be of heavy hearts' Proverbs 31:6. Yes Billy that means you. You may drink alcohol now according to MY Will."

So I drank like somebody chugging water. Only a little later (during my drive to the police station) did I worry about what God had meant. What was He saying by quoting a verse about "him that is ready to perish?" Nevertheless the wine helped and kind of smoothed things out for a while and left me feeling pretty relaxed.

At first sight the Johannesburg South African Police Headquarters didn't seem to have any windows. The windows were hidden behind thick gray wire mesh. It was stretched over a steel frame like the safety netting on work sites. Margo said that the mesh was to, "Keep the kaffirs from jumping until they're done with them." When we walked into the building the green walls reminded me of my high school. So did the windowless hallways and the steel lockers. Even the floor was the same as Triton Regional High's floor. It was a mixture of concrete and pebbles polished smooth with aluminum strips dividing it up. Margo sat down in the waiting area and lit a cigarette. I went up to the information window to ask about my appointment. I was told to follow a black policewoman. She had wide hips and thick legs.

We walked through three sets of doors that buzzed open when she showed her pass to guards behind thick glass windows set in concrete. We passed a black man in a white coat that looked like an ambulance driver. He was pushing a gurney with a black man on it with his wrists handcuffed to the sides. A white cop walked next to the gurney. The man on the gurney had cuts on his face and it was so swollen it looked like a black balloon. The hall smelled like disinfectant. We came to a dead end. The cop pointed to a gray metal door and then she turned around and stomped back down the hall.

In the room on the other side of that door was a mirror set into the wall, a wooden table, two chairs and a single light bulb inside a grill in the ceiling. The room was about 15 by 15 feet. The walls were made out of unpainted concrete and there were no windows. The ceiling was so low that my head almost touched it. There was a hook set in the middle of the table with a thick piece of chain attached to it. The metal table was bolted to the floor. I didn't sit down. I didn't pace in case I was being watched through the mirror. I tried to look relaxed but Isaiah 59:2 was running through my head, "But your iniquities have separated between you and your God, and your sins have hid His face from you that he will not hear." How could that be true though? God told me I could drink and He'd killed the black man on the mine dump not me. On the other hand He'd told me to drink wine because those "ready to perish" were allowed to do that! Maybe He was planning to get me for doubting Him.

The door opened and a very tall -- at least 6 feet 3 inches -- man stepped into the room. His head brushed the ceiling and he had to duck under the door's lintel. He had on a pair of jeans and a white shirt open at the neck and he wore a tweed jacket with leather patches on the elbows. He had a pistol stuck in the front of his pants. His face was tan and lined. He looked like Clint Eastwood on the poster for "A Fistful of Dollars" only with no cowboy hat.

"Right man, what's all this rubbish?" he said in a deep gravelly voice and held out a huge hand. He smiled in a friendly way. "Detective Officer Vandermeer, how do you do?"

I held out my hand, "Fine. How do you do?" I said.

Officer Vandermeer crushed my hand when we shook. He spoke in a heavy Afrikaans accent and hardly opened his mouth when

AND GOD SAID, "BILLY!"

he talked. He rolled his Rs and the letter "I" sounded like "E". So the word "rubbish" sounded more like "rrrubeesh." And the word "right" sounded like "rrroyt," actually more like "hrrroyght" because he threw in an "H" along with his "Rs." And the way he said "A" was more like "Eh." So when he said "Right man," it sounded like, "hrrrioyghtt mehn." And "rubbish" sounded like "hrrrubeesh." He started calling me "man" but used the Afrikaans word "maan" that sound more like *mun*.

Officer Vandermeer grinned and winked and then pulled a pack of Rothman's cigarettes out of his shirt pocket and tapped one out and lit it. He offered me a cigarette and I said no thanks. The smoke Officer Vandermeer blew out of his nose hung in the air.

"What's this fucking rubbish, eh maan?" Officer Vandermeer said again and took a deep drag then blew out more smoke and smiled.

"I'm not sure," I said feeling relieved that he was being so nice and a little silly for thinking God hadn't altogether forgiven me for my recent backsliding episode, "I was just flying out here to direct a movie and next thing I know I'm accused of stealing some black guy's stuff on the plane."

Officer Vandermeer exploded into a smoky laugh. "Rubbish!" he shouted, "We've got bombs going off every day, thirty million kaffirs to mind and twenty murders in Soweto every weekend to investigate and they arrest a famous film director for pick-pocketing some kaffir! Rubbish!" Officer Vandermeer clapped a hand on my shoulder and kept laughing. He left his hand on my shoulder and it felt heavy.

"That's what I thought," I said. "And I didn't take anything."

"Of course not, just what I told my boss when he ordered me to question you."

"O thank You Lord for giving me favor in the eyes of this just and good policeman! Bless him!" I prayed. I broke into inner singing of the good old Doxology: "Praise God, from Whom all blessings flow; Praise Him, all creatures here below; Praise Him above, ye heavenly host; Praise Father, Son, and Holy Ghost!"

"Suppose we'd better make out a report, eh? Get this fiasco over with then we can go out and have a drink! Eh? Then you can tell me all about Hollywood and I can tell you about minding our kaffirs."

"That would be great," I said, and I noticed that his hand was still gripping my shoulder so that when he stuck his cigarette back in his mouth with his other hand the tip was just inches from my face and I felt the heat.

"Who's the star of your film eh? Beautiful woman?" Vandermeer asked.

"Her name's April. She used to be on Hawaii Five-O."

"Not *the* April Kimberley! Not the beautiful bit of a thing in that little orange bikini?"

I was surprised. How could Office Vandermeer have heard of April, let alone remember her? And why had his grip tightened on my shoulder? And why was he imitating Clint Eastwood?

He clenched his cigarette between his teeth while he talked and his tone was just like Eastwood's when Eastwood spoke with those little cigars clenched in his teeth that he was always chewing in the Sergio Leone westerns. Officer Vandermeer was imitating Eastwood's voice perfectly too. I figured this was his idea of a joke because he must know that people thought he looked very like Eastwood. So I smiled to show him I was enjoying his imitation of a movie star, what with me being a director and all.

"Hawaii Five-O's the most popular new show in South Africa just now. Big following," Officer Vandermeer growled in a really good Eastwood voice and perfect American accent.

" 'New show?' It's at least ten years since--"

"Every Thursday night. I never miss it," he growled though clenched teeth.

"That's great."

AND GOD SAID, "BILLY!"

Officer Vandermeer grinned and went back to using his Afrikaans accent. "Now then I want to meet the lovely Miss April. You'll arrange it, won't you maan? Eh?"

"Sure."

Officer Vandermeer grinned some more as he let go of my shoulder. "That's settled then. Now what did you do, eh? Did you touch this kaffir's fucking rubbish?"

"I may have had to move his stuff out of my way or something."

"Bleeding reasonable. No problem," Officer Vandermeer said.

"Now then did you happen to take anything at all, just out of curiosity, absent-minded like? All you artistic chaps are absent-minded."

"Of course not," I said.

He punched me so hard that I doubled way over without making a sound. I couldn't breathe. He hadn't seemed to move when he hit me in the stomach. He never stopped smiling. I fell down. Officer Vandermeer took a long drag on his cigarette, so long that his cigarette sizzled. I couldn't breathe so it was strange that I noticed the cigarette sizzling, but I did.

"Well?" he asked.

I waved my hands and looked past his legs to where his face was up by the ceiling grinning down at me as friendly as ever. Officer Vandermeer placed the toe of his huge foot on my testicles and started to shift his weight. I waved my hands arms and legs hard but I still couldn't breathe. Officer Vandermeer pulled his pistol out of his pants grinned at me and pointed it at my head.

He switched back into his imitation of Eastwood. "I know what you're thinking: 'Did he fire six shots, or only five?' Well, to tell you the truth, in all this excitement, I've kinda lost track myself. But being this is a 44 Magnum, the most powerful handgun in the world, and would blow your head clean off, you've got to ask yourself one question: 'Do I feel lucky?' Well, do ya, punk?" Officer Vandermeer stuck the gun back in his jeans. "Now then my friend," he said hearty and friendly and back in his South African accent, "Refresh your memory. Why were your prints on the inside of Dr. Mzamane's wallet, on his credit cards and on his racial identity card?"

Having my testicles squashed made me suck in a deep breath so I was able to scream out, "I just wanted to look!"

Officer Vandermeer reached down and lifted me to my feet. I felt the hot diarrhea squirt into my pants a split second before I realized that he had just kneed me in the groin. I collapsed sideways onto the ground again. Officer Vandermeer lit another cigarette and sat down on the edge of the table.

"What did you do with his money?"

He waited until I stopped gasping enough to answer.

"I spent it," I whispered.

"How much?"

"Seven hundred and twenty Rand."

"What did you do with it?"

"I hid it in my socks on the plane."

"Where's the money?"

"I bought presents for my daughter after I talked to the airport police. I sent the gifts from the hotel."

"I hate paperwork. We'll keep this informal, eh? You just bring me seven hundred Rand and that will be the end of it," Officer Vandermeer said then turned and walked out. He paused on his way through the door and said, "There's a lavatory across the hall. It has a wall tap and a bit of hose. You need a bit of a wash *maat*. Have the money here tomorrow or I'll pay you another visit. And if you mention our little chat to anyone we'll have a similar talk and next time I'll get a bit rougher."

Chapter 15
Good Muti

I found myself standing on a white tile floor stark naked. "Help me Molly!" I cried out. Then I corrected myself and cried out "Help me Lord!" There was blood mixed with my diarrhea. I watched it swirl down a floor drain. A Bible verse popped into my brain: "But your iniquities have separated between you and your God, and your sins have hid his face from you, that he will not hear" Isaiah 59:2). I felt really angry when I saw my blood. "No," I said, correcting myself again, "Fuck this! If He wants to hide His face, then so be it! Help me Molly!"

There was a hose and tap just like Vandermeer had said. The water was freezing. God had unleashed Officer Vandermeer on me so I was trying to hear Molly's voice instead of God's. Backslidden, atheist lesbian or not she'd never have done this to me! Testing or "chastising" is one thing. Getting kneed in the testacies so hard you squirt diarrhea and blood is another!

Then Molly answered me by repeating something she'd written in a letter a few weeks before I'd left the States. As I hosed myself clean, I heard her sweet voice say, "I've been able to start picking up the shattered pieces of my life but I have such terrible anger and flashbacks. I don't know if I can ever trust anything religious again."

"I hear that," I groaned, "me too!"

Margo was waiting on the sidewalk. She was smoking a cigarette and watching the pale yellow police vans with heavy wire grills over their windshields and lights drive in and out of the parking lot. I had a hard time walking. It hurt to stand up straight but I didn't want Margo to ask what had happened to me so I tried to act normal. I hoped she wouldn't notice that my pants were wet. I had thoroughly rinsed them out.

"While we're here," said Margo, "We may as well walk up to the top of Jeppe Street and have a look-see. Leslie's chosen that bit over there as one of our exteriors, you know where they come out of their flat during the front end credits and hook the boat onto the bakkie and leave for the beach. He says he thinks it looks a bit like Miami. Does it?"

"Sure," I said without even looking.

"Pity you don't have your viewfinder with you today to block the scene."

"I left it at the office," I said and stuck out my hand to steady myself on a lamppost.

"How did it go?" Margo asked.

"Fine," I said. I took a deep breath and dug my shaking hands into my wet pockets. "It's all taken care of now."

"What a bloody waste of time."

"I said I wasn't going to waste my time with them unless they had something to charge me with."

"Good for you. I bet those bloody Afrikaners opened their eyes a bit at that. Bit of a surprise for them to run up against a Yank who knows his rights. Your trousers are wet."

"I tripped over a bucket in the hall."

"Bloody kaffirs never tidy up properly."

I followed Margo up Jeppe Street to Diagonal Street. It was a narrow road in a neighborhood of rundown apartment buildings and stores tightly packed together. The street was full of black and brown people. There were vendors with knots of shoppers hanging around their stalls. Household junk, sheets, lamps, records, tapes, sunglasses, bolts of cloth and all sorts of stuff from empty bottles to toilet brushes overflowed from the stalls onto the sidewalk.

"Ever been in a muti shop?" Margo asked.

"No."

"Have a look-see shall we?"

Margo ducked through a low door. I leaned up against the doorpost. I felt dizzy. I took a couple of deep breaths then followed Margo through the bead curtain that hung in the open doorway. A sickening rotting meat smell hit me and turned my heaving stomach. The store was in a dark small room piled floor to ceiling with cardboard boxes and mounds of dried plants, bones and animal skins. There were ratty looking pelts hanging from the ceiling so thickly they looked like some sort of sick laundry on a line. There were jars stacked on one side floor to ceiling filled with nasty looking stuff floating in them. I sat down on a weird folding chair made out of two thick interlocking wooden slabs with African mask-type faces carved on them. I hoped Margo hadn't noticed that I crashed down on the chair to save myself from falling. There were sticks of incense stuck in a lump of putty on a rusty oil drum next to the chair. I stuck my nose over the incense and breathed in the smoke to try and drive away the other smells.

A thin black woman with a baby tied to her back by a dirty pink blanket walked in. A brown man came out of a back room. He was wearing a white robe and a white lacy-looking skullcap. Margo said he was a Muslim from India and that's why he wore the cap. The whole time we were there, about 15 minutes that felt like hours, the Indian didn't look at us once even though Margo talked in front of him as if he wasn't there.

"Bloody kaffirs believe in this rubbish," Margo said and waved her hands at everything around us. "God knows what this all is," she said and shuddered. "But it works for the poor dears. They're a queer lot. Take her," Margo said and pointed at the black woman who didn't even look our way, "I'll wager she spends all day in church on Sunday like a good little Christian and the rest of the week it's all tribal mumbo-jumbo. If they get ill it's off to the muti shop for a bit of sheep's arse, bark and sangoma spit, you name it."

The black woman turned her child's face to the daylight that was coming through the store's one small dirty window. The Indian checked out the baby's face. Her eyes were swollen shut and crusted up.

"That chap probably doesn't believe a word of what he's telling her, but they run all the muti shops anyway," said Margo. "Bloody Packies and Indians are an enterprising lot."

The man brushed the flies away that were on the baby's eyes and pulled down an eyelid. Then he scrounged around in a bunch of drawers under the counter and tossed powders and leaves into the bowl. He mashed it all up with a thing that looked like a miniature baseball bat. Then he pushed his way out from behind the counter through the animal skins hanging in rows from the ceiling. He stirred up a terrible smell as he shoved the skins aside and made them swing on their hooks. I had to stick my nose right on top of the incense to stop from throwing up. I wanted to get out but my legs wouldn't work. My testicles were so painful that I couldn't even cross my legs. I closed my eyes. Something Margo had just said was going around in my head but kind of taking on another meaning. She'd said "That chap probably doesn't believe a word of what he's telling her, but they run all the muti shops anyway," and she was talking about the Indian shop owner. But, I thought, Margo could have said the same thing about Pastor Bob and probably about every pastor in the world. Change the words "muti shops" to "churches" or "evangelistic ministries" and you'd be pretty near the truth.

A piercing scream made me jump. It sounded like someone had

stabbed the baby. I opened my eyes with a jerk. The man was coming back into the store past a carcass of a small yellow monkey nailed to a board on the wall. It was crucified like Jesus only the monkey was dry and its skin was stretched tight over its ribs. Its moth-eaten mouth was frozen wide open. The man's hands were bloody. He held a little hunk of fresh meat that had a clump of hair attached to it.

"Live muti," said Margo, "it's the best kind they say."

The man tossed the hunk into his bowl and pounded it with the bat. Then he tipped everything into a food processor. Then he poured the mixture he'd whizzed up through a funnel into a coke bottle. He stuck a wine cork in it and handed it to the woman who paid him and left.

"What's live muti?" I whispered.

Margo answered extra loud like she wanted to make sure the man heard her. He didn't even look our way. "They keep beastly cages of dogs, squirrels, monkeys, rats, mice, birds, you name it. When they need a particular bit they go and slice it off, must have been a monkey or maybe a little dog just now judging by that squealing. Leslie says a good muti man can keep the same wretched creature alive for weeks. They begin with the extremities, toes, teeth, paws, ears, tails and work into the vitals."

"Are they allowed to do that?" I whispered.

"Where the bloody hell do you think you are luv?" Margo said and laughed. "We've got enough problems with the kaffirs as it is without taking away their precious muti."

Chapter 16

Seven Hundred Rand

I found myself in a waking half dream asking both God and Molly how to get the 720 Rand (hedging my bets as it were). Even while half asleep I was seesawing from faith to unfaith, from repentance to rebellion, from anger to whimpering groveling apologies, from Mood Swing to Mood Swing. Molly said "Just ask Rubin." Then God said "Forget Molly and cast yourself upon MY mercy and hope for the best. Trust ME!"

"Why?" I yelled throwing off the covers.

I jumped out of bed but my testicles hurt so much that I fell back face down clutching my pillows. What had happened to my family? How would I pay the money back to Officer Vandermeer? It was impossible to picture Ruth committing adultery, almost as impossible as believing that I'd been kneed in the testicles by a South African cop.

"Where are You God?" I moaned. No answer.

"Molly?" I called out. No answer.

According to the hotel's bedside electric alarm clock it was 7:45 in the morning so I knew that Rubin was awake. Margo was meeting us in 15 minutes.

I had to knock a couple of times before Rubin came to his door. "What the fuck?" Rubin said as he opened the door. He was wearing

AND GOD SAID, "BILLY!"

red thong underpants. I stepped over his room service tray. It was mounded with leftovers from his supper, including 4 kinds of dessert he'd only taken a few bites of. His buttocks sagged over his thong. Rubin went back into his bathroom and shaved. I sat on the end of his bed with my legs wide apart to avoid squishing my battered testicles. The room smelled like room service food and aftershave.

"I'm wondering if you could advance me a little money on my per diem," I said, in a friendly, casual and calm voice, just like I'd rehearsed in the shower.

"And I'm wondering if you want me to find me a director that doesn't get his ass arrested," Rubin snapped. "Where the fuck were you yesterday? How many production meetings do you plan on missing?"

"It's kind of urgent. It's only seven hundred Rand," I said.

"What the fuck do you need seven hundred Rand for you little shit?"

"It's to do with my problem on the plane."

"I thought you said you didn't do anything."

"I didn't. I guess this is like some kind of payoff or something."

Rubin stepped out of the bathroom and shouted, "I'm sure as hell not going to lend you any goddamned money!"

"Rubin, if I don't take it down there today I might get sent home and you won't have a director."

"Fine with me you cock-sucking weasel," Rubin snarled.

"C'mon Rubin, you still need your director, don't you?" I said and I tried to laugh and make it sound like I'd taken Rubin's Bad Secular Jew words like a friendly joke.

"Fuck you!" he screamed.

Then Rubin hauled out his briefcase from under his bed and snapped it open. He took out a folder and flipped it open then counted out 700 Rand in 50 Rand notes from a thick wad of cash. Rubin threw the money on the bed then picked up the bedside phone and dialed before I even had a chance to say thank you.

"Veronica!" he bellowed, "Our director has just fucked me in the ass for seven hundred Rand. That's his per diem for the rest of this fucking shoot! Got it? That's it. Not another goddamned penny!" Rubin slammed down the phone. "That's it jerk-off you're on your own," he said. "Get out!"

As I limped to the door I wanted to ask how I was going to eat with no per diem. I wasn't allowed to charge food to the room and my cash was about gone.

Chapter 17

A High Level Relationship Bears Fruit

After I gave my name at the information window at police headquarters I had to wait half an hour before Officer Vandermeer came down the hall. When he saw me he beckoned me outside. Seeing him made me feel like I was drowning, nervous and breathless. Once we were on the sidewalk I tried to keep my distance in case Officer Vandermeer wanted to knee my testicles again. I held out the money at arm's length that I'd tucked into a hotel stationary envelope. Officer Vandermeer took the envelope and smiled and said, "When I visit your film set be sure you introduce me to Miss April."

At 10 AM when I got to the production office I walked down the hall and knocked on Spink's door. There was no answer. Spink was asleep with his head resting on his desk cradled on his thick pink arms sticking out from below his shirtsleeves. Next to his elbow was an empty glass and a 2-foot tall pile of tattered scripts under four boxes labeled, "500 Rounds -- 20rds - .410 / .45 Defender Winchester Supreme Elite 2 ½ PDX1 Combo Self Defense Ammunition, Made in the USA." Under the label was an American flag logo and a huge GOD BLESS AMERICA stamped on the boxes in thick black letters.

I stood there watching Spink sleep and thinking about Hal Busby saying "Careful plotting is needed to weave the elements of the story together. This fundamental structure contains a number of stages, which includes, a call to adventure, which the hero has to accept or decline on his road of trials, regarding which the hero succeeds or fails, achieving the goal which must result in important new self-knowledge." What he'd said encouraged my heart. *I* was the hero of this story persevering through all adversity to my goal! On the other hand Hal Busby had never told his class that if they actually ever made a movie that there were people like Spink they'd be working with and that they would be standing in Lone Hill South Africa watching their production manager slumped on his desk surrounded by loaded weapons, ammunition and empty wine bottles and that the producer they would be working for would describe his movie as not a movie at all but a deal.

On the other hand I knew that according to Hal Busby's Story Structure Rules and also according to the Bible (mostly in the stories about King David and Jesus) that I was at the "trials stage" of the hero's journey. It was up to me to succeed to achieve the goal. Hal Busby had often said, "When you get the rare opportunity to make a high-level relationship the big shots need to know that you are a professional, a master of the craft. It's hard, but with commitment you can do it." As I remembered his wise words it was like Hal Busby was with me in the production office saying "If the world's top screenwriting coach is for you who can be against you? So right now your big shot in this high-level relationship is passed out, never mind, you can do it!"

"Les," I said. He didn't move. "Les," I said again.

Spink raised his head a few inches off his desk and shot me a bloodshot glare.

"Ask Margo," he mumbled and lay his head back down.

"Les, I hate to bother you but do we have to use Martin Luther as our cameraman? Isn't there anyone else?"

"What's that sodding Nazi prick done now?" Spink asked without looking up.

"I don't seem to be able to talk to him."

"He's a bloody Hun. Watchyou expect? They're all the same, introspective Gerry psychopathic wankers."

"Why do we have to use him?" I asked.

"Owns the camera and lighting package-- now sod off!"

"I need a director of photography I can talk to."

Spink sighed and sat up.

"Reminds me," Spink said, "never look through that prick's bloody camera to line up a shot, makes him wild when people touch his camera. No time for arguments on the set now that we're shooting the picture in six days."

"Six days?" I said, not believing what I'd just heard. "*Six days?*" I screamed when I decided I'd heard right.

"Please don't shout. I have a headache. Didn't Rubin tell you? Cut the shoot from sixteen days to six yesterday. The bloody investment package blew up. Turns out the investors don't think Karl counts as star content. We're shooting the whole bloody picture on money that Safari Films is borrowing against the South African tax credit. Budget's been cut in half. We'd cancel the shoot if Rubin-fuck-all hadn't made a pay-or-play deal with Karl and April, sod him."

"Rubin never said anything about this!" I shouted.

"Please do NOT shout," Leslie said and handed me a glass. "And we're shooting in sixteen mil now. Sorry mate. Bit of a balls-up."

"I thought the deal is we have to deliver a thirty-five millimeter print to qualify for the tax credit," I said.

I was trying to calm down and get my voice under control and to be the professional Hal Busby had taught me to be. Spink winked. "You've picked up a bloody thing or two," he said. "But those Afrikaner twits over at Revenue Service never look at the bloody films. We'll ship out in thirty-five millimeter tins so the descriptions on the customs forms conform to the thirty-five mil definition of a feature film per tax law. But it's got to be shot in sixteen. And you can't shoot more than two-to-one lad, no money for film stock now so we'll be shooting short ends scrounged from other production companies. The tax twits only look at a VHS as proof it got made and they'll never know the difference. Besides it will be so bloody appalling they'll only watch the first thirty seconds before they fast forward to the end of the tape."

Leslie laughed.

"It'll be better than that," I said.

"Six days lad! You'll be lucky to shoot a master of each scene. No close ups. You'll be dropping pages like autumn leaves."

While Spink laughed I noticed that I had chugged my wine. Then it was like all my troubles suddenly boiled up and I was filled with a directorial rage about having my stepping stone movie undermined. I yelled, "Fuck!" at the top of my lungs before I even realized that I'd said anything. Then I screamed "*Fuck!*" again even louder. I was so shocked by my profanity that before the second F-word stopped bouncing around Spink's office I screamed, "O Lord Jesus Christ forgive me!"

"Forgive us all lad, forgive us all," said Leslie and laughed.

Chapter 18
He Would Also Mock Her for Eternity

I emptied my toilet case in preparation for the Lord's bounty. Molly had been "talking" to me off and on all day. I seemed to be hearing lots more voices ever since the terrible doom-laden letters arrived. Molly spoke to me, Hal Busby's words echoed in my brain, and then of course – in a class all His Own, God talked to me too. Just now it was Molly's turn in my brain. Molly was saying, "Now, one of the things I struggle with most is how much or how little of my struggle to share with my kids. I concluded that my childhood spirituality was my spiritual 'default mode.' Half of what I say I believe is just self-justification for choices I make. I want them to have faith, but I want them to question everything too. I'm always trying to be honest with my kids without pulling the rug out from under them. I don't want to completely discredit what they have learned in church either."

I watched "Hawaii Five-O." The episode that night was about real estate developers on the Big Island making trouble for the natives and driving them out of their homes. Jack Lord kissed April Kimberly in a scene that was cut so short it seemed like even back then when she looked good and too much tanning hadn't turned her skin into leather that the editor couldn't stand to give April more screen time than he had to.

Then God and/or Molly and/or Hal Busby laid some wisdom on my heart to make me aware that I had bodily needs no matter how confused I felt. Whichever one of them said it someone said, "Every moving thing that liveth shall be meat for you; even as the green herb have I given you all things" Genesis 9:3. So I knew that it was time to collect the day's provision from leftovers on room service trays and eat a half of a piece of fried chicken here, a shrimp drowning in cocktail sauce there and a handful of rice pilaf and what was left of some dinner rolls and most of a baked potato stuck in a puddle of congealed butter. And soon my rubber-lined toilet case was full of soggy lukewarm supper. Once I got it back to the room the food tasted like rubber and aspirin and stale toothpaste. But it was the Lord's provision so I ate in thanksgiving because Elijah didn't complain about the food the ravens brought him tasting like bird spit. It seemed that maybe God had forgiven me for saying the F-word. Maybe He had forgiven my doubts too! The food was there wasn't it? He was still leading me, even giving me treats! One person had left a half a porterhouse steak along with some watercress. God was feeding me steak. And He knew I love watercress. And in another indisputable sign, *He even moved someone to leave an entire unopened mini cup of Haagen-Dazs vanilla ice cream on a tray.*

The ice cream reconciled me to God – for the time being – but nevertheless, it didn't give me peace though. I wanted justice!

I had brought the tapes and the cassette player with me to South Africa and carried along an adapter I'd plundered from the Sharper Image in Beverly Hills, so as to be sure I could listen to Ruth's words and feel close to her even in Africa. And now I knew that at the very time she was saying that it was a good idea for me to bring the tapes she was fornicating with Pastor Bob!

So I played the tapes before the Lord while I ate the Lord's bounteous steak and delicious watercress and Haagen-Dazs vanilla ice cream. I offered up Ruth's *own words* and my imprecatory prayers directed against "Pastor" Bob and Ruth. I chewed steak and prayed for revenge. I sucked down melting ice cream and demanded retribution!

I knew that God knew Ruth's eternally reprobate mind inside and out and yet He had allowed her to have rain and crops and a dwelling and everything else that was good in spite of her sin but that He would also mock her for eternity. I knew that Christ loves those who hate Him not because He loves their sin but because He is just biding His time! The Whole Trinity hates the wicked and will get even eventually, even if the wicked are laughing it up now and mistaking God's blessing and crops and their dwellings as some sort of "evidence" that they're getting away with their sins. They are not!

Revenge is the Lord's! So I hit the "Play" button and played the tape before the Lord as evidence of Ruth's perfidious hypocrisy.

"Listen to this Lord!" I called out "This is all the evidence You need! She is condemned by her own words!"

On the tape Ruth was saying "Kids of Christian parents get just as pregnant as unsaved kids these days. Something is wrong in America. The goal of God-centered education is the same thing as the Great Commission in Matthew 28:18. Teach your children by the Bible! And use the materials we have here on the book table from RJ Rushdoony. It's amazing that fifty million American children, most of them from so-called Christian families are *still* in the secular government-controlled schools. Back when RJ Rushdoony was the lone voice crusading to get our Christian children home schooled he wrote, 'Why then did kindergarten succeed? The answer was and is clear-cut: the desire of women to get rid of their children. Educators had to set an age requirement for kindergarten children; else they would be deluged with mothers trying to push very young children into their hands. Thus, kindergarten has proven to be in part a polite and oblique form of infanticide, one which hypocritical women can indulge in while getting credit for solicitous motherhood.'"

I turned off the tape.

"Well?" I asked God. "What do you think?"

"She's a lying bitch all right," said God.

Chapter 19
The Blue Pages

"We've changed the story," said Spink as he put down his glass. It was lunchtime on Day 6 of pre-production. "No budget for the water gags."

"What will we shoot if we cut everything?" I grumbled as I sipped my wine. If I hadn't been too scared to incur God's wrath by open association with a backslider lesbian I would have written to Molly (maybe even called her) to tell her that I was drinking wine now. I would have also told her that some of my Mood Swings were swinging me close to a total denial of God.

But I didn't. It was bad enough that I let her talk to me in the same brain that I listened to God and Hal Busby with! There'd be no percentage in having anything more to do with her than that. She had really gone to the dark side and seemed to be taking me with her. As if to prove the point Molly said, "Too much Kool-Aid drinking! My kids and I are working our way away from it, but like the generation wandering the wilderness, we have to die first before the rest can enter the Promised Land I guess. And for my kids, it's too late! They've lost their innocence! I have too! They understand that I don't buy the party line any more that we are 'right' and the 'other side' is 'wrong.'"

"Same thing," said Spink, "only now we'll set the story here and use the local flora and fauna. We're not shooting Joburg for Miami now but Africa for Africa. No need to change road signs and license plates to American ones. We own the production van. We'll use that as our picture car. Free bleeding art direction what with our zebra logo on the side. We'll just change the words from 'Safari Films' to 'Safari Tours.' Clever eh?" Leslie laughed. "Karl and April will be on a hunting safari now, break down in the bush instead of on a beach, walk toward some lights – our production office -- and find they've walked into a drug traffickers' safe house. The rest will be the same except set here. Torture, April's whacking cantaloupes swinging in the breeze, Karl kicking and chopping his way out of danger, and then they'll drive off in our van instead of in the motor launch. Fade to black."

Spink poured us each another glass of wine.

"So the boat chase becomes a car chase?" I asked.

"Can't afford any chases lad. No stunt budget. Besides, can't risk the production van. Don't write anything over forty miles an hour."

Spink drained his glass.

"Then what's the action part of the movie going to be?" I asked. "I planned to shoot long lens with smash cuts to extreme close ups and hand held intercut with boat mounts."

"Sex is cheaper. Talk April into taking more off. Her bum's better looking than some bloody speedboat. Last time she was here she broke the treadmill in the Sandton Sun. The manager complained that she'd been on it for five hours and the motor burst into flame. Her bum looks like it's carved of sculpted titanium. Show it! Fill the screen with it! Explore it! But first thing is you've got to break it to those twits that we're shooting the picture in six days."

"They don't know?"

"Got to get them out here first lad then tell them or they might do a bunk. Given all that nonsense April screamed at the 'Vulcan Princes' wrap party about 'a line I won't cross again!' I wish we'd cast little Kay Lense. Reasonable girl Kay and they love her in Brazil, almost as much as they love Linda Blair. There's not one sodding foreign territory where April's name means shit." Leslie poured more wine for both of us. "You talk the prima donnas into it lad. That's your bleeding job."

"They'll quit," I said. "Nobody shoots twenty pages a day."

"Not once you've started shooting they bloody well won't quit because we'll have their passports. I shan't give them back until they've bloody well completed the shoot."

"They'll find out as soon as they see the production schedule."

"Shan't see one," Spink said and winked. "Bloody hell lad if Karl does a bunk, we'll put Rubin in."

Hal Busby's words rang out in my mind, "Independent filmmakers face special challenges that mainstream filmmakers do not. The result of this crucible of storytelling is that on a typical low budget production you can expect to shoot about five pages of script per day. This means you'll be working day and night to set up and shoot your five daily minutes of final product footage. Anything more than that becomes impossible and marks the production as no longer just 'low budget' but lost. Remember: your script is your baby. It may be a stepping stone to better things but it's still yours! Beware of more than five pages a day."

"Give me a fucking break!" I yelled.

"You t-t-t-talkin' to ME?" God asked in a pretend-angry chipmunk chatter voice. His voice went way up on the word "*ME*." Then He laughed.

"I was talking to Spink," I said.

"I know you're bloody well talking to me lad," Spink said and laughed. Spink patted my shoulder. "Needn't worry lad Rubin can do it if it comes to that. In 'The Blood Runs Dark' he played the lead after Wayne Crawford was run over by the camera car."

"But I thought we had to have stars because of the investment deal," I said.

"You are slow lad! I told you the bloody deal's off. If Karl and April's tickets were refundable and if they hadn't bloody been paid in advance -- God Rubin's a twit! -- we'd tell them to stay home to save on the hotel bill."

I slammed my glass down on Spink's desk.

"Well, I came out here to make a fucking movie!" I shouted.

"That's the spirit! Drink up lad!" Spink yelled.

Margo barged in.

"For God's sake, Leslie!" she said. "Don't get the poor wee lad sloshed-- again! He's got to get to work on the rewrite. We need blue pages by tomorrow."

"Stuff the bleeding rewrite, the blue pages *and* the pink ones as well! Stuff them all! Cheers!" Spink said and gulped down what was left in his glass, stood up unsteadily and held up his empty glass and yelled, "To the re-fucking-balls-up pages!"

"Do sit down and shut up Leslie," Margo said and grabbed my arm. "Veronica's waiting with her typewriter poised. You may dictate the changes to her if you like to save time. She's a bloody good typist."

Spink held up his glass again. "To our director and fearless leader!" he said.

The way he said "To our director" and the friendly sincere smile he gave me made me want to cry. He wasn't making fun of me and we were talking about actual director stuff like me writing the blue pages. Spink was treating me as a fellow professional and using technical insider movie words between us movie professionals. I loved Spink. I wanted to hug him but I couldn't stand well enough to do it. I stumbled and Margo said, "Look at him for Christ's sake!" I waved to Spink from the floor. Margo helped me up. Then Margo guided me down the hall to where Veronica was waiting with her typewriter. Suddenly the truth hit me! And Hal Busby confirmed it when he said "Billy you're a real director now! I was wrong about you!"

If Francis Ford Coppola, Spielberg and John Ford had been there they would have heard Spink talking about the blue pages and known that they were in the heart of the movie business listening in on a fellow director in a pre-production meeting with his line producer. Like Hal Busby explained (this was in night class months before, not right then in my head), "Color-coded revision pages are referred to as 'Blue' or 'Pink' pages even though they're not all pink or blue. Here's the color key for each set of script revisions: First Revision—Blue; Second Revision—Pink; Third Revision—Yellow; Fourth Revision—Green; Fifth Revision—Gold and Sixth Revision—back to White. Once a script is locked the first revisions go out on blue pages so that the cast and crew can replace the original script pages in their ring binders."

Blue Pages! I was the one in charge of the blue page revisions that would set us on the path to getting our movie made! And that would set me on the path to getting God's movie made! And that would set me on the path home to my little girl!

Chapter 20
This Rewrite Came As a Relief

As I stepped up to Veronica and her typewriter I said, "To the Blue Pages and beyond!" Margo and Veronica exchanged glances and giggled. I didn't care. I pumped my fist into the air in triumph claiming the script victory that I already knew was mine.

>FADE UP
>Alex, handsome, rugged, thirtyish, ready for anything, and Sylvia, twentyish, beautiful, eminently available, looking like trouble and for trouble, step into their SPEED BOAT. They wear sexy sunglasses.

"Change it to Safari Land Rover," I said.

Veronica typed, "Step into their SAFARI LANDROVER."

Margo peered over Veronica's shoulder. "We can't afford a bloody Land Rover. We're going to use the van," Margo said.

I drank down half a cup of scalding coffee before I answered. I was feeling headachy.

"Okay, so change it to, step into their rugged safari van," I said.

"It's only a Toyota Forerunner," Veronica said.

"Rugged Forerunner then," I said.

"It's not rugged," Veronica said.

AND GOD SAID, "BILLY!"

"Just fucking type what I tell you!" I screamed.

Veronica breathed in so hard that her nostrils pinched shut. But she did what I told her and started to type.

"No one will read it. Martin Lucifer never reads the revisions and Leslie's drunk," Veronica said.

"April and Karl will," I said.

Hal Busby's spirit was with me. I was doing my best to craft my rewrite according to his leading. His words were ever before me. I had faithfully done my best to craft God's many rewrites of "The Calling" according to Hal Busby's wisdom. Now I was drawing on Hal Busby's screenwriting lore-craft to redraft this stepping stone script. Actually this rewrite came as a relief. It was so much easier that trying to apply Hal Busby's wisdom to God's script.

It had taken God and me fourteen drafts for us to figure out how to apply at least some of Hal Busby's 22 Building Blocks to our script. After two years of rewrite toil God and I had used seventeen of the 22 Blocks in God's script. That wasn't too bad considering that the story started out so far from what Hal Busby says is "ideal for a story premise." That's because God and me were stuck with a story about the End Times that can't be changed, even by God.

Adapting a book is always tough. That is especially true with the Book of Revelation. You see in the book version God had told John the Evangelist (to whom He was dictating His book) to write, "For I testify unto every man that heareth the words of the prophecy of this book, if any man shall add unto these things, God shall add unto him the plagues that are written in this book. And if any man shall take away from the words of the book of this prophecy, God shall take away his part out of the book of life, and out of the holy city, and from the things which are written in this book" Revelation 22:18-19. So God was stuck with His book version of His Own story. If we messed with that story's basic premise I'd go to Hell. It said so in the book we were adapting for the screen! And God can't break His

Own rules. So we were in a jam. That was why we were only able to use seventeen out of the 22 Hal Busby story building blocks.

Hal Busby taught me that the main character in a movie must undergo change. But *God can't change* and God is the star of His story. So "The Calling" had script problems. But now I was allowed to change the story of "Suck On This!" any way I wanted to because my stepping stone movie was *of* the Lord but not *by* the Lord. So at last I was applying *all* of Hal Busby's powerful teachings as a lamp unto my feet. That's why I was in an unusually carefree frame of mind even if I was getting angry at Veronica's obstruction of my creativity not to mention that I'd been kicked in the balls literally and figuratively.

See, Veronica's obstructionism, Ruth's faithlessness, God's meanness, Vandermeer's cruelty, several competing voices in my head, a sick longing for my child and mutual loathing between my crew and me and also the fact that my producer might as well have been Satan notwithstanding, at last I could unleash my full screenwriting potential without fearing for the eternal destiny of my soul. That included The Three Variations to Classic Structure; The Seven Steps to a Great Premise; The Four Requirements of a Good Hero, which even for "The Calling" had worked great because Jesus is the hero in God's script and Jesus has a great opponent -- Satan -- who, just like Hal Busby said, "must have similarities to the hero." They both were locked in a cosmic struggle that made "Die Hard" look like a Sunday school picnic! And then there were The Five Major Character Changes; The 4 Keys to The Perfect Opponent -- Satan in "The Calling" and a drug lord in "Suck On This!" -- and The Secret to Creating a Strong Middle of a Movie. Lastly there was The Advanced Lessons on Building to The Advanced Class on Reveals and How To Write 3-Track Dialogue.

I had bound these story structure commandments to my heart and meditated upon them night and day. As Hal Busby often said,

"Real story structure, also known as deep structure is organic. Three-act is a magic bullet we all desperately want to work. But it won't work. So let it go. Organic story structure requires knowing your hero with tremendous depth and being able to come up with story events that will inexorably lead that character to fundamental character change. If you can make the shift from three-act to organic story, the payoff is huge. It's what makes you a professional."

Amen!

Before dictating each line to Veronica I paused. She probably thought I closed my eyes to think or because I was drunk. But I was praying for God's and Hal Busby's leading that in each and every line of dialogue that I'd find ways to give the characters a true moral change and be worthy of my great teacher. And I offer the following excerpts from the dialogue (not to mention my creative process) I was writing as an example of the result of taking all 22 screenwriting classes-- twice! Did I get my money's worth? You bet! If Hal Busby wanted to advertise he couldn't have done better than to use the following passages from my blue pages as evidence of the literary level of storytelling that the great Hollywood script doctors like him inspire. If Shakespeare had had a Hal Busby in his life he could have written like this too.

>ALEX
>(Lighting a cigarette, exhaling passion and smoke)
>God! You were good last night!

>SYLVIA
>I love you darling! I never came so hard in my life!

> ALEX
> The only thing that makes me hotter than
> your wet pussy is going over a hundred in this boat.

"Change that to stalking big game, the only thing that makes me hotter than your wet pussy is stalking big game," I said.

> SYLVIA
> Speed makes you big?

"Make that, 'Big game makes you big?'" I said.

> They laugh and Sylvia throws her arms around Alex's leathery rugged neck and they kiss. CU on wet intertwining tongues like wet writhing snakes. TWO SHOT through windshield as they SPEED OFF through the choppy BLUE WATER.

"Change that to, 'drive off into the veldt.'" I said.

> WIDE PANORAMIC SHOT of the sun rising over the ocean.

"Make that... 'sun rising over the African plain,'" I said.
"Where do you suppose we're going to get a bleeding wide panoramic shot of the African plain?" asked Veronica. "This isn't Kenya."
"We need some sort of establishing shot," I said.
"It's cheaper to put in a subtitle that ID's the place. 'Deep in darkest Africa,' something like that," said Margo.
"But we're *in* Africa!" I yelled. "So why can't we just shoot it?"
"Last picture we shot in downtown Joburg was set in New York.

We never went to New York, did we? That's what stock libraries are for," said Margo.

"Did it get a theatrical release?" I asked.

"Where?" asked Margo.

"Anywhere!"

"Leslie released it in the townships. The kaffirs loved it," said Veronica.

"I mean in the world."

"Haven't the foggiest," snapped Veronica.

Veronica's nose pinched shut again.

"Leave in the establishing shot. We can shoot it second unit," I said.

Veronica burst into a nasty choking laugh.

"We're already the bleeding 'second unit!'" she said. "The whole bloody picture's the 'second unit.'"

"I'll shoot the fucking sunrise myself if I have to!" I yelled.

"Not with Martin Lucifer's precious camera you won't," Margo said.

"I'll ask Martin Luther to help out on the weekends!" I shouted.

Veronica laughed so hard it sounded like she was choking to death.

"Okay, forget the wide establishing shot," I said. "But I need to make Alex's character development more organic showing the difference between his moral need and psychological need."

"Bloody hell," Margo said and then shrieked with laughter. "Where do you think you are?"

Chapter 21

Mood Swings

By Day 8 of pre-production my current Mood Swing had put me right back in God's camp! And the Hal Busby "seminar" I was conducting by doing a textbook rewrite was advancing by encouraging leaps and bounds. My work was good! The power of creativity is a wonderful thing!

Think about all the setbacks I'd faced and yet the simple joy of unleashing my creativity in the rewrite provided me with long celebrative work sessions when I just forgot my troubles and just cruised along going with the flow of what – if I say so myself – were my best ideas. I was full of hope again!

I knew all the good action scenes had to be cut but I still had the dialogue. I planned to fight for that! Alex and Sylvia could be saying self-revelatory lines and it wouldn't cost any more than the bad expository dialogue I was cutting. As I shared with Margo and Veronica even they began to come around. I said that, "Good dialogue is always more intelligent, wittier, more metaphorical, and better argued than in real life." Margo and Veronica just exchanged looks but I would not let their skepticism stop me from sharing the good news. Let them roll their eyes! For once the truth would be spoken in this sorry excuse for a production office! So I said, "But because it occurs within dramatic moments, it sounds real and justified.

AND GOD SAID, "BILLY!"

So I think I'll make Alex a lover of poetry." And that seemed to hit home! They didn't laugh or exchange looks but just fell silent no doubt overwhelmed by the simple truth I'd opened their eyes to. I started to dictate again.

> ALEX VO
> (lighting a cigarette)
> Over in the meadow,
> In the reeds on the shore,
> Lived an old mother muskrat,
> And her little ratties four,
> "Dive!" said the mother;
> "We dive!" said the four,
> So they dived and they burrowed,
> In the reeds on the shore.

"Where did that come from?" asked Margo. "It's quite lovely."

I studied her face to see if she was being sarcastic but she smiled warmly and sincerely. At last I was getting some respect! She gave me another sweet smile. I didn't answer because I would have burst into tears. It was such a relief to find that my hard work was paying off! Little by little I felt that I was being restored to God's favor too since the Lord is the creative source of all creativity, so how could I be doing work this good unless God was inspiring me again? Yes Lord!

By Day 9 of pre-production after my wine lunch I felt more directorial and confident than ever. As soon as I arrived at the office I had a meeting with hair and makeup to discuss Karl and April's look. Hair and makeup was respectful to me! I felt affirmed and happy! Then by mid morning I'd put three more of Rebecca's favorite poems in the script. Veronica typed them in with no comments or mean laughter. She had fallen totally silent and just kept her head down and typed and would not even look at me. I was winning her over!

The day was going great. I put in a crew memo with the blue pages: "We'll record the poem voiceovers (VO) so it will be like we were hearing Alex's thoughts while he kills people. That way we will come to understand that he has an inner life that he never shares with anyone revealing his inner textured complexity."

Rubin came into the office in the late afternoon and glanced at my blue pages for about 30 seconds without saying anything. That hurt a little after all the work I'd done but on the other hand at least the quality of my writing had rendered him speechless, and when it came to Rubin no news was good news. And I didn't press him about what he thought because like Hal Busby said about not pushing studio chiefs too hard for compliments or what they think but just going with the flow, "You don't want to knock the crust off that turd!"

After Rubin shut the script without a word to me about my work then he ordered me to go with him while he went "collecting" like he called it. He wanted me to accompany him to downtown Johannesburg so that; "I won't get robbed by the Schwartzas." Then Rubin took the van and we headed out with him driving. On the way Rubin didn't say a word. I didn't either. I was still glowing and happy from all my blue pages successes not to mention winning at least some of the crew over to my side.

We paid a guy 10 Rand to watch our van and then wandered around in the Johannesburg flea market looking at African masks, dolls and carved sticks and such. A man selling the dolls said that they were made by Zulu women and "represent Zulu brides." The dolls were about the size of Barbie dolls but made out of glass beads sewn together and they had beaded "bridal aprons," like the man called the little beaded squares that hung over the dolls' hips. The patterns on the aprons looked like American Indian art with zigzags in bright colors and such. I wished I had some money to buy some for Rebecca.

Rubin bought a bunch of what he called, "antique English silver left over from the Boer War that's worth five times what these fuckwits are selling it for if I can get it through customs and back to Beverly Hills." Then Rubin made me carry his heavy plastic shopping bags full of silver teapots and sugar bowls and creamers while we walked between long rows of stalls set up on a parking lot opposite a movie theater playing "A Fish Called Wanda." It had just been released in America the week we left so I was surprised to see it was already in South Africa, what with their TV being 10 years behind and all.

Then God said, "'Be strong and of a good courage, fear not, nor be afraid of them: for the LORD thy God, he it is that doth go with thee; he will not fail thee, nor forsake thee' Deuteronomy 31:6." So with God's encouragement quoting His Own book the way Molly quoted her own letters and thereby boosting my brimming self-confidence, and while Rubin was looking at some ivory and asking the guy selling it how he could ship it back to America because it's illegal, I blurted, "I want a writing credit on this movie."

I knew he heard me but Rubin didn't turn around. That was fine with me because it was easier to make demands to the back of his head than to his face. So then without taking a breath and still talking to the back of his head while he picked up chunks of tusk and looked at them, I blurted out more of what I'd been rehearsing during the drive to town. In a nervous rush I said, "Producers pay screenwriters one to three percent of negative costs for their scripts and writers of low budget films payments' are mostly deferred and I understand that. But I want to be paid when the money's raised or on the first day of principal photography and if I can't get that, get paid from the first dollar of revenue, if there's any because payment from producer's net profits – or from any net – maybe no payment anyway, so I should at least receive sole screenwriting credit in lieu of the money."

"I'll take your name off the goddamned picture if you try to squeeze me," Rubin growled without even turning around.

"But I'm rewriting all of it. This morning I had to invent a new opening scene," I said. "Have you read Alex's voiceover poems yet? Margo says they're superb."

Rubin put down the tusk pieces and turned around and slowly shook his head from side-to-side in mock wonderment like he just couldn't believe what he was hearing. Then he folded his arms across his tubby chest and said, "First off if you want to talk contract shit you have an agent. Call Sol. Second off I'd tell him to fuck off just like I'm telling you to fuck off. So fuck off. And Margo's full of shit and I never told you to add anything, just to change the fucking location descriptions."

"We can't shoot some movie written for an island out in the veldt or whatever without changing the characters' motivation and how they react to their new environment," I said.

"Where do you get off puking out this bullshit?" asked Rubin. "And what's with all the fucking poems?"

I took a deep breath and said, "Telling your story with a unique voice and style is what the poems are about because the writing process involves digging into your premise and using story techniques that show you the elements of the idea that are totally unique to the hero."

"What the motherfucking *fuck* are you FUCKING talking about?" screamed Rubin.

People looked at us but I answered calmly, "I'm talking about the inciting incident."

AND GOD SAID, "BILLY!"

"Will you just shut up?" yelled Rubin but not as loud as before.

It was as if my calm inner assurance and my detailed knowledge of the 22 Building Blocks of a Blockbuster Script had impressed him. And then I closed my eyes and – speaking as clearly as the disciples who preached on the Day of Pentecost did when each person there heard the sermon in their own language -- I said, "The plot has an inciting incident and ends with a new equilibrium and has several revelations and reversals along the way to the hero's journey-story paradigm. His self-revelation strips away the hero's former facade and is the most heroic thing our hero does in order for his character to change or remain steadfast because a character needs to be able to distinguish between the source of conflict and its symptomatic effects." Then I took a deep breath and called out in a mighty proclaiming Old Testament-type prophetic voice, "So we keep my fucking poems or I quit!"

I opened my eyes. Rubin was staring at me with his mouth open in what might have been mocking pretend wonderment or maybe he really was impressed like Pharaoh was when he finally figured out that God really would do all the stuff He said He would do through Moses after it started raining frogs. Rubin didn't say anything more right then so I thanked God, Molly and Hal Busby (just to cover all my bases). We were standing next to a stall where they were selling rocks laid out on a long table on a green blanket. I picked up a perfectly round baseball-sized stone that must have weighed 10 pounds. My hands were trembling. It was dark pink and felt warm and sparkled in the blinding sun. I'd picked it up so I would have something to do besides watching Rubin stare at me in wonderment like the disciples probably stared at Jesus on the Mount of Transfiguration after He'd revealed His true powers to them. A young tall light brown man stepped out from behind the table. He was wearing a white robe and a knit lacy white cap like the one I'd seen in the muti shop. This brown man had smooth oily shiny cheeks glistening in the sun. He stepped up to us rubbing his hands. He smelled like curry and some kind of flowery perfume. "Highest quality Namibian rose quartz. Best, purest in the world! And from where are you?" the man asked us in a high singsong voice that sounded like a girl's.

"America," I said.

"Ah! An American! Well done, old chap! Well done!"

"Thanks," I said.

I picked up a weird-looking gold and black polished stone that changed color when I turned it.

"Tiger's Eye. You will never see quality Tiger's Eye like this for sale anywhere else!" the man said.

"He won't buy any," said Rubin, "and you'd better watch him. He's a klepto. I wouldn't let him fool with *my* rocks!" Rubin laughed.

The Indian smiled politely and looked from Rubin to me and back again like he was confused. Then he smiled some more and wobbled his head the way Indians (from India) do in that side-to-side thing they do like they don't have regular neck bones.

"Well done old chap! You Americans are so full of humor, so full of marvelous wit! So Bill Cosby! So Woody Allen! So Steve Martin! I love America!"

"Jesus," muttered Rubin.

"What's this?" I asked, picking up a piece of dark gray sparkling rock.

"Malachite also from Southwest Africa. The Namib Desert is a veritable treasure trove! Would you like some? Only fifty Rand! For you only thirty!"

"No use pal. Our 'director' here's broke. This poor fuck eats leftovers off room service trays and writes voiceover poems to go with ass-fucking. He's a psycho bag-director," Rubin said and laughed. The brown man gave up on us and turned to a man speaking German or Hebrew or some such who wanted to buy a bag of warthog tusks.

I never thought anyone saw me sneaking around with my toilet bag looking for leftovers. I didn't know what to say now that I knew that Rubin knew.

"You poor dumb fuck-- here," Rubin said and fished out a ten Rand note from his pocket, "Go buy yourself a fucking hotdog or some fucking thing."

"Thanks, Rubin," I said rejoicing that on this day when I was coming into my own new realm of directorial self-confidence even Rubin had been touched by my bold new self.

"'The hero's journey-story paradigm is self-revelation,'" said Rubin imitating me. Then he laughed hard but in a friendlier way than before and said, "Jesus Christ, you're one fucked up puppy, do you know that?"

I took the money to one of the hotdog-sausage stands that lined the fence around the flea market's perimeter. "One, please," I said. The hotdog vendor was a thin tall black kid with dreadlocks down to his waist that looked like dirty fuzzy braided strings.

"Coke? Pap? Sausage?" he asked.

"Yes," I said.

"Where you from mun?" he said and when he said "mun" for "man" his accent sounded like a TV commercial for vacationing in Jamaica. He dipped a wooden spoon into a huge pot and pulled it out loaded with thick gloppy stuff. "How much pap you want mun?"

"Just the hotdog and a coke," I said.

"The sausage's better mun. Tasty mun."

"Okay the sausage and coke. No pap."

He forked a big grilled foot-long sausage off his griddle and laid it into a hotdog roll and wrapped it in a twist of paper.

"Five Rand mun."

"Get the fuck over here Shakespeare!" yelled Rubin, "You buying a hotdog or the whole cart? Jesus!"

I paid and walked back to Rubin but no faster than I wanted to. I wasn't afraid of him anymore.

Chapter 22

My Rewrite Was Good

On Day 10 of pre-production I was sitting in a chipped metal enamel swivel chair across from Rubin's desk. Rubin's personalized servant he borrowed from Spink (who looked like he was 70) had brought in folding chairs for Margo and Spink. Rubin had a big new leather desk chair with a high back. It was the only new piece of furniture in the office. Margo and Spink sat on folding chairs by the window. Except for the dogs barking once in a while in the parking lot there were no sounds coming from the black's sheds that I could see through the window. Even the kids were silent. They never said anything or cried. I saw a little girl get her fingers slammed in a bakkie door that morning and she didn't cry, just held her injured hand in front of her and stared straight ahead. Everyone but me was reading my blue pages. I was pretending to read too but I was sneaking looks at the others. I was hoping they'd smile or nod so I could see that they thought my rewrite was good.

Rubin had an antique silver hand bell on his desk with an ivory handle. It was the same kind of antique silver he bought in the flea market. After a few minutes of reading and muttering "fuck me" over and over again Rubin rang it and his boy walked in and said "Yes Master?" Rubin ordered him to bring him some coffee and 3 croissants. Rubin didn't ask the rest of us if we wanted anything and

AND GOD SAID, "BILLY!"

I saw Margo and Spink exchange a look that was pretty clear about how rude they thought Rubin was. While the black man was in the kitchen getting the coffee Rubin muttered, "Page eight what the fuck?" So we all turned to that page.

Page 8 happened to be one of the parts of the script that I'd done my best work on. So my stomach tightened when Rubin so rudely asked us to look at that section. As far as I was concerned this passage contained non-negotiable greatness. The suspense in this scene stabbed home as the story and characters unfolded because each sentence was a journey and no one in their right mind would want to question a single word!

>   INT. VAN -- DAY
>   ECU Writhing tongues.
>   Pull back to reveal Alex and Sylvia lost in a world of hot passion.
>
>   CUT TO
>   Alex takes his hunting rifle off the van gun rack. He loads it with one deadly high powered BULLET.
>
>   ALEX (VO)
>   (As he loads the rifle and then adjusts the sights)
>   Over in the meadow,
>   In a snug beehive,
>   Lived a mother honey bee,
>   And her little bees five,
>   "Buzz!" said the mother;
>   "We buzz!" said the five,
>   So they buzzed and they hummed,
>   In the snug beehive.

EXT. VAN -- DAY
Alex steps furtively out of the dust covered safari van. Drum beat continues to build OC.

ALEX
(Hissing over his shoulder to Sylvia)
Stay down. No matter what, don't move!

Alex creeps into the bushes.
(OC) We HEAR bird calls and an elephant's trumpeting.

ECU Alex's determined yet FEAR-FILLED eyes.

DISTANT harmonica solo echoes in a haunting reprise/tribute to "Once Upon a Time in The West."

DRUM BEATS build.

Alex's POV through the crosshairs of his telescopic gun sight.

MEDIUM SHOT of Alex slowly taking aim. His finger on the trigger TREMBLES.

NEW ANGLE on Sylvia: She's mouthing a silent prayer for Alex's safety.

ECU on ALEX holding his breath and CLEARLY AFRAID.

Alex's POV through the gun sights: His KILL looms into the sights. It is a huge BULL ELEPHANT.

AND GOD SAID, "BILLY!"

"What do you mean a huge bull elephant?" Rubin said and slapped down the script.

"Sorry Master, sorry," said Rubin's black servant as he set down the coffee and croissant on the desk.

"It has to be something dangerous," I said, feeling relieved that Rubin was only brining up budget concerns but not attacking my writing or the dialogue and story. I read that as a supreme complement! So I was feeling good as I said, "The hero is the character with the central weakness or need who has the most to learn by going through his struggle. This scene is the only way we can establish Alex's potential for courage and yet his weakness as we show the fear in his eyes. We need to start the movie with a sense of who our hero may become psychologically that will give believability to the new Alex later. Establishing the psychology of the protagonist's inner struggle is important."

"We don't have a budget for any fucking psychology," Rubin snapped. "And cut the elephant too."

"I thought we could use the money we would've spent on the speedboat for a few extra scenes," I said. "Leslie says there's a private game park only twenty minutes from here that has three huge elephants."

"Why do you think we *cut* the speedboat? Do we have a fucking moron for a director or what?! Jesus!" Rubin took a drink of coffee and a few bites of croissant and then looked around at Margo and Spink.

They wouldn't look back at him. I think that they were almost feeling embarrassed for Rubin given that it must have been pretty evident that he'd just been trashing a scene that most people would have been savoring and later discussing as a template to use to measure all future rewrites and blue pages against. I mean Rubin hadn't even commented on my haunting evocative nostalgia-laden "Once Upon a Time in The West" musical signature reprise! He just blew past this gift I'd handed him and acted like the only thing worth discussing was if we could shoot his movie for free! Talk about "jaded" Rubin had just redefined the term!

"So then what do you think we should kill?" I asked, feeling happy and exhilarated by our producer/director back and forth professional banter Rubin's creative insensitivity notwithstanding.

Margo spoke up in a cheerful voice and said "Have him hunt a kaffir dressed as a Zulu warrior."

"You're as bad as Billy," snarled Rubin. "Why does he have to aim at any goddamned thing? Why can't he just be aiming? The audience knows he's a hunter."

Spink stood up and raised his wine glass and said, "Good old stock footage to the bloody rescue! Cheers!" Spink drained his glass. I raised my glass to Spink and took a drink. Spink had brought along a bottle to the meeting.

"You've had quite enough," said Margo and she grabbed the bottle away from Spink as he was about to pour a refill.

"Damn you, woman!" yelled Spink and laughed.

"We don't have anything in the budget for stock footage," snapped Rubin.

"I'm with our director," said Margo. "He's written lovely blue pages and we need to kill something. Bleeding hell Rubin, at least the first two minutes should look like a real movie. Besides, we can dress up one of the garden boys. It won't cost a farthing. We'll throw in one of our kaffirs gratis, won't we, Leslie?"

"Give me back my bloody Boschendal Blanc de bloody Blanc you bloody woman!" said Spink laughing.

"Okay if it's for free and if you can shoot it in one take," said Rubin.

I drained my glass and slapped it down on Rubin's desk.

"I'll get it in one fucking take!" I bellowed. "Satisfied?"

Chapter 23
Goddamned Fucking Script Won't Quit

By Day 11 of pre-production Veronica and I were working on pink pages and even a few yellow and green pages. Veronica distributed the new pages to everyone except to Martin Luther who never came by the office. The box in the hall marked "Camera Crew" was overflowing with the new pages and schedule changes. By mid-afternoon Margo, Spink and I were in Rubin's office for another story meeting. I read Alex's lines and Margo read Sylvia's. Spink read the descriptions and camera directions. Rubin was chewing on toast and eating scrambled eggs and repeatedly whispering "fuck me," under his breath.

    Alex's POV through the crosshairs of his rifle sights ON a ZULU WARRIOR dressed in all the savage glory of his tribe steps out of the BUSH and surveys the VELDT

    ECU on Alex's trigger finger tightening for the kill. CU on his tension-filled eyes.

>   ALEX (VO)
>   Over in the meadow,
>   In a nest built of sticks,
>   Lived a black mother crow,
>   And her--

"Just shoot the fucker," muttered Rubin. "Goddamned fucking script won't quit."

"Rubin, if I just put, 'he shoots the warrior,' you'll have empty pages," I said.

Margo laughed. Rubin shot her a dirty look. The wine was filling me with boldness. I had won over Margo and Spink and Rubin was just jealous of my professional insight. In fact I began to interpret his needlessly argumentative posturing as a face saving ploy in the glare of my clearly superior knowledge of screenwriting. He resented the mantel of artistic authority that was being placed on my shoulders. And Spink supplying me with wine also made it clear that I'd made more friends in South Africa than Rubin ever had. No one ever offered him anything.

"I like empty pages," Rubin muttered. "The script has to have at least eighty seven pages. Something has to fill them," I said. "And even that's cutting near the bone. We'd do better if there were ninety pages at least. What happens if you get a major studio distribution deal and they ask for some alternative out-takes or scenes to be cut in if the picture turns out to be something they want to release wide?"

Margo gave me a warm smile. Spink lifted his glass in my direction. I think my vision for the unlimited possibilities of our small movie was inspiring them.

"They can yell out shit while they're fucked over," Rubin said. "And what's this crap on page seventeen?"

Again my stomach tensed as if to ward off a blow. Rubin seemed to have an instinct to home in on the very best scenes I'd created for his undeserving "attention." I've always loved super slow motion and I'd used it here. I prepared to defend my work! It was like I could feel the presence of every great director who had gone before me there in that room rooting for me.

> CU on the Zulu. The sharp CRACK of a powerful rifle shot splits the African air. LOW ANGLE on the Zulu warrior as he cartwheels backward driven in a slow agonizing arc of death up and back, spinning, bleeding, dying, by the force of the tearing bullet exploding (400 FPS SLOW MOTION) into his brave black body with all the carnage of an out-of-control express train.
>
> ALEX
> One down, two hundred to go!
>
> ANGLE ON Sylvia as she breathes a sigh of relief. The hunter, her hunter, has triumphed.
>
> SYLVIA
> (Whispering passionately)
> Oh Alex!
>
> Alex creeps cautiously into the clearing. He pulls his huge glittering BOWIE KNIFE from its notched BATTLE WORN SHEATH.
>
> ALEX
> (VO playing over the rest of the scene)
> Now the day is over,
> Night is drawing nigh,
> Shadows of the evening

Steal across the sky.
Now the darkness gathers,
Stars began to peep,
Birds and beasts and flowers
Soon will be asleep.

ECU on the EYES of the Zulu warrior.

NEW ANGLE on a row of notches, each signifying a battle triumph on Alex's knife's SHEATH. Alex adds a NEW notch.

ALEX
(shouting over his shoulder)
It's trophy time!

ON Sylvia as she squeals with delight. She loves trophy time! It excites her though she pretends to cover her eyes. But trophy time makes her as hot as it makes Alex.

NEW ANGLE as Alex approaches the fallen body of his foe. Blood puddles under the target of his insatiable aggression.

Alex kneels and dips his fingers in the warm, still steaming, still flowing, crimson river of the Zulu's ebbing life.

Alex lifts his bloody fingers and marks his face with his own "tribal marks." (Tribute to "Blade Runner"

AND GOD SAID, "BILLY!"

when Rutger Hauer as "Roy Batty" marks his face with blood of the fallen replicant "Pris"/Daryl Hannah.)

Alex tilts his head back and HOWLS like a wolf (tribute howl to Hauer's wolf HOWL over his dead lover "Pris").

ALEX
I salute you, fallen foe. I will not forget you!

Alex lifts his vanquished foe's tribal apron and EXPOSES HIS MANHOOD.

ECU on the glittering blade of death as it comes into frame. We follow it down to the "trophy," lying peacefully like a—

"Jesus! H! Fucking! H! Christ! He's going to cut off his fucking dick!" Rubin yelled.

I squared my shoulders for battle. "We don't have the elephant," I said. "It's better than having April bite the penis off in scene thirty three the way it used to be and anyway I thought we could do something a little different upfront."

"We don't have any prosthetics in the budget. It'll take half a fucking day to shoot," Rubin snarled.

"Not if we cut off his actual bishop," Spink said and winked.

"Fucking go back to sleep," said Rubin.

I drained my glass and stood up. Spielberg never felt stronger. It was like I could sense the mantel of directorial leadership settling ever more firmly upon on my shoulders more or less like when King David got anointed. "We won't actually show it," I said. "Not showing the penis slicing will *both* save money *and* preserve the artistic film noir 'Blade Runner' tribute I'm bringing to this movie as a signal to the audience that this is going to grab them viscerally but not sink to a shocksploitation level. We'll cut away to Alex's reaction as he grabs the penis and gets ready to slice and play the rest of the scene off his singing VO but with lots of reverb, like the song is drawn from his distant memories of a more innocent time. We can play the rest of the scene on Sylvia's close-up and reactions with the 'Move on up A Little Higher' song tying it all together. It'll be our chance to explore Sylvia's nymphomaniac character foreshadowing later events. And *that* gives her the chance to change later when she confronts her own mortality in the gang rape scenes and realizes that she's been on a self-destructive path and vows -- in her voiceover -- that *if* she survives she'll never again cruise bars for cheap meaningless sex. We'll watch a lifetime of regret pass over her face and -- in that one shot as she's being violated repeatedly -- come to know her innermost self that, up until that moment, has been hidden even from her. This is her moment of self-discovery."

Spink and Margo both clapped. I mean they actually applauded me! Rubin looked cornered. "Okay, but not if it takes any time to shoot," muttered Rubin lamely.

I had won!

"We can do it in one setup!" I said triumphantly. "We'll play the whole self-revelation scene on her face as my signature shot framed by sweating torsos of her attackers in the soft-focus background and we'll know what they're doing because we'll hear them OC saying stuff like 'Hey baby, how do you like that?' with lots of adlib and grunting."

"You can forget the 'he cartwheels back' shit when the Schwartzas' shot," Rubin said.

"I'll rig it," I said. "All we need are some sheave blocks, a snatch block, two pulleys and quick releases and some cable. That stuff's in the equipment shed already."

"What planet do you come from asshole? Do you see some fucking stunt budget for rigging a bullet hit?"

"I'll do the fucking pull!" I yelled.

"Fuck you!" Rubin yelled.

"Okay he can just jump back when he's shot," I said.

"Some Schwartza garden boy won't want to take a hard fall," Rubin said.

"He will if I shoot him with my bloody twelve bore!" roared Spink.

"But only if it doesn't take any time," said Rubin.

"One set-up I promise," I said.

"No bullet hits though, right?" said Rubin.

"Just the blood as a cutaway after he's down," I said. "No squibs."

"There'll be a bloody realistic bullet hit if I shoot the bloody kaffir! Bang! Bloody bang!" shouted Spink.

"Do shut up Leslie my pet," said Margo.

Chapter 24
Church

Karl and April flew in early on Sunday morning of Day 13 of pre-production. Rubin sent Margo and me to meet them. They were flying in on Swiss Air from Zurich. While we were driving to the airport Margo said that Karl always dropped off his play-or-pay fee at a bank that had an office in the Zurich airport and that April picked up some kind of "happy pills" that she could only get in Switzerland. Margo said that the layover in Zurich to bank the cash was one of the "perks the American talent demands ever since the 'We Won't Play Sun City' rubbish."

"What's that?" I asked. "I keep hearing everyone talk about it."

"Sun City is our Las Vegas, an all-in-one hotel-casino. Your most famous entertainers used to perform there, until 1985 that is. Then Artists United Against Apartheid was organized by that ponce Little Steven Van Zandt. That wanker threatened he'd expose everyone who performed there and then asked all his pals to organize a boycott of South Africa. After that the buggers in Hollywood were not to be outdone in the self-righteous wanker department and got into the boycott act. That's why our government put the tax deals in place to attract twits like Rubin. That's why we pay in cash now."

When we got to the airport Margo went to buy some magazines she said weren't available anywhere else while I waited for the talent

AND GOD SAID, "BILLY!"

to clear customs. I was trying to keep away from the patrolling policemen because I didn't want to meet any of the airport cops again. So I was killing time standing in a gift shop with my back to the door and pretending to look at souvenirs settled behind one of the big pillars across from the customs exit.

"You look like shit," said Karl.

I jumped.

"Hi Karl," I said as I spun around.

When April walked out of customs a moment later she didn't even say hi.

"Hi April, glad you made it," I said.

"He looks like shit, doesn't he?" said Karl.

"I don't care what Billy looks like. There better be a goddamned limo to take me to the hotel," said April.

Margo walked up holding a *Vogue* magazine and said hello.

"Are you driving us?" April asked Margo.

"We've got the boy for that. I just wanted to welcome you back to South Africa my dear," said Margo. "Welcome!"

"So where are my suitcases?" asked April.

"The kaffir will meet us with them on the pavement," said Margo.

"Why the hell didn't you say so," said April and she marched out to the sidewalk.

Margo shuddered then followed April to the exit. Karl grabbed my arm.

"Just keep me away from that strung-out bitch," he hissed.

"How long was your layover in Zurich?" I asked, while I was pushing away the usual crowd of men shouting "Taxi Master! Taxi Boss!"

"When they wouldn't sell her the fucking pills without a prescription she tried to slug the woman. I categorically refuse to work with April. Once we shoot the master of a scene then she goes the fuck back to her Winnebago while I shoot my close-up. You can read her lines. Got it? And when she does her close-ups: same deal."

"I've improved the script," I said. "I think you'll be pleased."

"I doubt that," said Karl.

The shoot was set to start on Monday morning. I wanted to go to church. I had plenty of time because Karl and April's flight arrived so early. After we got them to the Sandton Sun hotel Margo dropped me at the Rosebank. She said she'd come back later to get me for the afternoon production meeting.

Some days I was convinced Molly was right. Other days I got nervous and begged God to take me back. Mood Swings, like I said, were happening to me more and more. That Sunday was a "please forgive me!" mood day. I hoped that God would use the church service to speak to my heart in some special way because that morning in my room -- right after the wakeup call at five -- I had prayed into my pillow for an anointed uplifting.

I was interceding for help in directing the movie and telling God that I was nervous whenever I was with Karl and April and so to please, PLEASE, give me favor in their sight like He'd given me with Spink and Margo, the makeup girl and even, to some extent, with Veronica and in a backward sort of way with Rubin too who had clearly become jealous. My request seemed reasonable to me. I was just trying to make the best stepping stone movie I could so why wouldn't God want to help?

But God chose to shout at me in a loud thundery voice, "Directing a movie is a complex network of creative collaborations with the artists involved in the creation of the film and they're all led by the vision of the director. So don't fuck this up you little shit!"

He used both the F-word and the S-word in one sentence which even for Him in a bad Leviticus-type mood was a first. So at the airport I had been wondering about why God had talked to me in that unfriendly way since I was doing my best to crawl back to Him and do His Will. Had I crossed some line of doubt and let Molly lure me into committing the unforgivable sin? Was I now in the Cain category and having my sacrifice rejected? I admit I'd been backsliding by using the F-word and probably drinking more wine than God meant to have me drink when He said I could, but was that any reason for God to spout profanity at me?

So I hoped that church would settle me down because when God screams at you in a deep booming voice *and* uses the F-word *and* calls you a "little shit" it's very upsetting. I hoped that if I met Him in church God would be more polite and let bygones be bygones.

There was a church only a short walk from the hotel. It was one of those modern kinds made out of rough-on-purpose concrete, steel beams and glass. It was full of abstract Secular Humanist-type stained glass that was just chunky shapes and colors stuck in the concrete. Some well dressed skinny elderly white people were standing around in the fancy entrance smoking cigarettes. There were no black people there. Inside this so-called church no one jumped, danced, or offered a Clap Offering. No one praised, prophesied or lifted up their hands in thanksgiving. And they were all way too dressed up for church and putting on a show of worldly blue blazers, furs, jewels and three piece suites instead of worshipping humbly in sweat pants like born-again Real Christians do. So instead of being uplifted I felt defiled by their lukewarm apostasy of the very kind Jesus said He'd spit out: "I know thy works, that thou art neither cold nor hot: I would thou wert cold or hot. So then because thou art lukewarm, and neither cold nor hot, I will spue thee out of my mouth" Revelation 3:15-16.

The church was half empty and dead, dead, dead! It was called St. Patrick's Anglican Church. I didn't know who St. Patrick was or even if he was born-again. The so-called preacher wore robes and people called him "father." I guess they hadn't read Matthew 23:9, "And call no man your father upon the earth: for one is your Father, which is in heaven."

It was while the so-called preacher was preaching -- not even from the Bible but about someone called Saint Mary of Egypt, how a lion had buried her when she died in the desert or some such Roman Catholic-type superstition -- that the Lord suddenly filled me with a double portion of His Holy Spirit. I felt a Powerful Outpouring pouring into me. I felt a filling up with unspeakable joy! It was as if God was saying that He'd only been joking around when He called me a little shit. It was as if He was sending me a message of welcome home and letting me know I'd been forgiven and my sacrifice was acceptable to Him now. Maybe this would end all these Mood Swings I thought. So I could no more contain His Spirit than stop Niagara Falls with a spoon!

I leapt up and shouted "Praise you Jesus! Praise Your Holy Name! Aga ahoi metha! Sha-na-na!"

The pastor had just said, "And what seems most wonderful to me is that in the context of this marvelous fable of Saint Mary of Egypt, that the essential spirit of the gospel of universal humility and justice has been brought to life, not by theological doctrine but by allegorical intuition, for it is in our stories that we lovers of justice share our hunger for reconciliation." After I shouted what God told me to scream the entire congregation turned to stare at me. The false preacher stopped talking and stood with his mouth open just like Nebuchadnezzar did as Shadrach, Meshach and Abednego walked out of the fiery furnace and yet were not consumed. And I was caught up into the Heavens, not in the body, but in the Spirit. I began to prophesy. "Hear me O Israel! The Lord is good! Bless His precious everlasting Name. Amen! Yes, Jesus! We just love You! You can't love God in the Biblical way of perfect submission until you fear God! Woe to you! You treat science as all-knowing and the Bible as false! There are many pronouncements of Scripture against you who would deny Christ!"

They couldn't move any more than the lions could pounce on

Daniel when God's hand closed their mouths against His prophet. God stopped their lying Liberal mouths! And then God whispered in my ear, "Good job Billy! We're All proud of you! Welcome home MY little lost lamb! We're back!"

Thus encouraged from on high, I called out in a mighty voice, "Oh people, who have hardened your hearts, thus saith the Lord of Hosts, I have sent My Prophet Billy unto you to do a mighty sign so that you may be filled with the Holy Spirit! I have sent you a healing revival this day! The Holy Ghost Fire is about to fall! *By My stripes you will be healed!*" Then I smote an old woman standing in the pew behind me on the forehead with the palm of my hand and yelled "Demon of false doctrine, come out in the name of the Lord! Sister, you won't need this now!" And then as I grabbed the cane she was leaning on out of her hand I screamed, "You are healed!"

The woman lacked faith to accept her healing. So that faithless old reprobate in a tweed skirt, white blouse and pearls tried to hang onto her gold-headed cane and I had to wrestle the stick away. She staggered and fell down between the pews and closed her purple eyelids, purple with worldly makeup, way too much for church. "She has been slain in the Spirit! Praise You, J-e-s-u-s-s-s!" I cried out.

"You're an idiot," Molly whispered to me.

I pretended not to hear her and I yelled, "Who else will come forward to be washed in the Blood? Who else needs healing?"

Then the congregation rushed me. My attackers were mostly old women but there were lots of them with a few over-dressed young men. And they joined with the old women in quenching the Spirit. Many spotted and blue-veined hands reached for me. Each hand took hold of me lightly and I could have brushed them away, if they grabbed me one at a time. But I got sandwiched between my pew and the one in front. I was caught in the hymnal rack by one knee. Hands grabbed my hair, ears, and sweater. I was tugged and pulled this way and that. And what was so weird was that they didn't say anything. All I could hear was the hate-filled clicking of their dentures. The weight of a hundred withered arms was too much for me. I was pulled down.

Chapter 25
Missed Me Did You?

When I arrived at John Vorster Square police headquarters the policemen took me out of the van once we were parked inside a fenced area. I was praying that someone beside Officer Vandermeer would be on duty. Without saying a word the two white policemen who had arrested me led me into a freight elevator that opened onto the parking lot. My head was hurting from being smashed by a big Bible with a gold cover that the so-called pastor crashed down on me right after I'd crawled out from under the pile of overdressed old ladies and homosexuals. I had looked up just in time to see him swinging it with both hands from over his head. With his robes and all he looked just like a Sunday school picture of Moses casting down the tablets of the Ten Commandments.

When we got off the elevator two other cops took me from the officers that had arrested me. They led me up a hall to a small room. They sat me down at a metal table bolted to the floor and handcuffed me to it by one hand to a hook. They left. I slept or maybe I passed out from the blow to my head.

When I opened my eyes Officer Vandermeer was standing in front of me. He smiled. "Goeiemore!" he said. "Good news or bad news first?" He was rolling his Rs hard and sounded a lot more Afrikaaner than at our last meeting. Officer Vandermeer waited for my answer but I didn't know what to say and he started talking again before I could think of anything. "The good news is that the arresting officers at the Sturdee Avenue police station in Rosebank called our chaps here and they called me. The bad news is that I told them not to log your arrest officially. I've decided to handle your situation privately." He stuck his face inches from mine so when he grinned I was looking right at a piece of food stuck in his front teeth. "I still want that drink with Miss April," he said. But it sounded like "I steel whant that trrrheenk wheeth Mhees Eprrrheel."

"We start shooting tomorrow morning and I have to get back to prepare," I said. "I was going to call you and invite you to the set."

"I'm sure you were," said Officer Vandermeer. He laughed and walked around behind my chair and circled his heavy arm around my neck. He started to squeeze.

"What are you doing?" I squeaked. I tried to pry his arm loose with my free hand. It was no use. His arm felt like a steel vice.

"Mag ek jou met iets pla? Now then, what's all this about? You're charged with attacking an old woman, an old *white woman* in a kirk! Were you having a go at the collection plate?" Officer Vandermeer said, tightened his grip and chuckled.

"No!" I gasped. "I was entering into the worship and praising God."

"Doen u is lief vir my? Missed me did you? Wanted to see me again, eh?" He squeezed so hard I started to strangle. I wondered why he was throwing in so many Afrikaans words I couldn't understand and speaking in such a heavy accent. What was he trying to prove?

"What a little liar you are," he whispered. His cheek pressed harder and harder against mine and his whisker bristles rubbed me raw. There was a meaty smell on Officer Vandermeer's breath when he growled out words. Between spitting out his rolled Rs I heard him chewing. He whispered "U smaak goeiethen," a couple of times then added a long string of other words with hard breathing and chewing in-between while he was rubbing his bristly cheek on mine.

"Gat poephol," he said, and "Donner bliksem moer," and "Kak!" Then he said more stuff in a heavier and heavier accent like he was trying to make it impossible for me to understand even his English. "We will not give away that which is holy without resistance," Officer Vandermeer yelled right into my ear. He chewed some more cheek-to-cheek then growled, "Any more nonsense from you and I'll declare you ANC and take you to the Tenth Floor and give you to the AWB boys up there. Do you understand, the Tenth Floor."

He kept his arm around my neck and squeezed until I passed out. When I came around he was still talking. "We will achieve our own independent Boer republic," he whispered. Then he stepped around to the front of me and pushed his face into mine and his eyes rolled up in his head and all I could see were the whites of his eyeballs. He shouted "Ek gee nie'n moer om nie!" and "Etterkop! Fok jou!" and then whispered, "The answer for God's chosen people will be written in blood and tears."

Officer Vandermeer jammed his mouth right against mine and screamed into my mouth, "Doen jy hou van my? Give the Boer land on which we can be free! Fokken olie boor! Fokof! Gaan Pluk jou riem! Neuk met my! Gaan kak in Gauteng! My heritage is sacred to me! The blood oath of Blood River shall abide! Gaan kak in die kaap! Gaan kak in jou poes!" He stepped behind me and put his arm back around my neck. My knees hit the floor. One arm was twisted way up held by the handcuff. My twisted shoulder hurt. I felt him grab my cuffed wrist. Then I heard a click and after that it hurt less and both of my arms were free.

"Get up you American bastard," Officer Vandermeer said calmly.

I struggled to my feet. I closed my eyes and waited for the blow. Nothing happened so I sat back down on the chair. Officer Vandermeer sat down in the chair across the table from me. He lit a cigarette and then took a cellophane bag out of his pocket and held it out. "Kudu biltong," he said. "Shot it myself near the Kruger. Have some."

I didn't feel like eating right then but didn't want to offend him so I reached out and took a piece. It was a thin strip of dried red meat.

"Thanks," I said.

It tasted like his breath had smelled while he choked me. Blood, salt and cigarettes was what it tasted like. I chewed and chewed and then I swallowed since he kept staring at me so I didn't dare spit out what felt like a mouthful gristle.

"Now then lad you've become a right little nuisance. But I still want my drink with the lovely Miss April. Jinne meisie, jy maak my nou sommer lekker jags. The little whore makes me hot, as you say *horny!*" He laughed. "I'd turn you over to immigration and they'd chuck you out as an undesirable alien but I want that drink! Does Miss April still look as bonnie as she does the 'Good Night, Baby, Time to Die,' episode when she's kidnapped in her wee wet bikini? Eh lad, does she?"

"I guess so," I said and pressed my hands together in my lap to try to keep them from shaking.

Officer Vandermeer squinted. He stared at me suspiciously.

"You're not lying again?"

"No. She looks great," I said.

"Well preserved, trim, fit? Did you fuck her yet lad? Did you leave a bit of nice pussy for me?"

"She spends all day in the hotel gym. She looks great."

"On the other hand you have become a regular little liability haven't you?"

"I can explain."

"Keep your trap shut. I should just kill you," Officer Vandermeer said in a friendly normal voice. "But I think the problem is that you're not quite right up here," he said and tapped the side of his head. "You need therapeutic help."

"I've learned my lesson. I'm sorry."

He smiled and said, "You will be maat."

Officer Vandermeer lit another cigarette inhaled deeply then blew out a big smoke ring. He sat looking at me through the smoke ring until it faded away. Then he said, "I have something special for the kaffirs and kaffir-lovers who get a bit above themselves."

"I just got a little carried away. I was just trying to share the Gifts of the Spirit."

"Pentecostal tongues-speaking loony are you?"

"Reformed Calvinist," I said, feeling surprised that Officer Vandermeer was talking about theological stuff.

"You can't be both," he said. "Do you lie about everything?"

"Both of what?" I said.

"Reformed Calvinist *and* Pentecostal," he said. "So you're a liar even about the things of God?"

"My pastor led us into a new denomination that experienced an outpouring of the Holy Spirit but is also still solidly Calvinist *and* Reformed," I said.

"That is a filthy heresy. John Calvin would have burned you and your pastor too," Officer Vandermeer said and laughed.

"We start tomorrow real early," I said. "I have to be on the set at seven."

"You'll be there. I give you my word as a Christian gentleman."

Chapter 26

The Battle of Blood River

Officer Vandermeer told me to ride in the front of the police van. I wasn't handcuffed. He switched to his English accent and talked to me like I was a tourist and he was a friendly tour guide. "Here we are on lovely Jan Smuts Avenue, center of public life in our fine metropolis," Officer Vandermeer said. "Now we turn onto beautiful Joubert Strasse. We follow Joubert up this picturesque hill and cross Hancock Strasse. Here we are opposite the vital historic landmark of Old Fort. It was built by Paul Kruger in 1899 to protect the South African Republic from the British. Later the British used this place against our people when our Boer leaders were imprisoned here. After the Boer victory we kept only whites imprisoned here except for Nelson Mandela, when some kaffir-loving fools put him in the hospital section and saved his life. Now we come to Joubert Strasse. This region is known as Hillbrow and is an illegally racially mixed area. Our NP leaders wink at this perversion and white, black and colored live together. It is quite the 'melting pot' as you Americans might say. We patriots call it a 'gray area,' just as sewage is called gray water."

We passed shopping malls and long lines of black women waiting at taxi minibus stands and then drove up to a plain yellow brick one story building about the size of a Ralph's supermarket. The building didn't have any windows. There were some glass bricks, the kind you can't see through but that let in light cemented into the wall every few feet along the top. The building was set back about a hundred feet from the street. As we parked a black policeman walked out of the door along with a black woman and two little girls dressed in school uniforms.

The woman was crying so hard she was having trouble walking. The cop helped her across the parking lot to a mini bus taxi stand on the street and left her and the kids there. One of the little girls looked as if she was about three, Rebecca's age when I'd left home. The other little girl was about six or seven, Rebecca's age now. I teared up.

"Come along maat," said Officer Vandermeer, switching to his heavy Afrikaans accent. We stepped through the door and into a long hall with a concrete floor, olive green walls and a high white ceiling. "Follow me," he said.

No one else was around. I thought about running away, but where could I go? My heart was pounding.

There was a door at the end of the hall. We stepped through it into a room lit by a single bulb hanging from a wire. The room was only the size of a large cupboard. There was a curtain covering the wall on one side. The curtain had brown and yellow sunflowers on it. Officer Vandermeer stepped up to the curtain and tugged it open. Through a large plate glass window behind the curtain I saw a big room the size of a tennis court. It was covered in white tiles. A foot from me and on the other side of the glass was a dead black man. He was laying on a gurney. He was so close to me that I jumped back with a yell. There was a small square of red rubber covering his privates. He had a tag tied to his ankle and a hole in his chest the size of a grapefruit. It was full of clotted blood that was even blacker than his pitch-black skin. One eye was open and rolled up and one eye was shut.

"Must be the kaffir the women came to identify," said Officer

Vandermeer. "Probably her kinders' father. I say 'probably' because no kaffir is ever so very sure who his father is," he laughed.

I tasted the biltong as I threw up.

"Into the bloody drain you filthy naaier!"

I stumbled back from the viewing window and finished throwing up into the drain in the concrete floor he pointed to. Officer Vandermeer opened a door and stepped into the big tiled room. "Welcome to the Johannesburg police morgue," he said cheerfully. His voice echoed off the walls. The room was cold and smelled like bleach. "On your right you may see the autopsy section," he said talking in his tour guide English accent. "We do about ten a day using the eight dissection tables. Each section has its bone cutting saw, skull breaker, and flush retractors and of course the always useful double prong flesh hooks."

He took my arm and led me across the room to a wall made out of shiny metal with many doors set in a row. "Here are the refrigeration compartments. We have two to three hundred bodies stored at any one time. Anyone who dies violently is brought here. We receive at least twenty fresh kaffirs a week. Very creative they are with their necklacing. Put a tire around each other's necks; fill the rim with petrol then light it and the kaffir becomes a torch and will take a bit of time to die. Winnie Mandela's young thugs are very good at this work. You left that verse out of your song 'We Won't Play Sun City.' Eh?"

Officer Vandermeer smiled a friendly smile and grabbed me by my hair. He dragged me along the wall and the line of doors. I screamed "Ow!" but he acted like nothing unusual was happening and kept calmly talking like a tour guide. "By law we must do autopsies on everyone who dies under suspicious circumstances, so we tend to fall a little behind in our work. Most bodies are kept here many weeks past their prime." He still had a hold of my hair. "Meet the natives," he said as he grabbed the handle of a metal door and jerked my head towards it. The smell hit me before I saw the stacked bodies. "In America where all you rich fat hoender naaiers traitors to your race live each body gets its own private drawer, even your kaffirs. That's how it is on Hill Street Blues at any rate maat. I like Captain Frank Furillo. Do you like him?"

I didn't answer.

"But this is South Africa where less than five million civilized white Christians have to mind thirty three million animals," Officer Vandermeer said. "Even Captain Furillo would have his hands full here maat. So we built one refrigeration unit into each wall connected behind these doors. We place the bodies on these sliding trays, stack them up like this. Of course we reserve a less crowded section in another room for whites."

Officer Vandermeer pulled out a tray. There were two naked black women head to toe on top of each other face down. "Bit crowded as you see. Two to a tray meant for one but the racks are sturdy Boer workmanship." One of the women had a hand missing. It was lying between her feet and looked like a claw. The bodies seemed small more like big dolls than real people. I don't know why the bodies looked so small, but even the man lying in front of the viewing window had looked small, though I could tell from how much of the gurney he took up that he was actually tall.

"Kaffirs don't like this place. Even ANC atheists pray when I bring them here! Do you believe in spirits?" Officer Vandermeer asked and grabbed the woman's severed hand and then yanked my head down and smeared my nose and mouth with cold sticky blood from the hand's stump.

I felt her wrist bone scratch my chin as I fell.

"Do you believe in spirits lad? The ANC terries do. They'd rather take a good sjambocking than visit this place. Do you know what a sjambock is?"

I got to my knees and shook my head no. I was retching and weeping.

"Sjambock's a dried stretched bull dick and makes a first-rate kaffir whip. Our police need many, many of them because it's what we use to drive back crowds in riots. They make sjambocks out of rubber now. It is another sad loss of our cultural heritage. Officer Vandermeer slammed the drawer shut. "It is the Sabbath today. That is why you won't have the pleasure of seeing how a skull breaker works. The police surgeons are in their kirks. I'm an elder and lay preacher in my Reformed kirk. We're a God-fearing people. I'd be taking up the Sunday offering just now if I hadn't been called back because of you. I will miss my family braai today because of you."

I was begging God to give me the words. I guess that proved something. When the chips were down I was calling to God not to Molly or to Hal Busby. No help came. So I did the best I could and blurted, "I believe blacks should be kept down! You guys are right! I support South Africa!"

"Now, now lad calm down," Officer Vandermeer said with a chuckle. "You're just saying what you think I wish to hear. Next you'll be saying that you're a lifelong rugby fan and angry that the Steenboks' tour has been boycotted! It is too late to get on my good side. You came here like the rest, for our money. You were ashamed of God's chosen people and asked that your passport not be stamped so that you could lie about where you made your movie. There is a record of your No Stamp request. You're like the rest. You foreign moegoe want our money but when you go home you pretend you're one of the 'We Won't Play Sun City' cunts."

"God led me here!" I cried out.

"And He is leading me now!" Officer Vandermeer shouted as he ripped my shirt and sweater off from over the top of my head in one big roll. Then Officer Vandermeer screamed "Take off your clothes!" and pulled my belt off and tugged down my pants.

I tripped and fell down tangled up in my jeans and underpants. He knelt and ripped them off along with my Reeboks and my socks. As he crouched in front of me pulling off my socks Officer Vandermeer was breathing hard. He bit his lip like he was chewing gum. There was blood on his mouth.

Officer Vandermeer stood and yanked me up off the floor by my hair and I saw myself reflected naked in the refrigerator door. What Officer Vandermeer said next was in one long sermon-type gush of yelling. He yelled-preached in his heavy accent and threw in lots of Afrikaans words. The whole time he held me by my hair and shook my head when he made each point.

"I will tell you the story you should be making in your movie! This is the script that I shall write someday and I will find you and you will make this movie! The world must know the truth! December 16, 1838 was the Battle of Blood River!" he yelled. "I will bring you a script and you will tell the story of my Boer People who were of the dispersed House of Israel just as your godly American settler peoples also were. In our film you will show that we Boer were gathered to Cape Province first by the Netherlanders who settled the Province at the same time as the Scottish settlers settled in the Plantation of Northern Ireland called Ulster and at the same time as your James Town settlement and your Pilgrim Fathers were also planting the seed of the New Israel in your country. God was working to fulfill His Covenant purpose as we read of it in Deuteronomy, that He fixed the bounds of the nations. God reserved the very best parts of the earth with the agriculture and minerals best suited for all of us of the New Israel. My People's Voortrekkers left the Cape Colony in our little wagons just as your God-fearers with their little wagons trekked to your West. Our Voortrekkers' purpose was to trek into the interior and there to peacefully establish our free states. There were no natives there in those times. There were no colored or black peoples there! The Zulu and Bantu and other dark animals were moving down to the region too but we and they were trekking into the empty region at the same time as my people! Let no one tell you that our Sacred Land was stolen from the kaffir! It was empty! Satan's dark ones attacked my people and they killed many, many Voortrekkers. But we selected a new leader a man called Andries Pretorius, a man of God, a strict Calvinistic man, a man who knew God's Word. On the 16th of December 1838 our Voortrekkers found themselves surrounded by twenty thousand Zulus. There were only four hundred and sixty Voortrekkers! What did my people do? They prayed together! They formed their wagons into a laager. Inside this sacred circle the Boer prayed and we made a holy vow to Almighty God. And this is what my People said: 'If His protection is with us we will give Him the honor and the glory and we will share this miracle with our children for generations to come and we will keep this day forever as a Holy Sabbath.' That was the Oath of Blood River that God's New Israel People took! The God of Heaven who in Deuteronomy said, 'Fear not for the Lord your God shall fight for you,' performed the miracle of deliverance for my people and we defeated the Zulu! Some of the surviving Zulu were captured. They said that they had seen white shinning angels on a cloud above our circle of wagons and that these angels were shooting down on them! THAT is the movie we will make! I will find you and I will have a script and you will tell this true story to the world!"

Officer Vandermeer was gasping for breath. He wiped away the tears that had started running down his cheeks when he preached or told his story at what had to be the worst story pitch meeting ever or whatever his tirade was. There was spittle and blood on his mouth and chin. He let go of my hair and grabbed one of my arms and bent it behind my back and shoved me toward the open locker door. When I saw what he had in mind I started to fight. I tried to punch him. But I was naked and he had shoes on and was ten times stronger than me.

"Don't waste your time kicking and screaming," he said, as he pushed-pulled and shoved me. "You'll only scratch that big soft fat white skaapie belly of yours and tear your fingernails. Lie on a dead body and think of your nation's rebellion against God Almighty's deliverance of the Boer! You have denied your holy heritage! Just as He gave Judea and Samaria to His People, so too He gave the Boer our land! You cannot fight God almighty! I will cure you and then you will make my movie!"

He dragged me by my testicles to the locker and shoved me under the bottom tray. I screamed "No! No! No!" while he kicked me until I crawled into the locker to get away from his kicks.

Chapter 27

O Heavenly King, O Comforter, the Spirit of Truth

I could taste the air. I tried to cover my nose. It was so completely dark that I didn't know if my eyes were open or shut. My hand brushed a cold arm or maybe it was a leg. I yelled then lay still. When I retched I banged the back of my head on the metal stretcher above me. I heard splashing sounds and screamed "Who's there?"

Then I realized that the splashing noise was being made by my hands shaking in the icy stinking puddle I was lying in. A roar made me jump. I hit my head hard on the underside of the metal shelf above me and splashed rancid liquid into my mouth. Gagging and calling for help I crawled deeper into the space behind the shelves. I groped forwards with my hands until I touched a wall. Then I realized that the roaring was the sound of a compressor.

My ears were ringing. Inch by inch I raised my head and crawled into a half-sitting position against the back wall in the space behind the shelves. I tried to swing my arms but snagged my elbow on something sharp. I felt my skin tear. I sobbed, "Dear Heavenly Father, Dear Heavenly Father," again and again but couldn't get more of a prayer started than that. The ache in my testicles made it hard to move. I was screaming "Help me!" at the top of my lungs before I knew who was doing the yelling.

Then I found myself yelling, "God damn you Ruth! God damn you Pastor Bob! God damn you Pat! God damn you Hal Busby! I planted my fucking seed of faith! I followed your fucking Words of Knowledge! Is this what you call the law of fucking reciprocity? Is this how you open the windows of Heaven and pour out blessings? Is this your fucking Wonderful Plan for my life?!"

While I was feeling around in the dark for a place to lie down I yelled, "Molly is right! I hate you Pat, I hate you Ruth, I hate you Pat, I hate you Bob, I hate you Hal Busby, I hate you Pat, I hate you Ruth, I hate you Pat! I HATE YOU GOD!"

By moving my numb hands up and down I found that there was a space between the bottom of the lower tray and the body above it. I inched my way over and then up on a body. The body wasn't as cold as the floor. It was a woman. "Body fat! Body fat! Body fat! I hate you Pat! Body fat, I hate you Pat!" I shrieked.

I rested my head on a big cold breast and pulled heavy arms over my chest. I had always thought dead people were stiff. But this woman was as soft and floppy as a mound of cold dough. I worked my feet under wide legs. Her fat didn't suck my heat out like the floor puddle did. A picture of all of those black women that I had seen walking along the roads with their babies tied to their backs flashed into my head. I thought about their babies. I wondered where this mother's child was.

Then I heard a voice say, "O Heavenly King, O comforter, the spirit of truth, treasury of good things and giver of life, come and dwell in us and cleanse us from every stain and save our souls, O gracious Lord."

"Speak Lord, for your servant heareth!" I screamed filled with joy. Speaking of Mood Swings here I'd gone from cursing God to screaming for joy when He spoke. His voice drove all my anger and rebellion away. God had shown up at last! He was a little late maybe, but at least He was on the job again! He wasn't using His cricket voice or His deep fatherly Jason Robards voice. Now He sounded like a friendly old man speaking in a quivery tone in some kind of foreign accent. "Holy God, holy mighty, holy immortal have mercy on us," the trembling old voice sang. "Speak Lord, for your servant heareth!" I yelled. "Glory to the Father and to the Son and to the Holy Spirit now and ever and unto ages of ages, Amen," said the voice.

"Forgive me for blaspheming," I said. "I didn't mean any of what I just said. I don't hate You Lord!"

"All holy Trinity, have mercy on us. Lord, cleanse us from our sins. Master, pardon our iniquities. Holy God, visit and heal our infirmities for Thy name's sake," the voice said.

I hoped that the Lord wouldn't mind if I turned over while He was talking to me. I needed to thaw my front out against the dead woman. I rolled over on her and pulled her arms over my back. I lay my head between her breasts and bent my knees so I could jam my frozen feet under her thighs. We were crotch-to-crotch but I meant no disrespect. I waited for the Lord to speak again and tell me what His Plan was but He didn't say anything. I figured maybe He was mad at me. I wanted to explain my blasphemous outburst just like it says to in the Bible; "If we confess our sins, He is faithful and just to forgive us our sins, and to cleanse us from all unrighteousness" 1 John 1:9.

So I sobbed, "I-I-I know that I never should have screamed out all those terrible things when I got locked in here. I-I-I know I should never have read Molly's doubt-filled lesbian letters. I know I've thought terrible thoughts about You Lord. I did all this even though You moved Pat to send me a clear message of uplifting on TV. I have no excuse. Forgive me!"

"Who is Pat?" asked the voice.

"What Lord?" I said.

"Pat. Who is Pat?"

"Your mighty servant leading America back to You Lord to get it back from the Secular Humanists to the way it was before the ACLU made Christianity illegal in America."

"Christianity is illegal in the United States?" the voice asked.

I figured God was testing me because of course He knew what had happened to America but I answered Him anyway and said, "There's a war on Christmas by the ACLU and the homosexuals have parades but you can't put a cross on a state house lawn or pray in school Lord, or put Your Commandments up in a courthouse, even though it says 'In God we trust' on our dollar bills Lord."

"Call me Father," said the voice.

"Thank You Father God," I said.

This was the most comforting conversation I'd ever had with God. He was being so nice. And His voice sounded so very real, warm and kind! But I didn't understand why He was pretending that He didn't already know everything. Maybe He wanted me to confess my deepest secrets and fully repent. That must be it I thought, He wants a fuller confession!

It all came out in a sobbed rush. "Ruth knew I did it!" I sobbed out. "You spoke to my heart to say it was okay. So why am I being punished? Is it because I masturbated so much? Is it because I used the F-word? Did I get Your Word wrong about being allowed to drink wine? Is it because I sometimes pictured Sadie when I cast my seed upon the ground? Is it because of my backsliding doubts? Is that why I'm here? Did Molly cause me to stumble?"

"Are you confessing to me?" the voice asked.

"Yes! Please forgive me Lord!" I sobbed. "I believe, help me in my unbelief!"

"My son, my spiritual child, who hast confessed to my humble self, humble and a sinner like you, none have power on earth to forgive sins, but God alone. Whatsoever thou hast said to my most humble self, and whatsoever thou hast not succeeded in saying, whatsoever it may be, God forgive thee in this present world, and in that which is to come. Have no further care for the sins which thou hast declared."

"Thank you Lord God!" I cried out and I started weeping with relief as the burden of my sins was completely lifted off me. God had just PERSONALLY forgiven me! For the first time in my life I was 100 percent sure I was one of the Elect!

The compressor roared on again and it got colder. There was a loud sneeze. I knew God doesn't sneeze, at least not since the resurrection because Jesus is in a perfected body. I yelled, "Who is it?! Who's there?"

"Only me," said the voice. "I've had a terrible cold for weeks. Are you one of my parishioners?"

"Lord?" I asked.

"Who are you my son?"

"Billy Graham. Not *the* Billy Graham. I was named for him. Mom said You laid it on her heart that I was going to be an evangelist even before I got born. She was saved at Billy Graham's 1953 rally in Cleveland. It turns out my call was to reach people through making movies, but Mom covenanted with You from my birth. When I married Ruth we both laughed because now there was another Ruth and Billy Graham. Ruth is Billy Graham's wife's name too. So--"

"Billy, what is it that you are doing here?" the voice asked interrupting me.

"I'm being punished for witnessing for You Lord."

"Billy, excuse me but who do you think you are speaking to?"

"To You my Lord God Creator and Jesus Christ my Savoir and Holy Spirit! To All Three of You!"

I heard a cough and more sneezing. "Lord have mercy!" said the voice and laughed. "Billy, this is Father Dmitri of St. Basil's Greek Orthodox Church in Pretoria. It's just me, stupid old Father Dmitri."

AND GOD SAID, "BILLY!"

I was dumbstruck. I thought I had been talking to God. His voice had sounded more real than ever! And even in that dark horrible place was feeling happier than ever in my life because God had just said I was forgiven for sure and saved for sure. And this was right after I'd yelled "I hate you God!" So there was a flood of relief, my biggest Mood Swing ever when I thought He'd spoken to me so kindly. Now it turned out that I had been spilling *my most personal spiritual secrets* to some Greek Orthodox so-called priest! All my Molly doubts rushed back! I crashed from a newfound assurance and certainty of my election and salvation to utter despair. I went from thinking that I'd been put in the morgue for a reason -- so I could have a rededication to Christ experience that would give me assurance of my salvation for the rest of my life and embolden me to do even mightier deeds for God -- to feeling that I wasn't sure I was even saved.

"The SAP does not dare to kill me, at least not yet," said Father Dmitri. "They bring me here from time-to-time so that I can think over my sins. They don't like me helping the ANC women and children. Nor does my parish council for that matter," he added with a chuckle. "Most of the Greeks here in South Africa are as racist as all the other whites, sometimes worse. I suspect it's my parish council president who got me in trouble with the SAP to begin with after I kept the soup kitchen open no matter that the parish council voted to close it. He thinks the Greek Orthodox Church is his personal Hellenic white man's social club. The only sacred feast day he keeps is Greek Independence Day and to him the heart of the Liturgy is coffee hour. But I do not care why the women are in need or if their husbands are ANC or not. They must have food and clothes on their backs. And so I'm sent here from time-to-time as a kaffir-lover who needs to be taught a lesson."

"Have you been in here before?" I asked, getting interested in his story in spite of everything.

"There is always some friend who keeps me warm. Tonight I think I am lying on an old man. And you?"

"I think I'm on a woman."

"It is not good for man to be alone," he said and laughed. "Do you think you could find your way to me? We would be warmer together."

I decided that keeping each other a little warmer wasn't such a bad idea. "Keep talking," I said, and I inched my way down the woman until my feet hit the back wall. "Keep talking so I can find you."

"Where are you staying in Johannesburg, when you're not a guest of the SAP?" he asked.

"The Rosebank hotel. But I'm up at the production office of Safari Films on Lone Hill most of the day. I'm directing a movie for them. We're supposed to start shooting in a few hours. Say something else."

"We bless you, O God most high and Lord of mercies, Who ever workest great and mysterious deeds for us, glorious, wonderful, and numberless, Who providest us with sleep, as a rest from our infirmities and as a repose for our bodies tired by labor."

"Keep talking."

"We thank Thee that Thou hast not destroyed us in our transgressions, but in Thy love toward mankind thou hast raised us up, as we lay in despair, that we may glorify Thy majesty."

"Are you on an upper shelf?" I asked.

"On the bottom shelf my son. My feet are toward the back wall. I will move down so that they will intrude into your path."

"Keep talking." I said. "And wiggle your toes."

"We entreat Thine infinite goodness, enlighten the eyes of our understanding and raise up our minds from the heavy sleep of indolence, open our mouths and fill them with Thy praise, that we may unceasingly praise and confirm Thee, who art God glorified in all and by all, the Eternal Father." His foot whacked me in the eye.

"Hello Billy! I will move our friend a little so there is more room for all of us in my cell," he said. I heard creaking and some groaning. "There my son, do not injure your head as you crawl into my humble cell."

My frozen hands couldn't feel much of anything but I could tell the difference between the dead body under us and Father Dmitri. He was trembling. I crawled up to his shaking knees, over his thighs, across his chest and up to his neck until I felt his beard against my face and we were laying body-to-body.

"Hello, Billy, pleased to meet you," he said and kissed me on both cheeks.

"Hi."

"I will turn so," he grunted. "You lie along me."

We rolled on the body and clutched each other. I felt Father Dmitri's arm go over my shoulder to steady me. I put my legs across his and pressed against him. Father Dmitri's beard smelled like roses. The body under us was much thinner and harder than the woman's body had been. Its hip points pressed into mine and felt sharp.

"Were you here when I got shoved in?" I asked.

"I heard it all poor boy but I could not say anything. Your persecutor sounded unhinged. I was here for an hour or so before your time began but I was put here by other policemen who brought me from Pretoria. What I do not understand is why your persecutor believes that he can succeed in doing such a thing to an American. How does he know you will not expose him?"

"Officer Vandermeer could put me in jail before I get to direct my movie. I stole something and if they wanted to they could put me in jail or kick me out of the country and that would end my chance to make a movie."

"I already heard your confession and it was made with weeping so whatever you forgot to say was also cleansed by your tears. Fear nothing. Are you warmer now?"

"Not much."

"I'm afraid you have made a poor bargain. Your young body will give me far more warmth than my dry bones will give you," he said. "How old do you think I am?"

"I don't know."

"Eighty-three."

"They put an old man of eighty-three in here? That's terrible!" I exclaimed.

"I like to think I am winning the martyr's crown but without an audience of Romans or Turks, it doesn't seem very probable," Father Dmitri said and chuckled. "How do you become a saint unless someone writes down what you did? Jesus was most fortunate that Matthew, Mark, Luke and John could write!" He laughed hard and kept chuckling on and off while he talked. "I'm glad I finally have someone who can bear witness to my persecutions. Now I might be made into saint! They'll put my old bones in a gold box and carry them to Mount Athos and venerate them!" Father Dmitri laughed so hard that we almost rolled off the body. I wondered if he was crazy. "You know," he said after he stopped laughing, "We have a rather serious problem."

"What?" I asked.

"The evil man that put you here may discover I was here also. The government is doing all they can to get Americans and others to come here to do business. They would never have wanted you treated this way no matter what you stole. Your persecutor must be a rogue officer playing his own game or is a madman."

"I don't know."

"The SAP attracts some rather curious characters to say the least. They get away with everything they do to my black brothers and sisters for so long that they begin to think they are invulnerable. That is why you will have to leave immediately as soon as he lets you out. If you are so fortunate to leave this place alive you must go directly to the airport. I will send someone to you there. Luke chapter sixteen, verse thirty-one. It is our password. Do not forget."

"What do you mean?" I said. "I'm directing a movie. Officer Vandermeer said he wants to visit our set. I need to go to the production office."

"Go to the airport. Wait at the car rental desks. Remember our Luke chapter sixteen password, 'And he said unto him, if they hear not Moses and the prophets, neither will they be persuaded, though one rose from the dead.'"

Chapter 28

You Will Never Be Beyond Our Reach

I woke up when I heard one of the locker doors slam. I tried to move. I couldn't. Another door opened. Light poured in from a locker down the row. It hurt my eyes. I saw a black child on the shelf next to mine. She had a hole in her forehead. I thought about Rebecca and sobbed. The door slammed. A minute later another door opened three or four doors from where I was lying.

"I hear you sniveling. Where the hell are you?" Officer Vandermeer shouted.

All I could do was groan. Another door opened. Officer Vandermeer's head appeared above me. The light was blinding.

"How did you manage to get up here to number three?" he asked and laughed. I couldn't keep my eyes open in the light. My mouth wouldn't work. "Ready to introduce me to the lovely Miss April?" he asked.

Officer Vandermeer reached under my armpits and dragged me off the tray. I flopped on the floor. I tried to sit up. I saw an old black man on the tray that I'd been lying on. His beard was sticking up and was clotted with blood. His throat was cut so deeply that his head was tilted back off the edge of the tray.

"It doesn't look as if your friend's too well," Officer Vandermeer said. "Did you spend a pleasant night together?" He kicked the drawer back into the locker and slammed the door. Then he dragged me across the floor by my arms and sat me up against the wall. He walked away.

My brain was as frozen as my body and my thoughts kept going around in circles but I couldn't figure anything out. I was trying to think about where Father Dmitri was. The Luke verse kept repeating in my head. "And he said unto him, if they hear not Moses and the prophets, neither will they be persuaded, though one rose from the dead."

Officer Vandermeer came back with a blanket and a mug of tea. He tossed the blanket over me and handed me the mug. I couldn't get my hands to close on it so he fed me. When he held the cup to my lips boiling tea burnt my mouth and chin and chest when it dribbled down my front.

After I drank half the tea Officer Vandermeer left again. He came back pulling a hose. He yanked my blanket away and then opened up the nozzle. The water was hot. "Stand up maat!" he commanded. I tried but could only get to my knees. I fell sideways. "Move your arms!" The hot water made my hands hurt. He kept it on me for 10 minutes or so. I warmed up enough to feel my toes. They felt like they were on fire. The water steamed as it ran across the floor and poured down the drains under the autopsy tables.

When the hot water treatment was over Officer Vandermeer tossed the blanket back on me and then stood over me with his hands on his hips. At least I could move now. When he talked his voice was matter of fact and back in his regular Afrikaans accent. He smiled and said, "If I hear even a rumor of your speaking about what happened to you here I'll pass your name to our friends. They have plenty of people in America. I'll tell them that you're working with the PLO's Black September as well as the ANC. Does the name Ruth First ring a bell?"

"No."

"She was a white South African kaffir-lover. That traitor to her Peoples was dealt with by a parcel bomb." Officer Vandermeer lit a cigarette. "She was in Mozambique at the time. Hard to reach you say? Safe as you'd be in America you say? And how do you think Professor Basil al-Kubaissi at the American University of Beirut was dealt with? Our Israeli friends told us he was providing logistics for Black September and the ANC as well. We had some people in Paris. They had some people in Paris. It was a joint effort between both of the Chosen Peoples of God. Kubaissi was shot twelve times when returning from dinner. Do you understand?"

"Yes," I said.

"You will never be beyond our reach," said Officer Vandermeer. "I will let you make your movie now and then I will find you and you will make the story of my people! Not a word to anyone! Do you hear?"

"Yes."

"I say again, you will never be beyond our reach."

Chapter 29
I Still Have a Career

It was starting to get light when Officer Vandermeer shoved me out of the police van down the block from the hotel. I took the elevator to my room. I sat in the tub drinking the coffee I picked up as I limped through the lobby. An hour later I went to Rubin's door and knocked.

"You look like shit," said Rubin. "You don't disappear the night before a shoot!"

I had decided what to tell Rubin while I was in the bath. It took me a while to figure out the story but once I did I knew he'd believe it. "I took off with a hooker yesterday and got the crap beaten out of me when I was mugged by some Schwartzas. When I woke up I was in some hallway someplace downtown. I wondered around looking for the Rosebank and just got back."

"Jesus H Christ! You fuckwit!" Rubin yelled. But I could see he believed me and I would have thanked God for inspiring me but I was tired of God and His so-called Plans. So I hadn't asked for His help and came up with the lies all by myself. "I thought you were broke. Where'd you get the money?"

"Spink lent it to me. He was drunk so probably won't remember. Rubin, I got to sit down." I fell onto the couch opposite Rubin's bed.

"April says she won't shoot any scenes today since you weren't around to do the script meeting last night. They hate the shit you put in the script especially the fucking poems."

Twenty minutes later I was standing in the production office parking lot. The joy of being a director had shriveled along with my joy in the Lord. There was a lot of coming and going and everyone wanted to ask me stuff. I felt dizzy and sick. Everyone started to pester me. And at the same time I was hearing Molly's voice clear as ever. God was silent. "Underneath" Molly said, "there was a frantic attempt to keep my kids from learning about my horrible 'mistake' – divorce then taking a lesbian lover…" Other voices chimed in. "I need to ask you questions about April's look…" and "Don't blame me if the van is wrong since you weren't here we had to just rig it…" and "I had to tell Karl to lose the bandage he wanted to wear. He thought it would make him look more macho…" and so on. "Oh, there you are!" said Spink, and walked out of the production office into the parking lot. "Didn't know what your first shot was so I told them to rig the van. I presume you want to shoot through the windscreen?"

"What did Martin Luther say?" I asked.

"You don't want to know. Bit chilly, eh?" Spink pulled a flask out of his pocket. "Have a spot?"

I took a drink. It wasn't wine, maybe it was whiskey or brandy or some such. Anyway it burned my throat and made my eyes water.

"Les, is there some place to sit down? I'm not feeling too good."

"My dear boy, what were you up to? We rang your room continuously from luncheon onward."

"I had a little too much to, well you know, I stayed in the hotel bar a little too long then went up the street with some guy I met to another bar. I didn't get back till late. Then I sat in the hotel bar all night."

"Say no more," Spink said and winked. "Margo!" he shouted.

Margo turned around from where she was standing by the office door talking with the gaffer and making a list of the lighting equipment he was unloading from Martin Luther's truck. "Yes?" Margo bellowed.

"Our director needs your Jeeves Special!"

"I twig!" Margo said and winked.

We walked over to the production van. The grip was rigging it with a hood camera mount.

"How's it going?" I asked. The grip smiled but Martin Luther, who was fussing with a bolt on the mount, turned his back and walked off.

"Touchy bastard is the little Hun. Have another pull?" Spink held out his flask.

Veronica walked over. She looked angry. "Karl says that unless you're in his Winnebago in ten seconds, he's leaving," she snapped.

"Where's his Winnebago?" I asked.

"He's calling the back pantry his 'Winnebago.'"

Spink and I passed his flask back and forth a few times. I was taking a third sip when Margo walked out of the production office with a glass in her hand. "Oh, it's really too bad of you, you bloody old bastard!" shouted Margo as she came up to us. "How's this meant to do him any good?!" Margo said and held out the glass. "Here lad, leave Leslie's poison alone!" It was filled with something like tomato juice. "As Jeeves said, 'It's a little preparation of my own invention.'"

I sipped. The drink was hot with Tabasco or some such. It made me feel a little less queasy.

———⋘◉⋙———

"Where the fuck have you been?" said Karl. This is the biggest load of shit I've ever read. I won't do one line of this shit!"

"Hi Karl, how are you?" I said as I stepped into Karl's back bedroom "Winnebago" dressing room.

"Has April agreed to do this shit?" Karl snarled. "April may agree to do this shit. I will not do this SHIT! I still have a career!" Karl held out the script and shook it at me. "This is my career we're dealing with here!" Karl screamed. Then he started to read from the script in a high angry sarcastic voice. "'Oh Alex, kill me another one. I want two trophies.'"

Karl pitched the script across the room.

"What is it you don't like, Karl? I can work on it," I said.

"What don't I like? Is that what you want to know?"

"Tell me what you want changed."

"And when will you be able to make those changes? I've never seen crap this bad and I've seen everything! Congratulations you have written something so awful it's totally original!"

"Thank you. The key to genres is going beyond conventions."

"WHAT?!"

"The poems are our special story events. We must not only hit these beats but transcend them."

"I'll kill you!"

"We could work on the first scene together."

Karl made a grab for me. I got an armchair between us.

"You're the dumbest piece of shit I've ever met!" screamed Karl and he threw the script at me. I tried to duck but I was so out of it that I couldn't. The hard edge of the binder caught me on the bridge of the nose. My eyes watered. I slowly bent down to pick up the binder. As I reached for it Karl took two quick steps around the chair and put his foot on my hand.

"Don't ever touch that piece of shit ever again!" he hissed.

I walked back up the hall to the reception area. April rushed in shouting, "If Billy doesn't direct I quit! Karl says he won't work with Billy because of how shitty the blue pages are. So Karl says he'll rewrite it. I won't have it!"

AND GOD SAID, "BILLY!"

"Of course not luv, of course not," said Spink, as he followed her into the reception area. He stood by Veronica's desk wringing his hands.

"I won't have Karl rewriting my lines and firing the director! I know whose lines will get cut!" April said and spun around and stamped out of the office just as Rubin walked in.

"What the fuck is *she* screaming about now?" Rubin asked.

Spink took a long pull from his flask and said, "I think we have a wee little problem Rubin."

"Will you stop drinking?! It's only seven in the fucking morning," Rubin said. "I want the first set up in the can by eight."

"We don't seem to have any stars left," said Margo and giggled.

Veronica started laughing hysterically. Johanna walked in with a tray full of mugs of tea. She held out a mug to Rubin.

"Tea Master?"

"Fuck tea!" Rubin yelled and slapped the mug out of her hand. It flew across the office and smashed on the wall.

"Sorry Master," said Johanna and backed away. "Sorry Master. Sorry."

"I'd like some tea," I said.

Johanna walked over to me and held out the tray.

"Thanks," I said and took the tea.

"Sorry Master."

"Not now Johanna," said Margo. "Take tea away."

"Sorry Mistress."

"What's she so fucking sorry for all the goddamned time? Jesus! This fucking country's driving me nuts!" yelled Rubin.

Karl walked in and announced, "We delay the shoot a week while I rewrite. And I'll direct too."

Rubin bared his teeth like he was trying to smile. When he spoke he was trying to sound nice. "Look Karl I wonder if we could just have a little meeting then get the first setup in the can? Sure you can direct but it's too late for a rewrite, so just improv or whatever."

"You," Karl said and pointed at Veronica.

"Me?" she asked.

"Yes you!"

"Yes?"

"Call me a cab. I'm going to pick up my stuff and head for the airport."

"Come on Karl, let's just fuck this puppy then we can all go home," said Rubin.

"Fuck you Rubin and your six day shoot!" shouted Karl. "I'm out of here!"

"We have a goddamned contract!" screamed Rubin.

"I signed to shoot an action movie and now the only 'action' is me standing with my thumb up my ass and some guy's dick in my other hand while I read children's poems voice over! I signed to do a low-budget production, not a non-existent-budget production! I risked my career by boycott-busting but I presumed there'd be an actual director not some retard putting Mary Had A Little Lamb all over a movie that don't make any sense and then when I ask this shit-for-brains about the fucking poems he's quoting me shit out of some cliché how-to-make-a-movie textbook! Like I need to listen to this shit! I quit!"

"I'll have you killed!" screamed Rubin.

I didn't know if Rubin meant Karl or me or both of us. Rubin lunged for Karl so I guess he meant him. Spink jumped between them.

The phone rang.

"It's for you," Veronica said calmly and held the receiver out to me.

"Hello?" I said. "Hello?" I put a finger in my ear so I could hear whoever it was above all the yelling.

"I'm not entrusting twenty fucking years of hard work on my

career to this asshole!" screamed Karl.

"Billy I have a message for you," a man's voice said.

"Who is it?" I asked.

"Have you read Luke sixteen, verse thirty-one?"

For a second I didn't get it. Then my knees sagged. I would've fallen except for Veronica's chair. I held onto that.

"I'll have you killed! I'll have you all killed!" Rubin kept screaming. "I'll have you killed!"

"Is that a threat?" yelled Karl. "You heard him Leslie! He's threatening me!"

"A certain priest says you are in grave peril," said the voice. "They know you were together. Do what you were told."

I felt like I was going to throw up.

"I'll have you killed!" Rubin was yelling again and again.

"Leave now," said the voice. "The police are on the way to Lone Hill. Have you told anyone about what occurred last night?"

"No."

"Get out, now," said the voice.

"I can make threats too! I'll have *you* killed too!" screamed Karl. "How do you like them apples?"

"I don't understand," I said.

"Have you looked up the gospel passage?" asked the voice.

"I know it by heart," I said. "'But he said to him, If they do not hear Moses and the prophets--'"

"Go directly to the airport," said the voice. "The police will be at your office at any moment."

"Will you get the fuck off that phone!" screamed Karl.

"Who is that shouting?" asked the voice.

"It's the people I work for," I whispered.

"Wait at the Avis desk."

"I'll hang up the goddamned phone myself!" yelled Rubin.

"I'll hang it up!" screamed Karl.

I sidled around Veronica's desk as Karl tried to grab the phone.

"My passport, they have that!" I yelled.

"Who gives a shit?" Karl screamed.

"Do you have any other form of identification?" asked the voice.

Karl grabbed the phone. I grabbed it back and got Veronica's desk between us again.

"Give me the fucking phone!" Karl screamed as he sidled around the desk.

"Give Karl the fucking phone!" screamed Rubin.

"I've got one thing," I shouted while sidling away from Karl again, "My South African union card!"

"Who gives a flying fuck?" screamed Karl and made a dive for me.

"Lads! Lads!" said Spink.

Karl wrenched the phone away from me and ripped the cord out of the wall.

"Bloody hell!" shouted Veronica. "What did you do that for you bloody fool? This isn't America! It will be weeks before they come to repair it you twit!"

"By which time I don't give a fuck what happens because I'm leaving," Karl said and walked down the hall.

"I'm leaving too," said April and she followed him.

"I'll go talk to them," I said.

"You'd fucking better," Rubin said.

"Good lad," said Spink and patted my back as I followed our stars. "After you mollify the talent please ask them to go to makeup then join us on the set."

Halfway down the hall I ducked into the toilet. I locked the door and sat on the edge of the rusted out tub. When I got my hands to stop shaking I fished out my wallet and looked in the billfold. Sure enough there was my SAFTA card tucked between my last 20 rand note and a picture of Rebecca. I opened the window. I dropped to the ground and looked up and saw a black kid staring down at me. He didn't say anything. I walked out through the gate in the back wall and staggered away across the field, past some eucalyptus trees, past a tangle of thorn bushes and out to the road. A taxi minivan loaded with black women and their babies drove past in a cloud of dust. I waved but the driver didn't even look in my direction. As the dust settled another minivan came chugging up the road. This one was empty. I stepped out into the middle of the road and flagged it down, and not like somebody asking a favor, but like a white man who expects the kaffirs to call him "Master."

Chapter 30
A Private World

I was standing at the Avis desk trembling and pretending to read brochures when someone whispered, "Luke chapter sixteen, verse thirty-one."

I spun around. A tall black man wearing a black robe and a big silver cross was turning away. I followed him. When I caught up to him I whispered, " 'And he said unto him, if they hear not Moses and...'"

"Never mind all that," whispered the man. He walked a few steps ahead of me as we crossed the departures hall. To anyone watching it would have looked like two strangers just happened to be walking near each other. We stepped behind a cleaning cart that hid us from view. "Look for your contact at Windhoek. He'll be dressed as a soldier and will know the password."

"I don't understand," I said.

"Do you have your identification?"

"I have my SAFTA card. The police have my passport."

"Say nothing and hand them this ticket and they may not even ask for an ID. They'll think you're just another geologist traveling to the Rossing mines for a consult. That's one advantage of having no luggage."

"The man or priest in the morgue, whatever, wasn't there when I woke up. I thought a dead man had been talking to me."

"You were asleep," said the man in the robe. "Father Dmitri crawled away as soon as he heard someone opening and shutting the doors. No good would have come of you being found together! Here's your ticket."

He put an envelope on the trash bin and walked away. It took me a long time to work up the courage to even go to the desk marked SAA Domestic Check In/Ticketing. When at last I did no one asked to see an ID. When I walked out onto the runway and then up the stairs to the plane I saw another much bigger plane like the one I flew from London on unloading passengers. It seemed to me that I was like a ghost, just a shadow watching people in a real and better life doing the ordinary things like I used to be part of. It seemed like a lifetime ago, not just under two weeks ago, that Rubin and I had arrived. There wasn't anyone at the plane's steps to check my boarding pass and once I got on the stewardess just said, "Sit anywhere you like."

The flight to Windhoek took an hour and a half. It was a bad time. My arms and legs felt heavy. I didn't have any money and my passport and ticket home were gone. My testicles were aching. I was shivering. Was I dead? In screenwriting class there was a Philip K Dick quote was posted on the wall in big black letters: "Maybe each human being lives in a unique world, a private world different from those inhabited and experienced by all other humans." I felt like that.

I worried no one would meet me. Then I worried they would. "You will never be beyond our reach," Officer Vandermeer had said. I believed him.

I was wondering if I cared that it seemed like my movie career was over. There was no point in calling the production office. That would just give me away. There was no point asking God for help. Hopefully He didn't exist. He'd certainly abandoned me. Even if He was there He was silent now. There was no point trying to call Ruth.

There was no point calling Solly. He'd tell Rubin and then that would get to Spink and I'd be found. The movie was over. I knew that. My stepping stone was gone. Maybe Molly would help me. But how? All I cared about now was Rebecca. "Rebecca, Rebecca, Rebecca," I whispered.

Once we'd been talking about Heaven. I said to Rebecca that probably I'd get there first. "I'll fix a house up for us and wait for you," I had said. "Will you leave the door open for me?" Rebecca asked. That had made me cry. I cried again just thinking about it. I wanted so badly for there to be something true and wonderful to tell Rebecca about if and when we got back together. I didn't want her idea of eternity to begin where mine was ending.

Chapter 31

I Don't Understand

The Windhoek airport was full of South African soldiers waiting for their weapons and backpacks to come down the conveyor. The airport was small, about the size of the Ralph's supermarket on Sunset Boulevard. Windhoek is in Namibia but I hadn't heard of it. Even if I had heard of it I wouldn't have cared. My hands ached from being frozen. I was bruised from head to toe from the punching and kicking. I was surprised that they let me just walk in. No one even asked to see any ID. Later I found out that when you flew to Namibia from South Africa it wasn't like going to another country. The flight counted as a South African domestic flight because the South Africans ran Namibia. As I stepped into the arrivals hall a voice whispered, "Luke sixteen, etcetera, etcetera... Do not turn around lad."

I didn't turn and remembered to whisper, "If they hear not Moses and the prophets, neither will they--"

"Yes quite, etcetera and so forth, jolly good. Continue to the pavement. I'll meet you in white Toyota van."

The van pulled up a couple of minutes later. I climbed in. The van smelled like gasoline. My driver had a wide thick nose like a boxer. He smiled. He had crooked teeth, pale blue eyes, and pink skin. He looked like he was about 60 and smelled musty sort of sweaty. He had shaving cuts on his chin and was wearing a South African army uniform that was too small for him. He spoke in a classy upper class English accent.

As we drove away from the airport the dry bushes, rocks and dusty hills looked like the scenery you'd see when driving up the Pacific Coast Highway between Malibu and Santa Barbara, only we were driving downhill and there was no ocean. Once the airport was about a mile behind us the man smiled and stuck out his hand and said, "I'm Brother Bernard. I took the name of Bernard of Clairvaux though he's a western saint. Do you know him?" I shook my head no. "I took his name with our Igumen's blessing. We have enough Seraphim's and Basil's already!"

"Are you a soldier?" I asked.

"This?" he said and pulled at the shirt of his uniform and laughed, "This is a disguise for our Igumen's benefit. He insisted I cut my beard and put on this silly get up. He's a fan of dramatic conspiracies designed to thwart the powers of darkness real or imagined. He's been a bit jumpy ever since a couple of insane bishops and rabidly conservative priests ganged up on us a few years back and tried to have him defrocked."

"What?"

"Never mind lad, sufficient to the day is the evil thereof and all that and so forth and so on etcetera, etcetera. The point being they failed and we're still grinding away at the old stand and here you are. Look how many times I knackered my chin. First shave I've had in ten years. No one has a razor except Brother Basil, and that's for his animals when he prepares them for surgery."

"I don't understand," I said.

"Byzantine intrigue and all that," Brother Bernard said and laughed.

"I don't know what's going on," I said.

"The path less traveled, eh?"

"What?"

"Care for a spot of tea? There's a thermos in the carry-all on the floor next to the tins of petrol."

"I don't understand."

"You don't understand tea?"

"I know what tea is. I don't understand what's going on. What's happening to me?"

"Nothing to it old chap; our Igumen got a call that another of Father Dmitri's friends was en route. He said that you had run afoul of the nameless powers and needed a spot of help and would arrive on the twelve-fifteen from Joburg sans passport etcetera, etcetera. Our Igumen and Father Dmitri are thick as thieves. Our Igumen is his spiritual father or vice versa."

"What's an Igumen?" I asked.

Brother Bernard laughed. "Father Dmitri's frightfully naughty! You mean to say he sent you all the way out here and you don't have the foggiest? Igumen means abbot in Russian and our abbot's name is Igumen Tryphon and he is an Archimandrite. He reached the Great Schema years ago. That's the highest stage of spiritual excellence in the Russian Orthodox Church which even those blasted fundamentalist 'traditionalist' fanatics can't take away, damn them! On the other hand Father Dmitri is a Greek priest, different ethnic jurisdiction but never mind that. The Greeks give him hell too just as the Russian bishops do to us. Why? All because he stands up for black people and we stand up to the traditionalist cretins."

"I only met him once," I said.

"Who?"

"Father Dmitri."

"Wonderful eyes he's got, hasn't he?"

"I felt his face but it might have been a dead guy's. I never saw his eyes."

Brother Bernard stared at me. "Now I'm the one that's a bit lost old bean," he said.

"We were stuck in a morgue together."

Brother Bernard whistled.

"Put you in the jolly old ice-follies did they? Are you ANC?"

"No I got into trouble for--"

"No need to confess to me! Then again, we've got a long drive and there's nothing like juicy personal confession to pass the time, eh?" Brother Bernard laughed so hard that the van swerved. I had to grab the steering wheel to keep us on the road. It looked like just when I had finally had my final Mood Swing away from religion, or whatever, that some kind of joke was being played on me because I had fallen right back into a religious entanglement. Like I asked myself again and again as we drove into the desert, couldn't someone other than monks have fucking rescued me?

Chapter 32
How Will I Get Home?

I woke up when the hum of tires on paving changed to gravel crunch. I opened my eyes just as we pulled into a rest stop. "Where are we?" I asked.

"On the Windhoek to Swakopmund road driving due west," Brother Bernard answered.

The rest stop had a small picnic table sitting under a weird little tree with thin spiky gray leaves. The 2-lane blacktopped road ran as straight as a ruler in both directions until it disappeared on the horizon. The only other thing there besides the table and the scrawny tree was the flat gray sand sprinkled with black rocks from marble to basketball-size.

"Pee and change," Brother Bernard said.

My cheek was wet where my face had been pressed on the window. My testicles hurt worse than ever. The air was much hotter than it had been at the airport. No other cars came by. It was the quietest place I had ever been. The rocks crunched loudly into the sand when I walked. The sun was so bright that it was hard to keep my eyes open. A second after I stepped out of the van my hair was too hot to touch.

"Are we almost there?" I asked. Brother Bernard shook his head no, turned his back to me and peed into the sand. Then he walked back to the van and opened the rear doors. He stripped down to his socks and underwear and pulled on a black robe. Then he took out one of the gas cans and filled the tank.

"Wouldn't do to the have the South African defense chaps asking me which regiment I'm from," he said and laughed. "They set up checkpoints near the mines. SWAPO likes to blow up things belonging to De Beers and the like."

"Is that what you wear all the time?" I asked, as Brother Bernard buckled on a wide belt with a big silver buckle that had some sort of writing on it.

"I've got a robe for you too. No better disguise lad. We're quite the local fixture."

He picked up a black hat, a sort of squared-off cap and put it on. Then he handed me a robe and a belt and cap.

"Put them on lad."

I was going to pull the robe on over my clothes until he said that I'd boil if I did. I took off everything. When Brother Bernard saw my bruises he whistled. When I tugged the robe over my head it felt scratchy. Brother Bernard helped me put it on then handed me a big silver cross on a leather string. I was going to ask him more questions but I suddenly felt like I was about to throw up.

"I don't feel very good," I said and vomited onto the sand.

Once we were back in the van Brother Bernard rolled up a tattered old blanket to make me a pillow. He was very gentle as he helped me get settled. Then Brother Bernard started to talk and I drifted in and out of sleep. I only heard bits and pieces of his story.

"We're not supposed to speak of our past lives in the world but I'll make an exception," he said. "Forgive me but I must keep talking or I'll fall asleep…

"I'm British from Kenya, born there…

"Presbyterian missionary parents…

"At the age of seven I was sent to boarding school in Lindfield, Sussex England, wonderful headmaster, Mr. Stark, changed my life…

"Met a Greek Orthodox priest when I was seventeen on a school trip to Greece...

"Converted to the Orthodox Church when I was at Cambridge University...

"Chrismated a year later...

"Met a monk from Simonopetra...

"Athos for seven years...

"Saint Catherine's, Mount Sinai...

"Uganda again...

"Southwest to organize our library... etcetera, etcetera..."

The sun was low in the sky and loomed huge and red in front of us when I woke up again. We stopped at another rest stop just like the first one. When we drove on Brother Bernard started talking again. This time I stayed awake.

"You see" he said, "in the eighteen forties or thereabouts the Germans decided they needed to keep up with the British and acquire colonies. Trouble was all the good bits, Kenya, Rhodesia, South Africa were spoken for. Southwest, which is really just a glorified name for the Namib Desert, was all that was left. Notwithstanding they sailed down with boatloads of colonists to Walvis Bay and stole it from the Himba, settled the bay and also up the coast at Swakopmund. That's where they built their town. Later the country was divided between the British and Germans. Later still it was given to the South Africans as part of the Versailles treaty. The Germans built the breweries though. That's why the beer's so good." Brother Bernard smiled. "The beer's the one 'perk' as you Americans call it that we allow ourselves, except on fast days of course when we eat and drink nothing."

"How will I get home?" I asked.

"Igumen Tryphon will have a plan I'm sure. In the meantime we'll keep you up the river."

"What river?"

"It's not actually a river. The last time there was water in the Swakop was in 1938 I believe. I should say up the riverbed etcetera, etcetera. It's full of mesquite bushes. Now you might ask, mesquite, how can there be mesquite in Southwest Africa? In the nineteen twenties they shipped fodder from Mexico to Walvis Bay for the horses and donkeys of the farmers who were trying to make a go of it in the valley. They'd pump out the aquifer for irrigation but it got used up and turned brackish, farming stopped but the mesquite seeds mixed in with the fodder sprouted from the donkey dung."

He glanced at me and laughed. "Oh dear,' Brother Bernard said, "I'm afraid I do carry on a bit. The other blokes complain. 'Brother Bernard,' they say, 'if we wanted constant chatter we'd have brought our televisions with us!' What's the use of fleeing to the desert with you chattering?' Then I answer 'There is nothing wrong with the real world. Religion may be carried to absurd extremes. Don't you agree?"

"I don't know" I said.

"Metropolitan Anthony Bloom, for many years head of the Russian Orthodox Church in Britain, once told me that he recalled an encounter he had years earlier during a retreat for university students. He said 'After my first address one of them asked me for permission to leave because I was not a pacifist.' 'Are you one?' Anthony replied. 'Yes.' 'What would you do,' Anthony asked, 'if you came into this room and found a man about to rape your girl friend?' 'I would try to get him to desist from his intention.' the man replied. 'And if he proceeded, before your own eyes, to rape her?' 'I would pray to God to prevent it.' 'And if God did not intervene, and the man raped your girl friend and walked out contentedly, what would you do?' 'I would ask God who has brought light out of darkness to bring good out of evil.' Metropolitan Anthony responded: 'If I was your girlfriend, I would look for another boyfriend.'"

I had to grab the wheel again to keep us on the road as Brother Bernard laughed so hard he fell sideways.

Chapter 33
It's Not a Long Drive to Rossing

The gold colored dunes first appeared as if they had suddenly grown out of the flat gray desert. A few minutes later Brother Bernard pointed out the town where we were headed. Swakopmund looked like a distant brown smudge between the dunes. A few minutes later we were driving past rows of palm trees down a wide street. We passed a train station and houses that looked like they belonged to a model toy-town. The ocean sparkled between the houses where streets ended at a beach. The streets were a pale gray and streaked with white and were as wide as a three-lane highway but there were almost no other cars. Brother Bernard said that the roads were made out of "a mixture of packed salt and sand" and that it was "as good as cast concrete because it never rains so the salt never melts." There were hotels, cafés, bakeries and antique stores with German stuff in the windows including swastika flags, framed portraits of Hitler and daggers with swastikas on the handles.

"Lots of Nazis holed up hereabouts at the end of the war," said Brother Bernard. "They still celebrate Hitler's birthday as a holiday. A few elderly Nazis aside it's a lovely Bavarian hamlet in a rather bizarre context don't you think? I'll give you a quick tour before we head for Rossing."

"Is that the town we're staying in?"

Brother Bernard winked.

"In a manner of speaking," he said.

We parked on the waterfront next to a big glass building that had a sign on it saying "Municipal Baths" in English and a bunch of other languages. It had a giant tube waterslide next to it. Lawns and flowerbeds lined the beach. A pier stuck way out into the ocean something like the Santa Monica pier but with no rides on it. Huge waves rolled under the pilings. The sun was sinking below the horizon so the whitecaps turned golden-red as the waves crashed on the sand.

"Smell the hops? How about a pull at the jolly old tap?" asked Brother Bernard.

I had noticed a tangy peppery smell as soon as we'd driven into town. I didn't know it was hops until Brother Bernard told me. They were playing accordion music in the Café Brucke where Brother Bernard bought the beer. We sat on a concrete seawall and drank. I sipped and Brother Bernard swigged his beer down in three long gulps and then went back for a refill. The beer tasted like roasted nuts. Huge pale pink birds that Brother Bernard said were flamingos flew so close to us that I felt the wind from their wings. They skimmed the waves and their wingtips touched the foam.

"How am I going to get home?" I asked.

"It's not a long drive to Rossing,"

"I mean back to America?"

"America? What's the rush?"

After we finished the beer we drove along the coast on a road that Brother Bernard said connected Swakopmund to Walvis Bay. To our left there were more giant dunes. To our right the ocean was such a dark blue that it looked almost black. A huge pipe ran next to the road. In places the sand lay across the asphalt in what looked like snowdrifts that we had to swerve around. Brother Bernard said the pipe brought water from far away.

We turned off the paved road, drove under the pipe, and headed up a sandy track between the dunes. Brother Bernard said that we were entering the Swakop riverbed. For the next few minutes the dunes towered above us on either side. The sand looked white now that the sun was gone. Then the riverbed cut deeply between high rock walls and the view of the dunes disappeared. We were in a canyon about half a mile across with cliffs on each side rising up hundreds of feet. At a fork in the canyon we passed a faded blue sign with an arrow pointing to a place called the Goanikontis Oasis. We drove in the opposite direction. I slept.

I opened my eyes just in time to see baboons. It was dark and Brother Bernard had the headlights on. We were driving very slowly grinding our way through loose sand. A baboon jumped right in front of us and just before he jumped out of our way he bared his huge yellow fangs.

"They're a bloody nuisance," said Brother Bernard. "Only Brother Basil likes them. He feeds them no matter how often we implore him not to. Unfortunately our Igumen refuses to forbid him."

"What do they do that's so bad?" I asked.

"Run off with our robes when we leave them out to dry," Brother Bernard said. He pointed at a cliff ahead of us and said, "There's our chapel's beyond the palms. And that's the old convent against the hill."

"What are those?" I asked, as some animals loomed up in the headlights then disappeared.

"There've been camels here since the nineteen-twenties when the German farmers brought some down from Morocco."

I pointed to a bunch of twinkling lights up in the hills. "What are those lights?" I asked.

"The hermits' caves, six of the brothers live there in what I call the 'holy heights,'" he said and laughed.

"Is that where you live?"

"Not me! You have to be at least a little bit saintly or pretend you are, for the Igumen to give you his blessing to live alone. Some of those 'saints' are real wankers. One or two are the 'real deal' as you Yanks say. We suspect one of them is a spy for the Russian bishops agitating to have our Igumen excommunicated. The Orthodox Church is a real mess. Still, the good bits are so good that one may be fairly content here but of course I'll say nothing about several other monastic communities that shall remain nameless! I've got my cell and a splendid view in the old convent."

We pulled up in front of some buildings made out of stones painted white. I followed Brother Bernard up a steep sandy path with black boulders the size of small cars marking the way. The boulders glittered in the moonlight. At the door of the monastery Brother Bernard lifted the heavy iron knocker and let it fall. Then he crossed himself and kissed an icon of Mary that was in an alcove next to the door. The icon was lit by a red oil lamp hanging in front of it on three golden chains. Brother Bernard said, "It's customary to kiss the icon of the Blessed Theotokos when you enter. You may if you wish. Kiss her, don't kiss her, its all one to me lad."

I didn't do any kissing. In the old days I wouldn't have kissed her because I'd figure it was idol worship. Now I didn't want to because I was tired of anything religious. If God was looking out for me why was I walking almost doubled over?

We waited a long time. I was staring at the moonlit valley with my back to the door and was so dazed I felt like I was floating. So when the door opened and someone spoke I was startled.

"Welcome. I am Brother Basil," Brother Basil said.

He had front teeth missing and a patchy gray beard and matted-up hair. His skin was as black as a cast iron stove. By the flickering light of the icon's oil lamp I saw that his forehead cheekbones and nose were scarred like he'd been in some sort of bad accident. His hands were small and thin but when he shook my hand his grip felt strong.

Chapter 34
The Suffering Martyrs

The papers rustled under my chin. I think that's what woke me up. Sunlight was blasting through the open window and bounced from the red tile floor to the high white ceiling and made it look pink. An icon of Jesus was staring down at me. He didn't look very friendly and was holding a golden Bible pretty much like the one I had been smashed in the head with. The air was hot.

I slept so hard that I hadn't moved and so the papers Father Basil gave me to read were still under my chin on the blanket where they fell out of my hands the night before. My candle had burned down to the bottom of a wood holder carved in the shape of a turtle. Brother Basil had said to make sure I blew it out before I slept but I hadn't. There was nothing left but a piece of black wick stuck in a pool of yellow beeswax that smelled sweet. I picked up the sheets and read the title. I noticed that the papers were tattered and smudged. The sunlight showed through where a typewriter had punched out a couple of letters. The letter O had made the holes.

Brother Basil had said "Please be very careful of these papers. They were written before Igumen Tryphon's time and that is why the English is rather imperfect because our former Igumen, Blessed John of eternal memory, did not write English so well though he did speak five languages. Our present Igumen Tryphon, who you will meet in the morning, went to Cambridge University. Then after receiving a First in Natural Sciences he gained a M.Sc. with distinction from Sussex University before becoming a priest, then a monk. He also received his D.Phil. also from Sussex, on the subject of artificial evolution and he speaks English perfectly even though he is Ethiopian by birth, of course. They have their own Orthodox churches – the Ethiopians that is -- naturally given that they were the first Orthodox when their church was founded in the first century, no matter what those insane Greek nationalists like to claim about being 'first' but Igumen Tryphon is a Russian Orthodox monk made so by Anthony Bloom himself. He was consecrated into the charge of the Russian Orthodox Church whilst in Great Britain and Ireland which is a typically odd and therefore a thoroughly Orthodox twist given that makes our Igumen an Ethiopian black man in charge of a Russian Orthodox monastery founded by Russians but now under the supervision of our Igumen, who is under the Bishop of Great Britain. Our Igumen is somewhat resented nevertheless. Many Christians want to appear clever but they don't really like people to be too intelligent, especially not black people. That goes for most of our bishops who are suspicious of all monastics because we rival their power in the hearts of most Orthodox. Then our Igumen is a special case you see, because he is brilliant as well as black and also he is humble and kind in a way that puts the bishops to shame. He also has his own ideas. However, you are now holding papers typed by our *former* Igumen Blessed John's actual blessed hands." Brother Basil crossed himself when he'd said *blessed hands*. "He was universally loved and respected."

This time I read the papers all the way through without falling asleep again. There was a lot I didn't understand. The story was interesting anyway. Here it is.

AND GOD SAID, "BILLY!"

INTRODUCING THE RUSSIAN ORTHODOX MONASTERY OF ST. JOHN OF KRONSTADT TO OUR MOST WELCOME VISITOR

Dearest Visitor,

Welcome! In the Name of the Father, Son and Holy Spirit, Amen! How strange to find yourselves to be welcomed by a Russian Orthodox monastery in the heat of South West Africa. By how ineffable God's Grace, in what strange Mystery His indescribable workings!

BEGININGS

When the suffering martyrs of the Trinity Lavra of St. Sergius monastery were crushed in the year 1920 by the hard boot of the God hating oppressor communists none escaped the evil one's fury against the brothers. Of the few to escape with their lives were Brother Simeon and the monk-priests Cyril and Herman of thrice-blessed memory.

To the Kresty prison in Leningrad (of the Petrograd Cheka system, Second Special Camp for Involuntary Labor -- Petrograd Ispolkom) the three were transported and imprisoned. There to await final martyrdom they celebrated the Eucharist for their fellow prisoners hearing many confessions and making even a baptism of a guard who became with them a martyr (by imprisonment) for our Lord. Lord have mercy! Lord have mercy! Lord have mercy!

In the dread winter of 1941 when the camp was overrunning with the Waffen-SS, Brother Simeon and monk-priests Cyril and Herman, of thrice blessed memory were, by the hand of God's Ineffable Mysteries, denied the martyr's crown and from there were transported with much suffering of cold and hunger and beatings to the camp of Mauthausen, Austria.

Having passed from God hating communists they were now imprisoned by God hating Nazis. There the brothers languish and we see them suffering for the Lord through the countless nights of growing dark in which there was no longer even a rumor of light. Still ministering to the faithful the monk priests baptized the famous painter Kazimir Malevich.

In the supreme coldness of the month of January 1943 the brothers were sent, still by Providence remaining together, for slave labor first to the Krupp Molotov steel works near Kharkov and thence by shipping to Walvis Bay, Southwest Africa, to work as slave laborers in the Khan Mines of nearby Swakopmund, Namibia.

Thanks be to God! For when The Great Patriotic War was ending the brothers three were still alive having suffered for God but not vanquished and having learned to speak some little German and some little English from their fellow humble prisoners. After many tears then they learn of the final closing of their beloved St. Sergius in the Motherland and of the falling asleep of many brothers and the continuing persecution of the remaining faithful by the communists unrelenting. All hope of returning to the homeland was despaired.

SISTER MARIA OF THRICE BLESSED MEMORY

It was in this time of great tears that the brothers three met the Blessed Sister Maria of the Roman Catholic order of the Sisters of The Good Shepherd (also called Sisters of Our Lady of Charity of the Good Shepherd) by chance some say, but we say by God, in the street outside the Hansa brewery in Swakopmund. Sister Mary of Thrice Blessed Memory took it in her pure spirit to say that with the ending of the war the source had been ended for the sisters' since the German Roman Catholic Church was with its compatriot nation in ruin.

The good sister, of not Orthodox but nevertheless of Blessedness spoke with all her heart that now only she and another elderly sister remained at the old convent and that to Germany to help their wounded nation they must repair. The brothers to them must be given the old convent. It was this blessed sister who was favored with the first vision for our Orthodox monastery. The sisters had first built it as a clinic for the Bushmen and Oshiwambo and Himba. The good Sisters were not Orthodox but beloved of God for He condescends to love all His sons and daughters of Christian, of Jew, of Muslim, of Hindu, of atheist.

HAVE NO FEAR DEAREST VISITOR

Have no fear Dearest Visitor to our humble home for there is only God's LOVE, only His Eternal Presence. For He LOVES all as the Father LOVED both the Prodigal Son and also LOVED his faithful son who had remained at home. For the Prodigal received that LOVE with joy but the other son hardened his heart. So too our joy derives only from the manner in which we receive the LOVE OF GOD. Fear not for LOVE is the essence for it was before all and will be after all.

FRANK SCHAEFFER

ENDING AND THE NEW BEGINNING

So it was in 1948 on the first day of Holy Week, the day of remembrance of St. Benedict of Nursia, that the brothers three met for the first time together here by the light of the stars and one candle in this very same desert in the this very same old convent and chapel and rededicated this place in the name of St. John of Kronstadt, wonderworker. He had warned the people of the homeland of the storm of revolution to come. All his words came true. He had once sent 300 rubles for the rebuilding of Simonopetra on the Holy Mountain of Mount Athos of Greece.

Monks Cyril and Herman, of thrice blessed memory, reposed in the year of 1952. In the year of 1964 (the year of his consecration by Archbishop John of San Francisco, together with Bishop Theophil Ionescu of the Romanian Synod Abroad in the cathedral in San Francisco) Eugraph Kovalevsky, spoken fondly of as Bishop Jean of Saint-Denis, made his pilgrimage to this humble place and consecrated our chapel bringing with him a rich gift of a relic of St. John of Kronstadt, both a lock of his hair and beard and a piece of his vestment. This was all sent to us from the Russian Monastery on the Holy Mountain of Athos.

And today the brothers have added brothers, others have come to us and some reposed and we are more than ten in the convent and less than ten in the caves that were readymade for us by the mine diggings of old. We are a Russian monastery but having brothers from all nations and of all colors we use not only Russian but English, Zulu, Oshiwambo dialects, Khoekhoe, Afrikaans, Kwangali language, Herero and Greek in our liturgies and thus are avoiding the grave sin of division.

AND GOD SAID, "BILLY!"

And so it is, Dear Ones, that we who are most sinful, podvig (struggle) to provide for you this resting place in our hospital of the soul meeting here with you as fellow travelers on our journey to God in blessed silence and peace.

Amen.

With Salutations in the Lord,

Igumen John

St. John of Kronstadt Monastery, Swakopmund, Rossing Mines, Southwest Africa (Namibia) on the day after the Holy Feast of the Annunciation in this the year of 1969.

Somebody had added this handwritten note on the last page. "Igumen John, of thrice blessed memory reposed on the feast of St. Nicholas the Wonderworker in December of 1973. Igumen John (who took the name of John the Holy Fool for Christ, Wonderworker of Moscow) reposed in the same otherworldly manner as his namesake. Foretelling the hour of his repose Igumen John went to our chapel and lay before the altar and commanding the brothers to leave him he said, 'I pass through this night to the light.' Some hours later the brothers returned and he lay dead with his hands folded for burial, though there had been no one there with him save for the angels."

Chapter 35
Eat!

In the night I heard a loud noise, the boom-boom-thwack-thwack made by the semantron. I found out later that a semantron is a board carried along the hall by a monk and hit with a mallet. It's a sort of alarm clock to wake the brothers for prayer. I heard it then fell asleep again. Later Brother Basil told me that the rhythm Brother Evagrius drums on the semantron "is the same as the one Noah used when he drummed on the side of the Ark to call the animals." I asked him "Do you believe that story?" He said, "Some things are true even if they never happened in the manner of quantum mechanics and the Everett many-worlds interpretation which holds that all possibilities occur in a multiversity of parallel universes. At least that is what Igumen Tryphon likes to say. Some people call our Igumen 'modernist,' even a 'heretic' but then so have all our best Orthodox saints been called heretics at one time or another."

After I read about the monastery and then peed in the bucket next to my bed that Brother Basil showed me the night before, the next thing I noticed was how bright blue the little patch of sky was that I could see through my window. I put on the monk's robe I wore the day before. My regular clothes that I'd brought in with me from the van were gone. My wallet was sitting on the folded robe. I checked to see that I still had Rebecca's picture and my SAFTA card. I did. There was no money left. The cab to the airport from the production office had taken my last 20 Rand.

The only light in the hall came from a small round window high above the end of the passage about a hundred feet away. There was no one around. There was a sweet smell like someone had spilled a bottle of perfume. I didn't know it then but the smell came from the gardenia incense the monks use in the morning Liturgy. Down one side of the hall was a row of twelve low wooden doors. I had slept in the last cell at the far end of the hall so I passed eleven doors on my way out. They were shut but not locked. I opened one and found a cell just like the one I'd been in except it had a robe and some socks folded on the bed and lots of icons on the walls and a shelf of books above a little desk.

I came to the top of a steep narrow staircase at the end of the hall. The stairs were made out of some kind of black stone. Going down was tough because my legs were so stiff. What hurt worst were my thighs where I'd been kicked again on that spot where you get a Charlie horse dead leg if you're hit there. I was black and blue from my knees to my crotch on both legs and my feet were numb. My brain still felt frozen too. The voices in my head were silent.

Many days later Igumen Tryphon would say, "The mechanism by which ECT – what people call shock therapy -- works is still unknown, but recent research indicates that both ECT and anti-depressant medications exert their clinical efficacy in depression by inducing brain cell growth (neurogenesis) in the hippocampus, which is a deep region of the temporal lobe. Perhaps your encounter with Vandermeer was a sort of 'shock therapy' for you, just what the doctor ordered so to speak to drive the 'voices' out. Or perhaps the Holy Spirit rescued you."

All I know is that morning I felt strangely empty. Next to the front door the oil lamp was still burning but I couldn't see its flame in the sunlight. I knew it was lit though because of the flame's shadow flickering on the icon of Mary. The door was set between fancy stone pillars. The columns were made out of some sort of glittering pink rock. The night before Brother Bernard had said that the columns were made of pink quartz and that, "We never would have spent that much money on our building. An insane benefactor rebuilt the old convent for the nuns in the nineteen thirties and he was clearly possessed by Baroque delusions and a highly decorative style which derives from southern Germany and is a synthesis of Bernini and Borromini's architecture as we observe it in the late Baroque architecture of northern Europe. Our chapel's dome is the one thing we built ourselves in order that at least something here looks ever so slightly Orthodox."

I walked past the icon and stood on the top of the stairs that led down to the sandy riverbed. The smell of incense was strong on the breeze blowing past the chapel. Some kind of hawk circled above me then flew off over the white dome of the chapel and then swooped up and disappeared over the ridge of the cliff. I walked across to the chapel and went in. I was starved and wanted to find somebody to ask about breakfast.

The chapel was empty. No one saw me go in or come out a moment later.

I sat on a big green rock and looked around. The ground in front of the monastery was made of hard-packed gray sand and millions of stones, mostly black rocks from pebble to boulder size. There were also some yellow crystals just lying around as big as coffee cups. There were lots of pink and blue rocks too. They were the most beautiful stones I had ever seen in one place, except that time when I saw the display table of stones in the Johannesburg flea market. When I got up and walked back toward the main building I stopped to bend down to touch a round dark black rock about the size of a baseball. It was so perfectly round I just had to touch it to see if it was real even though it hurt to bend down.

"Move it first," a voice said as I reached for the stone. I jumped. Brother Basil was walking toward me. He smiled. The gaps where his teeth had once been showed his pink gums when he grinned. His skin looked even blacker in the sunlight.

"Good morning. We were having our midday nap. Did you rest well?"

"Yes," I said.

"You must always move any rock with your staff before you touch it," he said.

"Why?"

"That rock has probably lain undisturbed for a hundred years. Scorpions! Here," Brother Basil said and held out his stick, "use mine."

When I poked the rock with his stick it rolled over. A big tan bug that looked like a little lobster with its tail held up ran away.

"Two days in bed of fever and pain," said Brother Basil. "Before you awoke ocean fog rolled over the desert. Now it is gone as happens every day. This Parabuthus scorpion drinks fog. Imagine that!" he said and he sounded excited. "She moves her mouthpart chelicerae collecting and drinking fog! That is her only source of liquid! This actually happens! Layers of a wax coat her exoskeleton trapping the water! This scorpion will await better times for more than one year without eating more than fog!"

The scorpion scuttled under another rock. I handed the stick back.

"Have you been awake long?" he asked.

"I just got up. What about you?"

"We rise for Midnight Office at three. Did you hear the beating of the semantron?"

"I thought I heard hammering. I went right back to sleep."

"You missed the morning meal after Liturgy."

"Is it lunchtime yet?"

He looked up at the sky checking where the sun was then said, "The evening meal is still six hours away."

"What about lunch?" I asked.

Brother Basil smiled, reached into his robe and pulled out an orange, two small crusty rolls and a huge peeled carrot. He held them out. "With the Igumen Tryphon's blessing I took these for you from the kitchen. You missed goat cheese lentil soup and tea. You may drink water at the well by the chapel. We keep a cup there for travelers."

"Thanks."

"Eat!"

It only took me a minute to wolf down the food. It was my first meal in three days. When I was done eating I took a drink from the tin cup attached to a chain next to the well's hand pump. Then Brother Basil said, "I have just returned from my infirmary. Would you like to see it? I only have one patient just now but she would love to meet you."

Chapter 36
Please Come Into My Clinic

Brother Basil stepped around the corner of the monastery. I hurried to catch up but my legs were too stiff to run. When I stumbled around the corner he was already halfway up a set of rock stairs cut into the cliff that looked more like a ladder than a staircase. They started next to the monastery and went almost vertically at least eighty feet. I held onto the steps ahead of me as I climbed. There was no rail. If I had fallen I wouldn't even have touched the stairs but crashed all the way to the valley floor. Brother Basil hitched up his robe and tucked it into his belt and took the steps two at a time and called over his shoulder "Something like 'The Ladder of Divine Ascent. At least no demons are pulling at our legs!'"

I had no idea what he was talking about. I do now. He was talking about John Climacus' writing (600 AD) that describes how to raise the soul to God through "ascetic virtues" -- whatever. I only know that because Brother Bernard told me about Climacus and how he "uses the analogy of Jacob's Ladder as the framework for his spiritual teaching."

Anyway, that day I crawled up the stone stairs feeling terrified. I was out of breath when we got to a flat sandy shelf about thirty feet across and twenty feet wide with more cliff above it rising up to the ridge. Brother Basil was standing waiting for me with his hands on his hips and smiling his mostly toothless smile. At one end of the flat shelf was a small windowless stone hut built out of rough stones cemented together. It was built against a giant boulder split from the cliff and roofed with flattened rusty barrels.

"Please come into my clinic," said Brother Basil.

When we ducked through the low door I was surprised. I expected the inside dimensions to match the outside but it opened up into a space the size of a tennis court because the hut was built against the narrow entrance to a large cave. Before I could walk in something black flew at my face. I ducked, yelled and jumped back into the sunlight. Brother Basil laughed and said, "Say hello to Miss Honeychurch. Two years ago I found her huddled under an acacia. I don't know how she got there. I raised her from a handful of fluff on one of your fine American dog foods called Purina Dog Chow. She's a Pied Crow."

I stepped farther into the cave and Miss Honeychurch swooped at me again and I ducked again. When I opened my eyes the bird was hovering in front of my face like some kind of huge hummingbird and beating the air with her wings. Her head, tail, beak and wings were black and she had a patch of white feathers on her shoulders and chest. Her beady bright eyes were dark brown.

"She wants to land on your head and take a good look at you," Brother Basil said. "They're very curious not to mention intelligent, destructive and devious. Come in and sit down and we shall all be introduced. Do you approve of her name? When I was a guest of the South African government and living on Robin Island in the cell next to Mandela I read E M Forster to pass the time. I was thinking of naming her Mr. Beebe, until I discovered she's a she. However, I'm not altogether certain I have her gender correctly identified."

There was bird poop and shredded up newspapers everywhere. The only light in the cave came from a gap in the rocks high above us about thirty feet up between the split off boulder and the cliff.

AND GOD SAID, "BILLY!"

Later I learned that Miss Honeychurch could come and go but since she'd been hand-raised she always came home. She wanted to be fed and to sleep on her favorite perch above the door and to do her favorite thing which was to play take-it-apart games, hide-things games and shred up newspaper.

When my eyes got used to the dim light I saw that along one side of the rock wall there were a couple of empty cages made out of wood crates. Next to the cages were boxes of dog food, a fifty gallon plastic drum of water, metal bowls and two hot-water bottles hanging from a hook. Ragged blankets and a couple of broken-down chairs were next to the cages.

"Sit," said Brother Basil.

I sat on one of the chairs keeping my knees apart so as not to hurt my bruised testicles. The rush seat was so frayed that I almost fell through it. Brother Basil took a pomegranate out of his robe pocket. He pulled out a Swiss Army knife and split the fruit on the wooden arm of his chair. From the many slice marks on the chair's arm I could tell that it had been used as his cutting board for years. The knife was razor-sharp and went through the pomegranate in one fast stroke. Red juice dripped as the two halves fell apart. Miss Honeychurch screamed when she saw the seeds spill into Brother Basil's hand. Instead of worrying about getting home or even caring about all my bruises I found myself completely absorbed by watching the bird. "Here," Brother Basil said, handing me half, "feed her. Pomegranate is her favorite!"

I cupped my hands. Miss Honeychurch circled the cave beating up a dust storm. A thin beam of sunlight that came through a crack in the door turned the dust she stirred up into a shaft of sparkling mist. Miss Honeychurch landed on my arm. That's when I realized how big she was. She was at least a foot and a half tall and her head was as big as a chicken's, maybe bigger. Her claws dug in.

"Do not pull away or you will frighten her. Quite a grip in those claws, eh? But she will not hurt you, at least not permanently," said Brother Basil. The bird ruffled her glossy black and white feathers and then she cocked her head to one side in a quick jerky motion and stared at me. She made a cheeping sound then pecked hard at the pomegranate. "She adores the seeds," said Brother Basil. She tightened her grip, stood straight up, and then banged her head down, rocking back with every peck like a jack hammer. My wrist felt like it was wrapped in barbed wire.

"Look," said Brother Basil, "Look at what she will do. She's so clever!" He took a scrap of dry dog food out of his robe, stuck it between his lips and made a whistling noise through the gap in his teeth. Miss Honeychurch ruffled her feathers, hopped up to my shoulder, took a peck at my ear and then made a dive for Brother Basil's arm. He slowly moved his arm up to his face while Miss Honeychurch rocked back and forth clinging to his wrist. Brother Basil closed his eyes. Then the bird leaned forward and with a snap grabbed the dry piece of dog food from between his lips. "Watch now," he hissed. "Watch! I must keep my eyes closed. She loves bright objects. Once she pecked my eye."

Brother Basil closed his eyes and mouth tight. The corners of his lips twitched. He was trying not to laugh. Miss Honeychurch cocked her head one way then another. When nothing happened she screeched and pecked at Brother Basil's lower lip. Then she waited. When Brother Basil didn't do anything Miss Honeychurch fluttered to the top of his head. This made him smile but he still kept his mouth tight shut and his eyes closed. She turned around holding onto Brother Basil's matted hair and then she leaned way out over the edge of his forehead and hung upside down staring into his face. She completely covered his face with her body. Brother Basil laughed.

I crept around to Brother Basil's side so that I could see what she was doing. She had pushed her beak between his lips and was trying to pry them open. Miss Honeychurch leaned back and peered at him with her big dark eyes then she stuck her thick beak between his lips and tried to force Brother Basil to open his mouth. Brother Basil opened his lips but kept his teeth clamped tight shut. Miss Honeychurch started to tap on his front teeth. This made him shake with laughter but Brother Basil still wouldn't open his mouth. Miss Honeychurch got impatient and pecked harder, sticking her beak deep between the gaps in his upper front teeth.

"Ow!" Brother Basil yelled.

Miss Honeychurch let out a raucous scream. She hopped from his head to Brother Basil's arm. He opened his mouth wide. She cocked her head and then slowly stuck her whole head into his mouth. When Miss Honeychurch stuck her head into his mouth Brother Basil shouted with laughter which made her squawk loudly and flap away high up into the cave. Brother Basil opened his eyes.

"She wants to know if I have more dog biscuit in there. She'd crawl down my throat to look for it if I let her."

"Is it safe to let her put her head in your mouth?" I asked.

"Oh yes, as long as you close your eyes. The worst that may happen is that she'll peck your tongue if you wiggle it. She thinks it's a snake," Brother Basil said and grinned. "You must try it!" Brother Basil sat back and stared up at the bird swooping above us. "Do you know why I love her so?" he asked.

"Why?" I said.

"Because when I startle her she always forgives me. How do you explain that, eh?"

I suddenly thought: I'm not thinking about anything except just being here and I wouldn't want to be anywhere else right now. Then I was instantly filled with sickening regret because of what I'd done to the monks that morning.

Chapter 37
Go Say Christos Aeinesti

After we fed the bird and played with her for about an hour Brother Basil said, "Our Igumen instructed me that my service today is to explain the order of our life to you. It is best if you take notes." He pulled a pad and ball-point pen out of a drawer in the bird-spattered broken-down dresser and blew a cloud of dust off the notepad. We stepped outside, Brother Basil closed the door then we sat down on the top step overlooking the valley. The sunlight was so bright I had to squint to look at the paper.

"I will speak slowly so you may take notes," Brother Basil said.

"I don't need to take notes. You can just tell me. I remember everything."

"Our Igumen says you are to take notes. Each novice must learn the order."

"What's a novice?"

"The order will be in your notes. It is Igumen Tryphon's wish."

I was in no position to argue. An hour later Brother Basil smiled stood up and stretched. My hand was cramped. It was worse than my Old Testament class back at Zion Bible College. They made me take notes there too just like everyone else did even though I told them that I remembered everything I heard. If Brother Basil hadn't been watching over my shoulder I would have just pretended to write. But with him keeping an eye on me I had to write more than fifteen pages down and he corrected my spelling as we went along. Here's some of what I wrote:

> The monk is in his room when the sun goes down and begins in the darkness to fill his spiritual being with light. His prayer rule is according what has been regulated for him by his Igumen. The rule of prayer may vary from monk to monk. The Elder (Igumen Tryphon) is a doctor of the soul and he knows what to administer to each according to his spiritual need. The monastery is a hospital of the soul. A new monk makes a onetime Life Confession to the Igumen. The novice's Life Confession may be written or oral. It may take days or be written down over months. After that he tells his Igumen of his thoughts and actions every day. His Elder rules his life with love.
>
> Each monk has different tasks we call "Service": gardens, machine shop, kitchen, Guest Master, tending the church… The Service of work does not separate the monk from church services that other monks are in at the time. He is there spiritually at all times -- whatever he is doing. As long as the monk's Service is done with the blessing of the Igumen and with love for others it is as holy as prayer even if it is the cleaning of the toilets.
>
> The Liturgy is about 1 hour long each morning. Holy Water is served in the silver cups after the Liturgy. Holy Water is taken after communion up to Leave Taking of the Feast of Theophany. Holy Water is blessed at the start of every month. Our silver Holy Water urn and cups were a gift from the monks of Simonopetra on the Holy Mountain of Mount Athos in Greece. The cups and urn are our monastery's finest treasures, besides the relics of St. John of Kronstadt.

The flow of life and movement in the service of God means monks come and go as their Service requires. We are not bound by time. Time relates to liturgical calendar here, not to clocks. Life relates to biological rhythms and seasons not to a man-made schedule.

The meals are according to our Igumen as he rings the bell on the table. Our Igumen strikes it with a small hammer.

Bell One: Start to eat!

Bell Two: Begin to drink!

(Do not drink before Igumen Tryphon rings 2nd bell!)

Bell Three: End of meal!

(Do not even finish the bite on your fork!)

Meals have a liturgical atmosphere. Lives of saints, spiritual instruction (*Ladder of St. John* during Lent, *Philokalia* and such after Lent) are read throughout the meals.

Eat in silence! Eat quickly! Do not to talk! Igumen Tryphon is quite strict about this!

Each monk has individual struggles. Salvation is a journey -- not a one-time magical event. No one is lost forever. We judge ourselves. God judges none.

The word "salvation" is a metaphor for the journey wherein we may repair the content of our characters so that we become more accustomed to the fire of God's love and are not consumed by it. There is no Heaven or Hell. The final reality is God's love for everyone. The Igumen welcomes each on the difficult path of salvation like the father in the story of Prodigal Son. We may enter the timeless realm now. Love is the deeper alternative to religious zeal.

Brother Basil patted me on the shoulder. "Now take a note of this story," he said. "Are you ready?" "I guess," I said and I flexed my hand.

"There was a monk" said Father Basil, "who was rumored to have

AND GOD SAID, "BILLY!"

brought a prostitute to his cave. The other monks learned of this and demanded justice from their Igumen. Their Elder agreed to go to the monk's cell and correct the situation. He asked the enraged monks if he could first go alone. The Igumen went to the cell and discovered the woman. Wordlessly he hid her in a trunk then sat down on the lid while the terrified monk stood by. Soon the other monks arrived. 'Make a thorough search,' their Igumen said. As the monks searched they naturally left their Elder in peace sitting on the trunk. In fact the monks made their zemnoy poklon (low bows) each time they passed the trunk he sat on. Soon they discovered there was no woman there. The brothers apologized to the accused monk, prostrated themselves before him and departed. When the monks were gone the Igumen rose from the trunk and turned to the tearful monk and said, 'Take care of yourself lest worse befall you. If you wish to take a woman I will give you my blessing and you may renounce your vow and go in peace. God will love you no less. But if you wish to live as a monk you must not break your vows. To live in the midst of a lie is hurtful to your soul.' With that the Igumen blessed the brother and departed. The monk sent the woman away and from that day forward he kept his vows. The Igumen had protected his monk from the wrath of the brothers by covering his monk's frailty with his own person."

"Is that it?" I asked.

Brother Basil smiled. I flexed my hand. "No," said Brother Basil and started to tell another story. "A simple monk always greeted the other monks and his Elder with a shouted and joyful 'Christos Aeinesti!' (Christ is Risen!) One day his Elder became annoyed by this endless repetition by the monk who was so simple as to be not quite right in his mind. His Igumen said, 'Go say Christos Aeinesti to the bones in the ossuary but leave the rest of us in peace!' The ossuary is the place monk's bones are stacked up to await the resurrection after their flesh has turned to dust. The simple and obedient monk walked directly to the ossuary cave, reverenced the stack of bones and skulls and cried out, 'Christos Aeinesti!' to which all the skulls shouted the reply, 'Alithos Aeinesti!' (Truly He is Risen!) The simple monk then returned to the monastery. His Igumen saw him and asked, 'Well? Did you do as I said?' 'Yes,' replied the monk. 'And what happened?' asked his Elder. 'The skulls answered Alithos Aeinesti,' said the monk very matter-of-factly. The Igumen knew that his monk was incapable of lying and so he prostrated himself before his holy brother and begged his forgiveness."

Brother Basil stood up and smiled. "That is our rule," he said, as he helped me to my feet. "Fear nothing Billy, everyone is saved. It takes very hard work to lose ourselves."

Chapter 38
Silence Is Peace

Father you said, "There is another choice: To admit that the best of any tradition secular or religious depends on the choices its adherents make on how to live *despite* their fondest beliefs not because of them."

"But where will that leave me?" I asked.

You answered, "Another name for uncertainty is humility. Certainty is the enemy of truth. Now that you've completed your penance, how would you describe yourself presently?"

I answered, "I'm a fucked up agnostic kind of wannabe recovering thief novice-trying-to-become-a-monk, at least on most days when I think about all that stuff. Mostly I don't think. I just am. So there you have it Father, your rebaptism worked. Or was it a *debaptism*? Mostly I don't think. Like I said, I just am."

And you said, "That is good. Just being is another way of describing silence and silence is peace. Now go back and include even those things I already know such as the papers written by Blessed John explaining our history. Insert them. I wish this record to be complete for Rebecca so that if she ever reads it she may know the full truth. You owe her this confession more than you owe it to God. Now then, in your remaining pages record what meant most to you and what you've learned."

So Father (I just went back and put in the story of the monastery in the right place where I talk about my first day here) here's my best shot at answering you. Call this last part of my Life Confession the "Epilogue." I'll start by mentioning one of the first books you made me read, "The Stranger" by Albert Camus. In "The Stranger" there's a line I really like: "He simply asked if I was sorry for what I had done. I thought about it for a minute and said that more than sorry, I felt kind of annoyed." That's how I feel about my wasted life in Hollywood and in my church and of course what I did to Rebecca.

You also made me read the "Narrative of the Life of Frederick Douglass, An American Slave." You said that this part of Chapter nine is a good example of "everything that's wrong with relying on religion instead of on your heart." You said that Captain Auld reminded you of my Pastor Bob. Douglass writes, "In August, 1832, my master [Captain Auld] attended a Methodist camp-meeting held in the Bay-side, Talbot county, and there experienced religion. I indulged a faint hope that his conversion would lead him to emancipate his slaves, and that, if he did not do this, it would, at any rate, make him more kind and humane. I was disappointed in both these respects. It neither made him to be humane to his slaves, nor to emancipate them. If it had any effect on his character, it made him more cruel and hateful in all his ways; for I believe him to have been a much worse man after his conversion than before."

I liked this from Philip K Dick from "How to Build a Universe That Doesn't Fall Apart Two Days Later." Here's the quote you underlined for me: "The authentic human being is one of us who instinctively knows what he should not do, and, in addition, he will balk at doing it. He will refuse to do it, even if this brings down dread consequences to him and to those whom he loves. This, to me, is the ultimately heroic trait of ordinary people; they say no to the tyrant and they calmly take the consequences of this resistance. Their deeds may be small, and almost always unnoticed, unmarked by history. Their names are not remembered, nor did these authentic humans expect their names to be remembered. I see their authenticity in an odd way: not in their willingness to perform great heroic deeds but in their quiet refusals."

Besides the reading I've done this year what helped most was our once a week walk up over the ridge and all the stories you and the other monks have told me like this one you told me when we were tracking those lion prints. You said, "Over one thousand years ago there was a monk who lived in a monastic community in a desert much like ours. He wanted to find holiness and so he prayed for years and years to his guardian angel. He asked his angel to show him which of the hermits and monks in his desert was of 'pure heart.' He wanted to find a perfect spiritual father-confessor who had achieved theosis or divinization as it's called. This is the process of a becoming free of *hamartía* ('missing the mark') and of being united with God. But since only God sees the heart this monk knew that outward signs of holiness might actually cover up inner filth. At last after many years of prayer and ascetic struggle he was answered and in a dream he flew hand-in-hand with his angel over the mountain where he and the other brothers lived in caves. The angel and monk flew over all the hundreds of great teachers and ascetics striving in that place and the angel did not stop. They passed over the boundary of the community altogether and flew over a town nearby to the garbage dump. Then the angel pointed to a woman scavenging in the dump for food. They followed her home to a hovel full of ragged children. The angel said to the monk, 'She is the only truly holy person hereabouts. Confess to her with assurance of receiving perfect wisdom.' The monk was horrified and said, 'But she's a pagan, a whore and worst of all a woman! How could she be holy or wise?' The angel replied, 'You asked to be shown a holy person. She's a perfect child of God.' The monk woke up and was sad and confused. He knew there were only two possible interpretations of his dream, first, that everything he thought he knew was wrong, or second, that he was right about what was needful for salvation but that the angel was wrong. Either way he felt that everything he'd counted on had just been torn from him."

 I liked that story. And I like that after the ocean fog melts away each morning besides the thing I feel most deeply is the bright clean sunlight piercing the absolute silence. You once said energy preceded matter and love preceded energy. Maybe you're right. Silence and bright clear light didn't seem like a very big deal to me once. They do now. God no longer "talks" to me. Molly no longer "talks" to me. I'm still scared of "Him" though. You can tell I am, Father, because I'm still using a capital letter "H" for Him, instead of just writing "him" like you told me to. I might not believe anymore but I can still feel God's wrath hanging over me. Anyway, the silence in my head and in the desert is a relief.

 Lying on my back outside Miss Honeychurch's cave watching the ocean fog melt away every morning is my favorite moment of each day. The fog covers every pebble, cobweb and grain of sand with dew. For a few minutes each single grain of sand, every thread of cobweb and every rock sparkles. I love that moment! I still like to eat too! When I first got here I wolfed down the two daily meals and thought that there was never enough to eat. I hated how you rang the bell when I still wanted to eat more and I'd have to stop, even if I had a forkful of food halfway to my mouth. But after a few weeks I was surprised that I was starting not to mind the smell of goat cheese and lentil soup. I got so I liked chapel too which is ironic since back when I believed everything Pastor Bob said sometimes I hated church services and now that I don't believe anything much I really like the Liturgy even though -- as a non-believer -- I don't partake of the sacraments. Go figure Father. I like how dark and warm it is and how sweet it smells in chapel and how the monks look like big bats standing around the walls wrapped in our black

AND GOD SAID, "BILLY!"

robes. I like watching them float back and forth when they're lighting candles, trimming the wicks and kissing the icons.

Okay now to answer your question about what I liked *least* when I got here. Speaking of the twists and turns there was the one big scary thought that spoiled everything: *That you would find out what I had done to you the day after I arrived.*

During those first weeks I almost blurted the truth out every time you prayed for the return of the Holy Water cups. You lifted your big black hands up to heaven and I just didn't know what to do I felt so bad. You would reach up to the sky like you wanted to be picked up like a child does. I wished I hadn't stolen them. I wished I had put the Holy Water back when there was still time!

As you know from what I told you, sobbed, blurted, sniveled, whined, begged, pleaded after I was caught, the first morning I was here I walked into the chapel looking for someone to ask about breakfast and I saw the cups and stole them. I stuck the cups into my robe pockets, one in each so they wouldn't clink together. I had the idea that maybe I could sell them when I got back to town. I thought I could use them to pay for a ticket home. Mainly I was just doing what impulsive habitual thieves do: steal.

Like I said that first morning when I walked into the chapel I saw the cups were (are) handy and small. Each one is no bigger than my thumb and shaped like a little wine glass with a twisty stem in the shape of vines. The cups look like a miniature bunch of grapes. The urn holds about a gallon and looks like a bigger bunch of grapes with cherubim folding their wings over the top. I hadn't planned to plunder anything when I went into the chapel that first time. I just wanted breakfast. But the cups looked valuable and were off to the side and didn't seem like anything that would get noticed, at least not for a while. Anyway, how was I supposed to know that they are over one thousand three hunderd years old? How was I supposed to know they are our greatest treasure and that you even refused the

Metropolitan Museum of Art's request to lend the cups and urn to a show called "The Glory of Byzantium?"

After a big search for the cups you decided that some German tourists, who happened to visit the same day I arrived, must have stolen them. I figured that I was home free. I wasn't. I felt bad. I'd never felt bad about "despoiling" anything before. A few nights later the night before I was unexpectedly and weirdly betrayed and the truth came out, Brother Basil and I were sitting in the cave with Miss Honeychurch. She was perched on his head. He said, "Remember these things are true, it is not a fantasy. We are united in one long prayer from the beginning of time to the end." I think he knew what I'd done.

When you asked me if I had any idea about where the Holy Water cups were your smile was trusting. I lied through my teeth and answered "I have no idea." The way you looked at me made me feel like I'd stolen the "Lamby" from Rebecca. (I think you knew!) Your expression made me feel like I'd taken her Lamby away for no reason and she'd never sleep peacefully again. Rebecca loved her Lamby that Molly gave her when she was born. To Rebecca it was as if it was alive and could talk. (One time I pretended to talk in Lamby's voice and Rebecca said "Daddy Lamby can't talk. She's only a stuffed animal.") Rebecca had lots of stuffed animals but she chose Lamby to be her special friend. By the time Rebecca was three and I left home Lamby was so worn out and dirty that unless I had seen Lamby when it was new I never would have known that Lamby had once been a fluffy white stuffed toy. Rebecca would not and could not sleep unless she had her Lamby. I never let Rebecca take Lamby anywhere because if it ever got misplaced we would have had to stop everything until we found her. I only took Lamby with us when Lamby could help Rebecca get through hard things, like when she chipped her front tooth and then later it had to be taken out. She held onto Lamby the whole time. And as she woke up from the anesthetic the first thing I did was press Lamby into her arms.

When I met you for the first time Father, (a couple of hours after I stole the cups) and you said, "Welcome to our desert, we shall do all we can to help you in your time of troubles," I almost told you what I had done. Like I said, the way you looked at me made me want to tell you way before anyone noticed the cups were gone.

Father, after I had been here almost six months I told you that one time Rebecca said to me "I'm shy of God." We'd been talking about going to Heaven. "I'd rather stay here," she said. I asked why and then that's when she said she was shy of God. You said that was "The most truthful statement of our human relationship with the divine I have heard." So I do think Rebecca and you are pretty much the same. You still say "I'm shy of God" once in a while and always smile when you do. So the point here is that my two favorite people turned out to be a three year old little girl (at least the way I remember her) and you, a seventy six year old black monk. Go figure Father!

That first day when Brother Basil had shut his eyes so he wouldn't get pecked I hid the cups in the sand by the wall of the cave. I didn't dare keep them on me. I noticed Miss Honeychurch watching me as I leaned over from where I was sitting and scraped out a little hole in the soft sand by the rock wall. I dropped the cups in and then covered them. It only took a couple of seconds. I didn't know Miss Honeychurch well enough to worry. Of course after we were outside and I was taking all those notes she dug the cups up.

A few days later when I was back in Brother Basil's cave alone I discovered that the cups were gone. I have no idea where she put them. Probably it was high up in the cave where she hides her treasures. At the time I thought I just couldn't find the right spot in the sand, or that Brother Basil had found them. I couldn't figure it out.

The first couple of weeks after I arrived each morning after Liturgy I climbed up to Miss Honeychurch's cave. If I was alone I'd dig around looking for the cups some more but after a few days I gave up. I'd sit for a while watching the bird searching for pebbles or tearing up her newspapers into shreds. Sooner or later Miss Honeychurch would start to play her game of hiding little items on me. I never knew exactly what she was hiding. While she hopped all over me I kept my eyes shut so she wouldn't peck them while she was tugging at my hair and robe. She stuck pebbles into the folds of my robe, pieces of string in the cuff of my sleeve, a piece of fluff into my ear, a car key in my hood or string in my hair. These things -- "her treasures" like Brother Basil calls them -- were her toys. She hid them on me and I never touched them because later she'd look for them. It was fun to let her find her stuff. Even hours later she knew where everything was, even half a day after she hid them! It made her so happy to find the paperclips, pebbles and other things in my hair and in the folds of my robe. She'd cheep and cackle and squawk with joy.

About 3 weeks after I arrived I was at the Ninth Hour prayers. I was standing in chapel in front of the icon of Jesus that's on the iconostasis wall between the altar and the sanctuary. That's when the two little silver Holy Water cups fell out of my robe's hood along with five pebbles and a paperclip. The cups fell to the flagstone floor and rang out like little bells. Miss Honeychurch must have stuck them into the hood of my robe without me knowing it.

They fell while you were saying what you always say at that part of the service Father: "We bless You now, again O Christ, Word of God, Light of beginningless light and dispenser of the Spirit, the triple light united into one glory; You who dissolved the darkness and brought light into existence." Falling down was all I could think of doing. So I pretended to black out and collapsed on the cups. But every monk in the chapel heard those cups ring out. Like you told me later "Orthodox monks' robes don't usually have hoods. Monks wear hats. Our robes have hoods because of the hot sun. So Billy, you were in the one Orthodox monastery where you could have been betrayed by that bird!"

AND GOD SAID, "BILLY!"

After a long silence you finished the prayer. Then you took me by the hand and lifted me up. You picked up the cups kissed them and put them back next to the Holy Water urn. Then you led me out. A moment later outside and standing in the starlight under that vast bright starry sky I admitted everything to you Father. I even blurted out stuff about Pastor Bob, Ruth, Rebecca, "God's movie" and the rest. I must have confessed for an hour or more. After listening to me babble on and on when at last I fell silent you gave me a choice: Call the police or "pay the price," your way for my being a thief.

I picked your way. You told me that your way was that I was to live in Brother Basil's old animal hospital cave with Miss Honeychurch! "That will be your Service" you said, "to care for the bird, read and talk until I decide that you are cured of your soul's illness."

During the weeks and months that slowly grew into a year, you lent me books and papers and we talked about what I was reading and writing. After a while I started writing this confession a little every day like you told me to. You said to write it "like a memoir-based novel." I think I have so far. You told me that confessing is good and that in other places "it's called therapy."

When I agreed to your "terms" (more like an "offer" from the Godfather I couldn't refuse!) I expected lots of Bible or prayers or something else religious but you said that too much religion makes people snap and that "all fundamentalism is a form of abusive mental illness be it Christian, Jewish, Secular or Muslim or anything else." Mostly you gave me stuff by Albert Camus, Frederick Douglass, and Philip K Dick, Mark Twain and William Shakespeare to read and music by Bach, Duke Ellington and Charlie Parker to listen to. You said I wasn't to ever "go near a Bible again." You said "There are no chosen people." You said "You can't teach good writing so your faith in Hal Busby was as misplaced as your faith in Pastor Bob." You said, "Fundamentalist religion is a mental illness involving emotional contagion and peer-group and group-think manipulations so dastardly it may only be described as a complete commitment to psychotic manipulation." You said, "Our brains shape and reshape themselves in ways that depend on what we use them for throughout our lives. With optimal experiences, the brain develops healthy, flexible and diverse capabilities. When there is disruption of the timing, intensity, quality or quantity of normal developmental experiences, however, there may be devastating impact on neurodevelopment — and, thereby, function." You said, "There is hope for you Billy, however because the brain is very 'plastic' meaning it is capable of changing in response to experiences, especially repetitive and patterned experiences."

After a few months I decided I didn't know what the word "Christian" meant anymore because in some ways you seem even more secular than Molly was becoming, and yet here you are doing all this really old-fashioned ritual stuff morning noon and night! Why?

What kind of "believer" are you? Some of the monks here are way stricter than you. Some say you're a "holy fool" and they mean that as a compliment. Some say you're a "heretic" and don't mean that as a compliment. And what did you mean when you said that I need to make my own "quiet refusal and reject God?"

I mean WHAT THE FUCK Father? What kind of a monk are you? How can your church let you get away with turning me into an atheist?

Chapter 39
Small Minded Reactionaries

NOTE TO BILLY

Billy, while correcting your deplorable spelling in your most recent confessional chapter "epilogue" as I typed it up for you as ever -- and by the way, once again, you're forgiven and so forth and so on etcetera, etcetera, as Brother Bernard would say -- I've taken the liberty of inserting this brief note of explanation to partially answer your pithy "What the fuck Father?" question. Perhaps you'll want to keep this note inserted within your text as a permanent contribution to your biographical record if for no other reason so that when someday Rebecca reads this (as you've told me you intend to give it to her in person someday), she will know what the person who "converted" you to sanity believed in (or more importantly did NOT believe in) since I seem to have played a somewhat significant role in your journey—so far.

At any rate a few years ago in an all-too-rare moment of pan-Orthodox unity ("ha, ha" I say laughing bitterly!) several zealous Russian and Serbian "traditionalists" (in France of all places) teamed up with several American former evangelicals who had converted and were therefore more-Orthodox-than-the-Orthodox (in California of all places) to work together against me. They found their "answer" to much the same "what the fuck?" question you asked me and then began vigorously agitating to have our entire community excommunicated for "heresy."

These small minded reactionaries petitioned the Patriarch of Moscow and even the Patriarch of Constantinople to excommunicate me. This was after an article of mine was published stating that many of our Canons (the "changeless" laws of the Church) are rather silly. This plunged me into considerable hot water with these former American evangelicals (and some former Roman Catholics too who were goading on the Serbian and Russian idiots in France) all of whom were desperate to find something that has "never changed" (Orthodoxy as they foolishly hope it is though it really never was as changeless as they fondly imagine) and cling to it in the same way that the stupider – and generally nastier -- of the "conservative" Roman Catholic "intellectuals" (most of whom are papists and hardly Catholic at all) cling to their "Natural Law." Hyper-confidence in one's opinions as a constant personality disorder is transposed by all these converts to their new faiths.

As evidence of my "apostasy" they accurately cited this quote from one of my articles: "Models of psychotherapy can help one hold on to a religious worldview while simultaneously living in a world increasingly described truthfully in scientific terms. Rescuing faith requires that we grapple with that tension as it focuses on science's recent challenges to the 'historicity' and intrinsic 'value' of the Bible and the Canons."

You see Billy, we must go behind both our Canon's "laws" and our Bible's stories too to glimpse the storytellers who in their own times faced enormous crises of faith as we do in ours. We may learn from their struggles and be inspired to honestly face our own global human-made ecological cataclysm while we also confront the cataclysmic confrontation between all forms of delusional religious fundamentalism and (sometimes equally delusional) modernity which has emerged as the unexpected story of our times. I say "unexpected" because not long ago wholesale loss of faith and the "inevitable" rise of secularism were predicted and what has actually happened has been a worldwide resurgence of fundamentalist extremism within all religions from the Islamic "brotherhoods" to the North American "religious right" fundamentalism of the kind that (if I may say so) came within a hair of destroying you and your life forever.

This resurgence of brutal fundamentalism can only herald a civil war (including actual violence I predict) breaking out over the control of the hearts and minds of all religionists of every faith. It will pit tolerant open faith against paranoid reactionary fascist "faith" seeking power over others by whatever name and in whatever religion, Muslim, Christian, and Hindu, Jewish et al. The real conflict will not be between secularism and religion but between all fundamentalist religious people and all moderate religious people.

I say the fundamentalist resurgence is unexpected because by the nineteenth century deism had all but collapsed into atheism as a growing number of educated people began to consider God an unnecessary hypothesis. This "death of

God" was heralded as the triumph of reason. This ideological confinement of reality to a narrow naturalistic definition allows no concessions for any spiritual, immaterial phenomena. Thus we Orthodox are so accustomed to defending ourselves from this real or imagined challenge posed by militant secularism (a struggle our own people who founded this place faced in the Gulag) that we have overlooked a far greater crisis and failed to mount an urgently necessary rebuttal to the rise of reactionary fundamentalism and its war on the spiritual heart of all people.

This new fundamentalism is itself a type of secular rationalism wherein theological determinism replaces sensitivity to, and love of, the spiritual and immaterial. True spirituality is thus replaced by a frightened rules-based commitment to fundamentalists' own version of the ideological confinement of reality to a narrow naturalistic definition. For instance, by applying the Orthodox Canons rigorously or Shariah Law or the 613 laws of the Torah, as if the essence of spirituality is rules, rules and more rules, the religious rationalists' destroy actual faith. For these days they are bent on applying medieval prejudice and ignorance designed to "contain" female sexuality by denying women full equality with men, campaigning against contraceptives and by even idealizing the "honor" of physical virginity. And of course they have declared war on homosexuals and anyone else they perceive as the "other" as well.

Perhaps my critics clamoring for my expulsion also do not like the fact that in yet another article I poked a bit of fun at the people who say the Canons are "perfect." One of these perfect Canons says that an Orthodox must not have a Jewish doctor and another forbids dancing! (Try to get the Greeks to abide by that at their weddings!) Or how about this: "A woman, who involuntarily has expelled a baby through miscarriage, receives her penance for a year." (22nd Canon of John the Faster died 595 A.D.) Yes, Billy, you've read that "inspired" "God-given" "changeless" Canon correctly. A woman who has suffered a miscarriage is to be *penanced* (i.e., temporarily excommunicated) from the Orthodox Church for one full year. Upon finding out that such a disgusting church law once existed within medieval Christianity, many people simply sigh and say, "Considering it was the Dark Ages what else should I have expected?" Then they go on with their lives never to think of this "rule" again. The Orthodox Church and our bishops (ever aware that they need donations from sane laypeople) obviously aren't going around advertising church "teachings" on avoiding Jewish doctors, not dancing or punishing women for miscarriages. What makes these foolish and inhuman Canons so unacceptable is not that some monks living in the Dark Ages believed this sort of rubbish along with the "fact" that the world was flat and witches must be burned, but rather that this utmost ignorance is still a technically enforceable today within the Orthodox Church! This is because our "leaders" (our cowardly bishops) haven't had the courage to confront our traditionalists and change what these noisy reactionaries claim must remain "changeless."

But we should be the ones embracing change! Breaking down barriers is the prerequisite of the law of LOVE. Christ's message was not "Keep everything the same!" It was, "I will make you free!"

I believe in changelessness too *the changeless upward direction of our evolving human ethical enlightenment.* We are at the beginning of creation. It is happening now. I believe that our ethical evolution is slowly leading humans away from the cruelty inherent in all primates. Have you observed "our" Swakop Valley male baboons raping, biting and beating their females? That is what we primates all *are* -- absent ethical evolution. Some of us, dressed up in suits and robes and riding in cars, are still mired in these behaviors.

So this is my "answer" to your question: "And yet here you were doing all this really old-fashioned ritual stuff morning noon and night! Why?"

One may nurture, respect and love tradition *and yet grow* in the light of the logic of our traditions' heart. We can do this when we realize that creation is happening continuously and that we're at the start of our formation not at the end of it. For instance, when I watch a Shakespeare play I wish to hear it performed in the original language not rendered in some dreadful "with it" modern English. This is not a moral issue but one of aesthetics. On the other hand in Shakespeare's day boys and men played all the women's roles. So some traditionalist might insist that a commitment to the "changelessness" of Shakespeare's plays demands that we continue to exclude women from acting the women's roles in his plays. Yet today even though I am a traditionalist when it comes to defending the peerless language of the plays (not to mention our venerable liturgies) I'm also grateful that actual women actors now play the women's roles. I'm grateful because I honor God's guidance of the ethical evolution of our species and also because this evolution results in better

AND GOD SAID, "BILLY!"

plays! "Win-Win" as you Yanks say! I also think that this evolution honors Shakespeare's deepest (if unconscious) creative intent. Women's rights make Shakespeare's plays better because women play females better than males do. The wonderful roles he wrote are now played by the women he wrote the roles about *before* he could have imagined that someday the liberating logic contained in his "condescending" to write great parts for women -- and thereby paying them the complement of giving "his" females psychological depth equal with his male roles -- would eventually benefit actual women everywhere by inspiring people to change the way they viewed women.

We *can* have it both ways: defend the best of tradition, for instance our glorious liturgies and the English of Shakespeare's glorious language, and yet move forward because we know that God's creation *of* Creation is ongoing and will never complete. If creation is judged changeless and "complete" -- say in the frozen "roles" of men and women -- and if rules cannot be changed, then that militates against the idea that God is infinite. Stasis binds God to time and place, and therefore He, She or It is no longer God.

For instance we can keep our liturgies intact and yet edit out the openly anti-Semitic language found in many Lenten services that is a holdover from a less enlightened age. In doing so we prove that we've actually been instructed by the *deeper meaning* of our liturgies, whatever the surface blemishes were that once had a time and place but do not have resonance today. And here's some further evidence of my "heresy": We Orthodox should be ordaining women priests instead of excluding them from the heart of our liturgical life as if we were unenlightened Elizabethan audiences who once excluded women from playing the roles written about females. And clearly the same is true for the brothers and sisters of ours who are born homosexual, for instance your dear friend here Brother Bernard who is as spiritual and kindly man as I or you will ever meet.

Do we follow what the Bible says or what it *means*? Do we follow what Shakespeare (as a man of his time) did in his day "about" women (exclude them) or the heed the deeper internal logic of his writing wherein irrespective of who played women's roles in his theatrical company, he gave his female characters full equality with his male characters in a prophetic forward looking manner unknown in his time?

I'm supposed to be a monk. Very well I'll talk about Jesus. The underlying logic of the teaching of Jesus is that no matter what else is "in" the Bible, freedom, dignity and emancipation is the final message of faith and prophetic destiny of the human primate's evolution. Without that realization there can be no peace or peacemakers. The outcast and the oppressed, from the "Gypsies" to India's untouchables to women and homosexuals and black men and serfs are freed by the biblical logic that overrides *even its own rules* that are the residual detritus of hidebound time and place. Or to bring this down to earth and into our late twentieth century present tense: I acknowledge the racist teachings in the Bible implicit in the biblical endorsement of slavery and yet I override these time-bound "directives" in favor of the deeper eternal and ever-evolving, ever-expanding truth that – by implication -- demands that Nelson Mandela be released from prison and that I – as a black man – am a full human being and that the many homosexuals seeking refuge here in our community be healed of their guilt-feelings not of their sexuality and be told that they are normal, equal and welcome members of God's family.

At any rate thank God for the holy confusion that, by another name, is Orthodoxy! Thank God for my Bishop Anthony Bloom's steady friendship! The other bishops never got around to kicking me out—yet. Perhaps they lost the paperwork!

There is only one defense against the rising worldwide fear-filled fundamentalist tide engulfing all religions: The embrace of paradox and uncertainty as the virtuoso expression of Christ-like humility. Our egos must be curtailed by what we do *not* know, which is far more than we do know. This humility is rooted in a fact: we are at the beginning of creation and don't have any clue as to how things will grow and change. To me this embrace is found in defending our wonderful liturgies and traditions which bind our communities together with blessedly familiar and comfortable predictability -- so that a granddaughter may share her grandmother's faith and practice in unbroken glorious contiguity -- *and yet simultaneously* by using what is *in* those traditions *at their heart* to open rather than close doors.

This liberating "anti-theology" came to be called apophatic theology, or the theology of not knowing. It speaks only about what may NOT be said about God. And this way of perceiving God is found not just in ancient Christianity but in the best of other religions too. This anti-theology takes a mystical approach related to individual experiences of the divine beyond ordinary perception of the very kind Phillip K Dick loved and/or that drove him mad in the end. Depending of your view of "madness" perhaps this is the good kind of madness. Yes there is a good kind of madness Billy, just as there is a bad form of "sanity" that we call rationalism. This good "madness" teaches us that we're only at the dawn of creation and that the divine is ineffable, something that can be recognized only when it is felt, then remembered, a dream within a dream from which we will only awake for the first time in the presence of God. And therefore all descriptions of this sense will be false, because by definition the experience of God defies description because it is never ending.

The less you worry about God the better. If there is a Creator -- and that is an open question to anyone but an ideologue -- do you think He, She or It cares about your "correct" beliefs any more than you care about Rebecca's beliefs about you as the condition for loving her? Think about Rebecca. When you get home someday soon now and see her will you only love her if she still remembers the correct date of your birthday and your dietary likes and dislikes and your rules, the correct name to call you and what fruit to eat from what tree in which garden and, when she grows up, when to have sex and with whom?

My final word to you is this Billy: If there is a Creator -- and that is a big if -- perhaps He, She or It embodies love. I believe that the source of love must be outside of our cold mechanical universe. Certainly there are factors in evolutionary biology to "explain" the how of love. Neural components shed light on the subjective experience of being "in love," and "loving." Dopamine triggers testosterone production, which is a factor in the sex drive of both men and women and the same reward chemicals are involved in drug addiction that lead us to crave our beloved and so forth. It seems that developmentally and evolutionarily, advanced forms of empathy are preceded by and grow out of more elementary ones. We must assume continuity between past and present, child and adult, human and animal, even between humans and the most primitive mammals. Empathy probably evolved in the context of the parental care that characterizes all mammals and so forth…

And yet…

It seems to me that the gap between the sum total human consciousness and everything else is rather awkwardly wide given the short trajectory of our evolution so far. So perhaps the unlikely phenomenon of our brutal primate consciousness evolving the ability to feel empathy even for strangers originates beyond the stardust from which we are made. I hope so. At any rate, what do you think meant more to you Billy, my "correct" theology or that when my friend Father Dmitri called me and begged me to help you that I risked everything for a complete stranger and rescued you?
 With Much Love,
 Your, not-so-holy Father,
 Igumen Tryphon

Chapter 40
Brother Bernard's Story

Brother Bernard told me a story Father. I wrote it down and sent it to Rebecca, care of Molly, who takes my letters to Rebecca and sends back her letters to me. It was only after Rebecca read this story that she wrote back to me for the first time after not answering my letters for the first four months I was here. Maybe Rebecca finally answered me because I drew an outline of the bird's feet on the note I sent with this story. Whatever the reason this story moved her to write back. And because it got her to write back to me I guess that this story is the most important of all the things that have happened to me here. So anyway here's the story Brother Bernard told me that Rebecca must have liked:

"During my second term at the mission boarding school that my parents sent me to in Sussex England, this was in 1958 etcetera, etcetera, Webster and I ganged up on Higgins. We all went by our last names as was the custom in British 'prep' schools at that time. We called him 'Higginbottom,' and it drove him mad. Higgins was about my age ten or thereabouts, and had something a bit wrong with him. He was from a missionary family as well and had been in mission boarding schools since he was five. Perhaps that's why he flew into sudden and uncontrollable rages over the pettiest provocations. The rest of the time he kept to himself. He had no friends.

"Higgins was short and stocky and moved like a clumsy bear cub. He had a rather dark complexion, ruddy as if he had spent most of his days outdoors. Higgins would glance up from under a shock of thick, wiry hair falling over deep-set, dark, and brooding eyes just a bit too close together, giving his face a pinched look. When he was upset, his cheeks suddenly flushed crimson, as if Higgins had had a splash of vermilion paint dashed onto his face. Tease him a bit more, and he would put his head down and charge in such a blind, incoherent, roaring fury that his aggression was totally ineffectual, reducing Webster and me to fits of laughter—and Higgins to tears.

"One night Webster and I were asleep in our dormitory, which happened, that term, to be up near the water tank in the top of the school, almost in the attic. Our headmaster -- Mr. Stark -- woke us up. He told us to follow him. The other four or five boys in the room watched us from the refuge of their old cast iron bunks as we put on our dressing gowns and follow the Head. I didn't bother with my slippers. Mr. Stark had already stalked out and I didn't dare delay following him. The other chaps seemed to shrink back into their beds and stare through eyes wide with curiosity, and not a little morbid pleasure, at someone else's dramatic and highly unusual misfortune.

"Mr. Stark was young for a headmaster, handsome, tall, and thin, his thick, wiry salt-and-pepper hair divided by an uneven part into a shaggy mop that bounced as he walked. He had dark eyes that—from the point of view of a terrified little boy—seemed piercing. Mr. Stark was wearing a dark green plaid tie, a white shirt, rumpled gray flannel trousers, and a shabby tweed jacket. His golden Labrador retriever 'Bret' (if I remember his name correctly) pressed against his legs as Mr. Stark walked and always left hair on his trousers. All thoughts of the name we boys called the Head behind his back "Starky" nor "Stark Staring Bonkers" etcetera, etcetera, vanished from my mind.

"What on earth could merit this abrupt hauling away in the

middle of the night? From time to time during summer term, the Head was known to roust us all out for rollicking midnight swims, but whoever heard of two boys being summoned at this hour? It was winter term. The school pond was frozen. And no one could have mistaken Mr. Stark's equally frozen 'Walser, Webster, come to my study— at once' as an invitation to anything pleasant. (By the way Billy, Walser was my name in the world, Peter Walser, as I was known then before taking the name of Bernard at my becoming a monk and so forth.)

"We walked in near darkness, finding our way by the occasional glow from some single low-wattage bulb far down a hallway. We followed old Starky down three flights of narrow, rickety back stairs, out to a landing, then down the wide, grand staircase to the main hall. That was a shock. What could this breach of protocol mean? Expelled? A firing squad?

"Striding on legs twice as long as ours, Mr. Stark was far ahead of us. We began to run after him and then remembered the 'no running indoors' rule. No point compounding the trouble we were in. We slowed to a panicked fast trot. We soon found ourselves in the Head's study staring at the usual clutter and trying to avoid Mr. Stark's eyes while we stood at attention in front of his immense Victorian mahogany desk. It was piled high with papers, open books, letters, and assorted lost and found items: a cricket bat or two, several air rifles, pens and watches, and two swords Mr. Stark had recently confiscated from a boy who had wanted to carry naval cutlasses to class. 'Do you know why you two are here?' Starky asked. 'No, sir,' we replied. 'It came to my attention that you've been bullying Higgins. He didn't sneak on you. You know I have my sources?' 'Yes sir.'

"Indeed we did know. There was no point trying to deny anything—ever. We believed Stark when he said Higgins hadn't told on us. No one ever sneaked, and also we knew that Mr. Stark knew everything! Adam and Eve were never as naked before an angry God as Webster and I were before Mr. Stark! We stood there praying for the floor to swallow us. He'd used the word bullying. We knew that we stood accused of the worst crime. We were dead men. 'My sources tell me you two have been winding him up. Is this true?' 'Yes, sir,' we whispered. 'Very well,' Stark said quietly. He looked down at a book, opened it, and began to read. Mr. Stark didn't look up. Webster and I shifted uneasily. Then, almost as an afterthought: 'Stand outside the study door while I decide your fate.'

"We stepped into the darkened hall. The only illumination came from Mr. Stark's desk lamp. It cast a long square of dim light through the open door and across the black and white marble tile floor. The rest of the hall was a black void, something that went nicely with the feeling in the pit of my stomach. We stood silently facing the wall next to the study door—it was always open—shivering in our pajamas and dressing gowns, which provided inadequate protection from the frigid air. The tile floor felt like ice below my bare feet. The stale, sour mayonnaise smell of the ubiquitous 'salad cream' (all-purpose and awful salad dressing favored by the British in those days) wafted out of the open door of the staff dining room nearby. The hall clock chimed. We didn't speak but exchanged frozen, despairing glances as the doom-laden minutes dragged past. The half hours came and went as the bell on the school clock struck 10:30, then 11:00, then midnight, then 1:00, then 1:30. Legs were numb. Heartbeats slowed.

"Then he spoke. 'You may come in now.' Blood pumping, heart pounding, we were sure that after so long a wait we'd each get six of the best, trousers—or in this case, pajamas—down. 'Well?' asked Stark, looking up from his book, 'How did you enjoy that?' 'Not very much, sir,' we mumbled. Mr. Stark closed his book with a snap and sat back in his chair. He sighed then nodded slowly before he spoke. 'Now you know how Higgins spends his days. You see, you chaps are happy boys. When you get up in the morning, it isn't with a sense of dread. You're expecting a pleasant day. When Higgins gets up, he's expecting unpleasantness. He knows that chaps like you think it's amusing to wind him up, to take advantage of the fact that he loses self-control. Well, for him that is a sort of hell. Would you make fun of him if he were a cripple, Walser?' 'No, sir,' I said. His words hit home. 'And you, Webster? Would you fight a boy smaller than yourself, some little chap in First Form?' 'No, sir,' Webster said, and his face flushed. He was powerfully built and tall for his age, a great athlete and one of our best cricket bowlers. The idea of being labeled a big chap who picked on the little chaps was intolerable. 'Well, here's the thing, lads, now you know how Higgins feels not knowing what will happen to him. You've been waiting for several hours not knowing your fate. Not much fun, eh, chaps?' 'No, sir.' 'What do you think I should do to you lads?' 'Give us a whacking?' Webster suggested in a shaky questioning voice.

"I cast an involuntary glance in the direction of the school safe. Yes, there it was, the dreaded plymsole (gym shoe as you Yanks call it) surrounded by dust balls and nestled under the old safe. Mr. Stark almost never actually used it, but the idea of that shoe-of-death hovered in all our brains, the final guarantee of order among one hundred and eighty boys. Any master could get our attention by casually remarking, 'Would you like to explain this to Mr. Stark?' There was ultimate justice waiting for anyone who pushed his luck.

"So at any rate we expected the fateful, 'Fetch the gym shoe' and so on etcetera, etcetera. But Mr. Stark was saying something unexpected. 'You certainly deserve it, but no, I think that wait was enough.' Heartfelt stunned relief: 'Thank you, sir!' Mr. Stark held out a biscuit tin. We each took one of the slightly stale digestive biscuits with trembling fingers. We ate them in silence, solemnly. No partaking of any sacrament has ever felt more joyful or salvific. Then, brightly smiling, his usual friendly self Starky said, 'I have a job for you two! From now on I want you to provide Higgins with just as many pleasant surprises as you've given him nasty ones. Mercy, gentlemen! Mercy! Take him along. Change his life! I'm holding you two personally accountable. You are to become his secret guardian angels. And he mustn't know. I don't want to find him alone in the library again. I want to see him coming back from the woods with the whole gang, muddy, happy, and bedraggled as you lot!' 'Yes sir.' 'Words are dreadful weapons, aren't they?' 'Yes, sir.' 'Never bully anyone again.' 'We shan't, sir.'

"Stark smiled and held out his hand. We shook. A handshake was a sacred bond between gentlemen, between men like our Head, men we wanted to be like someday, and be liked by. Higgins's life was about to change for the better. The wisdom and mercy of our headmaster was what I followed Billy, not a theory. He did not try to convert me to a better way or to correct ideas. He *was* the better way. His teaching didn't depend on my believing what he believed. It depended on his setting an example for me to follow—an example that cost him a night's sleep. Mr. Stark spoke no grand words. Rather he traveled with two frightened lads a few steps down a path to greater kindness, to empathy, to learning to walk in another's shoes."

Chapter 41
Life Confession

Yesterday you said, "Tell me your innermost thoughts."

"I'm thinking about holding Rebecca close," I answered. "I can't wait to go home."

And you said, "Don't forget that love invites loss. What a terrible price to pay for the sweetest gift."

Father, I think I've started to wake up to what you call "the grace of paradox" that you say is the "terrible price we pay for love." I guess I first really woke up the moment that you (very unexpectedly!) poured a stream of dry silvery sand over my head that you'd just scooped from the cave floor. It was so dry and powdery that it flowed like water over my head and shoulders. You said, "I *unbaptize* you in the name of truth, love and beauty! You are free!" and Miss Honeychurch swooped over us and you laughed and said "A dove for Jesus and a crow for you Billy! Perfect!"

This morning we took our walk. The ticket is here and so is my new passport. So this looks like this is our next to last walk and this is almost my last "chapter" of my confession/spiritual journal, whatever this is! We were talking about how very crappy my rewrite of Rubin's screenplay was as "yet more evidence of the capacity for self-delusion" like you said and how "Hollywood delusion" and "religious delusion" are more or less the same thing, sort of "like people

AND GOD SAID, "BILLY!"

actually expecting to win the lottery." And then you were showing me (again) how even if the desert looks dead, plenty lives here. You pointed out a wasp laying an egg on a spider. "The wasp's baby eats the spider alive," you said. "Theology eats its host like this wasp does. Religion has become so toxic that the only solution for many people like you Billy is to reject religious belief altogether. Atheism may be your only road back to God."

We were following a desert elephant and her baby. They lumbered along kicking up plumes of sand on their way down a steep sandbank to a waterhole surrounded by the tall reeds that they feed on after they drink. We were passing your binoculars back and forth. The mother climbed the bank, slipped back in a cascade of sand and trudged on. Her child had trouble following until the mother returned and nudged him up the steep incline with her trunk. Then they both slowly walked over the top of the dune and were gone. Like that mother with her child, you helped me. What Brother Bernard described about his headmaster traveling with "two frightened lads a few steps down a path to greater kindness, to empathy," is what you did for me Father. Thank you.

Paris,
August 3, 2013 From:
Rebecca To: Molly

Dearest Molly,
Please find enclosed a photocopy of Dad's "Life Confession" just as it came to me last week out of the blue after almost 30 years of deafening silence! It was forwarded to me from my West 102nd St. NYC apartment to my Paris

address. I still don't know who sent it to me or how they got it. The original postmark was stamped "Ealing London, UK" about a month ago. They sent Dad's handwritten original and an old dusty typed copy. I compared the two docs and other than spelling corrections (and an absence of bird poop!) there are no differences between the handwritten original and the photocopy of the typescript I've sent overnight to you. I had never even heard Dad had written this! I know Dad would want you to read it. BTW, you come off as the only sane person in it.

Some of Dad's story came out in the Truth and Reconciliation Commission hearings (Cape Town 1997) about how Dad and Igumen Tryphon were murdered in early 1990. They were walking in the desert at someplace called Rossing Mines. The police in Swakopmund never settled on who the killer (or killers) were. At the time the local South African authorities flatly blamed SWAPO. I was a child then but as you know later I pieced what I could together while I was at the University of Chicago, which is maybe why I became hooked on being an investigative journalist and dropped my comparative religion studies. You'll remember that I sent you clippings about how Officer Vandermeer was killed in 1989 by one of his fellow cops. (You'll "meet" Vandermeer in Dad's "Confession"). Other members the South African Defense Forces were also mentioned in the Commission hearings by a man called Brother Basil. He also mentioned some possible Russian and/or Serbian fascist nationalist connection to the killings because he said they had put Igumen Tryphon on some sort of hit list as an "enemy of true Orthodoxy." Even the monks who didn't like Tryphon and/or Dad at the monastery in (near) Swakopmund were mentioned by Basil. The Israeli secret service got mentioned by one former SAP

AND GOD SAID, "BILLY!"

officer being questioned by the Commission about the collusion between the state of Israel's security forces and the apartheid regime in various political murders of "terrorists" around the world and of course their joint development of nuclear weapons. Other people suggested Dad and Tryphon were shot by local poachers going after the last of the desert elephants that the monks were trying to protect.

No one really investigated the crime at the time as far as I can tell and by the time the Commission was talking about this (briefly) it was just one more story folded into many horrors. No one knows which one of them was the target and which one was killed because he was just in the wrong place at the wrong time. No one will ever know. One way or another Dad's murder seems to have had something to do with religion. I'm betting you could say that about half the people who ever got killed on this planet. On the other hand I don't buy the all-too-facile "new" atheist argument that just because religion sucks then that proves there is no God. Humanity sucks period! Religion is just more evidence of this but I'm still betting on "Something" being "out there." So we'll have to keep on agreeing to disagree on that!

I still have the 47 letters Dad wrote to me from the monastery (not to mention more than 50 from Hollywood from his 3 years there in "New Midian") and all those feathers and footprint outlines he sent from his bird. I've got the little semi-precious gems he sent from over there too that he tucked into all those notes-- rose quartz, tiger's eye and the rest.

When he tracked me down 2 years later Brother Bernard wrote that on the day he died Dad was carrying all 37 of my letters that I'd written to him. They had blood on them. Mom freaked out. Mostly my "letters" were just little girl pictures with big scribbled "I love you Daddy" messages and a few things from school. Brother Bernard sent that icon of the Ladder of Divine Ascent along with my letters. I keep my icon in a corner here in the kitchen above the oil lamp you always said would burn down my apartment back when I had that first little room in NYC on Bleecker. I still keep the picture Bernard included in the letter about Dad's murder of Dad in his robe with his bird next to my icon along with all those little sparkly pebbles.

After Dad was killed and before Bernard got in touch I wrote and wrote and then got mad when no answers came and figured that Dad had just walked away again. (Remember how angry I was?) Then finally Brother Bernard broke the horrible news 2 years to the day after Dad was shot. I cried for days and soaked my "Lamby" with what must have been gallons of tears even though by then I really didn't know Dad at all and by then Lamby was on a top shelf forgotten. I'm glad Mom had the sense to let me answer Bernard even when that bastard Bob was still in the picture and tried to prevent me. Dad was planning to come home (he wrote that to me in one of the last letters) but then he never mentioned it again. I don't know if he ever became a monk. I have no idea what happened to anyone Dad knew in Hollywood or over there in South Africa. Now I have this "Confession" I'll do a Google search on some names.

I wish Dad had known that Mom called for him when she was dying and was so very sorry for what she had done to me after Pastor Bob was arrested for raping me the second time. Poor Mother! I think I've come to understand Mom's relationship with Bob as what the professionals call "traumatic bonding" where victims attach themselves to their tormentors because they know they will be shamed and stigmatized.

Thank you for helping keep that bastard behind bars by flying all the way out to Boston from Seattle for each parole hearing. You'll never know what that (let alone your lifelong friendship) means to me. I'll see you at Bob's next parole hearing unless I can tempt you to visit us here first! As ever there's a chilled bottle (or three) of Louis Roederer's Cristal kept here for you 24/7should you drop by the 8th arrondissement. Please do!

I can't really remember Dad very well. What I do remember is that he was gentle.

Lots of Love,
Rebecca

Acknowledgments

My wife Genie made this novel better by giving me fresh ideas and direction during the 15 years I worked on it off and on. Novelists Andre Dubus and Brian McLaren read drafts of the manuscript (Andre almost 10 years back and Brian more recently) and gave me notes and encouragement over the years as did movie director Kevin Miller ("Hellbound?") who gave me great notes. Jane Smiley has kept up my writer's spirits by periodically telling me that she likes my work and that it makes her laugh, not to mention the encouragement that her kind reviews of my nonfiction books gave me. Katherine Venn (editor of Hodder in the UK) was supremely kind and gave me notes that were very helpful at a critical moment. Thanks to Hal Fickett for his work managing my internet life, and to Christy Berghoef for a careful read of the book and her notes. Thanks to my friend Frank Gruber for encouraging me when I wrote the first brief outline of this story years ago and for his needling reminders to me to finish the book. I paraphrased several quotes from various legendary Hollywood screenwriting coaches and turned them into the basis for the Hal Busby quotes in my story. I also used several quotes from *The Crazy Side of Orthodoxy* a book by Charles Shingledecker in the Igumen's "memo" to Billy. My readers will note that one story the monks tell Billy was something I used in my book (*Patience With God*). Thanks to my dear friend and artist Holly Meade for her friendship and encouragement (of both my writing and painting) over many years. She read this book and loved it, and gave me a great gift of support to me and to this book before she passed away in June of 2013.